Choosing Love

Choosing Love

A Novel

Rick Herrick

SUNSTONE
PRESS

SANTA FE

Sunstone books may be purchased for educational, business, or sales promotional use.
For information please write: Special Markets Department, Sunstone Press,
P.O. Box 2321, Santa Fe, New Mexico 87504-2321.

Book and Cover design › Vicki Ahl
Body typeface › Californian FB
Printed on acid-free paper

Library of Congress Cataloging-in-Publication Data

Herrick, Rick.
  Choosing Love : a novel / by Rick Herrick.
    pages cm
  ISBN 978-0-86534-968-1 (softcover : alk. paper)
  1. Love stories. 2. Christian fiction. I. Title.
  PS3558.E748C48 2013
  813'.54--dc23

                            2013030769

WWW.SUNSTONEPRESS.COM
SUNSTONE PRESS / POST OFFICE BOX 2321 / SANTA FE, NM 87504-2321 /USA
(505) 988-4418 / ORDERS ONLY (800) 243-5644 / FAX (505) 988-1025

∼ ACKNOWLEDGMENTS ∼

Choosing Love became a publishable novel because I had lots of help from my friends. Dave Kranz, Carol Traenkle, Liz Huss, Julie Herrick, Kate Hancock, and Jamie Fish made perceptive comments on early drafts of the book. Dr. Bill Horn provided medical advice, Chris Houghton offered psychological insight, and Howard Grubbs answered all of my legal questions.

Special thanks go to Amy and Ken Laderoute who traveled with Lyn and me to Prince Edward Island where I researched the early scenes for the book. A huge debt of gratitude goes to Jeff Traenkle who suggested the legal case upon which the book is based, and offered help with the expert testimony at the trial. The book is grammatically clean because of the hard work of Les Woodcock.

As you proceed through the book, you will be introduced to The Family. The Family is a fundamentalist Christian organization of men who devote their lives to creating a Christian based world government emanating from Washington. The events and characters described in the book relating to The Family are fictional, but I believe they accurately reflect the members of this organization and its goals. If you become intrigued with The Family, Jeff Sharlet's book by that name is a must read.

The original idea for *Choosing Love* came from our daughter Molly Kelly. Fifteen years ago she came to us one morning and said: "Mom and Dad, I just quit my summer job. I leave tomorrow on a tall ship for Nova Scotia. They need an extra crew member." When Molly returned three weeks later, she regaled us with her stories of the trip. Because she had such an important role in inspiring the story and because she continues to inspire me with her thoughtfulness and belly laugh, I am proud to dedicate this book to her.

~ ARRIVALS ~

Karen Hathaway peered out of her first floor bedroom window at the driveway off to the left. It was 7:10 p.m. She was waiting for Chase Williams to pick her up at 7:15 for an outing with her church youth group at the local bowling center.

She quickly returned to the long, slender mirror for one last check. She liked her casual look, the brown khaki slacks, the light blue sweater, and the hoop earrings on loan from her friend Sarah. The light touch of blue eye liner was just right.

Karen was a junior in high school, and this was her first date if you could call a group bowling outing a real date. She liked Chase a lot, although she was undecided if she wanted him for a boyfriend. He was definitely cute looking with his short-cropped brown hair, green eyes, and athletic frame. The problem was he was a "goody two-shoes." Tonight would be a good test to see if he could also be fun, she thought as she ran her large blue comb through her shoulder length chestnut- brown hair one last time.

Moving slightly to the left from the mirror, she closed her closet doors and picked up her running shoes to place them under the dresser when she heard Chase's car enter the driveway. She flew from her bedroom, walking rapidly along the long, narrow hallway toward the front door. Of all people, she encountered her father coming from the opposite end of the house. He starred at her with cold, blue eyes, a look of disapproval rapidly crossing his face.

"Karen, you look like a teenage hooker. Those silly earrings and the blue eye shadow have to go."

"I use blue eye liner in pageants. Why not tonight?"

"Because this is a church event, not a beauty pageant. There will be no argument about this or I will send the young man home." Karen fled to the sanctuary of her bedroom, tears pouring forth from her innocent, green eyes.

This inauspicious beginning to her first date ten years ago couldn't have been farther from her mind as Karen placed two suitcases down on the curb and looked for a cab. She was exhausted. Her Continental flight from Washington DC had arrived at Logan Airport at 7:45, and she was looking forward to curling up in bed with her book and falling asleep. A Yellow Cab came to her rescue. The driver, a short, slight man in his mid fifties, with dark features and a face that needed constant attention from a razor, took her bags while she got into the back seat.

"The Long Wharf Marriott," Karen announced as the driver turned sideways toward her. "Do you know it?"

"Right on State Street, young lady. I'll have you there in twenty minutes." With that Karen settled back in her seat and closed her eyes, but sleep alluded her. Her mind was racing, driven by a general uneasiness over her job.

Karen was a staff person for Republican Congressman Christopher Jackson from Colorado Springs, Colorado. It was a dream job for a political science major from Denison University, class of 1986. She loved the excitement of being in Washington, its many opportunities for a stimulating social life, and her four roommates were easy. They shared a house together on Park Street, a fifteen minute ride on the Metro to the Capitol Building.

So what was the matter? What was behind the general angst, her nagging blues, the difficulty she sometimes experienced getting up in the morning? Well, in the first place, she was not writing speeches or doing policy research, but rather her ten-hour days involved handling constituency problems and answering letters. Her letter writing chores particularly galled her because her replies said very little, were bromides really, that did not respond effectively to the constituent's problem or concerns. Earlier this morning, with her mind a thousand miles away on the beaches of Prince Edward Island, she put on her best manners and smile to take a high school group on a tour of the Capitol Building and the White House. Such tours got old, she thought as she shifted her position on the seat in the small yellow cab.

Then there was the cynicism in the office, the counting of votes, the placing your finger in the air every time a controversial issue emerged to see which way the political wind was blowing in sunny, conservative, religiously uptight Colorado Springs. The conservatism was fine, that's why she was there. It was the self-righteous hypocrisy that got her down. Values were spun from the Congressman's office in a steady drumbeat and left for others to live. She was also a little disappointed in herself. She was a hypocrite too. She liked the idea of being a Congressional aide, the prestige associated with working for a congressman. People treated her as if she had power, and it felt good. That's why she was reluctant to even think about changing jobs.

Finally, there was the long-standing problem with her father, the control freak who hated blue eye liner on teenage girls, but she was not facing that situation now. She devoted an hour every other week to that mess with her psychologist who had nicknamed her father the man in the blue flannel suit. The suit matched his cold, steely blue eyes, and said so much about his stiff, formal ways. Was she achieving any form of closure from the pain he had created? Who knows, she thought as she nodded off briefly or maybe it was just her mind slowly grinding to a halt; but the peace lasted only momentarily as she was startled into functioning awareness by the sense of the cab pulling to a stop in front of the hotel.

"We're here," the cab driver quietly announced as he shoved the transmission into park. "I'll get your bags from the trunk and be gone. Have a nice stay in Boston," he concluded as the front door swung open and he exited onto the street. She wondered briefly about his accent. Though not heavy or difficult to understand, it did have a distinctive tone. Maybe he was Italian or Lebanese, she reflected, but that deduction was probably based more on looks than sound. The rough and tumble of city life was relatively new to her experience, not part of her sheltered upbringing in suburban Philadelphia and the posh Broadmoor neighborhood of Colorado Springs, and so she was not particularly good at discerning accents. It interested her, though.

But now it was time to cope again. Karen was good at coping, at putting a good face forward, at functioning day-to-day, and even under pressure. She often thought coping provided the background music of her life. It was one big reason she was so ready for this vacation. She needed a break from coping.

As she disembarked from the cab, she found herself waiting for a second time on a curb. Nice hotel, she thought, as her eyes scanned the tall, angular building before her. This vacation will be the best. She had never cruised on a sailboat or done much sailing of any kind, but her sense of adventure created an eager anticipation that lightened her mood. Two weeks away from work. It was just what the doctor ordered.

As the driver came around the cab with the two suitcases, Karen reached into her pocketbook for a twenty dollar bill. "Will this cover things?" she asked as she faced him with a pleasant smile. She was good at smiling at strangers. She had practiced it all her life.

"It will cover just fine," said the driver as he released the bags and reached out his hand to receive the money. "Thank you very much and like I said before, have a nice stay in Boston." Karen nodded in acknowledgment, picked up the suitcases, and proceeded to walk the short distance to the hotel lobby. She considered briefly looking for the Amity, the tall ship that would soon take her to the beaches of Prince Edward Island; but it was becoming darker by the minute, she was tired, and the thought of wandering around a strange city with two suitcases was definitely unappealing.

Thirty minutes later she was in her room, and in bed with *The Flame and the Flower*, a must read by Kathleen Woodiwiss according to Janet, one of her roommates. It must be a steamy one, she thought; and the story began quickly as she was led to wonder whether the beautiful Heather would be able to escape from the handsome and dangerous Captain Birmingham. The answer was only a few pages away, but Karen missed it that night as the book slipped from her hand and she fell into a deep and restful sleep.

The phone rang at 8:00 the next morning, per her instructions to the clerk at the desk the night before, and Karen answered with a dreamy, "Hello. No, I would prefer to have breakfast in one of the restaurants in the lobby. Is the service relatively fast? Good. The Waves Grill will be it then. Thanks for waking me and have a nice day." She felt like she should have closed the conversation with "and vote Republican." She laughed to herself as she hung up the phone, stretched, and slowly slid out of bed before heading toward the shower with dispatch. The warm, soapy water completed the job of waking her. Ten full hours of sound sleep, she thought. What a luxury and what a good time for it to happen. She wondered what it would be like sleeping on the ship. There were so many questions she had about the ship which led her to quickly end the shower, not lingering as she often did when getting ready for work, so she could get on with her day.

After drying herself with a towel, blow drying her long, light brown hair, and putting on her underwear, Karen reached for the television clicker and found the weather channel. She sat on the edge of the bed combing her hair, and soon learned that the high for Boston for Sunday July 19th, 1992 would be 86 degrees, with a southwest wind of from ten to fifteen miles per hour. "Better learn to say knots lady," she mumbled to herself with a laugh. "Even I know that." There was a 30% chance of an afternoon shower. Perfect, she thought, as she put down the comb and searched one of her suitcases for her khaki shorts, brown belt, navy blue tee shirt, and white keds.

Breakfast at the Waves Grill was light for Karen, not because there weren't lots of tempting choices on the menu but because she had a figure to protect. She settled on a bowl of bran flakes, a piece of whole wheat toast, lightly buttered with no jam, and two cups of coffee. Because she was excited and in a hurry, she placed ten dollars on the table after completing the meal, and left the restaurant to fetch her luggage.

The elevator ride to the seventh floor was uneventful, although Karen enjoyed reading the posters on the wall which outlined some of the interesting historical facts pertaining to Long Wharf. She laughed silently after learning how the city of Boston received the nickname "Beantown." It must have been a smelly place in colonial times, she concluded as she exited the elevator and turned right toward her room. Twenty minutes later she returned to the same elevator with suitcases in hand. When the spirit moved her, when a goal was on her radar screen she fervently desired, Karen Hathaway was an efficient, no-nonsense young woman. At 9:40 that morning, she walked up the Amity's narrow plank with wooden rails, and made a mental note of the handsome guy in the tattered shorts with the Red Sox cap who helped her aboard and welcomed her to the ship.

～

Patrick McGovern said goodbye, hugged his older brother Kevin, and proceeded to step onto the T. It would be a different ride for him. He had taken the T all his life to and around Boston, but he had traveled on the Blue Line from Chelsea not the Green line from Newton Centre. Kevin has gone upscale, he thought with a smile as he turned left and moved toward the first empty seat of the surprisingly clean green and white subway car.

He had had a pleasant visit with Kevin, his wife Debby, and his two nieces, Catherine age ten and Maddie age eight. Patrick was proud of his older brother. Kevin was doing well as a project manager for a large Boston construction company. He supervised the building of high-end family homes, and some small office buildings, mostly in the western suburbs. Yet he was dying to get his hands into the "Big Dig," the ambitious plan, one might even call it visionary, to solve Boston's traffic nightmare by routing nonlocal traffic under the city.

The "Big Dig" is the largest public works project in American history. It was all Kevin could talk about that Saturday night. "Lots of work for a geologist to do," Kevin said as he handed Patrick a beer while the two visited together on the back porch after dinner. "The project is only getting started. One of the big worries is that buildings will settle along the path of the tunnel. Geologists will do all the testing."

"I've got my hands full in Denver," Patrick responded. He was a project engineer for a small environmental company that specialized in solving wastewater treatment problems. "This vacation is really a freebee. My boss gave it to me because of all the traveling I do. The company treats me well Kev, and Denver's a great place to live."

"Mom sure would like you to come home."

"She doesn't need me when there are six of you within a fifty-mile radius. She's a lucky lady with all that family around." Patrick felt a brief pang of guilt as he took off his backpack and settled into the seat on the subway. He felt guilty not because he had left Boston four years ago, but because it would have been nice to have spent the night with his mother in Chelsea. Oh well, there was always Saturday night on the other end of his vacation two weeks hence, and Kevin had insisted. It was fun to catch up with him, and there was no way he would allow anything to mar the trip he was about to embark upon. He unzipped the side pocket of his backpack and took out the travel book on Prince Edward Island the Amity Friends Memorial Foundation had sent him several weeks ago after receiving his check. The trip involved eight days of round-trip sailing on a tall ship, and five days on some of the most beautiful beaches in the world. He was psyched.

Patrick had a 10:00 a.m. deadline for boarding the Amity, the nineteenth century barque that would carry him to Prince Edward Island and back. A quick glance at his watch reassured him he was in good shape. The T ride to South Station was no more than forty-five minutes, even taking into consideration the change over at Park Street, which left him almost an hour to find the Amity. It was docked at Long Wharf, right next to the Aquarium, which made the whole thing a slam dunk. He had been taking the subway to the Aquarium ever since he was a little boy. It was his trips there that had fueled his interest in science and the environmental problems associated with water.

Thoughts of his childhood returned as Patrick closed the travel book after spending ten minutes or so reviewing the enticing details about those amazing beaches. Two older brothers, four older sisters, and twenty-one nieces and nephews. Certainly his mother wouldn't resent the fact he was still single and had not contributed additional grandchildren. With twenty-eight family birthdays to worry about, she had her hands full.

She was a great lady, his mother Kathleen. Among his siblings there were six college degrees and four masters degrees in various professional and academic fields. He came from an ambitious family, a family whose members all seemed to agree on the need for a higher standard of material well-being than they had experienced as children. They didn't resent their childhood. They merely wanted more. Patrick's mother had contributed financially to all of these programs as best as she could, mostly on her own, because his father had died from lung cancer when Patrick was nine.

Sadly Patrick didn't remember his father very well mostly because his father was always working when he was growing up—first as a postal clerk during the day and then as an all-purpose repairman whenever the phone rang, and he had spare time. As the last of seven children, Patrick understood the many demands that rested on his father's shoulders. He didn't resent his father for their lack of time together. He only wished his dad had seen him play in one ice hockey game.

His mother had not missed a game however, either in high school or in college. She was his biggest fan. Although she never remarried, she remained financially independent thanks to her job in the packing department of Glenco Manufacturing, a company that made wallpaper products, located less than three blocks from their home in Chelsea, and his father's pension from the government. She retired from Glenco at sixty-eight, the year after Patrick completed his masters in hydrology from the University of Massachusetts.

As the train pulled out of Fenway and headed underground, Patrick thought briefly about the Red Sox. Fenway was another station with which he was infinitely familiar, and yet it was funny. Despite the fact he had been away from the area for only four years, there were few players on the current Sox roster he could recall. Roger Clemens, Manager Butch Hobson, Wade Boggs, Jeff Reardon, Tony Pena. That was it. As a kid he had known every player, their batting average, the team the Sox had acquired them from, and several other relevant statistics. But Patrick lived in Denver now; and, more importantly, he was a participant much more than he was a fan. His goal was to make things happen in life, not to sit on the sidelines and watch.

It was also a little strange the train was less than a third full, a rare experience for Patrick, but he had always been in church on Sunday mornings as a child, not traveling around town on the T. Kevin had been in church too; but he, Debby, and the girls had other plans for today. Had they all become bad Catholics, Patrick wondered? He, for one, hadn't left the Catholic Church. He just never attended anymore; and there may be a difference, although he had no interest in reflecting on it further because the train was pulling into Park Street station which meant a change was in order. He lifted his pack to his shoulders, moved briskly through the sliding doors, and descended a flight of stairs to board the Red Line to South Station.

South Station is the central transportation crossroads for the Boston metropolitan area. It links the subway with busses and trains. Most importantly for Patrick, it deposited him with less than a fifteen minute walk to Boston Harbor. He exited the station onto Atlantic Avenue and was surprised to see a familiar landscape so completely altered. The "Big Dig!" Cranes, bulldozers, steel girders, and construction barriers to reroute traffic were all around him. There was a large dump truck partially filled with dirt parked off the road waiting for crews to return on Monday to transport the dirt to some other location. Maybe to the site of a future park, he concluded. Constructing additional open space was part of the master plan. According to his brother Kevin, there will be more than 500,000 truckloads of dirt removed before the project is completed sometime in 2003 or 2004.

The walk to the New England Aquarium took him along Atlantic Avenue, then onto Purchase Street where his mind was forced away from the "Big Dig" by the sound of an ambulance screaming toward him. The traffic was relatively light on this early Sunday morning; but the sound from the speeding ambulance and the pigeons scavenging for food in an open garbage can off to the side in a sun deprived alleyway told him he was back in Boston. It was great. As he approached the Aquarium on India Street, Boston Harbor came into view and along with it the wide expanses of the Atlantic Ocean. He immediately sensed a gentle breeze, which led him to pick up his pace toward Long Wharf. Upon arriving, he turned right, and there was the Amity at the far end of the pier. He paused briefly to catch his breath, to take full measure of the ship that would be his home for the next two weeks, to reflect on his good fortune, and to thank his Catholic God, the tyrant of his youth, the deity who had tried so hard to burden him with guilt as a kid but had never succeeded, for the fine weather that would launch this much needed vacation.

"All hands on deck, all hands on deck," the captain, Todd McMillan, called out as he walked the Amity from bow to stern repeating his command to passengers and crew. Karen glanced at her watch and noted it was two minutes after ten. She became excited for the third or fourth time that morning. It was time to get underway, to finally embark upon this great adventure. Karen wondered whether the excitement she was sensing had something to do with the call of the sea, a sentiment often expressed in novels about the sea she had read. But how could she be feeling something she had never before experienced? These exciting sensations must relate to the call of life, she concluded, a call to adventure and challenge, a call to live to the fullest, a call she hoped she was finally ready to accept.

She had been standing at the railing near the stern of the ship for the last ten minutes by herself peering out at Boston Harbor. Planes from Logan Airport took off and landed while she stood there. A harbor tour boat was taking on passengers at the next pier with a hydrofoil ferry docked alongside it. Several small power boats and one cruising sailboat were heading out to the open sea, while a small fishing boat needing several coats of fresh paint headed home into the harbor. It was a busy morning. There were lots of interesting things to observe, but in response to the captain's command she turned around and directed her attention toward the interior part of the ship.

People were congregating on the deck around the mainmast, the widest section of the ship. She released her grip from the railing and proceeded to move in that direction, stopping a little beyond the mast where several passengers were already seated on the deck floor in a semi-circle around the captain. She leaned against the small wooden cabin that encased the galley and focused her attention on the captain.

Todd McMillan was a well kept, stocky guy, 5' 9" tall, one hundred seventy pounds, with short curly brown hair and brown eyes that were both lively and intense. He had an earnest look about him which filled Karen with a sense of confidence. He was thirty-eight years old and a graduate of the Maine Maritime Academy with six years of previous experience on an oil tanker. This was his third summer as captain of the Amity.

"On behalf of the members of the crew, I would like to welcome you aboard the Amity," the captain said as he surveyed the group before him. "Let me spend a few moments introducing you to the ship. After that I will divide you up into your three watches for meetings where you will receive specific instructions as to your responsibilities on the cruise and the procedures we have for running the ship.

"The Amity was built in Baltimore in eighteen thirty-eight by the shipbuilders Kennard and Williamson. It is four hundred ninety tons in total weight, one hundred forty-three feet long from bowsprit to stern, and thirty-one feet wide at its widest point. As you can see the ship has three masts—a foremast toward the bow, a mizzen mast behind me toward the stern, and a mainmast that rises before you approximately one hundred five feet above the deck. At full sail, the Amity can fly twenty sails—six square topsails from the main mast, five each on the fore and mizzen masts, and four triangular sails from the bowsprit. We will not use all of these sails, but we plan to go with several. To supplement our sail power, we have two auxiliary diesel engines, each one hundred thirty-five horsepower, which will always be running.

"The Amity was a Quaker ship. Quakers dominated merchant shipping in early nineteenth century America, which explains why it has no guns. This meant, of course, its only defense against pirates was to outrun them."

"I bet the owner had a hard time buying insurance," muttered a red headed woman not ten feet from Karen. There were some snickers among her immediate neighbors, but the captain seemed not to hear. He charged on with his presentation.

"From its headquarters in Baltimore, the typical routine was to pick up cotton in Charleston, South Carolina, which it then delivered to Liverpool England. The cotton was exchanged for finished textile products which were shipped back to Baltimore for sale and distribution."

Karen continued to lean against the wooden cabin, which placed her two or three feet behind the last row of the semi-circle of fellow travelers facing the captain. She found the talk of the Amity's history interesting, although her mind wandered some as she surveyed the crowd of thirty or more seated in front of her. It looked like an interesting mix with a few older and middle-aged people, and lots in their twenties or early thirties. The gender breakdown definitely emphasized men which suited Karen fine. She certainly wasn't opposed to latching on to some cute guy for the next two weeks. It didn't have to be serious, actually the less serious the better, just a nice addition to the trip was all she was looking for. There seemed to be several interesting prospects out there as she scanned the small group one last time before refocusing on the captain.

At this point in his introduction Todd paused briefly, looking over his audience to see if there were questions. Finding none, he proceeded to explain some of the navigational aspects of the trip. "The first leg of the journey begins here in Boston as we sail to Cape Sable Island on the southern tip of Nova Scotia. The distance is approximately three hundred miles, most of which is out of sight of land." Karen shivered a little as this last point penetrated her awareness. She hoped Todd was as competent as he looked and the crew was equally experienced. Of course they were, she concluded. Such silly thoughts, and she directed her attention back to her captain. "From Cape Sable we sail another three hundred miles up the coast of Nova Scotia, through the Northumberland Strait, and into Charlottetown, Prince Edward Island. The approximate sailing time for the journey is four days.

"Now please don't worry about the first few days when we are out of sight of land." He must have read my mind, Karen thought as she smiled to herself and thanked the captain silently for his sensitivity. "We will probably see several whales; and, of course, we have navigational help. As you will notice when you are in the stern of the ship, there are three crucial instruments located directly in front of the helm. In the center is a large compass, with a radar screen beside it on the left, and a Global Positioning System on the right. GPS is a system that uses several orbiting satellites to provide navigational information. These satellites emit signals that are picked up by our receiver, which enables it to locate precisely our current position as well as the compass reading to our destination. As a bonus, it provides the exact distance in miles between our present position and our intended destination.

"For those of you who are interested, we have charts under the main deck, toward the stern, in a small room right next to my cabin. Any crew member can explain to you how to read these charts. Our ship-to-shore radios are also located there which you will monitor as part of your duties while on watch.

"Okay, let me pause here for a moment and see if there are any questions." A hand went up, right in front of Karen. It belonged to a young man in his late twenties, or that's what Karen guessed, with long black hair pulled up in a ponytail.

"What role will guests play in raising and lowering the sails? It looks like a long way up there," the young man asked.

"That's a question we usually leave for the individual watch meetings which convene right after this one, but the answer is that only paid crew members are allowed on the yards. The yards are the wooden poles fastened at a right angle along the mast. Sails are let down or furled from there. As your question implies, it is a long way up the mast, and you do your work standing on a rope much like a circus performer on the high wire. It's dangerous work if you've never done it before. So unfortunately you won't be able to participate in that part of our work, but there is still plenty to do. Are there any other questions?"

Seeing none, he concluded with saying, "Let me then introduce you to the crew members you will be working with on your watch. On a typical three-masted barque like this one, there was a captain, three mates, four petty officers, and a crew. The petty officers consisted of a sailmaker, carpenter, boson's mate, and cook. Currently, on this ship, we only have a cook, Mr. Dominique Delgrosso. One hundred and fifty years ago, when this ship was at its prime, the standard diet was mostly salt pork and bread. Dom, will you stand please?" He did, and there was a smattering of applause which Dominique acknowledged with a slight bow. "I hope you can do better than that. We want these people to travel with us again."

"Aye, aye captain," Dominique responded with a smile as he resumed his sitting position on the deck.

"The captain of a merchant sailing vessel in the nineteenth century was God within the confines of his ship," Todd continued with a bemused look on his face. "His word was law, and he was often difficult to deal with as I'm sure all of you are aware from any reading you have done on the subject. Rather than God, please think of me as your instructor/tour guide. I won't become God unless some unusual problem arises which I don't anticipate. I will lead the first watch which we label A. Linda Symonds, our first mate, will lead Watch B. Linda, will you stand please?" As she did, there was a second brief smattering of applause. "Linda has been with us for three summers. She teaches sixth grade in Londonderry, New Hampshire in the winter. Finally, Watch C is led by our second mate, Jason Rosenthal." Jason, anticipating the captain's next words, raised his hand from his sitting position on the deck and smiled. "Thank you, Jason. It's nice to see a mate execute a command before it is even given," he said with a smile. "This is Jason's second summer with us. He is a recent graduate of Brown University with absolutely no clue about what to do with his future. Isn't that right, Jason?" Jason smiled once again as he nodded his head affirmatively at the captain. The irreverent look on his face hinted he was in no hurry to get serious about his life.

"Well, that's it for me," Todd concluded as he surveyed the group one last time. "We cast off in thirty minutes which gives you just enough time to meet with your watch leaders and learn more about the routines of the ship. I hope everyone has a great sail, and please come see me if you have any questions or problems."

Upon concluding, Todd McMillan leaned over to pick up a clipboard from the deck. He then proceeded to call out the names of each passenger, assigning them to a watch. Karen was placed in Watch B. She was pleased to be on Linda Symonds's team. She was reassured a second time that day knowing she would be instructed in the ways of the ship by a woman. As Linda raised herself from the oak deck floor and walked toward the stern, Karen followed after her.

～

Linda Symonds convened her meeting on the open deck in front of the helm. "Well," she said with a pause as she scanned her charges, "it's great to have you with us. Let me also take this opportunity to welcome you aboard the Amity. We had a great trip last summer to Nova Scotia, and I'm sure this trip will be equally memorable. What I would like to do this morning is have everyone introduce themselves, and then I will go over some additional routines of the ship. As Todd indicated, my name is Linda Symonds. I am a school teacher in Londonderry, New Hampshire, with two wonderful children, a boy and a girl, both in college. I have a passion for sailing and adventure which is why I'm here."

Karen, who was sitting this time with her back resting against the platform that supports the helm, noticed immediately that Linda was without a wedding band. Divorced, she thought. What a pity. She's an attractive woman with her trim figure, sandy blond hair of pageboy length with a few noticeable streaks of gray. Probably a little younger than her mother she thought. She couldn't picture her mother in a similar situation. She was far too traditional and lacking in self-esteem to move beyond her role of suburban housewife or, at least, that was what Karen had thought about her mother for as long as she could remember. Her mother lived in the shadow of her husband who defined her. Karen loved her mother dearly, but she had often wished her mother would stand up to her father. Just once would have been reassuring; but it never seemed to happen. Karen was looking forward to getting to know Linda. She was envious of a woman who had passion in her life. Passion was an emotion Karen rarely, if ever, felt. Her instincts told her this was a lack in her life needing work. Her therapist kept telling her she needed to find her own distinctive voice and live it, whatever that meant. Maybe this vacation would provide some answers. That was her hope, anyway.

When she had finished introducing herself, Linda looked to her immediate left to Edmund Huss, a retired retailer from northwestern Connecticut who also had a passion for sailing. In addition to Edmund and Karen, Watch B included Charlotte Ryan, a thirty-nine year old actress from New York City, the redhead who had made the crack about insurance earlier; Susan Carnegie, a twenty year old student at Smith

College; Walter Rogers, a thirty-five year old stockbroker; Scott Berk, a thirty year old pediatrician on his last vacation before starting his practice; and Doris and Jim Watkins, a couple in their early sixties from Severna Park, Maryland where Jim was a general contractor, and Doris, a school psychologist. The couple was taking this trip to celebrate Doris's recent retirement after twenty-five years of service. The paid crew working under Linda included Michael Blacklow, a senior at the University of North Carolina, Chapel Hill; and Peter Davies, a recent graduate of Trinity College in Hartford Connecticut.

With the introductions completed, Linda briefly outlined the safety regulations for the Amity. "Is there anyone here who is not a strong swimmer? Please raise your hand." After some hesitation, Doris Watkins raised hers. "I appreciate your honesty, Doris." Karen was impressed Linda had already learned Doris's name. She's a professional, Karen thought. "What we strongly recommend is that you wear a life vest while on deck. In heavy seas, water frequently washes over the deck, and people have been known to be swept overboard. I'll be happy to provide you with one as soon as this meeting is over.

"To make the sail more comfortable, we issue each passenger a pair of rubber boots, foul weather gear, and work gloves. We recommend you use the gloves while trimming the sails to avoid rope burns and blisters.

"Now did you all stow your gear properly in the forecastle? We suggest you use the ringbolts on the forecastle deck to lash down your gear. The ship pitches and rolls a lot—especially in rough seas." Karen wondered if she would ever sleep on the Amity. Her luggage was secured properly, a nice looking crew member had helped her with that, under the bottom row of beds in what appeared to be nothing more than a large bunkroom. Being someone who had difficulty sleeping in a noisy environment, the accommodations in the forecastle were a bit of a concern.

Passengers, as well as crew members in the nineteenth century, were housed in the forecastle, a cabin-like structure located toward the bow of the ship, which rises a few feet above the deck with sleeping quarters below. On the Amity these quarters consisted of nine rows of wooden bed frames stacked three on top of each other. When Karen had viewed them earlier that morning, the frames appeared more like large shelves than beds, with thin mattresses, and no safety rails. Karen concluded then to aim for a lower bunk to minimize any fall that might occur from a sharp pitch in a rolling sea. The only other alternative for sleeping was an area toward the stern, directly across from the charthouse, where there were ten hammocks. Linda anticipated Karen's anxiety and that of several others by saying, "Please don't worry about sleeping in those cramped quarters. You'll be so tired from serving your watches you'll be able to sleep anywhere. It's also dark there during the day.

"Before wrapping this up with a brief discussion of our watch requirements, let me pause briefly for any questions you may have." After surveying the group twice, Susan Carnegie finally broke the silence.

"The captain referred to a crew member called the boson's mate. What exactly does that person do?"

"He was responsible for maintaining all the equipment on deck—the rigging, anchor, lifeboats, things like that. Which reminds me, Todd mentioned we do not allow passengers on the rigging to raise or lower sails. However, passengers are permitted on the lower crosstrees. If you look up the mizzen mast in front of you, you will see two wooden triangular platforms lashed to the mast. Those are the crosstrees. It's a great place to look out on the ocean. You access them by climbing the rope ladder, but please be careful. You will be twenty-five or thirty feet above the main deck."

"What about keeping clean?" Charlotte Ryan asked in a voice that displayed a slight trace of irreverence. She obviously hasn't been below, Karen thought as she looked carefully at Charlotte. Charlotte was an interesting looking woman, about 5'8", one hundred and forty pounds, or thereabouts, with long, curly auburn hair and a well endowed figure. I wonder if she is as interesting a person as she looks, Karen reflected before focusing her attention back to Linda.

"There are showers in the male and female restrooms located right next to your sleeping quarters."

"Gender specific showers. Those Quakers were no fun at all. They must have picked up the spirit of Puritan New England," Charlotte responded with a grin.

"Think of yourself as on an adventuresome camping trip, Charlotte," Linda continued with a smile.

"Just what I want to hear, that I'm spending all this money to go camping, in tenement housing, on rocky seas, no less. Oui Vey. Such an adventure I won't soon forget."

"You will all survive this trip with flying colors," Linda said as she scanned the group one last time in search of additional questions. With no further questions forthcoming, she concluded the meeting by explaining the watch procedures.

"Each twenty-four hour day on the Amity is divided into three watches—ten a.m. to seven p.m., seven p.m. to three a.m., and three a.m. to eleven a.m. Our first watch will commence right after dinner at seven. While on duty, we ask that our passengers help with the cooking, take the helm, observe from the bow for floating objects such as lobster buoys and logs, trim sails, and monitor the radio. We like someone to be in the chartroom at all times. It can be boring sitting there waiting for the radio to clack on, so bring a book along if you so desire. Sailing cruises provide a great opportunity to catch up on reading. Finally, a member on watch checks for fire and flooding. We are especially concerned about problems in the engine room. Duties are rotated regularly so the different responsibilities are shared. Nothing requires prior knowledge or special skills, and Mike, Peter and I will be there to get you started and answer any questions. It's our watch too.

"That about wraps it up. We set sail in ten minutes, and Todd is always punctual. Enjoy the Boston skyline as we leave the harbor, and I will get you all back together to hand out boots and foul weather gear after we make the turn for Nova Scotia and the sails are set. Doris, please follow me to the supply room so I can issue you a life vest." Linda waited for Doris to join her, and then the two women headed at a brisk pace toward the bow of the ship.

∽

As the Amity began slowly to make its way out of Boston Harbor, Charlotte Ryan came over to join Karen along the port railing in the front section of the ship not far from the bowsprit. Karen had been looking out at the lighthouse off to her left and wondering who maintained it. The lighthouse was positioned on a tiny island, certainly less than an acre in total area; and aside from the many sea gulls, there were no other residents in evidence. She smiled warmly as Charlotte approached, signaling she welcomed the company.

"We certainly couldn't have picked a better day," Charlotte said as she moved alongside her. The temperature was in the low eighties, the sky partly cloudy, and the breeze gentle but firm.

"Hi," Karen responded. "I really like those cutoffs. Where did you get them?"

"Took some scissors to an old pair of jeans. It was either that or toss the jeans."

"That's how most cutoffs are born. So you're a New York actress? Must be exciting," Karen said.

"It's not that exciting," Charlotte responded with an impish grin, "or I wouldn't be wearing these cutoffs, traveling steerage class. The idea certainly gets people's attention when I'm introduced in a group setting. In my case, the actress thing is mostly hype."

"Do you do a lot of theatre work?" Karen asked, ignoring Charlotte's last comment.

"Some, when work is available. Mostly, I wait tables to pay the bills. That's really a form of acting too if you want good tips. On Wednesday nights I teach a modern dance class."

"Sounds like a busy schedule. I used to do some of that as a kid."

"Community theatre stuff?"

"No, I competed in beauty pageants."

"You're shitting me," Charlotte responded with emphasis and a mocking tone of disbelief. "That's nothing more than a cattle show."

"I know, except for the talent part."

"Did you enjoy parading around a stage with no clothes on?"

"Oh, we always had clothes on."

"Not enough, Preppy. You do have that wholesome preppy look. I love it. Too many clothes and those horny, gawking, judges will reject you right off the bat." And then she paused briefly to give Karen a critical look over. "You probably did rather well with those looks," Charlotte concluded. "What was your talent?" Karen was beginning to feel like she was being questioned by a Gestapo agent.

"Singing. That was always my favorite part. It's what I like best about church too." Karen was putting her on a little with that last comment. It was true she went to church occasionally, but the main point was to get a rise out of Charlotte. She succeeded, but Charlotte's response caught her a little by surprise.

"Don't tell me you're a Republican?"

"Is that a crime?" Karen replied a little defensively.

"It is in New York City, Preppy, but I guess you wouldn't be arrested for it in Colorado Springs. Isn't that where you said you were from?"

"Yes," Karen responded as the Amity proceeded past a green buoy. "It's a nice city," she said with a conviction to her voice she didn't always feel. It certainly is a beautiful place she thought as she directed her gaze away from Charlotte and toward the open sea. The Amity had left Boston Harbor safely behind them. The problem for Karen was Colorado Springs was confining socially and religiously conservative, an environment she was only able to fully comprehend now that she lived in Washington DC, a city culturally diverse and large enough to provide an anonymity that freed her from social pressure.

"Do they have carbon monoxide there? I need a fix everyday or I start to go nuts. Keep an eye on me over the next two weeks. I certainly won't get a fix around here." This woman was too much Karen concluded as her brief reverie abruptly came to an end. She wondered if they could ever be friends. She was even beginning to look for an escape when a wide grin came across Charlotte's face. Charlotte started to laugh. "Oh, don't take me too seriously, Preppie," she said as she continued to chuckle. "People from New York City are a little weird. I plead guilty. You'll get used to me. I look forward to hearing you sing. Maybe at some karaoke place on Prince Edward Island. I bet you're good."

"Maybe we can do it together," Karen responded feeling a little drained and yet somewhat better about Charlotte. The woman's going to take getting used to Karen concluded. As she was about to resume the conversation, Charlotte interrupted her train of thought with an excited:

"Whoa! This is about to get interesting." The Amity had eased her speed considerably and was turning slowly but decisively to the left. Crew members were scrambling up rope ladders, and the captain was calling out instructions from his position at the helm. "That young one in the tan shorts and the Princeton cap has nice legs," Charlotte commented with a grin.

"He's definitely hot," Karen responded. "Do you know who he is?"

"Hot. That's a good word for him. Nope. Must be from one of the other watches. Aren't those long poles up there, the ones that move out horizontally from the mast, called yards?"

"I think so."

"The captain was right when he said it's like balancing on a high wire up there. Look at those guys. They must be a little loco." The two woman continued their conversation and watched with increasing fascination as three members of the crew methodically worked together to unfurl and lower three rectangular sails on the foremast directly above them. As each sail was put into place, the captain instructed members of his watch on how to set the proper angle for the sail with the trim lines. In some cases the work of pulling the sheet to move the yard into position along the mast required two people.

"I guess that's what we'll be doing in a few hours," Karen commented as she refocused her gaze from the yards above to the interior of the ship where members of Watch A were working hard to trim the sails.

"Looks like fun," Charlotte said as she too directed her focus to the interior of the ship. "I'm starting to dig this scene." Twenty minutes after the excitement began, the three crew members came sliding down, one by one, on a rope attached to the railing not ten feet from where the two women were standing. As each one descended, Karen and Charlotte clapped their hands. The last one down had been the first one up, the nice looking one in the tan shorts and baseball cap. As he passed by the two ladies, he acknowledged their applause with a tip of his hat.

"Thanks," he said as he moved past them and headed toward the galley. "Lunch will be served in about ten minutes."

~

Lunch was good. It was a sandwich buffet with a variety of cold cuts, condiments, and breads laid out on a long table, with each person responsible for helping themselves. Chocolate chip cookies and fruit of all kinds were offered for dessert. During lunch, Karen sat and talked with Ed Huss. Ed was impressive with his gentle, aristocratic manner, and his detailed knowledge of so many subjects. He explained to her some of the principles of sailing and related them to a large ship like the Amity. He also reassured her about her politics. Ed was a Republican too.

Dinner on the Amity was even better than lunch. Again it was done in buffet style. The galley was located between the fore and main masts. It was a narrow room, about fifteen feet long and ten feet wide, with a roof overhead, and large pots and pans hanging from the walls. There was an industrial sized gas oven with burners, a gas grill, a huge sink to wash dishes, and cupboards located around the room for storage.

The facility had a disheveled, disorganized look, but it smelled great that night, a home cooked barbeque smell, with steaks cooking on the grill, small, individual steaks that each person selected for themselves and was responsible for grilling. It was a crowded, happy scene. Baked potatoes, a salad bar, and chocolate chip cookies again rounded out the menu. There was also a large hors d'oeuvres tray with beer, wine, and an assortment of soft drinks. Most passengers assembled outside the galley at six for cocktails while Karen's watch cooked and ate dinner early so they would not be late for the changing of the guard at seven. Karen's first work detail on the Amity was to monitor the salad bar and then to help wash dishes after everyone had eaten. She especially enjoyed working the salad bar because it gave her a chance to look over and to be introduced to some of the other passengers on the ship.

Although washing dishes was one of her least favorite activities, the job was made easier because Ed Huss had been assigned to work with her. Despite the wide difference in their ages, they were fast becoming friends. It was part of Karen's nature to seek out such relationships. She was searching for definition. Subconsciously she sought out strong, compassionate individuals to test different approaches to life. Linda seemed to sense a subtle "something" between them, and so she assigned them to walk the ship together as the safety patrol whose primary responsibility was to check the engines from time-to-time. The two new friends left the galley a little after 8:30.

"Now do you understand why I have such a deep love of the sea," Ed said as they slowly made their way toward the bow. "It started with my three years of service in the navy during World War ll. I remember nights like this on the Pacific. You tend to put the bad, terrifying times right out of your mind."

"Women say the same thing about childbirth. Most seem to forget the horrible pain of labor soon after their baby is born. I hope it is that way for me."

"I'm sure it will be. The mind seems to ignore the negatives associated with the things we love. Listen," he said as he paused and grabbed onto one of the rope stays that helped to stabilize the foremast. "A sailing vessel has a rhythm and a melody line. Tonight we have a symphony with the gentle slapping lines against the yards and masts, and the creaking deck. Put us in a gale and you'd think you were at a rock concert."

"It's so picturesque," Karen concurred as she leaned up against the ship's railing. "I keep thinking of all this vastness—the immensity of the starry universe above and the ocean. Both seem to be without end. And the moon playing peek-a-boo from between the clouds only adds to the mystery."

"The eternal. You can't touch it, but there are times when its presence is known. It's the kind of experience that can't be defined without messing it up; but, my dear, would you mind terribly if I shifted to something a little more mundane, to something a person can really touch, in fact the touching of it often makes it smell. What I'm aiming at is politics. Your expertise."

"Do I smell, Mr. Huss?" Karen asked with a wide grin he unfortunately missed due to the darkness of the night.

"I certainly don't think so. Bad analogy. It would take something very corrupting to make you smell, but let's quit all this cute stuff. What I would love to know is what your office thinks about the upcoming election?"

"You mean Bush/Clinton?" Karen responded.

"Yes, that's the race I'm interested in. I bet Republicans on the Hill are pretty confident."

"I would say extremely confident at this point, although the American people haven't really begun to focus on the election. From what I hear at the office, Clinton is the ideal opponent—lots of character problems and weak on foreign policy. All Bush strengths."

"That's kinda my take on things," Ed responded after a moment's reflection. "I'm rather surprised Clinton has made it this far. But they must be worried about something," Ed inquired as the two resumed their slow stroll toward the bow.

"Oh, there are always worries in an election," Karen responded. "What people are talking about is the soft economy and Perot. Mostly Perot. Republican leaders can't fathom why his support is as high as it is. They keep expecting his support to plummet, but, of course, it hasn't yet. The real concern is Perot's support will come more from Bush than Clinton. He's the wildcard in the race everyone worries about."

"You bet he is, and I'm sure he's loving things right now. He scares me a little. People with his background and mindset don't understand the subtlety and messiness of politics, the need for compromise, the need to befriend members of the opposing party. They make for good corporate executives but not presidents. The only thing for sure is events can change quickly. Two years ago Bush had this thing in the bag."

"Congressman Jackson is still quite confident. Clinton makes his blood boil. I don't feel quite so strongly. Actually, I find Clinton rather cute, although I would never vote for him."

"Is your congressman a solid Bush supporter?"

"Yes and no. I think in his heart of hearts he's a Buchanan man, but all politicians are first and foremost realists. Sentimentalists don't seem to last long on the Hill. He has supported the President pretty consistently on his domestic priorities, and he definitely respects him."

"That's good. I have a high regard for Bush too. He led this country admirably in the Persian Gulf War. Saddam Hussein will be lucky to survive the next six months the way the Iraqi economy is decomposing. I think the sanctions are a good way to finish the job. They certainly saved a lot of American lives, and they saved us from having to put the place back together. That would have been complicated with the diverse mix of ethnic groups. I'm one of those who never criticized the President for not finishing off Saddam Hussein."

"I hope the sanctions work," Karen said as she sat herself down on the capstan. "Now, Ed. What the heck am I sitting on? It looks and feels like a giant steel mushroom."

"That's the capstan. It's used primarily to raise and lower the anchor. Do you feel the large hole by your knees? There are about six of them. You insert wooden planks into the holes. The planks look a lot like oars. The anchor line is wrapped around the base of the capstan which enables six sailors, each holding a plank and walking around together in a circle, to raise and lower the anchor."

"Neat," said Karen. "It's amazing how all these things can be done without modern machines."

"Yes, these ships are remarkable, but don't romanticize too much or you'll miss the harsh truth about this work. Sailing in the nineteenth century was hard, dangerous, lonely work. Imagine yourself up in the yards in a real blow. The effect of the roll and pitch of the ship is much greater up there."

"Not me thanks."

"And I forgot to add the element of cold. Ships that rounded the South Pole went through cold, nasty weather. Working with ropes with freezing hands is no fun. Finally, imagine being away from family for six months or more at a time. The only good thing was there was so much to do—swab the decks, paint them, mend the sails, trim and adjust the sails. It was never ending."

"I'm beginning to like my Washington job a whole lot better," Karen said as she lifted herself from the capstan, and they resumed their tour of the ship. Being in no hurry and stopping to chat with other watch members who crossed their path, they finally completed their rounds a little after nine thirty. Ed sought out Linda to report all was well. From there, he was assigned to the radio room, and Karen reported for her first stint at the helm.

For Karen, standing watch at the helm required some learning. She was assisted in this process by Michael Blacklow, one of the paid crew who worked under Linda. He explained to her how to operate the radar screen and when to become concerned about an approaching ship that was getting too close. He then asked her to read off the information from the GPS screen. After taking a moment or two to become familiar with the screen, she responded: "It looks like our course to Nova Scotia is set for thirty degrees and the distance to our destination is a little more than two hundred and forty miles."

"What about the current course of the ship? You get that information from the compass directly in front of you."

"The needle seems to be fluctuating between twenty-eight and thirty-three degrees."

"Excellent," Michael exclaimed. "Now come join me at the helm." As Karen stood up on the short platform and moved toward him, he continued. "All you have to do is keep the ship heading on this course. You will soon discover the roll of the waves causes the ship to move off course in one direction or the other. This shift shows up immediately on the compass, and so you make your adjustments by moving the wheel to bring the ship back on course. Nothing radical. You'll get the rhythm with a little practice. It's really quite simple, and I'll be right here in case you have any problems."

"That sounds reassuring," Karen said as she stepped onto the metal grate and took hold of the large wheel with both hands. She remained at the helm for the next hour and was pleased to learn when she consulted the GPS, upon being relieved, the ship was headed on a course of twenty-nine degrees with two hundred and thirty-four miles left to the coast of Nova Scotia.

She left the helm feeling upbeat and energized for this late in the evening, however, she was soon to learn the most interesting portions of her watch were over. Her tour of duty at the bowsprit was boring and pointless, at least as far as Karen was concerned. It seemed pointless because she could barely see ten feet in front of her. Even if she spotted a log or some other foreign object, she wondered what could be done about it. How could she warn the helmsman in time and would that person be able to direct the ship away from the dangerous object? Impossible, she thought. It was boring because she was a person who was not very comfortable with extended periods of silence which was what this job was all about.

Her last responsibility for the evening was to monitor the radio in the chartroom. Because she was too tired to read and incapable of divining the charts on her own, she sank into the lone lounge chair in the small paneled room and was soon fast asleep. Keith Simpson from Watch C woke her at 3:04 a.m. with the good news she was relieved from duty and could go to bed. As she walked up the narrow passageway to the main deck, the thought of those thin mattresses on the wooden beds did not seem so bad. She even managed a smile as she bumped into Charlotte Ryan on her way across the main deck to the forecastle. Charlotte acknowledged her with a deliberate thumbs up. The two women descended into the bowels of the forecastle together, tired, looking forward to sleep, but pleased the day had gone so well and eager to do it all over again in the morning.

Patrick McGovern was exhausted. He had not planned his watch well, the third watch of Group C, which ran from three a.m. to eleven a.m. He had tried to sleep on one of those thin mattresses in the forecastle earlier in the evening, but it had been noisy and not very comfortable. He had succeeded only fitfully, and the wake up at three in the morning had been jarring.

Despite his exhaustion, he was getting through his duties, in fact there was an eerie beauty to the sea that night which he found stimulating. The breeze had been moderate to gentle throughout the night, and he enjoyed the work of trimming the sails in response to Jason Rosenthal's direction. There were always small adjustments to be made. He learned quickly that there was no such thing as automatic pilot on a sailing vessel.

He also enjoyed standing near the bowsprit looking out at the vastness of the ocean. The quiet stillness that enveloped him as the Amity pushed through a fog bank was disorienting and yet somehow moving. Nothing stayed the same for long. Soon the stars were back in a partly cloudy sky. The half moon that broke in and out of those clouds created streaks of light across the rolling water that reminded him of oil paintings he had seen in museums as a kid. His only disappointment was there were no signs of fish out here or other ships in the night.

He was relieved from duty at the bowsprit to take the helm a little after 4:30 a.m., as the sun was rising off to the right of the Amity's bow. Jason outlined the procedures for operating the helm and remained with him for several minutes to make sure Patrick had everything under control. "I'm going to take advantage of the new light and let out a few sails. The wind has changed somewhat in the last few hours. Keep her on a steady course, and no wild gyrations please. I'll be up on the yards," Jason said as he left the helm area and moved toward the main mast.

"Aye, aye Captain," Patrick responded with a wink Jason obviously missed as he proceeded to his destination. "I'll keep an eye on you."

"Thanks, Pat," Jason said as he briefly turned to smile. Soon he was climbing the mast on the rope ladder and then inching his way along the yard with his feet precariously supported by the thin rope sheet as he let out the lower topsail. Ten minutes later he was climbing higher up the mast to accomplish the same task on the upper topsail. Patrick admired both his skill and his courage. He breathed a little easier when Jason returned to the helm after twenty-five minutes with the job completed.

At six that morning Patrick's duty changed again, and he was ordered to the galley to help Dominique Delgrosso prepare breakfast. He enjoyed cooking and had done a lot of it as a single man living by himself because his frugal disposition kept him from eating out when he was not on the road. Dominique quickly realized his talents as a short order cook, and put him in charge of preparing the eggs, both fried and scrambled.

As the breakfast crowd thinned out sometime after 8:00 o'clock and his responsibilities eased, Patrick's exhaustion caught up with him. He began to look forward for the first time to finishing his watch and trying the forecastle one more time. But the pitch and roll of the sea can have a roller coaster effect, and his waning energy received a much needed second wind when Karen Hathaway entered into the small galley.

Wow, who is this slim beauty? he thought as he scraped the grease with his spatula to the back of the skillet. How have I missed her? "Is it too late for some soft scrambled eggs and a piece of toast?" Karen asked as she looked over at Patrick and forced a tired grin. She too had fought with the bunks in the forecastle with only partial success. She was wearing the same khaki shorts with a dark yellow blouse and a hunter green sweater. Though the sun was shining brightly, it was a crisp sixty degrees outside; and, with the steady breeze, the sweater was a must for Karen.

"Absolutely not. Soft scrambled are my specialty," he replied grinning. "By the way, I'm Pat McGovern."

"Karen Hathaway," she responded looking at him a second time. She too experienced a surge of energy which she misinterpreted as a signal from her body coffee would soon be on the way. She left Patrick and went in search of that coffee as well as a tray, a plate, silverware, and toast, settling instead for a cinnamon raisin bagel which she felt a little guilty about because she knew she didn't need it. The problem was it smelled really good, all the food around here was tempting in that way, so she picked up the bagel thinking they better find land soon before she floated off the ship like the Goodyear Blimp. As Patrick cracked two eggs into a small ceramic bowl, he immediately thought of the musical *Chorus Line*, the idea of a blimp couldn't have been farther from his mind. "Tits and Ass" she's got he chuckled to himself as he whipped the eggs into shape with a fork. I like the long, sandy brown hair and the soft green eyes. The eyes, though a little sleepy looking that morning, hinted at an innocence and tenderness which Patrick found enormously appealing. This trip has taken on a whole new dimension he concluded as he gently poured the eggs onto the hot skillet.

Karen was halfway through her breakfast when Jason Rosenthal yelled out, "Thar she blows over the port bow." The Amity which had been gently listing that way in response to the steady tug of the southwest wind seemed to lurch further to that side as twenty passengers scattered to the portside railing. Patrick left his station at the galley and followed directly behind Karen as she quickly moved the short distance to the railing to see what this was all about.

"Looks like great big Hump Backs to me," Charlotte Ryan called out from her vantage point near the bowsprit. She looked across at the gathering crowd, singled out Karen, and winked. There were ten or twelve large black hulks sunning themselves and watching the Amity as she sailed by not more than fifty yards away.

"They look more like long-finned Pilot whales to me," Edmund Huss said as he moved toward Karen and Patrick on the railing. "Good morning, Karen. It's getting exciting around here."

"Pat McGovern," Patrick said as he held out his hand toward Edmund.

"Ed Huss, nice to meet you Pat," Edmund said as he received Patrick's firm handshake.

"What makes you think they are Pilot whales, Mr. Huss?" Patrick asked as he returned his gaze toward the sea.

"Ed, please," Edmund responded as he too looked again out at the whales. "You can tell from their long, slim bodies. If we were a little closer, you could see their flippers are long and slender too."

"The big ones look to be about twenty feet long," Patrick replied as he watched them drift off in the distance. "It sure would help to have binoculars."

"The males run about that length, the females about five feet shorter. If you look closely, you can see the females weigh about half what the males do."

"That's good to know, Ed," Karen said, smiling over at him. "I bet the females live longer too."

"Five to ten years longer. A healthy female can make it to about sixty."

"Fascinating Ed," Patrick said as he turned away from the whales and started to walk back in the direction of the galley. "Nice to meet you both," he said with a smile. "I better get back to the kitchen and start cleaning up."

Patrick couldn't wait to get off duty at eleven. After finishing in the galley, he spent his last two hours on safety watch which involved checking the engine room for fire or strange noises and the lower decks for signs of leakage. It was boring duty, but he spent the time wandering the ship with his eye on Karen. She busied herself with a book, leaning up against the forecastle cabin on the starboard side in the early morning sun. She looked up and smiled whenever Patrick passed by, which charged him with renewed energy. Each time he stepped back onto the main deck he felt the pull of the forecastle, the North Pole, and the mysterious presence of Karen Hathaway.

"Hey Karen," he said after completing his last round of the ship's perimeter with some relief and excited anticipation. "Come join me on the crosstrees."

"Can two fit up there?" she asked as she looked up from her book with a smile.

"No problem," Patrick said as he gazed up at the lower crosstrees on the foremast just ahead of them. Actually he had no idea what the answer was to her question, but he wasn't going to give her an easy excuse. One problem at a time he thought as he looked back at her. "It doesn't look like it's more than thirty feet above the deck."

"Sounds like fun," Karen said as she closed her book and began to gather herself from the deck. Patrick extended his left hand in assistance which she graciously accepted with a smile. "It's not too rough out. I'll be right back as soon as I put my book away downstairs." Deciding not to wait, Patrick climbed the rope ladder and perched himself on the crosstrees. It would be a little tight, actually a nice problem to have with a good looker like Karen, and what a view he thought as he scanned the ocean before him.

"I'm up here," he called down as Karen emerged from the forecastle looking up and down the deck to see where he had gone. "It's great. Just climb up the ladder. The view's magnificent." Karen did as she was told and soon joined him. Being a little afraid of heights, the thought quickly flashed through her mind of "what am I doing here." It must be Patrick she concluded as she grabbed tightly with one free hand to the rope stay directly to her right. He certainly was dashing looking with the neatly trimmed golden red hair, gentle blue eyes, and athletic physique. The ship pitched and rolled as it plowed its way through the sea, more noticeably than was evident from the deck, but not enough to make their perch on the crosstrees dangerous or especially scary.

"First one to spot a whale gets a free dinner," Patrick said as he looked over at her.

"You're on, cuz that's exactly what I'm looking for," Karen responded. She was far happier looking out than down. "Can you imagine standing on that little rope and working one of those sails? Not me."

"Jason did it early this morning. Maybe after a little practice, but I know what you mean. That's a hard deck down there."

"What a dangerous way to earn a living. I read a book by some guy named Dana in college called *Two Years Before the Mast*. It's starting to come back to me. At least we're not headed around one of the poles with all that cold and bad weather."

"I wonder what they did when someone got hurt on a ship like this? They probably just pushed the bone back into place, put an ace around it, and sent the poor guy back to work."

"Something like that," Karen said as a frown passed fleetingly across her face. "We've got a doctor in our group which is always good to know."

"We've got a couple honeymooning in our group," Patrick responded with a laugh. "I wonder how they're doing on those thin mattresses?"

"There's no way they could both fit on one together. What a great honeymoon trip. They sound like an adventuresome pair."

"They seem nice, though I don't really know them well yet. They've stayed pretty much to themselves." And then after a brief pause, he continued. "It sure is beautiful up here. What a perspective! The sea is so awesome, and I guess pretty mundane and lonely at times. There's nothing out here to see."

"There's lots underneath, though. We have to see a dolphin before this is all over."

"Isn't it amazing how exciting it is to see wildlife in their natural environment? It's like seeing an elk in the Rockies."

"Do you know Colorado?" Karen asked as she looked over at him.

"I'm learning about it. I've lived in Denver for the last four years. What a great place!"

"I grew up in Colorado Springs. It's a small world."

"Do you live there now?" Patrick asked as he shifted his focus from the sea to the deck below where he noticed several passengers from the first watch were starting to set up lunch.

"Yes and no. I live in DC now, but because I work for a Republican congressman from the Springs, I go home often as part of my job. My parents still live there." Wrong party, but that won't be too difficult to get over he thought as he looked across at her and smiled.

"I'll tell you what," Patrick said as he shifted his position somewhat and grabbed onto the rope stay. "Let's continue this over lunch."

"Good idea," she responded. "As you may remember, the whales interrupted my breakfast. I'm getting a little hungry. Must be all this salt air. I certainly haven't done much exercise." He extended his right hand to help guide her back to the rope ladder and then followed her descent to the deck. They had lunch with the doctor, Scott Berk, and with Susan Carnegie, the junior from Smith College. Patrick enjoyed reliving his old haunts in Northampton. He had dated a Smithy for a time while a student at the University of Massachusetts in Amherst, and he instantly bonded with Scott. Scott was 6' 4" and had played basketball at Dartmouth College. They had winter sports in common. Patrick had attended UMass on a hockey scholarship, had played on the varsity for three years, and had remained after graduating as an assistant coach while he completed his master's degree in geology. The girls were impressed to be eating lunch with two college jocks. Although he hated leaving, Patrick excused himself after lunch and headed for the forecastle and those thin mattresses. He fell sound asleep almost instantly.

≈

"Damn it," he said to himself as he stretched on the wooden cot after checking his watch. It was 8:30, and he had slept through dinner. He rolled out of bed, stepped down a wooden ladder from his middle bunk to the wooden plank floor, and searched for his backpack in the near total darkness of the forecastle bunkroom. He grabbed a towel, his shaving kit, and headed for the shower.

He emerged on deck twenty minutes later and was glad he had put on a sweatshirt. It was sixty-two degrees outside, with a light wind, and a sky that was solidly defined by thick clouds. The galley had long been closed, but he found Michael Blacklow, one of the hired hands from Watch B, who helped him organize a plate of leftovers from dinner. He ate quickly, washed his dishes, took one more beer, and headed for the stern of the ship where he heard guitar music and a small group singing.

Peter Davies was an accomplished acoustic guitar player. He had minored in music at Trinity College and was planning to get a job in one of the large hotels in Vail Colorado for the winter. He couldn't imagine a better routine than to ski during the day and entertain at night. Maybe he would be back on the Amity next summer. Linda Symonds, for one, was happy to have Peter entertain the guests. With everything in good order on her watch, the ship was practically sailing itself in the light evening breeze, it was important for the guests to be having a good time. A small group, led by Karen Hathaway and Charlotte Ryan, had gathered around Peter on the section of deck between the mizzen mast and helm.

Patrick wandered over with his beer and listened to Karen and Charlotte belt out "Hotel California" by the Eagles. He was impressed. The girls were good and were obviously enjoying the singing and the attention their clear, strong voices were attracting to them. The two women had not had to wait for a karaoke bar. After "Hotel California," Peter went directly into "Black Magic Woman" by Santana, and the two friends didn't miss a beat. The trio worked together like a well rehearsed band.

The concert lasted for another thirty minutes. Patrick loved music but couldn't sing, so he just leaned against the mizzen mast and listened. It was nice to be a little way off from the small group circling the performers because he was able to focus a steady gaze on Karen. Her trim figure was hidden in a red and white Denison University sweatshirt, but not her finely boned cheeks, long and graceful neckline, and soft green eyes, eyes that were not piercing or intense but eyes that would often shine with good humor as she looked over at Charlotte for reinforcement. She was both beautiful and obviously talented. His current girl friend, a fellow geologist who worked for the state of Colorado testing underground gas tanks for leakage problems was certainly attractive, but nothing like this he thought as he tapped his left foot to a James Taylor tune.

Fortunately, for Patrick, he was not standing too far away to go unnoticed. After finishing "Fire and Rain," Karen winked at Charlotte and ruffled the short, dark brown hair of Peter Davies. "You're great," she said. "Thank you so much. We will have to do this again." Peter smiled up at her as she moved away from the small group and headed toward Patrick. She too had been charged earlier that morning, and like a collection of nails placed within the powerful field of a magnet, she moved deliberately toward her target. Peter went into a rendition of "San Francisco Bay Blues" he had taken from an Eric Clapton CD.

"Hey, sleepy head," she said as she came up alongside Patrick. "I missed you at dinner."

"Last night took the wind out of my sails," he responded with a brief smile.

"That's an apt analogy. So were you able to sleep in the bunkroom?"

"Like a baby."

"Good for you. I'm headed there in another hour after finishing my watch at the bow. Come up there with me and help me stay awake."

"I'll make a deal with you. I come on duty right after you finish. Stay there with me, and we can make the transition together."

"I'll see how long I last," she said with a smile as she started to make her way slowly toward the front of the ship.

"Okay. I guess that's the most I can hope for at this time of night," he said as he walked up beside her. The two proceeded together in silence past the galley, the forecastle, and stopped in front of the capstan which was located six or seven feet from the bow. They leaned together against the capstan enjoying the feel of each other's warmth, and peering across the bowsprit at the gently rolling sea. After another minute or two of silence, he placed his left arm around her and she nestled her head against his shoulder.

"Tired?" he asked.

"I'm getting there," she responded.

"You sure do sing well," he continued.

"Thanks. I've had a lot of training."

"That other lady has a good voice too."

"That's Charlotte Ryan. She's a New York actress."

"You're kidding. A trip like this attracts interesting people. I also like your friend Ed. Did you know him before?"

"Nope. I met him on the ship too. He's a dear. He has this passion for the ocean he acquired from serving in the navy during World War II."

"He goes back a while."

"Yes, but he is so gentle and wise. He's the type of man every girl dreams of having for a father."

"He'd also do well with a son."

"I'm sure he would," she replied as she closed her eyes and thought about sleep. Patrick wondered a little about this father association and wanted to ask about her real father, but he held off. He didn't want to sound nosey, and he also sensed he was losing her to sleep. So here he was, staring out into the ocean, doing extra watch duty. He laughed silently to himself as he thought how much he enjoyed her taking advantage of him. A few minutes later she whispered up at him. "Are there any whales out there?"

"None that I can see."

"Good, you do excellent work," she said as she snuggled up closer to him for warmth and so she could gain a more secure position against the capstan. He held her like this for another few minutes and then he spoke in a quiet voice.

"Karen. Why don't you go to bed. I'd be happy to finish out the remainder of your watch."

"That's not fair," she said as she shifted her position and raised her head from his shoulder to look into his kind blue eyes.

"I really don't mind," Patrick responded.

"I'll be happy to help you with the breakfast dishes in the morning."

"That won't be necessary. You just get a good night's sleep; and when you wake up, we'll be off the coast of Nova Scotia."

"That will be a nice change," she said. "Are you sure you don't mind?"

"No problem," he said as she stood up, faced him, leaned over toward him, and gave him a soft kiss. He stood up with her, held her firmly, relishing the feel of her body, and thinking it was doubtful he would ever see his geology friend again. After a moment or two she broke away, and he wished her a good night. "Sleep well, and I'll look forward to seeing you in the morning."

"Me too," Karen replied as she squeezed him briefly before stepping away from the capstan. She smiled over at him warmly as she turned to head the short distance to the forecastle. That kiss stayed with Patrick for a long time as he began to take seriously the idea of dating Karen. There was only one nagging problem: the fact that she worked for a right wing Republican congressman. It wasn't the fact she was a Republican that bothered him because Patrick was not excessively partisan. It was Congressman Jackson. That asshole, Patrick thought. He knew the record well. Jackson was known to have one of the worst environmental records in Congress which not only affected Patrick's job but his deep love for the outdoors and open spaces.

Jackson was also known as a loyal supporter of the NRA, an organization Patrick loathed, stemming from a scary experience he had had in his senior year in high school. To earn extra money, Patrick drove a middle school bus each morning in east Boston. He would have driven the afternoon route too, but it conflicted with hockey practice. One morning in early February, a sixth grader, exactly three days after watching a TV movie involving a terrorist hijacking of an airplane, shoved a real handgun up against the back of Patrick's head in an attempt to hijack the bus. The attempt failed only because the bus monitor in charge of discipline, a huge kid who played tackle on the varsity football team for a high school in Roxbury, acted quickly when the sixth grader's attention was diverted to wrestle him to the ground and take the gun away.

Patrick never felt absolutely safe walking in a large city after that experience, and he believed he had just as much right to feel safe as another person who owned a gun. Tokyo was safe, most European cities were safe, but their American counterparts were a war zone. Hunting rifles were fine, but handguns and semi-automatic weapons needed to be taken from their owners and destroyed. It was the government's job to provide for safe streets, and there was no way, at least in Patrick's mind, to do it without controlling guns. Beauty only goes so far, Patrick concluded with some disappointment. Maybe he would be seeing his geology friend again after all. That would be his last kiss from Karen if she turned out to be a rabid right-winger like her boss.

∽

Watch for Patrick that night was routine, a carbon copy of Sunday's experience, with two exceptions. First, it began raining hard, a little after three on Tuesday morning. Life on deck was slippery, thus a little dangerous, and generally miserable. The second incident involved an approaching fishing boat. The problem was the Amity and the fishing boat were on a collision course.

Patrick was wandering aimlessly on the deck in his foul weather gear looking for something to do when all the excitement broke out. The helmsman, a paid crew member named Burt Robinson, notified the second mate of the potential problem. At that point the fishing boat was half a mile away. Jason Rosenthal went quickly below to the chartroom to hail the fishing boat on the radio and demand he change course. The fishing boat refused to answer.

"The fucker's on drugs," Jason yelled out to Burt after hurriedly returning to the helm. "It happens all the time out here. Those guys are on drugs and paying no attention to what's around them. Prepare to head up. All hands, please help with the lines." And so the Amity headed up wind and avoided a collision. The physical exertion of trimming the sails and then letting them out again was a pleasant diversion for Patrick on an otherwise monotonous and dreary night.

They spotted land, Cape Sable Island, off the coast of Nova Scotia, at 7:00 on Tuesday morning which put them right on schedule. They had traveled three hundred miles and were half way there. The captain changed course, heading twenty degrees further east, and the Amity began the two hundred mile journey up the coast of Nova Scotia. The rain continued to fall, though lighter now, and Patrick looked forward to sleep. Mercifully Jason dismissed him two hours early with a well done, and he headed for the forecastle.

∽ 41 ∽

He slept soundly until two thirty that afternoon when he was awakened by a gentle shaking of his shoulder. "Pat, you might want to wake up and join us on deck. We're about to go swimming." Patrick yawned, stretched, opened his eyes, and as he looked up at Karen a smile came across his face.

"Are you going swimming too?" he asked in a groggy voice that was fighting to shake off sleep.

"Yes, I just put my suit on."

"Is it warm enough to swim? The water in Maine is freezing."

"Linda, our watch leader, said it was about seventy degrees."

"That doesn't sound so bad. Sure, I'd love to go. I need a good jolt to shake away these cobwebs."

"Good," Karen responded as she patted his shoulder and turned to go. "I'll see you up there in a few minutes." When Patrick arrived on deck fifteen minutes later, it was a different world out there. The sun was shining, the sails furled, and the two diesel powered engines were running at idle. The Amity was headed into the wind and drifting slowly backwards as it rose and fell, pitched and swayed to the moderate swells produced by the southwest breeze. Linda Symonds and Peter Davies were perched on the forward and aft crosstrees as lifeguards and lookouts for sharks.

With Karen watching, Patrick was ready to play Tarsan for his Jane. He grabbed a halyard for one of the jibs, walked out on the bowsprit, swung low over the water, and tried to enter it by doing a back flip. The problem was he released too late and wasn't able to complete the flip, thus landing directly on his back. Because the distance to the water was minimal, the only damage done was to his ego. After recovering from her laughter, Karen dove in from the side of the ship to join him. As soon as she surfaced, Patrick swam over to her, grabbed her shoulders, pulled her under water, and tried to kiss her. Karen defended herself by grabbing his trunks and attempting to pull them off. They both bobbed up to the surface, laughing, and choking down water. Karen then proceeded to challenge him to a race around the Amity and took off with a strong crawl. Patrick lunged forward in hot pursuit, and after several strokes was able to take hold of her shoulders again and pull her under the water. Mercifully, good judgment prevailed, and they decided to return to the boat before they both drowned.

What happened next was, for Patrick, a gift. The swim itself had been enlightening. She was not only beautiful, but she was an athlete too. Her dive over the side of the Amity was executed with good form, her legs had been together for the most part with toes pointed, very impressive, much more impressive than his own lame performance he concluded; and she was obviously a strong swimmer. Spunky too. All of this was important to Patrick, but when he saw Charlotte Ryan approach them in white short shorts and a psychodelic T-shirt, he sensed another important learning opportunity.

Karen and Patrick were sitting with their backs against the forecastle cabin and their legs extended toward the sun, drying off solar style, as the ship continued to drift in irons while the paid staff took their turn in the ocean. "Hey, you guys," Charlotte announced as she stopped in front of them. "Can I join you or do you have something private going on? It's like the fourth grade around here. Everybody's pairing up. It makes me sick."

"Please come join us," Patrick said as he took in all of Charlotte. "My name is Pat McGovern, and I understand you're an actress from New York." Another good looker Patrick thought to himself. How come my watch only has married women and males? I'm going to have to transfer to their watch for the trip home Patrick decided as Charlotte joined them on the deck.

"Actresses don't swim as you can see," Charlotte said as she too stretched out her legs into the warm sun. "It's good to finally meet you, Pat. You know a nice person would have given me a chance with some of the handsome guys on this ship, but Republicans aren't nice. Rather selfish sons of bitches. They know what they want and go right after it. As long as it doesn't lead to more taxes, they smile like Cheshire cats."

"I know what you mean. They pretend to be elephants but that's a smokescreen. They're jackals in disguise that go right after their prey."

"Just vultures if you ask me," Charlotte replied as she winked at Patrick and gave him a reassuring grin. Yes! Patrick thought. An ally in the form of an outspoken New York liberal. This is good.

"Come, come you two," Karen responded in a voice rising to the challenge. "You have no idea what my politics are all about."

"You got politics, baby?" Charlotte intoned, imitating the voice of a black woman. "What politics you got? You got politics to stop the shooting, baby? You got politics to make the streets safe at night?"

"You're right about gun control, Charlotte. I hate guns. They scare me to death. Republicans need to support moderate gun control," Karen said rather earnestly and somewhat defensively. Yes, again, Patrick thought. There is hope. Bless this loud mouthed Yankee.

"What about the air you breathe, the smoke from all those guns, the exhaust from snarled traffic?" Patrick asked as he looked over at Karen hoping he wasn't pushing her too far.

"Oh, I'm a Republican on that one," Charlotte interjected with glee. "As I told Karen the other day, if I don't gulp my quota of toxic fumes I think I'm going to die. It's dangerous out here in all this fresh air."

"Now listen you two. I didn't come all the way to the coast of Nova Scotia to hear my party maligned."

"Oh, we ain't maligning, baby, we're ed-you-cay-ting."

"Unfortunately, we're acting like asses, Karen," Patrick said as he quickly interrupted Charlotte before she could complete her thought, "and I apologize for both me and my new friend from New York."

"Speak for yourself, John. I think the company you keep has thrown your hormones out of whack. You're thinking with your you know what."

"It fills up my senses."

"It certainly fills out those cute little trunks."

"Hey you guys," Karen said with a grin. "I might even surprise you on the environment, Charlotte," Karen said, interested more in defending herself than in shifting the conversation in a safer direction. But Charlotte got Patrick's point and backed off in her own immutable style.

"We won't let you vote, baby, but you sure can sing."

"You both were terrific. We need to get you together with Peter again tonight."

"That kid's not bad for Hartford," Charlotte announced with a grin.

"We'd even take him in Boston," Patrick replied.

"You two are impossible," Karen said as she jokingly shoved her elbow into Patrick's side.

"Just two Yankees picking on a westerner," Patrick said in his best Boston accent that was more distinctive than the usual tone and cadence of his speech. He reached for her elbow and gently squeezed it.

"Good sport," Charlotte replied as she closed her eyes and soaked up the sun. Noticing the change in Charlotte's demeanor and sensing a wonderful opportunity with a bucket that Jason Rosenthal had just withdrawn from the water, Karen looked at Patrick, put a finger to her lips, and gently motioned for him to move aside. Her eyes and facial expression were all that were necessary to bring Jason on board, and Charlotte went swimming. Well almost. The shock and expression on Charlotte's face as Jason emptied the bucket on her made Karen feel a whole lot better about the political barbs and challenges she had recently endured.

~

The Amity sailed all day Wednesday up the coast of Nova Scotia. It was a dreary day for the most part, a day defined by thick clouds, intermittent rain, and gusty winds of up to twenty knots; but the passengers were entertained by the Nova Scotia coastline, always in sight from the port side of the ship, the many seals, and one spectacular flurry of performing dolphins. Karen had achieved one of her goals for the trip. They did not see whales again, however, until the return trip the following week.

The immediate goal of Wednesday's sail was to arrive at the Strait of Canso. This narrow body of water, it is only ninety feet wide at its narrowest point, separates the main body of Nova Scotia from Cape Breton Island. By traveling through it you avoid circling Cape Breton Island which takes two hundred miles off of the trip. Once you pass through the Strait of Canso, it is a straight shot to Prince Edward Island—about one hundred miles away.

Karen was impressed with the work of the crew as the ship made its way toward the strait. It was four thirty in the afternoon, there was a light drizzle in the air, Karen was dressed in rubber boots and foul weather gear, and the wind produced a steady pitch and roll on the main deck. Captain McMillan took the helm and headed the Amity into the wind so all the sails could be furled. That job took half an hour or more and was not easily achieved due to the weather conditions. When the task was completed, the captain went below to radio the keeper of the bridge that crossed the Strait of Canso, the bridge that provided the only direct link between Nova Scotia and Cape Breton Island. The bridge was situated on a turntable that opened to allow ships to pass through.

The passage through the strait was memorable. Karen and Patrick stood near the bowsprit with Linda Symonds. Linda was there to pass along information to the captain at the helm. The two conversed over a two way radio. Linda also had a chart which she handed to Patrick that explained the sights on both sides of the strait.

The Amity approached the strait through Chedabucto Bay with Nova Scotia on the left and Cape Breton Island on the right. Karen wondered if the beaches on Cape Breton Island were as beautiful as those on the coast of Nova Scotia, and became excited about arriving at Prince Edward Island on Thursday morning. Linda pointed out the oil transfer station at Point Tupper on the Cape Breton side which twenty-five years ago had been a heavy water plant for nuclear reactors. The world is changing

Karen reflected with Yeltsin in the Kremlin and the Berlin Wall a thing of the past. She felt optimistic about life as she grabbed Patrick's hand and smiled up at him. She waved with her free right hand to a middle-aged couple that was braving the poor weather, standing on the green bank of Nova Scotia looking with interest at the Amity.

As the ship powered through the 8,000 foot strait, Linda pointed to the town of Mulgrove, a quaint, old fishing community off in the distance on the Nova Scotia side. She had been there on her first cruise with the Amity two years ago. She remembered a little restaurant two streets from the water where crew members and assorted guests had enjoyed a wonderful lobster dinner. Fifteen minutes later she pointed out the town of Port Hastings on Cape Breton Island which signaled the Amity was about to enter St. Georges Bay.

The trip through the Strait of Canso took less than half an hour. When the ship was well off of Cape Breton Island in St. Georges Bay, Captain McMillan again headed into the wind to reset the sails. That, of course, meant Linda was back at work. A little after 6:00 p.m., the Amity, under full sail, was pointed in a northwesterly direction that would take it directly to Prince Edward Island. Karen released Patrick's hand so she could return to work, and headed for the galley to help Dominique prepare dinner.

PRINCE EDWARD ISLAND

Prince Edward Island is located off the coasts of New Brunswick and Nova Scotia in the Northumberland Strait. At its narrowest point, eight miles separate the island from the New Brunswick shoreline. Prince Edward Island spans one hundred and twenty one miles from its eastern to its western most points. It formally joined the Confederation of Canada as its smallest province in 1873.

The Island's 130,000 full-time residents come from a diverse mix of ethnic backgrounds. Micmac Indians migrated there more than 2,000 years ago and continue to maintain a presence, although few today speak the native language or practice their native religion. French settlers came in the early seventeenth century as part of the colony of Acadia situated primarily in the provinces of New Brunswick and Nova Scotia. During the late nineteenth century American blacks migrated to Prince Edward Island, and they were later joined by groups from Holland, Germany, El Salvador, Guatemala, India, Lebanon, and China. Yet despite this rich ethnic tapestry, today almost eighty percent of the residents are descendents of the British Isles—England, Scotland, and Ireland.

With its many small, isolated harbors, Prince Edward Island is an ideal setting for this diverse ethnic mix, allowing individual groups to settle in their own coastal communities. It also explains why shipbuilding flourished in these tiny harbor towns in the nineteenth century. It is estimated that over 3,000 wooden ships were constructed between the years of 1850 and 1900. The many harbors, in addition to the island's small size, evoke a sense of quaintness and intimacy, which is an important reason why the management of the Amity Foundation selected Prince Edward Island for the cruise. The island is also known for its secluded beaches, rocky cliffs that rise up from them, a rolling pastoral interior defined by wooded forests, ponds, and winding streams, and its red clay roads.

Charlottetown is the capital of Prince Edward Island and its main harbor. The crew of the Amity worked feverishly on a cloudy Thursday morning to take in all eleven sails in preparation for docking in the harbor. The harbor sits at the confluence of three rivers and is protected by its narrow entrance and Fort Amherst. Captain McMillan gave the order to proceed directly into the harbor at 7:10 a.m.

Karen Hathaway and Charlotte Ryan were standing together near the bowsprit, and both were excited. Off to the right they could see red sandstone cliffs and sandy beaches. The Blockhouse Light came clearly into view at the harbor's head, a freshly painted white brick building with a lighthouse behind it that rises twenty feet above the two story building. As the Amity entered the harbor, the women saw several wood framed colonial houses off to the left nestled among a lush outcropping of hardwood trees; and a wide variety of boats—a white ferry with red lettering that was not quite readable due to its distance from the Amity, a freighter moored off to the side, bobbing sailboats of varying sizes and descriptions, fishing boats, and small power boats. The Amity pulled up to a long, floating dock at 7:35, tying up alongside a white and red tugboat.

With the lines of the Amity fully secured, the two women strolled to the galley where Patrick prepared his specialty of the day, stuffed French toast with apples and cinnamon and steaming hot coffee. At breakfast, Charlotte organized a girls only sightseeing trip that included Karen, Linda Symonds, Susan Carnegie, and Donna Cappers, a thirty year old drug company salesperson from Watch A. According to Charlotte, they were going to her town, and as it turned out they were to see it through her eyes as she provided them with nonstop commentary. The women left the Amity a little after nine thirty, but not before Karen checked with Patrick. She promised to return to the Amity after lunch to awaken him.

Though it is the largest city on Prince Edward Island, with a population of only 20,000 it is hard to classify Charlottetown as urban. The city begins with a commercial and historic district that surrounds the harbor and spreads out in concentric circles that are less congested and more picturesque. Despite the dreary, gray day, the women were especially impressed with the city's cleanliness and color. The private homes were well taken care of, and their wooden frames were painted in a wide array of vivid colors with white picket fences bordering the sidewalk.

The first stop for the ladies from the Amity was the Confederation Centre which was a ten minute walk from the ship. This rather small, tan colored building was opened in 1964 to memorialize the setting where delegates from the territories that made up Canada first met to discuss union in 1864. The Confederation Centre houses an indoor theatre, an art gallery, and an historical museum.

It was at the museum, where a docent was explaining the continuing influence of Acadians, the seventeenth century settlers from France, on the culture of Prince Edward Island, that Karen's mind began to wander and focus on Patrick. She was definitely attracted to him, and it wasn't only because of his good looks, though his 5'11" athletic frame, the soft blue eyes, and the reddish blonde hair were certainly a plus. She was also attracted to his quiet self-confidence and sense of integrity she had gleaned from their conversations over the last few days. Patrick was a person who knew who he was. He was comfortable in his own skin, a quality she wished she possessed in greater abundance. She had never dated a jock before, but she was certainly open to it. He definitely was a smart one, and she smiled at the thought because it deflated a stereotype she was happy to deflate. She hoped he was also fun, something she knew would be fairly tested in the next few days.

The women left the Confederation Centre a little before noon and, after receiving directions, walked the short distance to historic Great George Street. They had a light lunch at a small sandwich shop along the waterfront Charlotte picked out, commenting that any passenger from the Amity who ate a meal in the next four days away from the water was crazy. Amity passengers were now on their own for meals with the exception of breakfast. After lunch, the amiable group proceeded to visit the old historic houses along Great George, many of which had become inns. Donna Cappers commented the place reminded her of the battery in historic Charleston, although all agreed the vivid colors and understated character of these houses distinguished them from the stately mansions of the Confederate South.

At 2:15 p.m., after briefly touring the Wellington Inn and the impressive Roman Catholic basilica across the street, Karen bade farewell to her companions to return to the Amity. "We can't compete with the love bug when it bites," Charlotte announced to a chorus of snickers and laughs.

"See you all soon, I'm sure. Maybe we can get together for dinner?"

"Anyone who brings a date, pays," Charlotte said jokingly as she winked over at Karen.

"Then I guess it might have to be breakfast," Karen countered, returning the wink as she started to head back down Great George Street. She found Patrick sitting on the deck with his back against the forecastle cabin, a favorite place of his, reading the tour guide book from the Amity Foundation. "Hi," she said, smiling as she moved over to him. "Did you get some rest?"

"About five hours. I'll be fine as long as it's an early night."

"Me too," she said as she sat down beside him and turned her head to receive a light kiss.

"I've been working on some plans for tomorrow," Patrick said as he opened the tour book again.

"Good. Susan and Scott want to come with us."

"Are they an item too?" Patrick asked as he looked over at her curiously.

"What do you mean too?" Karen responded with a short, nervous laugh.

"Good question. You know these trips are great for coupling people. Were you looking for a male companion?"

"Not really," Karen responded, taking his free hand. "But I'm glad I found one."

"Me too," Patrick said as a flash of pink darted across his face. "Now let's get back to the plans."

"That's a little safer at this point," Karen answered while squeezing his hand before releasing it. "What do you have in mind?"

"Well Charlottetown is approximately in the middle of the island. So tomorrow we can go east. There is a little village called Orwell Corner about fifteen miles on the Trans Canada Highway. From the description in this book, it sounds like the Williamsburg of Prince Edward Island. It has several old buildings like, let me see here," and he flipped through a few pages in the book, "a blacksmith shop, general store, a nineteenth century school building, and several farm buildings. I'll rent a car, and we can start there in the morning."

"That sounds nice. I'll get dinner tonight," she offered, wondering a little when they would get beyond history and onto a beach. "You know one thing we have to do is go to Cavendish."

"What's over there?" Patrick inquired as he looked up from the book and turned toward her.

"That's the home of Lucy Maud Montgomery. She's the author of *Anne of Green Gables*. I read the book as a little girl. The novel takes place right here. She makes Prince Edward Island into a bucolic paradise," Karen said as she looked over his shoulder and down at the tour book. Patrick had returned his attention back to the book, and was scanning the map to find Cavendish.

"Cavendish is on the west coast. We probably ought to leave it for another day. It would be quite a drive from Orwell Corner."

"We can easily save it for a rainy day. They seem to get rain around here," Karen said as she smiled over at him. "Cavendish is probably full of museums and indoor attractions."

"Fine with me," Patrick said as he closed the book. "After Orwell Corner, we can drive to Prim Point. According to what it says here, it has the oldest lighthouse on the island and a nice beach."

"Oh, goodie, a beach. I'm looking forward to sinking my toes into hot sand.

I hope the sun's out and it's a lot warmer than it is today." She was wearing blue jeans and a monogrammed beige sweatshirt. It was one of those cloudy days with the temperature close to seventy when you are hot in a sweater and cold without one. She took Patrick's hand again, closed her eyes, and rested her head on his shoulder. She briefly fell asleep; and, while she slept, he sat there reading the tour book about Cavendish. He was the type who liked to make plans, while she was happy to go with the flow as long as she felt comfortable and it sounded like fun. At least in this regard, they were a well suited match. They left the deck at 3:45 to change clothes in preparation for going out on the town.

～

Friday with Scott and Susan was fun. Karen wondered though if Scott and Susan would make it beyond touring companions. There was, of course, the considerable age difference between them, and she also questioned whether there was any chemistry there. Yet they did have a few things in common. Both had large body types. It wasn't that either was overweight, they were both just large. Karen had Scott figured at 6' 4", two hundred and twenty pounds, and Susan was close to 5'11". Though their hair coloring was different, hers black and his sandy blond, they had matching ponytails which Karen found amusing. She suspected Susan deliberately wore her hair that way to enhance their bonding potential.

But there was a small problem developing for Karen involving Scott and Patrick. To use a trite expression, they were like two peas in a pod, yucking it up with their locker room humor and all the chatter about sports. She didn't resent Scott. How could she? He was a great guy and very intelligent; and she certainly had no claims yet on Patrick. She also wasn't the jealous type, but she wanted some alone time with Patrick. It was time for her to get to know him a little better, that was all.

Yet, despite her wish to get to know Patrick better, the two couples had a good time together. It was light, and easy. Things especially got better when the sun came out after lunch, and they were at the Prim Point Lighthouse. The drive from Orwell Corner to Prim Point took about twenty minutes, and they passed two potato farms situated in rolling, green landscapes. These scenes brought back memories of *Anne of Green Gables*, a book which Karen enthused about to Susan. The two girls were sitting in the back seat of the blue Honda civic sedan because Scott needed the legroom up front.

The Prim Point Lighthouse is located at the end of a long, narrow peninsula that juts out into the Northumberland Strait. It is constructed with white brick, freshly painted, and is conical in shape with a red platform that sits below the flashing light. The four friends climbed to the platform and discovered the view from there was spectacular. Just beyond the lush green lawns surrounding the lighthouse, there was a rocky red beach which, though not great for swimming, was an inviting setting for a walk. To the right there was a ferry boat which appeared to be heading to the Charlottetown harbor. Far off in the distance an oil freighter was working its way toward the coast of Nova Scotia. After climbing down from the lighthouse platform, the two couples took a long walk along the quaint beach, which to Karen's great surprise was practically deserted. Scott hypothesized the rocky shoreline kept the crowds away.

They headed back toward Charlottetown late in the afternoon along Route 1, a two lane, red clay road that ran parallel to the ocean. At Pownal, a tiny fishing village just off the road, they had dinner while they watched the lobster and fishing boats return from a day's work. Karen laughed to herself remembering Charlotte's earlier prophecy about eating dinners on Prince Edward Island. The day ended in the forecastle bunkroom at 10:15. As Patrick adjusted his eyes after returning from the men's room, he found Karen in a lower bunk, kissed her good night, and promised Saturday would be their day together. He then walked up the wooden ladder to the bunk above her, and hoped he would be able to sleep. Sleep was usually not a problem for him; but that night, with her below him, presented unusual circumstances to say the least.

$\sim$

Patrick surprised himself. He slept quite well, but he woke-up early—a little after six o'clock. He quietly climbed down from his bunk, stopped briefly to listen to Karen's gentle, rhythmic breathing, and then headed for the showers. He arrived on deck a little before seven and enjoyed a cup of coffee with Dominique Delgrosso. Karen didn't join them until 8:30.

Over a full breakfast of scrambled eggs and homemade blueberry muffins, they made plans. He showed her the guidebook again and pointed out a beach called Little Harbor. "It's a long drive from here—probably about forty miles. As you can see from the map, it's on the eastern shore of the island."

"But the book says it's a beautiful beach, and one of the most secluded. It looks like it should be a nice day. I say let's do it," Karen said as she handed the book back to Patrick. "I can be ready in half an hour."

They headed off in the blue Honda with Patrick behind the wheel a little after nine thirty. "We go on Route 2 for about thirty miles until we come to a place called

Priest Point. In a little while I want you to help me look for it because I'm sure it will be easy to miss," Patrick said. "I'm pumped about today."

"Me too. I've been thinking about these legendary beaches for the last two months. Isn't the Hillsborough River beautiful with the sun shining on it? I wonder how much longer this road parallels it."

"About five miles, I think," Patrick said. "Soon we should have the Gulf of St. Lawrence on our right." They were quiet for a while, each concentrating on a different task, Patrick on the road ahead and Karen on the well manicured houses across the river, when Patrick broke the silence and asked, "Tell me about your singing. You do it so well. I think you said the other day you had training."

"I've been taking voice lessons since I was a little girl. It was my talent."

"Your talent?" Patrick asked with some confusion.

"I'm not sure I want to admit this, but I have a long history of competing in beauty pageants. Singing was my talent."

"You're kidding!" Patrick said as he looked over at her and grinned. "I've never dated a beauty queen before. This will be a new experience."

"Well, I guess that makes us even. This is the first time I've ever dated a college jock—a few pretenders but never the real thing."

"How far did you get?"

"I was first runner up in the Miss Colorado pageant when I was seventeen."

"Damn. That's impressive. To look at you, I'm not surprised. This puts a whole new meaning on our swimming today. Do you have a great bikini? I can't wait to judge."

"My bikini is on under my shorts and T-shirt, but there will be no judging. It's been ten years since I've done what you guys call 'parade my stuff' for leering judges and hungry television audiences, and I'm glad those days are over."

"You don't sound too thrilled about all of this. What got you into it? It sounds exciting to me."

"I did it because my parents wanted me to. They really pushed me—especially my father. I did everything as a little girl to please my parents. That's one of the things I'm trying to sort out, to get over," she said a little nervously. It was a revealing statement, and she hoped Patrick was the type of person she could share this with.

"It was easy for me to break away from my parents. My Dad died when I was a young kid; and being the baby in the family, I got away with murder. According to my mother, I could do no wrong."

"It's been difficult for me. You were lucky. I'm learning how different I am from the other members of my family. I have an older brother Billy who's thirty-one. He's the assistant minister at the Abundant Life Assembly of God Church in the Springs. He's just like my father."

"What kind of a church is that?" Patrick asked as he reached over and took Karen's hand in a gesture of reassurance.

"It's Christian, but you would probably call it 'holy roller.' It's very conservative—both theologically and politically. The two seem to go together. Both my father and brother are black and white people. Every issue is so simple, and they have a strong opinion on everything, even when it has little to do with them or so it seems."

"What does your Dad do?"

"He's President of Noah Communications."

"That sounds impressive. What does his company do?"

"Well, among other things, they own somewhere between seventy and a hundred Christian radio stations."

"Wow, you're really steeped in that stuff."

"Tell me about it!"

"Do you believe it?"

"Do you mean the Christian gospel? I'm not sure what I believe. Certainly parts of it, but my mind set is different from the men in my family. In some ways I'm more like my mother. She's a kind, but weak person. She allows my father to dominate her. So it's complicated." And then she paused, looked over at Patrick, and tried to laugh. "Are you sure you want to hear this stuff? You're going to think I come from a funny farm."

"It's an interesting story. Remember, you told me I'm not supposed to judge. I'll look you over pretty good; actually I've already done that, but I won't judge. I promise," he said as he looked over at her with a reassuring smile and gently squeezed her hand.

"Thanks." She felt a little better. His attitude had restored some of her confidence. "There's a part of me that hates to pick on my mother. She's a beautiful woman and has always been a loving presence in my life, but she's never had an independent opinion on her own. My father has defined who she is."

"And you don't want to be like your mother in that sense?"

"Exactly, but I also don't want to hurt them. As I told you before I've always been a good girl and that is precisely why my father loves me. Because I'm a good girl. Because I was a "beauty queen" as you just said. I am like a trophy for him. I'm fine as long as I'm away from the Springs."

"What happens when you're there?"

"I never stop being a good little girl. I hide my real feelings. I say yes, smile a lot, and seethe inside. That's the way my Dad likes it. Me smiling. My brother too. The problem is I hate myself for it, but at least I'm aware of my deceit. The really sad thing is I'm tense around home, not fully at ease. It's a tension I mostly create. I don't feel comfortable with them, or at least with my Dad. It goes back a long time. When I told my parents I was through with beauty pageants after Miss Colorado, my Dad has never forgiven me. He lost his trophy daughter that went with his trophy job and his trophy house."

"That is sad, to be uncomfortable in your own home. I can see how hard it would be to survive psychologically in such an environment."

"It has been for me, at least."

"How do you cope with it?"

"I stay away from the Springs. I'm also seeing this wonderful psychologist twice a month who's helping to sort it all out."

"These sound like lifestyle issues you're dealing with, not deep seated psychological problems. I'm sure having an independent sounding board is helpful."

"They're more than lifestyle issues. You're nice to say that. But Silvia, my therapist, is wonderful;" and, because of his reaction to their conversation over the last ten minutes, Karen was beginning to think Patrick was wonderful too.

"I'm lucky my parents were easy. My family is boisterous, large, an enthusiastic mess, but they're easy. You'll have to meet my Mom someday. She's quite a lady."

"I hope she will like me."

"She likes all the girls I bring home." And then after a brief pause, "Oh, my God. You blew it. See that sign marking the East Point Lighthouse? We missed our turn. You were supposed to give me fair warning."

"You'll have to learn not to count on me," Karen said in a tone that reflected a note of self pity, embarrassment, and concern she was revealing too much. The horrible thought she was blowing it with Patrick went rocketing through her mind. Patrick pulled the car off the road onto the shoulder, stopped it, and moved over to take her into his arms.

"It was my fault really. Your story was too interesting." And then he kissed her long and tenderly. She struggled hard to fight back tears. After this brief and poignant interlude, Patrick made a quick u-turn, and they found Priest Pond, another classic Prince Edward Island fishing village, three miles back down the road. They turned left there onto Route 302, a red clay road that led directly to Little Harbor. The parking lot to the beach was well marked, and Patrick was able to turn off the ignition to the car in no more than fifteen minutes from the point where they had made the u-turn. It couldn't have been easier.

Karen got out of the car, stretched, walked up four wooden stairs, and looked out on a lush, green meadow. The ocean was half a mile or more in the distance, and the view was breathtaking. Off to the right was a wide river that emptied into a cut in the ocean. There was a small, white sandy beach on the riverbank which faced sandstone cliffs that rose fifty feet above the ocean floor. The beach on the riverbank stretched around to the left and joined another sandy beach that fronted the ocean and seemed to extend for miles. Pockets of wildflowers added color and a softness to the meadow that stirred Karen inside.

Patrick gathered up his backpack from the backseat and soon joined Karen on the small incline above the parking lot. "Wow, it's really beautiful up here," he said. "I don't see more than four or five people on that little beach by the riverbank."

"This is so awesome, Pat. What a lucky find!"

"You're not kidding. Are you all set?"

"Do you have my stuff in the backpack?"

"I think so," he said as he grabbed her hand and led her toward the narrow red clay path that would take them to the beach. Three minutes into the walk they had a quick change of plans.

"Pat, it's ten forty-five. Why don't we quickly drive back to that small group of stores and buy lunch. That way we can stay at the beach all afternoon."

"Good idea. It's a shame we didn't think of it when we passed the stores," he said as he stopped walking and prepared to turn back.

"We had no idea there was a half mile walk to the beach." It took them forty minutes to return with lunch and another fifteen minutes walking along the narrow, sandy path to arrive at the beach. After staking their claim to a little privacy away from the seven or eight people they shared the beach with, Patrick took off his running shoes and walked across the shallow river to the rocky cliffs. There he found a rock large enough to provide some privacy while he put on his suit. He soon returned to another breathtaking view; Karen in her bikini. It wasn't that the soft yellow suit was particularly revealing. It was Karen. She was stunning Patrick thought as he walked over toward her to place his clothes in his backpack.

"Let's go swimming," Patrick said as he zipped up his pack and leaned it against a small rock. He led the way by jogging the fifty yards of beach along the riverbank and then turned left and headed directly for the ocean. Karen followed behind him. They swam, frolicked, roughhoused, and kissed in the warm ocean water with the gentle swells for forty-five minutes until they were both waterlogged and exhausted from the physical exertion. Patrick was again impressed with Karen's strength as a swimmer, but that was merely the tip of the iceberg. He was falling for this beauty queen from Colorado, which made the whole experience a little surreal. He couldn't quite believe what was happening.

After racing to their towels, they sat on the beach for a few minutes to recover before setting off on a stroll along the water's edge. It amazed them there were no houses in view along the shoreline, which led Karen to speculate the entire stretch of beach was National Park land. It was too hard to fathom that anything this beautiful could remain free of houses and be privately owned.

They arrived back at the beach along the riverbank a little after 1:30, and Patrick was famished. He literally devoured the roast beef sandwich, potato chips, and coke they had purchased from the quaint general store in Priest Pond. Karen was not quite so ravenous. She was able to avoid the chips, and shared the last few bites of her ham and cheese with Patrick. After cleaning up the remains from their lunch, Karen was ready for a nap. She smeared another light coat of sunscreen over her body, and arranged her towel next to where Patrick was sitting. She stretched out on the towel with the back of her head nestled against Patrick's side. She was happy to have his body shield her face from the sun. He gently stroked her shoulder length brown hair, and when his fingers got close to her lips she kissed them.

With her eyes closed, he devoured her. Her legs were long and gracefully muscular. Her waist was thin, and her breasts shapely and proportional. Her lightly tanned face had a few freckles, just enough to make it soft and interesting, and, although closed, he thought about her green eyes, eyes that shone with warmth and sparkle whenever a smile crossed her face.

When she kissed his finger a second time, he decided it was safe to engage her in conversation. He was interested in learning more about her job. He looked down at her peaceful face and asked in a quiet voice, "You know, Karen. I'm having a hard time picturing you in Washington."

"Me too."

"I mean how does one get a job working for a congressman?"

"I inherited mine," she said in a dreamy voice. Her eyes were still closed, and she nestled her head closer to Patrick's side.

"What do you mean you inherited it?"

"Simply that my father is one of Congressman Jackson's largest contributors."

"I see," Patrick said as he shifted his focus from Karen toward another young couple, about their age, maybe a year or two younger, who were lying together fifty or so feet away with their bodies partially hidden by a large, brownish rock. They needed one of those he thought with a laugh. A little more privacy. "What got you interested in that kind of work?"

"I guess it's because I majored in political science in college. It seemed like a natural thing to do."

"Do you like working for a congressman?"

"At times."

"What gets you really fired up, excited?"

"I wouldn't say anything does really," she answered as she raised herself from the sand, squinting as her eyes adjusted to the sharp light reflecting from it. As she refocused her gaze onto Patrick, she continued. "You're after more true confessions."

"No, not really. Your work intrigues me."

"The rewarding part is helping people solve their problems. You would be amazed at what we get. Two weeks ago a woman called because her kitchen sink was leaking."

"She called Washington from Colorado Springs?"

"Sure. It's an 800 number, and I got her a plumber. He came that afternoon."

"That is amazing."

"I also like attending committee hearings when Congressman Jackson cannot be there, although I often find the proceedings at the Banking Committee rather boring."

"Do you write any speeches?"

"No. The congressman does that himself. He rarely writes one out. Most of the time he merely makes out a list of the points he wants to cover. He's pretty good at it."

"What's so bad about what you do? It sounds rather stimulating."

"Lots of things. Do you really want to know?"

"Really," he said with a grin as he squeezed her hand.

"Well for starters, my boss is a creep, not the congressman, but his chief of staff. He's a lawyer and a member of my brother's church. Both he and my brother can be obnoxious at times with their self-righteous beliefs, but the worst part is that he is always leering at me. One smile from me, and he would make a hotel reservation. You guys never have to worry about that stuff. He's constantly hitting on me, and he's short, balding, and married with four kids. A real slime ball!"

"A guy like that can certainly poison an office. I don't see it much because I spend so much time out in the field."

"You're lucky," she said turning toward him with a sheepish grin. "And then, of course, he thinks like my father and brother. Everything is black and white. Most of the relevant people in my life have never heard of the word gray. My Dad would love for me to marry a guy like that. Oh my God, what a disaster that would be."

"Is the policy making process interesting at all?" He felt it a good time to change the subject somewhat.

"Not really. It's so political, and by that I mean personal, partisan, and money infected. Some of the work committee staffers do is interesting. Maybe I would enjoy it more if I actually knew where I stood on the issues."

"Explain what you mean by that."

"Well, sometimes liberal women, and I deal with a lot of them, make me nervous. Take abortion as an example. I guess if I'm really pushed, I'm for women choosing, but I could never have an abortion myself. Those women are as rigid in their thinking as my father."

"Is it murder?"

"Not in the sense of someone shooting another person in a premeditative way, but clearly you are destroying something very sacred and special."

"That's a good way of looking at it."

"I'm glad we can agree on something political."

"I don't think we are so different. As a matter of fact, I'm wondering a little why you are a Republican."

"First of all, I come from a Republican family. Most people inherit their politics, me included. I am also a believer in balancing the budget which was an important part of the Republican platform until Ronald Reagan came along."

"That truly is a switch. To think of Reagan as the biggest deficit spender in American history is remarkable."

"Irresponsible is the word I would choose. It's so much easier to cut taxes than spending. If he had been a real leader, he would have said: let's cut spending first and then we can legislate tax relief, but he was an actor. He did everything for applause."

"Can you vote for Clinton this year?"

"He's cute, that's for sure, but Bush has so much more experience, and he did a good job with the Persian Gulf."

"Clinton is going to have problems with the experience issue."

"Ed Huss and I had the same discussion. As I told Ed, the character issue may be his biggest hurdle. That's all the people in my office talk about. It seems a little hypocritical to me. The only thing my boss won't do is rape me. Isn't that a reassuring thought? Yeah Jesus," she said as she raised her arms above her head and looked toward heaven.

"Infidelity seems to go with politics," Patrick said with a smile as he watched Karen return to her former position on the sand.

"It's the favorite topic of office gossip. What I find hard to understand is these guys have so much at stake. Can you imagine making a large contribution to a campaign and then have the whole thing blow up over a sex scandal?"

"No. Quite frankly, I can't imagine donating to a campaign."

"It's amazing how many people with big bucks do. And, of course, corporations are the real fuel for the political process."

"So I've heard," Patrick said as he shifted his position on the sand. "Money certainly is the toxin that pollutes the system."

"That's for sure," she said as she stood up to stretch. "There's no free lunch with contributions." He got up too. He couldn't stand being on this beach with her any longer with other people around, even though it certainly wasn't crowded. He found public displays of affection distasteful which made their current situation profoundly frustrating.

"Let's get dressed and explore those cliffs," he suggested. "I'll give you a geology lesson." Karen put on khaki shorts and her new Amity T-shirt over her bikini. The T-shirt was a pretty navy blue with simple white lettering, she wore it proudly, and she carried her running shoes as they crossed the shallow river. When they got to the other side, she continued to carry her shoes because the cliffs were too steep to climb. They walked along the water's edge, on a narrow spit of sand, that separated the ocean and the cliffs. Patrick explained to her about sandstone cliffs, how they were formed, why these cliffs were colored with a reddish, brown tint, and he pointed out different rocks as they made their way along the shore.

Thirty minutes into the tour it ended with remarkable suddenness. As they rounded a corner, the beach expanded, and when they walked on the sand toward the base of the cliffs, there was a protected area among the rocks which offered considerable privacy. They both moved in unison toward it. Karen took Patrick's hand, sat down on the sand, and pulled him toward her. Soon they were passionately kissing, and then their clothes were off. As they made their way back slowly to the beach at the riverbank, Patrick reflected glowingly about the experience. Karen was good, not so much for what she did but for how she held him. There was a hunger and a passion in the way she made love which he had never encountered before. It was all so natural with her. She was not uneasy or awkward, just comfortable in his arms, eager to please him, and to share her pleasure. She was also stunningly beautiful. It was an afternoon that produced an experience and a consequence he would never forget.

~

Several members of the Amity crew had set aside Sunday as the day for visiting Anne's Land, the north shore region of Prince Edward Island that is the setting for Lucy Maud Montgomery's, *Anne of Green Gables*. The selection worked well because the weather was not great. It was a cloudy day in the seventies with intermittent rain throughout the day. The sun was not forecast to come out to stay until late in the afternoon.

Most of the members of Karen's watch went along, including Susan Carnegie and Scott Berk who rode with Patrick and Karen in the blue Honda civic. The odd couple, as Karen had referred to them once to Patrick, seemed to be doing better than she had expected. A convoy of four rented cars left the parking lot alongside the wharf at 9:30 on Sunday morning.

Their first stop on the way to Cavendish was the small town of Winsloe North. The purpose of the stop was to visit the farm of Martina Terbeek, known affectionately as the Cheeselady, who came from a long line of Dutch cheese-makers. The crowd from the Amity enjoyed watching how cheese was made from milk produced on the farm using traditional Dutch recipes. Karen was intrigued gouda cheese came in so many different flavors, eight in all, which everyone enjoyed tasting. Patrick was pleasantly surprised they were open on Sunday.

The drive from North Winsloe to Cavendish took twenty minutes with the Amity convoy arriving at Green Gables around 11:30 in the rain. There they toured the two-story green and white frame house, constructed in the mid 1800s, and restored to represent the farmhouse in the book. At the first break in the rain, Karen and Patrick left the tour to walk one of the fabled trails that encircles the property. Patrick found touring old houses somewhat boring, they both felt like they had landed at a tourist trap, and were happy to establish some distance from the Amity crowd. Patrick took Karen on a walk along "Lover's Lane." They held hands, got wet, and talked a little about yesterday at Karen's insistence. Strolling down "Lover's Lane" inspired her or that was what she claimed each time Patrick tried to gently steer the conversation in a new direction. She was falling for this guy, and it was important for her to explore her feelings with him.

With Charlotte Ryan assuming responsibility as cruise director, the group left Green Gables a little before two for a late lunch in Cavendish. Afterward, with the weather improving, the four traveling companions plus Ed Huss and Linda Symonds took a long walk on the beautiful and crowded beach that stretches twenty-five miles along the north shore of the island. The entire group met at seven thirty that evening in the quaint fishing village of New Glasgow for a lobster dinner, lots of beer, wine, and enthusiastic conversation.

On the way home, Karen used what little light that remained to read Patrick's tour book. When they arrived at the wharf, she excused herself from the small group to make a call at a pay phone across the street. She found Patrick twenty minutes later talking with Scott and three other men toward the stern of the ship. She motioned Patrick aside and told him in a hushed tone she had taken care of their plans for tomorrow, she was paying for it, and he would need a small suitcase.

"You've let me pay for so little on this trip, so our last full day is on me."

"Sounds great," he said as he grabbed both of her shoulders and gave her a big bear hug. "I'll look for you in a little while, and we can watch the stars from the bowsprit."

"I may or may not be awake."

"That's okay. If I miss you, we have all day tomorrow." Karen smiled at him and headed for the forecastle and a long overdue trip to the ladies room.

Monday morning was clear again, seventy-five degrees outside, and Patrick was excited as he had been every morning for the last three days. They pulled out of the parking lot a little after nine with Karen perusing the tour guide book. "Where to?" Patrick asked as he looked over at her smiling.

"Well, we're going to Summerside on the western end of the island. Do you know where Route 225 is?"

"Just outside of Charlottetown, I think."

"Good. I'm glad someone's paid attention these last few days. We head west on 225 for about forty miles until it intersects with 1A. 1A takes us right into Summerside."

"Great and what's at Summerside?"

"We're staying at the Island Way Farm. It's a bed and breakfast on 1A right before Summerside. I thought we could rent bikes and explore the area."

"Fantastic."

"Tonight there's a Scottish music festival at the College of Piping. The lady I talked to at the inn suggested I reserve the tickets last night. They sell them at a small discount, and she said if we wait till performance time we may not be able to get in."

"Wow, you done good girl," and he reached across the seat and took her hand. "Tell me about the inn? I really like staying in bed and breakfasts."

"I don't know much about it except your book says it's a working farm." They arrived there at 10:15 a.m., checked in with a distinguished looking man in his early sixties, and left their luggage in the room. The inn provided them with bikes, which enabled them to embark on a tour of Summerside and beyond.

Historically, Summerside was the center for the construction of wooden sailing vessels on Prince Edward Island. Today the city honors that tradition, but is better known for its well manicured Victorian homes. These homes, some of the most stately and beautiful on the island, reflect another important part of Summerside's past, namely its involvement in the lucrative fox-raising business in the early 1900s.

Karen and Patrick enjoyed exploring the waterfront at Summerside—especially Spinnaker Landing, the location of the Summerside Yacht Club and a group of handsome shops on the boardwalk where they had lunch outside, in a small café, with a direct view of the harbor. After lunch they left the small city and explored Bedeque Bay, visited a shipbuilding museum, and ran into a tiny fishing village by accident which happens rather frequently on Prince Edward Island. Throughout their journey, they biked on little traveled, two lane, red clay roads, arriving back at the Island Way Farm at 4:30 in the afternoon.

"Boy do I need a shower," Patrick said as he closed the door to their room.

"Me too," Karen responded as she turned around, walked back a few steps, and put her arms around him.

"It's a beautiful inn," Patrick said as he pulled her toward him. "You chose well."

"Just luck," she said "and your guide book." Before she could utter a new thought, Patrick kissed her passionately and began removing her clothes. Soon they were in the warm shower together washing each other and exploring their newly tanned bodies. "I hope you have protection this time," she whispered up to him as she moved her fingers lightly from his neck on down.

"I do, and I feel guilty about the other day. It all happened so quickly," he said as he moved slightly away from her and began to play coyly with her round, firm nipples. "I never dreamed we'd be making love that afternoon on that beach. It was so private. Just perfect."

"I know, and I can't even accuse you of planning the whole thing," she said as she smiled up at him with her green eyes shining. "Forget the guilty. It doesn't get any better than it was that afternoon. I think we'll be fine." He reached around her shoulder to turn off the water and then he took her hand and led her to their bed. They made wet, wonderful love for the next forty-five minutes, and he was again impressed with her involvement and passion in lovemaking. Karen appreciated his slow, tender approach, and as she lay there in his arms after it was over the image entered her mind of falling off a cliff, of diving head over heels and landing in a peaceful and distant place. She buried her head into his shoulder, smiling inside with deep satisfaction, her mind floating gently toward that distant place after her recent encounter of wave upon wave of exquisite passion.

~

The College of Piping is the only year-round college of Celtic performing arts in North America. It is located in Summerside, and so Karen and Patrick returned to Spinnaker landing where they had dinner at the "Whale's Tale," another quaint restaurant on the boardwalk with a water view. They arrived at their seats in a packed auditorium at 7:55.

The concert was both educational and entertaining. The first group to perform was a local pipe band with instruments that included bagpipes, and snare, tenor, and bass drums. Karen's favorite song was "Dr. Gaelic" which is an upbeat, bouncy tune that enabled the man playing tenor drums to entertain the crowd with his twirling mallets. The second act consisted of a class from the college performing Scottish country dancing. With women dressed in flowing white dresses with plaid sashes and men in kilts, they paired off as couples and performed several dances that reminded both Karen and Patrick of American square dancing.

Following a twenty minute intermission, a highland dancing group in their white and green plaid kilts performed a series of traditional dances. The program ended with a Celtic band involving a fiddle, guitar, a young woman on small pipes, tin whistles, and a hand played Bodhran drum. The group performed several old favorites such as "Danny Boy," "Auld Lang Syne," and "Loch Lomond," which brought the crowd to its feet and led to two encores.

It was a different night for Karen and Patrick, a fun interlude, an engaging cultural experience, but on Tuesday morning it was all about lovemaking again or at least it was after the breakfast in bed Patrick organized for Karen. He awoke soon after the first light of the morning which came early in this eastern Canadian Province, started the coffee pot in their room, and then went outside to explore the immediate surroundings. He admired for the second time the early twentieth century structure that was the inn with its three floors, brown wood finish with white trim, and elaborate porches on the first and second floors. Their room on the third floor was defined by intriguing angles and alcoves, and an antique, queen sized bed. Though smaller than he was used to, it was a bed he would not soon forget.

Around the inn and in back, he found three barns, a riding corral, and several walking trails through the fields. He followed one that led to the Wilmot River at the far end of the property line. He walked along it briefly looking for fish, and then returned to the dining area of the inn to gather together their breakfast. He entered their third floor bedroom with a tray of donuts, oat bran muffins, and two plain bagels at 7:25.

Karen was still asleep, but the creak from his closing the door awakened her. She got up slowly, propped herself up with pillows against the headboard, stretched with her arms fully extended, and smiled over at him. "I've got our breakfast," he said returning her smile.

"What a treat! The coffee smells wonderful."

"Hungry?"

"Well I could use a little something. How about a cup of coffee, and I'll nibble at what you have on that tray," she said as she got up from the bed, walked over toward him for a good morning kiss, removed her nightie, and headed for the bathroom. Patrick was awestruck, and yet caught off guard with the tray in his hand. It was a struggle to leave her alone in the bathroom. To shift the focus of his mind, he took the tray and placed her breakfast on the bedside table. He then retreated to a comfortable brown chair not far from their bed.

She returned soon, poured herself a cup of coffee, and looked across at him on the chair. "You certainly have a lot of clothes on for this time in the morning," she said with an impish grin. And that started it. Before she could finish her coffee, he had his clothes off, and was all over her on the bed. Karen teased, caressed, held, and made him feel as if he was the only man in the world. This woman thoroughly enjoyed what she was doing, he concluded as he freed his mind to allow his passion and intensity to rise to the level of hers.

Spent and fully at peace, she slid off beside him, wrapped her right leg around him, and closed her eyes. A few minutes later he interjected a soft comment that kept her from sleep. "You are a very special woman," he said as he moved away slightly from her which enabled him to trace her right breast with his hand.

"I wish I knew why I'm so special," she answered quietly in a dreamy voice that was fighting sleep.

"Your courage and honesty about your family situation was impressive to me."

"You liked my little soap opera," she said as she took his hand and squeezed it. She released his hand, allowing it to return to her breast, and placed her arm around his back.

"I admire the way you are dealing with the problem. I can't imagine living under all that Christian pressure."

"Obviously, it's not a big problem cuz here we are sinning in this wonderful, old inn. I just wish I knew myself better. I wish I knew what I believed and had the integrity to live that way."

"I think the problem is that your instincts are different from the other members of your family. Family loyalty pushes you one way, and your instincts pull you another way. I would have trouble figuring things out under those conditions."

"Thanks, Pat. That's a nice way of looking at it. You ought to enter politics. You have good instincts about spin."

"I think it's true. You don't seem to have the same fundamentalist approach as the other members of your family."

"You're right. I don't. I often wonder where heaven is, and why Jesus has never returned. According to the way I read the New Testament, he is two thousand years overdue. To think that he will ever come now is wishful thinking to say the least, though so many of the people in my church still expect it within their lifetimes. The rapture. That's what they call it, an interesting name when you think that most people will burn in hell, including us. The whole idea has a rather nasty ring to it."

"I think the rapture just came. I'm burning, but I wouldn't call this hell. I'm a little surprised you still refer to it as 'my church.'"

"One of those little slips of habit. The hypocrisy of the congregation is nauseating. Let me tell you about my best friend in high school. Her family went to our church. She got pregnant when she was seventeen. I'll never forget the afternoon after school when she told me about her doctor's appointment. I was really afraid we were looking at suicide. Anyway, because her parents could not face the shame of a sinful daughter, they sent her away that summer to have an abortion. They told everyone she was going to summer school."

"People will do a lot to protect their self-image," Patrick said as he shifted his position on the bed.

"That's what it is, image. It's all about appearances. You've got to be born again in that church. Everyone is, but what does it mean? People have an experience that stirs their heart, and they're born again. But it doesn't change anything. It doesn't make them a better person. When I was younger, I used to tell all my friends I was born again, but what did that mean for me? What did it do? Of course, Daddy's born again like all the rest, but why can't he love me for who I am and not for what I do to raise his self esteem. Why can't he hug me once in a while, and cut out all the self-righteous lectures. He never told me I was pretty unless I was dressed in a pageant costume. He hired a private investigator to spy on me in college." And she broke into tears. Patrick held her tight, and then he entered her again and again and again. "Oh, Patrick, I love you," she said as she looked down at him and covered her tears with a smile that broke his heart.

"I love you too, Karen. You are the most precious woman I have ever held in my arms. I want to protect you. I feel it so strongly inside me, and yet I can't keep my hands off of you."

"That's part of protecting me," she said as she closed her eyes and rocked with his rhythm until she too was spent with a peace that took her to another place. She slid off him one last time, resting her head on his chest, and draping her right arm across his shoulder. They awoke in time to take a brief walk around the property before heading back to the Amity.

The Amity left Charlottetown right on schedule at 4 p.m. on Tuesday. Most of the passengers were sad to leave Prince Edward Island for the island had treated them well. The four-day cruise back to Boston was largely uneventful with one notable weather exception.

Patrick had an easy time changing his watch over to Karen's which made the couple happy. It didn't even involve switching people around because his old watch had one extra person. They did change watch schedules, however, with Karen's group receiving the 3 a.m. to 11 a.m. shift.

Patrick and Karen devised what Patrick called a survival strategy for the trip home. They spent much of their time with other people or in a group, saving their alone time for the wee hours of the morning when the ship was quiet and the deck largely uninhabited. Patrick was still hung up on the public display thing.

"Let's sneak into the chartroom and lock the door," Karen said in a teasing voice as Patrick strolled over to her. It was 3:30 on Wednesday morning, and Karen was standing lookout at the bow. Patrick was wandering the deck looking for something to do. "I go on duty there at four or four thirty."

"I'm scheduled at the helm for that time slot," he said as he placed his arm around her and the two leaned up against the capstan.

"Give Jason twenty bucks to cover for you. We don't have to take long."

"Stop it, Karen, please. You're not making it any easier," Patrick said in a voice of some frustration.

"I'm only teasing, Pat, and I love the role reversal," she said as she looked up at him and gave him a sweet kiss. "It's nice to date a man with some discretion for a change. Anyway, we have Saturday night."

"My mom's house," he said as he tightened his grip on her shoulder.

"I still have that reservation at the Marriott," she said as she looked out at the ocean where a three-quarters moon floated in and out of white, billowy clouds creating fascinating patterns and colors on the water below. It was a nice temperature outside, close to sixty degrees, with a gentle wind from the prevailing southwest.

"We can't disappoint her. She wouldn't understand."

"Where will I sleep?"

"That's no problem. There are only two bedrooms, and my mother snores. You wouldn't want to sleep with her."

"So that's where you get it," she said as she took her free hand and wiggled his nose. "Where did all you guys sleep when you were kids?"

"It was first come first serve, though as the youngest I was usually on the living room couch. There are two sets of bunk beds and a single in my old bedroom."

"Just like the Amity. No wonder you have no problems sleeping here. Are you sure you wouldn't prefer the Marriott?"

"Mom goes to bed early. I can't wait for you to meet her."

"I'm looking forward to it. It will be fun to see your old neighborhood."

"It's very Catholic. There are churches on every corner. It looks a lot like Archie Bunker's neighborhood if you ever saw that show." They were quiet for awhile which gave Karen an opportunity to reflect some on their different backgrounds. Her parents will flip when they learn he's Catholic she thought, although her father will respect the fact Patrick played Division One hockey. Colorado College is a Division One school in hockey, and her dad is an avid fan. Maybe Patrick played against CC? That would help a lot, but they will gag at the Catholic neighborhood in Chelsea. Karen smiled as she considered their reaction. She loved it in fact. Maybe creating greater distance from them would be easier than she thought. Maybe part of her attraction to Patrick was this difference in their backgrounds, but she quickly dismissed that thought.

"You're a good man Charlie Brown," she said as she turned to face him. She placed both arms around him, and they kissed long and tenderly. "You know I was thinking about my religious heritage before you so rudely and deliciously interrupted me," she teased as she released herself from him. "This ship provides lots of opportunity for reflective thought."

"What did you discover?" he asked as he placed his arm around her shoulder again and the two shifted their positions on the deck in an effort to become more comfortable.

"Well, I was thinking about a course I had at Denison in political philosophy. Fundamentalist religion is an ideology, much like Fascism or Marxism. I wrote a paper on the topic. Fundamentalism is all about things you believe and not about living and loving.

"I'll never forget sending the paper to my Dad. I compared Christian fundamentalism to Marxism. The professor gave me an A minus. Mom told me a few years ago Dad would have sued the college had she not intervened. It's pretty obvious I was trying to zing my Dad with the paper. It was nice to learn my Mom went to bat for me. Maybe she is a stronger person than I have given her credit for. At least we talk."

"I can see how a paper like that would anger your father. It sounds like a harsh judgment to me." Ignoring his subtle critique, she pressed on.

"It goes deeper than that. Rigid ideologies like Christian fundamentalism appeal to certain personality types, people who like to see the world in black and white, people who willingly surrender their autonomy to a system of ideas, people like my brother and father."

"The political thinker in you is alive and well. I'm impressed, and I'm also dying to know what type of religion goes with my personality type?" Patrick said as he looked over at her with a wide grin.

"You're so secure and self-confident you don't need religion. So much of fundamentalism is based on need and fear."

"I certainly believe in love. I'm a good boy and go to St. Mary's whenever I'm home with my mother. I'm learning to believe in you."

"You're the greatest, Patrick," she said as she held on to him tighter. "You know what I think I'm going to do? Call you every night and cancel my therapist."

"You can make a few of those calls collect."

"I love you, Pat," she said as she gently steered him to the deck floor. They kissed and stroked and held onto each other passionately until Patrick could stand it no longer. He left her for a walk. He wondered what the married couple was doing. He wondered what he was doing. He wondered how he could have fallen so deeply in love in such a short time.

The next morning Patrick found himself in almost the same place. As he sat up against the forecastle cabin and stared out over the bowsprit, the moderate seas beat up against the bow, and the fifteen knot wind whistled through the rigging. It was four on Friday morning, and Patrick wondered when the first streaks of light would penetrate the thick, dark clouds. Though not yet raining, the weather looked ominous.

He was thinking about his next project at work, one that would take him to Billings, Montana for at least two weeks. There would be no Karen for awhile, and that was weighing on his mind. He was beginning to experience separation anxiety for the first time in his life. Work related travel had always been a lark, a call to new adventure, but things had changed. Travel didn't sound like much fun anymore. Life certainly had its surprises; and, as he shifted his position on the deck, there was a gentle tap on his shoulder.

"Hi, Pat. I'm off to the chartroom with my book. See you in about an hour."

" Try to stay awake in there," Patrick responded as he shifted his position again to smile up at her.

"I can't promise that," she said as she returned his smile and slowly began walking toward the stern of the ship.

Patrick watched her depart and wondered if she was upset about something. Why no kiss? Why such a brief exchange? Was she moody? He had never seen that side before. Maybe this was all about nothing. Maybe his mind was inventing a situation that didn't exist, but he decided he needed to find out.

As he gently opened the chartroom door five minutes later, Karen looked up from her book in surprise. "Oh, my God, Pat. I'm going back to church. My prayers have been answered," she said as she leaped from the chair and threw her arms around him.

They undressed slowly. The process was exquisite. Their lovemaking was passionate, with energy that was pent up, explosive. Patrick had his answer. He was reassured, vowing never again to doubt her.

As he held her tightly on the hard wood floor of the chartroom, there were rustling noises overhead. Several footsteps could be heard running along the deck. "Whoa, I better get up there, and see what's going on," Patrick said as he kissed Karen softly and disengaged himself from her.

"My book was just getting good before you came. Maybe this was all a wonderful dream."

"It was no dream. I can assure you of that," Patrick said looking down at her. He quietly gasped as he took in the curvy lines of her beautiful body. "Please get dressed," he said softly with a smile. "If it's a real emergency, someone's going to barge in here to use the radio."

"I will, Pat. I'm just savoring this moment, and all the incredible things that have happened. There's only room for one of us to dress, anyway. When you get out there, let me know if I'm missing anything."

"I love you Karen. So, so much," he said as he bent over to quickly tie his shoes. He then kneeled on the floor, kissed her one last time, and was gone. She continued to lay there, with shoulders wedged up against the far corner of the chartroom wall, and began to cry. She could not imagine how she was going to get through Monday morning in Washington DC.

Patrick entered another world from the one he had left forty-five minutes before. There was an eerie calm, and yet off to the Northeast a huge bank of dark clouds was driving toward the ship. Flashes of lightening ignited the sky with a malevolent glare. "Oh my God," Patrick said to himself as he hurried toward the helm where Todd McMillan was anxiously watching his crew on the yards furling the sails. "Look at that torrent of rain about to hit us."

"Captain, what can I do?" Patrick asked as he approached Todd with some trepidation.

"Nothing, Pat. We're about to be hit by a gale. Those guys better hurry up with the sails. Get your slicker on and hang on tight. This could be a dangerous storm."

Patrick ran to the forecastle, found his slicker, and headed back on deck. The ship was plunging up and down as Captain McMillan fought to keep it heading into the wind. And then the rains came. Blasting down on the deck, slashing up against Patrick's face, which led him to turn his back away from the storm.

Patrick clung tightly to the starboard railing as the sea washed over the deck, and the wind slammed the rain against his back. "Stay below, Karen," he said to himself. He thought about joining her, but the water pouring over the deck and the lurching motion of the ship convinced him to stay put. It was silly to risk walking on that deck.

Two minutes later Patrick had no choice. Jason Rosenthal's right foot slipped on the thin support rope that hung loosely beneath the yard. As he plunged toward the deck, the rope painfully slammed into his groan, flipping him around, which enabled him to catch onto the rope with his left hand. He emerged swinging in the wind, dangling perilously twenty feet above the deck. The problem was that he was unable to maneuver himself back onto the yard.

"Jump, Jason," Todd yelled from his position at the helm.

"Don't you dare," Patrick yelled back as he tore off his slicker and ran to the rope ladder alongside the main mast. He quickly climbed the twenty-five feet to the yard in question, climbed onto it in a layout position, and slithered his way toward Jason. When he was directly over him, he reached down with his left arm, grabbed Jason's extended right hand, and slowly pulled him up so that he could once again balance his feet on the thin rope and grab onto the yard.

There was one additional hero during these early morning hours. Rachel Murley had been sound asleep in the forecastle when the storm suddenly hit. As the Amity lurched upward, she was thrown from her second tier bunk. Scott Berk reset her dislocated shoulder, and then he and Susan joined her for breakfast, outside, on the deck, with the sun shinning.

~

The taxi ride to Logan Airport on Sunday morning was a difficult one. Karen fought hard to hold back her tears. Saturday night had been special. They had hardly slept. Karen had also enjoyed meeting Patrick's mother. It was obvious there was a strong bond between them. They spent most of the time teasing each other which enabled Karen to see the really funny side of Patrick. It was hard for Karen to believe Kathleen McGovern was in her early seventies. She was a "with it" lady.

Saying goodbye to their new friends on the Amity had not been easy either. Karen was sure Patrick and Scott Berk would see each other again. She would miss Ed Huss and Charlotte the most. As Karen and Charlotte became better friends, Charlotte's New York bluster seemed to disappear. In some ways, she marveled at their friendship. If you took away the singing, the two had little in common.

As they approached Logan Airport, Patrick instructed the cab driver to take them to American. Their plan was to check Karen's bags to Washington and then head for the United gate for Patrick's flight to Denver. His plane left at 10:45, hers two hours later. Though the parting was difficult, Patrick hugged her so tight that it left her literally breathless, they had a two-part plan for the immediate future which they executed faithfully.

The first part of the plan was to meet together every other weekend in a different city. Patrick enjoyed visiting Washington DC as well as the trips to Chicago and Austin, Texas. Karen especially enjoyed coming to Denver and staying in Patrick's two bedroom townhouse in Englewood. She liked the floor plan, the open kitchen, the brightness inside which resulted from the white paint and many windows, and its location near a city park. She spent a good deal of mental time purchasing and rearranging Patrick's sparse and functional, though not particularly attractive, furniture.

The second part of the plan was to speak on the phone three or four times a week. For Karen it was therapy. It wasn't that she would dial up his number and unload all of her problems. It was just so reassuring and comforting to talk to him. For Patrick, it was a new experience. He wasn't a great phone talker, typically very direct and right to the point, but Karen changed him. He couldn't believe how easy it was to spend an hour on the phone with her.

When Karen phoned one Wednesday night in early October, he thought she was calling to tell him about their upcoming plans for Louisville. Patrick wasn't sure why they were going there, but they had become great tour guide readers. Karen had assured him there were lots of things to do there. But Louisville was the farthest thing from her mind. When he answered the phone, she merely said, "I'm pregnant." No opening with "hi" or "how ya doing," but simply "I'm pregnant." Though initially stunned, Patrick answered in kind after a few moments during which he regained his composure and put together a few thoughts.

"Little Harbor."

"Little Harbor," she responded in a voice that, amazingly, was both calm and matter of fact.

"I guess there's no point in my packing condoms for Louisville. I sure do wish we had had them on that beautiful beach."

"I got back from the doctor this afternoon. But after missing two periods, I wasn't very surprised." As she was speaking, Patrick's initial reaction changed dramatically. He couldn't wait to interrupt her.

"How ya feeling?" he asked with real enthusiasm.

"Not too bad considering the circumstances. I've been a little tired the last few weeks, but I never attributed that to pregnancy."

"Listen, sweetheart. I don't know how you feel about this, but I'm actually pretty excited. As a matter of fact, the longer it sinks in, the more excited I become. Let's get married. It certainly couldn't be any more expensive than what we've been doing for the last three months."

"My parents are going to love this wedding!"

"Do you want to get married? Who gives a shit what your parents think about the whole thing. We can get married in Vegas if that makes it easier."

"Oh Pat, I'm so lucky. Vegas would be a fun place to visit, but I think my parents will rise to the occasion and put on a good show."

"Have any dates in mind?"

"I was afraid to think about that because I had no idea what your reaction would be to all of this."

"Karen, Karen, Karen. I think you know me better than that. What about the Saturday after Thanksgiving?"

"That's pretty short notice for my parents, but it's a good weekend. I'm sure I'll be showing by then. Mom's wedding dress will be out. If my brother performs the ceremony, he'll insist I wear a necklace with a big A."

"A what kind of necklace?"

"Oh, you know, a *Scarlet Letter* necklace, one that shouts out adultery to the entire congregation. He will look so somber, and yet secretly he'll be loving it."

"The first step in your liberation, Sweetheart. And who cares what your asshole brother thinks anyway." Patrick immediately regretted his liberal use of language. He had never met Bill Hathaway Jr., although Karen had talked about him some. It usually wasn't his style to be judgmental. He liked most people, and ignored jerks. Pushed them right out of his awareness. They were a waste of time he always thought. He would have to meet Karen's brother and give him a chance. In any event, he quickly completed his thought in as light a tone as he could muster. "We have so many other things to worry about. When's the baby due?" And then after a brief pause: "Let me restate that. When's our baby due?"

"I love you, Pat," she said softly into the phone. "Some time in April was what the doctor estimated. Actually all you have to do is take Little Harbor and add nine months. It's certainly not rocket science."

"That was some afternoon. I'm excited about becoming a father. Are you going to nurse the baby?"

"Jesus Pat, one thing at a time. I haven't given that a thought."

"I was imagining you two sizes larger. Wow!"

"You can take your measurements this weekend."

"Louisville has taken on a whole new dimension."

"I know. We have to figure out what to say to my parents."

"I can be there with you if that would make it easier."

"It might. We can decide all that Saturday morning."

"I'm looking forward to it. I love you."

"I love you too."

"Bye."

"Bye."

~

Colorado Springs is the city of Pikes Peak, a mountain on the southern edge of the front range of the Rocky Mountains that towers 14,110 feet. It is also the home of the Air Force Academy, Colorado College, and Noah Communications. As a result of their passion at Little Harbor, the Springs, as natives refer to it, became the setting for the wedding of Karen Hathaway and Patrick McGovern on Saturday November 26, 1992. It was a wedding characterized by formality and careful planning.

Such attributes, however, do not accurately describe the activities of the McGovern clan. They arrived late Wednesday night en masse from Boston, two older brothers, four older sisters, their spouses, Kathleen McGovern, the matriarch of the clan, and eighteen nieces and nephews. The clan set up camp at the Tyler House, a bed and breakfast on West Kiowa Street, about four blocks from the Abundant Life Assembly of God Church.

Their plan was simple. They came to party, celebrate, and to roast Patrick. All McGovern activities were centered around the Tyler House, a lovely restored Victorian home with ten bedrooms, the family still managed to overwhelm the place, in the historic section of the city. On Sunday morning Patrick's siblings checked out of the inn and split the bill evenly among the six families.

Patrick asked his family to do their drinking before Saturday, and they honored his request. They began in earnest a little before noon on Thanksgiving day on the wonderful porch that wrapped around the entire house. They relived experiences at their Chelsea home, they remembered their father, and they toasted their mother Kathleen who spent most of the afternoon aglow from all the love and pride she felt toward her family and from a little too much to drink. They teased Patrick about his phantom bride who had Thanksgiving dinner with her family five miles away in the western section of town. Karen had hoped to meet them all at the airport with Patrick on Wednesday night, but she was tied up with the seamstress making last minute alterations to her mother's wedding dress. The best Patrick could do was show them a picture of the two of them smiling at the helm of the Amity, but that merely fueled the fire. "She's all caught up in that wheel," Kevin said as he slapped his brother affectionately on the back. "You're still hiding her from us."

Thanksgiving dinner in the picturesque dining room of the Tyler House was warm and festive. The rehearsal dinner the next day was madness. Fifty-nine people attended. Karen looked stunning in a simple blue plaid dress that highlighted her soft green eyes and provided an attractive contrast to her shoulder length brown hair. The men in Patrick's family were suitably impressed.

William and Virginia Hathaway warmed up slowly to the occasion. Actually Karen was quite proud of them. This was not their scene: the informality, the beer and wine, Patrick had strongly requested no hard liquor be served, and the overwhelming presence of McGoverns. They pulled it off, however, with aristocratic grace and style. Karen did not give such high marks to Bill junior, her brother, the young man who would officiate over the ceremony the following day. Sean, Patrick's oldest brother, put it most succinctly at the postmortem when some of the senior family members were helping the exhausted staff from the inn put the place back together. "The guy spent the entire evening with a poker up his ass." Maggie, the sister closest in age to Patrick, was relieved her mother had gone to bed.

In addition to family, Doug Hemings, Patrick's college roommate for three years and the guy who centered the first line with Patrick as his right wing was there as best man and to toast his old college buddy. Doug praised Patrick's slap shot and his good fortune with women. He then told a story about the night Patrick rolled out of the back door of an antique hearse.

"We had just dropped off three Smithies after a Valentine's party in Northampton. The hearse wasn't traveling very fast, maybe twenty-five, thirty miles an hour tops, and Patrick was pretty loose. When the back door mysteriously opened, Patrick fell out of the hearse as he tried to close the door. He rolled off the road into the ditch. When we ran back to see if he was alright, he was laughing and covered with snow. He insisted we carry him back to the hearse. Twenty minutes later, as we were stopped at a light, two cops exited their car to arrest us for picking up a dead man. I have no idea how they were on to us so quickly, but Patrick saved the day. He resurrected himself. He proved to the cops he was alive by dropping his pants, removing his sweater and shirt, and allowing them to see the scratches and black and blue marks that covered his body. As the two cops turned off their flashlights, one cop remarked to his partner, 'this is the first time I have ever let a kid off for mooning me.' After putting his clothes back on, Patrick promised them hockey tickets, and they escorted us back to school. I tell you this story because Patrick is a guy who keeps coming back. You are marrying a very good man," he concluded as he smiled directly at Karen. She beamed while William Hathaway shifted uncomfortably in his chair.

Maggie and her older sister Mary each rose separately and told family stories about Patrick as a child, but Kevin stole the show. He welcomed both the "beautiful" Karen and the baby into the family. "The McGoverns don't need another child in the fold," he concluded. "My mother certainly has more grandchildren than she can handle, but the union of these two very special people can only result in the most precious offspring. I raise my glass to the next blood member of our clan." Karen burst into tears while Billy junior choked on his ginger ale. Fortunately he recovered in time to praise his sister for being the best Sunday school student in the eighth grade.

There was one touching toast on the Hathaway side. Stephanie Hathaway, Karen's first cousin and maid of honor, told this wonderful story about the first time they had been drinking. Karen was sixteen and a year older than Stephanie with her driver's license. The two girls had been at a party on the beach at Stone Harbor along the Jersey shore where Stephanie's family had a second home. At the party Karen had had her first beer, or most of one, which she didn't particularly like while Stephanie had stayed with diet coke.

"Our dilemma was, who should drive home? Karen the lush, with her first beer under her belt or me, the sober one without a license. We talked about this problem in earnest for ten minutes or more. Finally, it was decided I should drive home. Karen literally thought she was drunk. So there we went. I didn't even have my permit, and it showed. I took it easy, but at one point I screeched up against the curb, and in over correcting I crossed the yellow line. Thankfully there was less than two miles between the party and my mother's house. So, Karen, my second sister, the cousin that has kept me laughing and who I have looked up to for as long as I can remember, I have one wish. Please learn more about parenting than you did about drinking."

The wedding took on a different, more subdued tone. The meeting after Louisville, when Patrick met Karen's parents for the first time and she revealed her pregnancy, was tense. There was no throwing their arms around their twenty-seven year old daughter and expressing joy in the news they would soon become grandparents for the first time or a sincere handshake for Patrick welcoming him into the family. Instead harsh questions were asked by William Hathaway. Virginia remained largely quiet in the corner of the large living room fidgeting with the hemline of her dress. It was only on Wednesday or Thursday of the next week that Virginia phoned Karen and told her they would cooperate in putting on the wedding.

Once that decision was made, Karen fell in love again with her mother. She was at her very best organizing the wedding to its smallest detail. Her tone on the phone was enthusiastic, excited even. Invitations were sent out to four hundred and fifty people, an enormous number for a young woman who wanted a small, simple wedding, but her mother explained the Hathaway's had important business and political considerations to take into account.

What excited Karen most was that after the final alterations were made on Wednesday night before Thanksgiving she was able to fit into her mother's wedding dress. She was hardly showing yet, not in any noticeable way, which disappointed Patrick. He wanted to see and feel the real thing, although he filled with pride as he watched her walk down the long aisle in the Assembly of God sanctuary on the arm of her father in a wedding dress that was beautiful in its elegant simplicity. It was a satin empire dress with tandem spaghetti straps, a scoop neckline outlined in pearls, and a floor length skirt. The dress came with matching sleeves that extended well above the elbow, but Karen chose to leave them at home.

Reverend William Hathaway, Jr. performed his job well. He smiled often at his sister as he gently led the couple through their vows at 4:35 on Saturday afternoon. His homily was short and simple, reminding the couple that God was the third partner in their marriage and that a Christian marriage involved a very special responsibility to honor this three way partnership. The forty plus McGoverns sitting on the right hand side of the church shed a few tears, grabbed loose hands, and smiled broadly when the groom kissed the bride while the two hundred and fifty friends and associates of the Hathaways looked forward to a gourmet meal at the Broadmoor Hotel.

The Broadmoor is a famous landmark in Colorado Springs. It is located in one of the exclusive neighborhoods in the city, a few blocks away from the Hathaway's home. The original seven story, light pink stucco building with a red slate roof was built in 1918 with several wings added later. As one drives up to the entrance, the place oozes elegance with immaculately sculptured gardens, shrubs attractively arranged in clever patterns, fountains, and, of course, the Rocky Mountains in the background.

For the Hathaway's only daughter, it was a must. They rented the Montgomery Room, a large ballroom that overlooks an eighteen hole, championship golf course. The guests began filtering in around 5:30 and were served an assortment of nonalcoholic beverages while they made their way through the reception line. A dinner featuring a selection of rack of lamb, roast beef, and swordfish was served while a four piece band performed quiet background music. Although there was no dancing, the toasts were light and appropriate, and the bride and groom added a special warmth to the occasion by spending most of their time mingling and visiting with the invited guests.

By the time Karen threw her bouquet a little after nine, she was exhausted. It had been a long, hectic, and stressful week. The stress was mostly self-induced on her part as she would imagine from time to time she was being judged by members of her family. In any event, she was looking forward to returning to Prince Edward Island. In fact, she had insisted on it. "There is no way I am returning to Washington on Sunday," she told Patrick on one of their frequent phone conversations prior to the wedding. She had decided to keep her job at least through the end of the year. Patrick had worried about Prince Edward Island only because he was running out of both vacation time and money. The Hathaways solved the money problem by giving them the honeymoon as a wedding present. In a strange way William Hathaway would soon solve the vacation problem too.

Karen and Patrick left the Broadmoor at 9:30 to spend their first night as a married couple in Patrick's Englewood townhouse. The drive took a little more than an hour; and Karen, though wanting to compare notes on the wedding guests, slept most of the way. Their stay in Englewood was brief. They arose at 6:00 on Sunday morning to catch an 8:20 plane to Charlottetown. As Patrick buckled his seat belt for the first leg of the trip to Pittsburgh, he took Karen's hand and said. "Your parents did a great job yesterday."

"They did," she said as she turned toward him and smiled. "I was proud of them."

"Your mom is a very sweet lady."

"A great organizer too. I couldn't believe she put the whole thing together so quickly. She did most of the work. I merely made suggestions."

"She's still a beautiful woman. You know what my mom told me when I went away to college?"

"What did your mom tell you when you went away to college?" she responded as she looked over at him and laughed.

"She told me to look as closely at the mother as I did the girl because that's what I'd be getting in twenty-five years."

"What did she say about the father?"

"She didn't mention him."

"Do you like my father, Pat?" she asked quietly as she leaned her head on his shoulder.

"He certainly can be a charming man."

"But?"

"That's your but, not mine," he said as he gently squeezed her hand.

"I know. I was giving you a chance to add to the charming."

"Well, I must admit he made me a little nervous when I first met him that weekend after Louisville. In fact, I was furious at him. It's a good thing we left early and spent Saturday night at my place."

"I agree. By the way, I never told you how proud I was of you for keeping your cool. I wish I could have met your father so I would know what I'll be getting twenty-five years from now."

"Sadly, I don't remember him well. It's been twenty years, but I will tell you a story about one of my oldest memories of him. It was a fall afternoon, most probably in late October or early November, and I was six years old—an enthusiastic first grader.

"When I got home from school, I had this idea of surprising my father. I raked all the leaves in the backyard, placing them in a pile in the middle of the lawn. Unfortunately, it was windy, and the leaves blew all over the place. So, I made a fateful decision. I piled them next to the garage to solve the blowing problem, ran into the house for some matches, and lit the pile."

"Oh, my God, Pat. Did the fire burn the side of the garage?"

"It burned the damn thing down to the ground. It's a good thing the garage was not attached to the house."

"Did the fire trucks come?" Karen asked, smiling over at him.

"Two. It was quite exciting, but my mother was frantic. She put me in that room we shared on our first night home from Prince Edward Island, and said my father would deal with me when he got home from work."

"I don't know that I blame her."

"Well, I can tell you this. The wait was excruciating. An hour later when Dad gently knocked on the door, I instantly burst into tears. He came over to the single bed we had so much fun in, sat beside me, and put his arm around my shoulder. The first thing he did was thank me for raking the leaves."

"You're kidding!"

"Then he made me promise never to start another fire without him being there. After I hugged him, and sobbed my way through that promise, he concluded:

'Pat I have another thank you to make. We really need a new car far more than we need that old garage. The insurance money for the garage should be just enough to buy one. When I get the new car, you'll be the first to ride in it."

"Did he make good on his promise?"

"Absolutely. Two weeks later he brought home a new car, and took me out for an ice cream."

"What a beautiful story!"

"He was a beautiful man."

"I think I'll be getting someone really special twenty-five years down the road."

"I'll try my best."

"I also think I'm going to like being a McGovern. Your family is so warm and shall we say exuberant. I hope I'm not overwhelmed."

"You'll find your place. It's interesting how different our families are. It's as if you and I were born on different planets."

"I know, but I think we can make it work. We'll take the best from both planets."

"I love you, Karen," he whispered over to her.

"I love you, too," she responded, as she again placed her head against his shoulder. She was soon sound asleep, but not before smiling deeply to herself as a result of her new understanding of why Patrick was so full of goodness. If only I had had a father like Mr. McGovern, she concluded as she closed her eyes. I don't even know his first name, but I love him dearly for giving me a very psychologically healthy husband.

They landed on Prince Edward Island at the airport outside of Charlottetown at 4:30 on Sunday afternoon, and discovered a different island. It was chilly with the temperature in the low fifties, overcast, and the wind was blustery. The streets of Charlottetown, though certainly not deserted, were largely free of enthusiastic tourists. They missed their friends on the Amity.

They spent the first two nights at the Wellington Inn on Great George Street. Karen had made the reservation. She remembered it well from that first day with Charlotte and the gang. The Wellington is a lovely old two story building, painted a dark navy blue with white trim and a maroon front door. Karen was excited to be surrounded by the vivid colors of Prince Edward Island again. In a strange way the soft grayness of the afternoon provided an artistic backdrop to the colorful array of houses and shops.

It rained for much of the day on Monday, but that was okay. It was their day to catch up—on love making, baby talk, and making plans for their future. They did everything well, but the planning. The events of the last five months had happened so quickly. Patrick was happy to proceed slowly, one step at a time, but Karen was a little anxious. She wanted a vision of what came after the baby. Patrick's solution was to make love again, and it worked. It was an activity Karen naturally flowed toward. It wasn't that she was what one might call a loose or easy woman. She just liked to hold Patrick and to gravitate in whatever direction he might lead her. Patrick realized he was a very lucky man.

Karen also used Monday to rest up for the remainder of the week. Their plan was to leave Tuesday morning on a biking trip along Confederation Trail, an old railroad track, that runs for two hundred and seventeen miles through the interior of the island. They started out at ten o'clock on Tuesday morning at the Elmira Railroad Museum which was near the East Point Lighthouse and less than five miles from Little Harbor. They were tempted to return to the spot that had so changed their lives, but they would never have made it to Summerside and the Island Way Farm bed and breakfast by Friday night. They were flying back to Boston on Saturday afternoon, and they really wanted one more night at that special inn.

Karen enjoyed the exercise of the bike ride and the fact that Patrick was perfectly content to proceed at a deliberate pace. Although the morning sickness of her first trimester was behind her, she still could become easily tired. Their goal was to travel forty miles on each of the four days, leaving the western third of the trail for another time. The trip was worth taking because they saw a different island—rolling farmland, wooded forests, rivers and streams on their way to the sea. The gently rolling topography made for easy riding, and they stopped often to admire the scenery, wait out the rain, or hold each other and romp a little in the soft grass when the sun was out and it was warm enough for such activity. The trail was virtually deserted at this time of year which was enough to ease Patrick's mild anxiety over public displays of affection.

Their honeymoon ended on Saturday night in Chelsea at a second McGovern family reunion. Karen and Patrick went their separate ways on Sunday as they had five months earlier. It was a sad parting, but they both felt they had achieved so much in such a short time. Neither had any regrets which boded well for the future of their marriage. Their next reunion would be over the Christmas holidays which was less than three weeks away.

Patrick left the office early. Karen's flight from Washington was due in at 5:10 p.m. He was concerned somewhat by the steadily building traffic, and the two or three inches of snow that had fallen that morning. He didn't want to be late.

He was excited they would finally be living together as a married couple. She had resigned her position with the Congressman and had found a new person, a chemist who worked for an engineering firm, to take her place in the Brownstone row house on Park Street. Patrick had been receiving her belongings in boxes for the last week.

He was also excited to tell her about his new job which would begin in the middle of January. He had met William Hathaway for lunch four days ago and had accepted the position over the phone last night. Mr. Hathaway, he couldn't quite call him by any less formal name, had asked he not discuss the new job with Karen over the phone, but to wait instead until he could inform her in person. William Hathaway was an enigma—closed, secretive, not particularly warm and yet charming when he wanted to be. Patrick wondered about him. Could he ever feel close to a person like that? Probably not, but there was no question about his business skills. The numbers at Noah Communications spoke volumes about that.

As he left the car in short term parking near the United baggage claim area, he hurried to the gate as it was already after five. Luckily the plane was ten minutes late which gave him time to catch his breath and further reflect on Karen's homecoming. All he could think about was placing his hand on her belly. It had been three weeks since the last time, and there was very little to feel then. The thought of his own child was awesome, overwhelming, and a little frightening at times.

Karen's face lit up the moment she spotted him in the small waiting crowd. They hugged briefly, and then proceeded to walk hand-in-hand toward the down escalator and the baggage claim area. Karen's face radiated life and excitement to be back with Patrick, but sadly for him, her slightly enlarged belly was hidden in the long gray polo coat that encased her with warmth.

"That's it for politics," she said as he climbed into the driver's seat of his 1990 blue Toyota Camry station wagon and fished for the keys he had hidden under the seat. "Been there, done that."

"Hopefully you won't have to work again unless it's a deliberate choice," he said as he engaged the ignition.

"One doesn't get rich living with a geologist."

"Those days will soon be over. Been there, done that, as you so aptly phrased it a few moments ago."

"What's that supposed to mean?" she asked as she looked over at him with mild consternation moving across her face.

"I start at Noah Communications in three weeks."

"Oh, Pat, you didn't," she said as she took his right hand and squeezed it hard.

"Your Dad's going to pay me sixty thousand dollars. That's almost twice what I'm making at Harris."

"You sold your soul, Sweetheart," Karen said as she released his hand and sat back in the seat. Patrick unrolled the window to hand the parking ticket to the toll clerk. He then handed her a five dollar bill and awaited his change. As he rolled up the window, he led the conversation in a less controversial direction.

"Can you feel the baby kicking?"

"All the time. I love those little reminders that all is well, but you're changing the subject. You big chicken! You have a lot of explaining to do regarding Noah Communications."

"Do you want to go out for dinner or stay home?"

"What's the choice at home?"

"I've been learning how to cook shrimp scampi. The shrimp is already thawed."

"Home sounds fine. I may have a little screaming to do when we get to the subject of Daddy and his company. A restaurant would only cramp my style."

Bill and Peter Hathaway inherited Philadelphia's largest radio station when their father died in 1971. The two brothers worked hard and well together, adding almost two stations a year to the family business until Peter tragically died in a car accident on January 4, 1977. At the time of Peter's death there were eleven stations in all.

Though Peter's widow Harriet maintained her ownership of 50% of the stock in the corporation, she did not stand in Bill's way when he very quickly changed the focus of the company to Christian broadcasting. Bill sold eight stations, including the original one started by his father, and moved the company to Colorado Springs. Hathaway Radio and Broadcasting Company became Noah Communications on July 1, 1978.

Today Noah Communications owns ninety-two stations with more than 1500 affiliate stations. The company also has several related divisions. Noah News and Music Network produces and distributes news, talk shows, and Christian music programming to radio stations throughout the United States and Canada. Noah Advertising sells commercial air time for Noah stations and their affiliates. The company also owns and publishes a magazine whose beat is the Christian music industry. Their newest acquisition, Paradigm Software, is a company that designs and distributes software for the automation of radio broadcasting. The most recent semi-annual audit valued the company at more than five hundred million dollars.

"Tell me you're not going to sell advertising for the Christian music industry?" Karen called out from the kitchen. Because Patrick had done all of the cooking while she had worked at organizing her clothes, she dismissed him from the kitchen for clean up detail. However, as she placed the last of the dishes in the dishwasher, she was looking forward to some answers regarding his new job. Patrick, feeling relief to be finally away from the kitchen, had retreated to the living room and was surfing the television for a college bowl football game. Karen soon joined him on the couch, clicked off the television set, and asked him if he had heard her original question.

"Yes I did Sweetheart," he responded as he moved nearer to her on the couch, placed his arm around her shoulder, and drew her closer to him. "And I'm not selling advertising. Your Dad recently purchased a tiny company that has developed a software package which is going to revolutionize the radio industry. The software plays the music, reports the news, and inserts advertising in appropriate spots all automatically. You can actually run a station with no one there. In six months I'm going to run the division."

"I told you Daddy likes college jocks."

"No I think he was more impressed with the fact I minored in math and have an extensive science background. It also helps that the person who sold your Dad the software company is a computer nerd with little social or business skills, or at least that's what I've been told. The challenge and potential of this thing are unbelievable."

"I'm glad it is you that will be dealing with my father and not me," she mumbled into his shoulder.

"Please explain to me what's going on between you and your father. If it really is a problem for you, I can certainly stay with Harris. I haven't given them notice. I was waiting to talk with you before handing in my resignation." He now wished he had waited on his call to Mr. Hathaway. He could certainly call him back to decline the offer, but Mr. Hathaway would know exactly why he was changing his mind. Family problems are complex and definitely out of his comfort zone. His brother Kevin had warned him about joining a family business when they talked about his offer two nights ago. Maybe he had been right.

"Thank you for that consideration," Karen responded as she raised her head from his shoulder, sat up on the couch, and faced him. "My problems with Daddy are that he was a mean father and he loved me conditionally. As long as I performed and acted in ways that built up his ego, things were fine. The beauty contest routine was his thing, not mine," she said as tears began to well up in her eyes. "When you get right down to it, I'm quite shy and don't like performing or being the center of attention." Karen took hold of both of his hands as she looked away from him and blurted out the rest of the story.

"You know what he said to me after the Miss Colorado contest when I was first runner up? No praise or congratulations, no hugs or smiles, no your rendition of 'When You Walk Through A Storm' was beautifully done, honey. He simply said, 'next time Karen, you will win.' His control over me as a child was suffocating. I was like a puppet on a string. One look from those cold, blue eyes, and I would dissolve into dysfunction and obedience.

"And let me tell you one more thing about my father. You need to have a complete picture before signing your life over to him. This is going to blow your mind. He's a prominent member of some crazy Christian organization called the Family."

"You mean your Dad's a Mafioso?"

"No, but the Family is somewhat like it. It's an organization of Christian men who want to create a worldwide government under Christ. Can you believe that shit? What's Jesus supposed to do? Return to earth so he can run for office.

"Naturally, this government would be led from Washington—the new Jerusalem. These guys see themselves as warriors for Jesus. Jesus tells them what to do. Their only mission is obedience. Who gives a damn about the Constitution. What they want is theocracy. Maybe there won't be an election. Maybe God will just coronate his only son."

"Jesus talks to them? Come on. What does he say?"

"Who the hell knows what he says. I'm sure nothing. Carol argues they make it all up. But Family members maintain Jesus speaks directly to them in their little prayer groups. Isn't that cute! He gives them marching orders."

"Who's Carol?"

"A friend in DC. She's writing a book on the Family, and she showed me an early draft. Daddy's in her goddamn book. He's a member of the Board of Directors."

"Is the book interesting?"

"Jesus Christ, Pat. You don't get it. My father is a fucking Christian fascist, and you want to know if the book is interesting."

"Wow. I may have made a mistake."

"You certainly may have, but keep the job till we get our feet on the ground. You can spy on Daddy. Find out the real truth about this second life of his."

"I'm so sorry. I had no idea."

"Well, you'll soon have lots of ideas, and yes the book is fascinating. Quite scary really. The Family's not a secret group, but it kinda acts that way," she said in a more factual tone of voice, regaining some of her composure. She wiped the tears from her face, and retook his hand. "The members work quietly behind the scenes. And they come from all branches of the government— Senators, Representatives, of course Congressman Jackson, Supreme Court Justices, top military brass, State Department people, you name it."

"They're all men?"

"Male fascists according to Carol. She's a great lady. She's an Evangelical Christian who believes deeply in the social gospel, Sermon on the Mount type stuff, loving your neighbor, all of Jesus's teachings. Her ex husband on the other hand is a member of the Family. For him, the social gospel is for girls, sissies. His Jesus is a warrior and, of course, a free market capitalist. They literally got divorced over his membership in the group."

"Wow! Does your mother go along with all this stuff?"

"Who knows? She can't stand up to my father anyway. As I told you in Prince Edward Island, she's a weak, beautiful woman, and though I love her very much, I can't stand the thought I am in any way like her. The scary, scary thing is I probably am," she said as she fought hard to keep from crying again. "Anyway, enough of this shit," she continued. "As I told you on the boat, I've been seeing a psychologist for the last three years. Now that I've left Washington, there's no more friendly psychologist around. You're it buddy boy. Good luck," she concluded with a rush and a little edge to her voice. She burst back into tears.

"I don't want to create further problems for you," he said as he pulled her toward him and held her closely. "There's nothing wrong with my job at Harris with the one exception that it involves a lot of traveling." She held him tightly too and slowly, after gaining control over sobs that were both deep and silent, she formulated a response.

"No, Pat. I love you too much to stand in the way, and the extra money will come in handy. I really would like to stay home for the next seven or eight years and three or four kids. I believe in full-time motherhood. I guess I've been corrupted by all that family values crap that emanates from Daddy's stations. Daddy can take care of us while I find my way in the world and learn to get him out of my head. What a delicious irony! I've spent twenty years trying to please an autocratic prig. In the last session I had with Silvia I told her I wanted to find myself with you and as a mother. She responded by rising from the chair behind her desk and hugging me."

"Wow, that is a wonderful ambition. I'll be there. I can promise you that."

"There's only one thing I will not do and that is live in Colorado Springs. I need plenty of psychic space from him."

"That's fine. I don't mind commuting from here."

"No, no, no. It's much too far—at least an hour if the traffic is reasonable. There's a little town about twenty minutes from Daddy's office called Monument. I first went there two years ago to help organize a fundraising party for Congressman Jackson. I fell in love with the place at first sight."

"Monument it is," Patrick responded as he moved his hand from her back to her tummy and then under her sweater to her breast.

"We'll go there on the 26th," she said as she looked down at him and smiled. "I promised Mom we'd come for Christmas dinner and spend the night. That gives us an excuse to leave early in the morning on the 26th. I'll call a real estate office tomorrow to make an appointment. Don't let me forget. It's less than a week away." Patrick marveled at her organizational skills, her ability to put together seemingly disparate goals into a coherent plan, and the decisiveness with which she acted. She didn't agonize over a decision. She ploughed right through. He was also a little shaken by the depth of her problem with her father. He hoped the toxic nature of their relationship would not spill over and affect them. So far so good, he thought as his mind shifted to other, more pressing matters. It had been three weeks, far too long, since he had made love to his beautiful, young mother to be.

∽

Patrick and Karen left their Englewood townhouse after a light lunch on Christmas day for the hour drive to Colorado Springs. The traffic was light, the weather crisp and clear, and Patrick was feeling good about the world. They had called his mother earlier that morning and were able to find several members of his extended family there to wish a merry Christmas. They were the best, the raw material of his soul, and he had only married into Karen's family. It was only necessary he coexist politely with them. Maybe genuine fondness would come in time, but it certainly wasn't a necessity.

As their car entered the Hathaway driveway, he was again impressed with the understated elegance of their home. It was not a home he would choose or probably ever be able to afford, but he certainly did admire it—the openness of the downstairs with the kitchen, formal dining room, and large living room flowing into one another. This complex represented the center of the house, with two wings containing three bedrooms each, spreading out in either direction. Four thousand square feet, all on one level, laid out in a horseshoe-like arrangement, made for an impressive design.

While Karen walked briskly up the steps to hug her mother, Patrick took the two suitcases from the trunk—the small one containing their overnight clothes and the larger one filled with an assortment of Christmas presents. After briefly hugging his mother-in-law and shaking hands with Bill and Billy Junior, he gave Karen the smaller suitcase to take to their room in the left wing, her old bedroom decorated with high school memorabilia, while he unpacked the presents and placed them around the tree.

There was a quiet warmth surrounding the opening of presents that encouraged Patrick. He was touched Virginia had hung a stocking for him alongside those for Karen and Billy. She had even knitted his name on it. He was also interested in observing the chemistry between Karen and her father. It seemed quite proper to him. There certainly was no obvious tension. The conversation was pleasant and happy. Karen could certainly put on a good act when it was required. Maybe there was some real fondness between them at a deeper level Karen failed to see. That is what he wanted to believe, anyway. William Hathaway could be a courteous, gracious man, especially in a setting he quietly controlled. Patrick was sure Karen would focus on the word control, but he was encouraged nonetheless. Patrick was a guy who liked things to work, who abhorred tension, who was open in his approach to people with no secret or hidden agendas. If family occasions were friendly and polite, maybe their working relationship could assume a similar tone. After Karen's outburst last week, Patrick had become a little nervous about working for William Hathaway Senior, Family Board member, Christian warrior, corporate tycoon. Maybe it won't be so bad, he concluded.

At 3:45 p.m. Karen rose from the love seat she was sitting on with her opened presents surrounding her on the floor, walked over to Patrick and gently kissed him, smiled over at her father, and then proceeded to join her mother in the kitchen. She was glad Candy, the Hathaway's maid of several years, was off for Christmas so that she and her mother had the kitchen all to themselves. Cooking and visiting with her mother was a ritual which Karen always looked forward to and enjoyed.

The departure of the women was the signal for Billy Junior to turn on the Bills/Cowboys game. Patrick definitely approved of the selection, although his father-in-law had competing plans for his attention. He wanted to talk business. "I'm looking forward to your meeting Jason Hamerick," Bill said as he shifted his position on his favorite easy chair and directed his attention toward Patrick. Jason Hamerick was the founder of Paradigm Software. "He's nothing but a computer nerd if you don't mind my saying so. Nice kid, but totally lacking in business sense."

"I've got so much to learn. I hope he has some teaching skills."

"All you really need to do is learn our business. We have Jason under contract for five years as a consultant. What I want you to do is to find operational problems for Jason to solve with new software. Then you can sell it with the other products throughout the industry."

"I still think you should buy a Christian theme park, Dad. That Jimmy Bakker guy is raking it in."

"You've got to stick with what you know, son. Theme parks and hotels are foreign to my experience."

"It couldn't be that hard," Billy Junior said as he shifted his focus from the football game to his father. "You just keep the Lord front and center, and let Him take care of the rest."

"I'm not sure it's that easy, although I certainly don't want to doubt the Lord." Patrick was glad he was not asked for his opinion. He found the whole discussion a little confusing. Who was the Lord? God or Jesus? Maybe it didn't matter, they were one and the same, but Patrick didn't want to have to hazard a guess.

"There's easy proof on that," Billy continued. "Jim Bakker and his beauty queen wannabee wife do it. Their profits are huge. The Lord must be supporting them. The profits prove it."

"If their profits are that large, maybe Jason and Patrick can develop an accounting program to help them sort it all out."

"I'm not sure they want anyone to know what flows into their deep coffers. They certainly don't want the government to get it."

"Be kind, its Christmas, and they are our Christian brothers," Bill Hathaway

Senior said as he offered a sly smile to his son. Billy Junior shrugged his shoulders, sulked, and redirected his attention to the football game. Patrick praised the Lord, whomever that might be, God or Jesus, for the football game on the television screen that redirected the attention of the Hathaway men away from Christian theme parks.

~

Although their real estate appointment in Monument wasn't until 1:30, Karen wanted to leave right after breakfast so they could tour the town on their own first. Patrick thought he detected a real note of hurt from his mother-in-law because of their decision not to live in Colorado Springs, right near by; but Virginia Hathaway's upbringing and natural shyness made this feeling an impression rather than something concrete and definite. It was certainly never expressed. Karen didn't comment on it. Either Patrick was wrong about his intuition, or Karen was ignoring her mother's feelings as not relevant to her plans.

Nevertheless Karen was in an upbeat mood when they left the house at 10:30 that morning. Patrick felt good about things too. Christmas with the Hathaways had been more fun than he had expected, and he was excited about the possibility of purchasing a real home even though he wasn't entirely sure their finances warranted it. As they entered onto Interstate 25, it wasn't long before Patrick saw the sign for Colorado College. He hadn't been back there since they played the hockey game seven years ago. It was his first experience playing at higher altitudes and he found the effect, at least for him, more hype than problem. He wondered briefly whether CC shared their rink with the general public. Now that he was going to be home on a more regular basis, he longed to get back on the ice. Even free skating with Karen would be fun. That was the main reason he had given her figure skates for Christmas. He admitted he had bought the skates more for him than her, but he wasn't a very creative shopper. She would be able to use them some day, he concluded.

His hockey nostalgia was soon interrupted by Karen who said: "Do you see that exit sign for a hospital up ahead? I'm pretty sure that's for Penrose. I bet we will know that place pretty well come April."

"How far is it from Monument?"

"Maybe twenty minutes, a little more. Time it. We'll certainly want to know for sure," Karen said as she reached over and took his right hand. They were silent for a while with Patrick taking in the majestic expanse of Pike's Peak off to the left when Karen interrupted his train of thought a second time. "Okay, Patrick McGovern. Here we go again. There's Noah Communications on the left."

"Maybe I better clock the distance from here too."

"Probably no more than twelve miles."

"You know this area well."

"It's the Congressman's district. I've traveled everywhere along here within a fifty mile radius." Love surged through Patrick. He wasn't sure why, but he squeezed her hand tightly before placing his back on the wheel. And she was right on target with her mileage guess. In less than fifteen minutes they exited from route 25 at Monument. As he came to a stop at the intersection, he looked over at her for directions. She read his signals well.

"Okay," she said. "Take a left here, and we'll cross over 25. Do you see that traffic light up ahead? Proceed straight through it, and we'll be right in the historic district." Patrick did as he was told, they passed a small shopping center on the right, and then, not more than a mile further down the two lane road, Karen told him to take another left. This was obviously it. The houses were small, brightly painted with a well manicured look and interspersed with older, wooden buildings, storefronts now, obviously dating back to the last century. "Oh, look at that lovely little bookstore on the right. You can be sure I will be spending time there. Slow down, Pat. This is a small town. We'll miss the whole thing if you're not careful. Look, there's Raspberry Mountain Realty on the corner. We meet Heidi Jackson there at one thirty this afternoon."

Patrick spotted a parallel parking place right next to the bookstore and began to maneuver the car into it. "No, no, Pat. Let's not stop yet. We can see the historic district with the realtor. Keep heading west, toward that mountain in the distance. We will cross the railroad tracks soon, and I think Monument Lake is right there." Patrick smiled to himself; women, he thought, and he again did exactly as he was told. Sure enough they ran right into the lake. Patrick parked the car in the gravel parking lot, and they both got out to take a look. Karen moved over toward him, took his right hand, and they proceeded to walk to the bank which was raised up several feet above the water.

"The water looks pretty low," Patrick said as he surveyed the scene in front of him.

"Do you see the dam over there on the left? Maybe they fill the lake for the summer," Karen said as she too looked around and tried to take it all in.

"I guess they don't skate here, at least until January," Patrick said.

"I can't wait for you to teach me how to skate, but I don't want to do it on lakes. You hear on the news of too many people falling in."

"That's probably true around here, but they certainly skate on lakes at higher elevations. I wonder what we are at here?"

"Probably around six thousand feet, maybe a little higher. That's what the Springs is. But it's a cute little lake, don't you think?"

"Absolutely. I'm sure it's a great place to swim in the summer."

"Do you know the big difference between us?"

"What's that."

"You grew up swimming in lakes, while I learned to swim in the pool at the Broadmoor."

"You have been somewhat sheltered."

"Tell me about it. I can't wait to swim in a lake." There was silence between them for several moments when Karen lifted his hand and placed it on her tummy. Patrick looked down at her and smiled.

" I just wanted to remind you I'm eating for two."

"Hungry?"

"Well, I'm getting there, and I don't want to be late for our appointment."

"That's fine. How about Rosie's Diner? I spotted it right after we got off 25."

"Sounds perfect," she said as she smiled back at him, released his hand, and turned toward the car. As they headed out of the parking lot, Karen noticed a baseball diamond off to the right. The sign at the head of the driveway read: "Dirty Woman Park." Patrick saw the sign too, and immediately turned right into a second parking lot.

"You read my mind. I love it. A rather dumb name for a park, but there's a nice walking trail around the perimeter. Baby McGovern and I will spend lots of time walking around here. I like Monument even better than I remember it," Karen said as she looked around one last time as Patrick eased the car out of the parking lot.

"I can see us fitting in here quite well," Patrick said as he looked out the window to his left and entered onto the two-lane road. Karen kept quiet for once, smiled at her self-discipline, and retook his right hand.

~

Rosie's Diner is a fifties place with lots of atmosphere and good food. Karen ordered a chef salad which she ended up sharing with Patrick, and Patrick ordered a patty melt with fries. Good food and atmosphere, however, were not what was on Patrick's mind. As he handed the menu back to the waitress, he looked directly across at Karen and said. "The tour was great, and I agree with you about Monument. But we need to talk money. At least from my perspective, we've been living in La La land ever since we got married. How are we going to afford a new house? Maybe we should start by renting."

"I've got some good news for you and perhaps a surprise. First, the surprise. I think you will eventually learn I am a very practical person. I really won't spend money we don't have. Now for the good news. I have a nice, little nest egg. How much equity do you think will come from the sale of your townhouse?"

"Perhaps fifty thousand, tops."

"That's about what I figured. Here's what I propose we do. According to my last statement from Dean Witter, my portfolio is worth about seven hundred and eighty thousand dollars."

"Wow," Patrick said as he smiled over at her. "That's impressive."

"You married well, Sweetheart," she said returning his smile. "I told the realtor on the phone we'd be looking at houses in the hundred fifty thousand to hundred seventy-five thousand range and that we would put up a hundred thousand in cash. I'll sell the necessary stock, and then you can repay me when your townhouse sells. We split the down payment, which makes our mortgage manageable."

"That's really generous, but what if the townhouse doesn't bring in fifty grand?"

"Then you'll clean the bathrooms for the rest of our married life. I can't lose."

"You're something," he said as he looked over at her and smiled. And then quickly another financial dark cloud passed over him, and he looked up at her again. "But you're also going to need a car. I can't leave you stranded when I go to work. Especially with a baby."

"You're right about that. I will need one. The best part about Washington was that I could walk or take the metro. When I was in the Springs, I used Mom's extra car. But not to worry. I plan to pay cash for a new car. We can start looking next week."

"You're going to run down that portfolio."

"That's what it's for. Big purchases and a safety net. I'll have plenty of time to rebuild it. Daddy has always said the most important factor in investing is time. Not timing, but time, and we're both young with lots of the latter. And listen. I'm taking a seven or eight year children's sabbatical. I may never work again. That puts a lot of responsibility on you. The least I can do is help us get started."

"I love you, Karen. You're almost too good to be true." He was about to lean across the table and kiss her, but the waitress ruined the moment by coming with their lunch.

Heidi Jackson, the owner of Raspberry Mountain Realty, was a tall woman, maybe Patrick's size or a little taller, with a well proportioned figure, mostly gray, wavy hair, sparkling blue eyes, and an engaging smile. She repeated some of their earlier tour through the historic district, but her commentary was worthwhile. "The layout of Monument is quite typical for a nineteenth century western railroad town. We are currently on Front Street which runs parallel to the railroad tracks. As you move east, there are two streets named after Presidents Washington and Jefferson, and these streets are intersected by numbered streets—First, Second, and Third." Patrick immediately reconfirmed in his mind this was not a large place which was part of its charm and attraction for him. They looked at two houses within the historic district, both small, three bedroom houses in the $140,000 range. Karen and Patrick liked them, but were not excited enough to make an offer—at least not right then.

As they pulled out of the driveway of the second house on Jefferson Street, Heidi said: "Okay, let's go outside the city limits. If you like space, I have one in the low hundred seventy thousands."

"What is the population within the city limits?" Patrick asked, a little surprised to hear it expressed that way. This was a small town to him.

"A little more than eleven hundred. If you go beyond the city limits like we are now, there are about twenty-five hundred residents in Monument." Perfect Karen thought as she focused her gaze outside the backseat window. "By the way, the mountain in the distance is Mount Herman. It reaches around nine thousand feet. The house I plan to show you is on Schilling Road, the property abuts Pike National Forest. That means all the land in front of the house to the west is ever green. Hiking trails practically come right up to the backyard." Perfect again, Karen thought. She was ready to write the check.

Schilling Road is a brown, gravel road that parallels the eastern edge of the national forest. The house in question was a three bedroom, one story log cabin with a green tin roof. The three quarter acre lot was defined by a split rail fence. The nearest neighbor was five hundred yards away and barely visible. Karen was excited as she entered the door held open by Heidi. Patrick delayed his entrance and decided to walk around the perimeter of the house. At the back there was a large deck and a picture window that made possible the viewing of Mount Herman. The temperature was close to fifty degrees with a clear blue sky. The landscape around him was brown and very dry looking. Patrick was convinced that come spring the parched look would all change. A little snow would help.

Karen followed Heidi into each room and listened politely while Heidi described them, but she had already bought the house. Patrick had too, and he was still outside looking up at Mount Herman. "Oh, Pat, I love it," Karen said as she went from the living room out to the deck. Patrick came to the rail and spoke up to her.

"Me, too. Shall we make an offer?"

"Would you like to see the inside first?" Heidi asked as she joined Karen on the deck.

"No, not really. That's for Karen to decide, not me."

"It's homey. Nothing fancy. But it's clean and spacious."

"Seventeen hundred square feet," Heidi pointed out.

"What's the asking price?" Patrick inquired.

"A hundred seventy-two thousand five hundred," Heidi replied.

"Okay, let's offer one hundred and sixty thousand."

"Is that enough, Pat? I'm sure we'll never get it for that."

"How long has the house been on the market?" Patrick asked as he looked over at Heidi.

"We listed it right after labor day."

"Obviously there's no rush to buy it, Karen. There won't be much action on it till summer. I think one hundred and sixty is a good first offer. Remember this is a game. We may have to pay more."

"Fine with me, we just don't want to lose it."

"We won't, Sweetheart," Patrick said as he directed his gaze toward Heidi. "That does it. You can draw up a contract for one hundred and sixty thousand dollars. The only condition is we will want to have a contractor of our choosing inspect the structure and all the appliances."

Heidi drove the love-sick couple back to her office believing in Santa Claus again. She instinctively knew she had a sale, although probably at a slightly higher price. Karen and Patrick returned to Denver, tired, but deeply satisfied with their day's work. Ten days later they returned to Monument to sign the final contract for $164,500. The closing date was set for March 1st·

The walk between their home on Schilling Road and the Covered Treasures Bookstore took about forty minutes. Karen had been making that walk almost every morning for the last two weeks. Because they had been in their new home for nearly a month, they were settled now which made routines like a daily walk into town possible.

The attraction for Karen was much more than the books in the store. She had made her first friend. Alexander Sherman, the store's owner, had grown up in Monument. She was thirty-five years old with a wealth of experience, at least from Karen's rather sheltered perspective, that made her seem considerably older.

The key to Alex was the two years she had spent in Thailand in the Peace Corps. There she was introduced to Eastern philosophy and to her handsome, hippy husband, Bruce. They were married in a Buddhist Temple in a small village fifty miles outside of Bangkok where they both lived and worked. After completing their Peace Corps commitment, they spent the next three years touring the world, working odd jobs when they could, and spending their savings when such jobs were unavailable. They divorced soon after returning to the United States because Alex was convinced Bruce, like Peter Pan, would never grow up. The divorce brought Alex back to Monument, and when the Covered Treasures came up for sale in 1991 she entered into a silent partnership with her parents.

The store is located in an old, historic building on Front Street and consists of three rooms. The front room as one enters is set up like a living room with comfortable furniture where coffee is sold as well as an assortment of pastries and other dangerous (to a pregnant woman watching her weight) carbohydrates. When Karen first noticed this set up, soon after their March 1st move from Denver, she became an early morning coffee regular. The two-mile walk was great exercise, and the walk home was penance for the bagel or donut that was supposed to remain on the tray. If the weather was lousy, which wasn't often in this arid, western town, Alex would drive her home around lunch time.

Patrick had a new friend too. Her name was Ruth Hawser, his administrative assistant at work. Ruth was in her early sixties, a little overweight, with mostly gray hair, and a heart as big as the ocean. She was married with three children, all of whom had left the nest years ago, leaving her vulnerable to adopting a handsome young man like Patrick. William Hathaway had assigned Ruth to Patrick because she had been with the company for more than ten years and knew the ropes well. Ruth was both teacher and mother to Patrick, and was largely responsible for his smooth adjustment to Noah Communications.

Since joining the firm, Patrick had worked hard, and William Hathaway was well pleased. Patrick was pleased too, actually rather pleasantly surprised, at the professional atmosphere that permeated the company. The background noise was definitely Christian, it was the Lord this and the Lord that, and Patrick was still confused as to whom exactly the speaker was referring, God or Jesus; but there was also the more important concern with making money. Noah Communications was organized around and focused on the bottom line.

For Patrick, learning the radio business had been easy. He had spent his first two weeks working at the Stratmoor Hills station, nosing around, listening, and asking pertinent questions of the staff. He mastered the programs created by Jason Hamerick at night, on his computer at home, in the living room with Karen while she watched television or read baby books. She was determined to make her cousin Stephanie proud by learning all she could about parenting.

The computer programs were amazing which energized Patrick. It also increased his respect for his father-in-law. This man knew what he was doing. He was on the cutting edge of technological efficiency with respect to radio broadcasting which had lagged far behind most other industries.

Paradigm Song Master placed all the songs a station plays into the computer and established rules for their playing such as no more than two female vocalists back-to-back. It generated a list of songs for each day, and totally eliminated the need for manually inserting tapes. Paradigm Advertiser managed all commercials while Paradigm Newscaster inserted news, weather, sports, and whatever shorts the staff generated into their appropriate time slots. Finally, Paradigm Organizer integrated all three programs so that a station could literally operate without personnel.

Patrick and Jason successfully converted the Stratmoor Hills station to full automation during the last week of March. Their next project was to write training manuals to supplement the seminars planned for all Noah station managers. The plan was to bring twenty-five or more station managers to Colorado Springs for a week to introduce them to the new software. Patrick set the first one for early May, a time considerably after the baby's due date.

~

Although Patrick thought often about the baby, for Karen it was the central focus of her life. One of the first things she did after the New Year was to sign up with a local OBGYN. Calvin Lovejoy was sixty years old, a graduate of CU Medical School, and a caring physician. He was part of a team of doctors who worked at Monument Medical Center with hospital privileges at Penrose Hospital, which was located on Cascade Avenue on the Denver side of Colorado Springs.

Karen was on her way to his Monument office in her new white, Plymouth Caravan. What she liked best about the car was it suggested children with its three seats, sliding door, and spacious interior. It was April Fools Day, two weeks from her due date, and a great day to have a baby she thought as she pulled up beside the medical office building. She would have had to have the sheriff arrest Patrick at work for him to believe this was actually the real thing and not a Fools Day joke, she thought as she entered the four-story office building.

Unfortunately, at least that was the learned opinion of Dr. Lovejoy, Baby McGovern was not to be born on April 1st. "You look wonderful," he said following a brief examination. "The due date of April 18th is right on target."

Not surprisingly Dr. Lovejoy was not as smart as his professional manner and good looks suggested. Babies seem to have a way of confounding our best estimates when it comes to due dates. As Karen prepared for her walk to the Covered Treasures three days later, she began to feel gentle but firm tugs inside her tummy. Instinct told her to delay her walk and to figure out what was going on inside her. With this in mind, she took off her coat and paid close attention to her watch. Oh, my God, they're regular she concluded fifteen minutes later. Four minutes or so apart.

After talking with Dr. Lovejoy's nurse, who told her to pack her bag and call back when the contractions were firmer and closer to two minutes apart, she dialed up Patrick. "It's time, Pat. You better come home. I'm going to need a ride to the hospital."

Patrick quickly dialed up his father-in-law and sprinted to his car. He found Karen half an hour later in their bedroom changing her clothes. He stood at the doorway and watched. After pulling on another pair of blue, elastic pants, she looked over at him, smiled and said: "My water broke five minutes ago. The living room couch is a mess."

"Don't worry about that. I'll clean it up tonight. Let's get to the hospital." And then he stepped into the room and held her so tightly she burst out in a huge smile as she struggled to release herself.

"Keep squeezing, and we can forget the hospital."

"Not this time around," he said as he abruptly let go, grabbed the suitcase, and flew out of the room for his car which he had left running in the driveway. Karen smiled again. Men she thought. She had read about this sort of behavior in romance novels and, at that time, couldn't quite believe it was true. Thanks Patrick for confirming my taste in literature, she said to herself as she laced up her shoes, and waddled after him.

The baby was born at 3:30 p.m. following a routine labor and delivery. Patrick spent five hours in the waiting room, calling family and friends, but mostly pacing restlessly and grousing over the fact he had not taken the childbirth class and was not permitted to participate in the delivery.

His absence from this miraculous event did not adversely effect the delivery of Maggie Hathaway McGovern, however. She entered the world at seven pounds, five ounces, nineteen inches in length, with light brown curls long enough to support a pink ribbon. Karen and Patrick were ecstatic. Karen couldn't take her eyes off of Maggie's tiny fingernails, perfectly formed ears, her cute snub nose, and soft, smooth skin. Maggie was named after Patrick's favorite sister, the sibling closest to him in age. William and Virginia Hathaway confirmed these rave reviews when they arrived at the hospital shortly after work.

The next morning found Patrick anxious and in a hurry to return to the hospital. He had not slept well which was unusual for him, but the circumstances of his life had changed rather radically. As he was rinsing his cereal bowl in the sink about 7:20 on April 5th, the telephone rang. He leapt from the sink to the nearby countertop to answer it.

"Is this Patrick?" a gentle female voice asked on the other end of the line.

"Yes, it is," he responded.

"I hope I'm not calling too early. This is Frannie Vrooman, your pediatrician."

"No, Dr. Vrooman. I've been up for more than an hour. Is there anything wrong with Maggie?" Patrick asked as tension flooded through him. Frannie Vrooman had been recommended to them by Karen's friend, Alex. The two women were members of the same book club, a club Karen was looking forward to joining herself when time and circumstances permitted. Frannie was in her mid thirties and had recently finished her residency, perhaps two years ago, at University Hospital in Denver. She was married to a college professor at Colorado College, and they resided in Woodmoor, a town that faced Monument from the other side of Interstate 25. Patrick had been looking forward to meeting both of them, but this early morning call was worrisome.

"There is certainly no imminent danger, but there are some issues we need to discuss." Shit, Patrick thought. What does she mean by issues? I can't even believe I'm hearing this he said to himself. "I was hoping to meet with both you and Karen in her room sometime this morning. I start my rounds about eighty-thirty, so any time after that."

"I was planning to be there as close to eight o'clock as I can."

"That will work out well. Maggie is a beautiful baby. As I just said, she is in no immediate danger, but we do need to talk."

"Okay, Dr. Vrooman. I'll see you soon. Thanks for the call."

"Bye," she said, and Patrick hung up the phone. Tears flooded his eyes, and he was disoriented as he moved into the living room and sat on the couch. There was a light rain falling outside which seemed to match his tears. What was going on? he wondered. There is nothing worse than the unknown. Dr. Vrooman was obviously preparing them for something, but what? Because Patrick was not a reflective person and when no answers came, he left the couch, finished up the breakfast dishes, brushed his teeth, and headed for the hospital.

Dr. Vrooman arrived at the door of Karen's room at 8:55 holding Maggie. She looked in on Karen and Patrick. The two were sitting on chairs alongside the bed, holding hands in silence. "This certainly is a peaceful scene," Frannie said. "How are you feeling the day after?"

"Fine, Dr. Vrooman, but I'm..."

"Frannie, please," Dr. Vrooman interrupted as she stepped into the room and walked toward the seated couple. As soon as she reached down to hand Maggie to Karen, Karen burst into tears.

"She certainly is a beautiful baby, Frannie. Nobody can take that away from us," Karen said through her tears as she looked up at Dr. Vrooman seeking reassurance.

"That she is," and with her newly freed hands she extended her right one to Patrick. "Nice to meet you, Pat. I've heard a lot about you from Alex. You have a precious little girl. Those lovely brown curls are long enough to have a bad hair day."

"Is there anything wrong?" Karen asked in a voice of considerable desperation. Tears were streaming down her face again. Patrick was silent, numb really. He had not gotten up to shake Frannie's hand which was unusual for him, against his upbringing. His mother would not have approved, and yet maybe she would understand considering the circumstances.

"Well, as I explained to Pat over the phone, there is certainly no immediate danger," Frannie said as she took a few steps backward. "We are somewhat concerned, however, about the possibility of a chromosomal abnormality. Do you see the slight slant to her eyes? When I examined her last night and just before coming here this morning, I noticed a protruding tongue. Her limbs and fingers seem shorter than normal. It's the cluster of symptoms that is worrisome."

"What are we talking about here, doctor?" Patrick asked in a voice that was almost threatening.

"Well, the combination of these symptoms suggests the possibility of Downs Syndrome."

"Oh, my God," Karen gasped in interruption. She instinctively increased the strength of her grip on Maggie as if to protect her.

"We will need to do a chromosomal analysis to be sure. The results take about two weeks to get back to us." There was silence in the room, an eerie silence with Karen and Patrick both unable to focus, staring off into space in disbelief. Tears welled up in Patrick's eyes.

"Can there be a mistake?" Patrick finally blurted out through his tears.

"Yes, of course there can," Frannie responded as she moved toward Karen and the baby, " and I hope I am wrong about this. As I just pointed out, it's the cluster of symptoms that makes me suspicious. Let me show you one more thing." She stooped down, took the baby from Karen's arms, and sat her on Karen's knee, making sure to support her neck with her left hand. Though Maggie was fully awake, she was quiet as a mouse. Her little eyes tried to focus, and her lips moved up and down in a sucking motion. There was a little drool dribbling from the side of her mouth, but hardly enough for one to notice. Frannie used her free right hand to raise Maggie's arm and let it drop. She performed this procedure a second time. "This arm lacks muscle tone," Frannie said. "It's not something you would notice, but having done this with hundreds of infants it is quite apparent to me there is some loss of muscle tone here." As she returned Maggie to Karen's arms, she concluded: "loss of muscle tone is another symptom of Downs Syndrome."

"Oh, Frannie, this is so horrible," Karen said as she again swaddled Maggie tightly in her arms.

"Let me reassure you. Downs babies are precious. They also can become highly effective, well functioning adults."

"Then what's the problem?" Patrick asked in a testy voice that was totally foreign to his affable nature.

"Let me explain to you both a little about Downs Syndrome. As I said at the beginning, it is a chromosomal disorder. At conception, the first cell in a normal embryo contains twenty-three chromosomes from the egg and twenty-three from the sperm. Within each chromosome there are more than 20,000 genes. As each cell divides, the two new cells contain forty-six chromosomes.

"In a Downs child, the initial egg or sperm contains twenty-four chromosomes. That means when each cell divides there are forty-seven chromosomes in the new cell which causes the abnormality. We will want to keep her in the hospital for an extra day so we can do an EKG and a chest x-ray."

"What does all this have to do with the heart?" Patrick asked in a more passive tone that suggested he was beginning to come to terms with the problem. Though still deeply concerned about what he had learned in the last ten minutes, he was less threatened by it all. "I thought Downs Syndrome was about mental retardation?"

"It is both," Frannie said in a voice that was both gentle and full of concern. "Downs Syndrome has both physical and mental manifestations. About half of all Downs infants have treatable heart abnormalities. That is why we do these tests. There are other possible physical complications that effect Downs babies, but we do not need to go into all that now. We will have the chromosomal analysis done and get back together in two weeks when we have more concrete information to deal with. There is no need to worry about potential problems that may never arise."

Frannie then moved toward Patrick and suggested by her body language he rise. When he did so, she hugged him. He was amazed at the intensity of her hug, and he burst into tears again as he returned to his chair. Then she knelt down and placed both of her hands on Karen's knees. "You have a beautiful baby, Karen, a baby that will be precious in ways others are not. Let me reassure you one last time. Maggie is in no imminent danger. For the next six months it will be hard to tell she is not completely normal. After that you may begin to notice certain characteristics of Downs children, but she will have the most adorable smile."

"Thank you Frannie," Karen said as she looked at Maggie with deep love in her heart. Frannie squeezed Karen's knees gently with both hands and then was gone. The nurse came for Maggie ten minutes later, a time frame in which Karen and Patrick remained silent, absorbed by their own thoughts, trying in their own individual ways to come to some understanding concerning this devastating news. As the nurse quietly left the room with Maggie in her arms, Patrick turned toward Karen and said:

"Well, at least I think we have the right doctor."

"I hope so," Karen replied as she slowly rose from her chair and headed the few steps across the room to the bathroom.

∾

Patrick left at noon to check in at work and to grab some lunch. Karen was relieved—she needed a nap, and she slept soundly until her parents came to visit at 1:45. Oh, boy, she thought after returning her mother's kiss. What am I going to tell them? Her mother was giddy with excitement to hold her first grandchild again.

After exchanging pleasantries for the first few minutes, Karen allowed herself to be inspired by Frannie's direct approach. She wished, however, Patrick was also here. He probably wouldn't have said much, but his presence would have been reassuring. "Let's go get her, Mom. There's a few things I want to show you."

"That's what I was hoping you would say, Sweetheart. I hope she's awake and not too fussy. She certainly was good yesterday. I've been looking forward to holding her again ever since I awoke this morning." Karen gingerly got out of bed, wincing a little as she felt some pain from her stitches, but she managed to smile over at her father who was seated in one of the two chairs in the room. Her mother dutifully followed after her as they made their way to the nursery. When they returned, William Hathaway rose from his seat and came over to look at his granddaughter.

"Do you want to hold her, Daddy, before I place her on the bed?"

"Not today, Karen. I'll leave that for your mother. I will when she gets bigger. Newborns make me a little nervous." Karen smiled over at her father saying without words his discomfort in this situation was okay, and then she took Maggie and placed her in the middle of the bed. Once Maggie was settled, Karen stepped back from the bed and looked at her long and hard, trying to see if she could spot the symptoms and yet in another way wishing they would simply go away. Her mother stepped forward to play with those long curls, and then bent down to kiss her granddaughter. Maggie was awake, silent, and, like yesterday, trying to focus her eyes. "She's so adorable, Karen. Just a perfect little girl."

It was now or never Karen thought as she stepped over toward the bed. "Okay, Mom," Karen said as she bent down and gently pushed Maggie's curls back toward her forehead. "I want you to look carefully at Maggie's eyes. Do they look a little slanted to you?" William Hathaway had been absorbed in thought about a new radio station he was considering buying. He was dressed for work, in his usual three piece suit, today it was blue, and moments ago he had checked his watch thinking it would be nice if they could leave before the entire afternoon was lost. But Karen's words to her mother refocused his attention.

"No darling. What are you talking about?"

"The doctor said her fingers and limbs are shorter than normal."

"So what," her mother replied with a trace of tension creeping into her voice. "What does all this mean?"

"It means, Mom, that it is likely Maggie has Downs Syndrome," Karen said and then burst into tears. William Hathaway let out a short gasp. After refocusing her gaze from her granddaughter to her daughter, Virginia Hathaway said:

"That can't be true, Sweetheart. She looks fine to me—perfect in every way."

"Well, that's not what the doctor said," Karen replied as she got back into bed, propped herself behind two pillows, with Maggie between her legs making little motions with her legs and feet. "They do some test either this afternoon or tomorrow, and we'll know for sure in two weeks." William Hathaway rose from his chair, and as unobtrusively as possible, escaped from the room.

"I'll pray for her, hon, and don't you cry anymore," Virginia said as she stepped toward the bed, handing Karen a Kleenex, and taking her hand. "I'm sure everything will turn out alright."

"I hope so Mom, but I'm not counting on it. The doctor was pretty convincing." Virginia Hathaway bent forward to hug her daughter.

"I love you Karen, I love you so much Sweetheart, and I'll pray hard about this. We'll be back tomorrow. I better not keep your father waiting." And she too was gone.

Virginia Hathaway found her husband staring out of one of the windows in the waiting room. "We can go now Bill," she said in a quiet voice. The two walked to the hospital parking lot in silence. Not a word was said between them until they were five minutes into the trip home.

"I knew Karen should have had those tests doctors give women when they first become pregnant," Bill said as he kept his gaze on the traffic in front of him.

"What tests are you talking about?" his wife responded as she looked over at him.

"You know, the tests that tell you whether you have a healthy fetus."

"Are you crazy, Bill? Are you suggesting Karen should have had an abortion? Karen would never have done anything to end her pregnancy."

"Sometimes such actions are justified."

"I can't believe you're talking this way. You're a huge financial supporter of right to life causes and rightly so."

"Do you know what our granddaughter is? She's what people used to call a Mongolian idiot," Bill said with some vehemence to his voice. "That means she will be severely handicapped mentally and look like a freak of nature." Now it was Virginia Hathaway's turn to cry, and the tears came flooding. She slunk back into her seat and wished there was some way she could escape from the car. After several more moments of silence, William Hathaway concluded his ugly attack. "This is the kind of thing God does to couples who live in sin."

"Enough Bill, not one more word from you," Virginia Hathaway blurted out through her tears. "We will pray about this and hope either the doctor is wrong or the Lord will bring us a miracle. And most importantly, we will be strong for Karen. She is our daughter, and we will do everything we can to support her."

"That's all fine and nice, Virginia, but it does nothing to change the reality of the situation."

"That's up to the Lord, not us. You pray, Bill, and not one negative comment to Karen. I mean it. Not one nasty comment." William Hathaway was silent for the rest of the way home. When they arrived at the house, he dropped off his wife, and headed back to work.

∽

When Patrick left the hospital at noon, he too had intended to return to work until he saw the signs to Colorado College. Without knowing exactly why, he turned left off of Cascade Avenue, the busy street on which Penrose hospital was located, and followed the signs to the college. He parked in front of a collection of brick buildings that looked like classrooms. Several students were walking in various directions along walkways that organized this collection of four or five handsome brick buildings. Patrick joined in with them.

At first, his intention was to look for a familiar landmark, but his mind was in too much turmoil for that. Where did the 24th chromosome come from? Was it his? Did it matter? No, of course, it didn't matter, but he was convinced it was his. Karen was too normal, wholesome, too beautiful and innocent to have contributed in any way to Maggie's problem. And he continued walking with his focus mainly on the pavement and his mind churning.

Twenty minutes later he had obviously found, or more accurately run into, the athletic complex. Parts of it looked vaguely familiar from his visit there seven years ago, but he decided not to go in. He was thinking about his family. What would he tell them? How would they respond? His mother would probably be great, but she already had more grandchildren than she knew what to do with. How would the Hathaway's respond? This was their first, and Karen was their daughter. He continued to walk.

Long after he had left the Colorado College campus, he began to wonder how he would respond. This was the crucial question. Would he be a loving father? Would loving Maggie be a natural instinct, or an act of will, something he would have to force? How would he handle the mental and physical problems when they manifested themselves? Would he have suggested an abortion if something had been detected in an early pregnancy test? Could they afford all the doctors's bills, and then there would be psychologists, physical therapists, maybe even marriage counselors? Why did this happen to me? How would Maggie cope with all of her problems? Would there be behavior problems related to her retardation? How am I going to relate to her? My own child. Oh, my God, where is the car?

Finding the car took almost an hour and brief conversations with three fellow pedestrians. It was now four o'clock, and he was hungry. Because he also wanted to get back to the hospital, he decided to eat at the cafeteria there, and was pleasantly surprised. Hot chicken soup, an enormous salad, and a cheeseburger were all delicious and less than seven dollars. He had made a good decision.

While eating, he made an even more important decision. The one thing he must do is get rid of all this guilt and focus on Karen instead. He loved her deeply, there would be no marriage counselors, and for this not to happen he had to be healthy and optimistic, rather than a wounded puppy wallowing in self pity. It was a good thing he panicked over the car, he thought as he finished his second and probably last meal for the day. It directed his attention where it needed to be, on coping with every day issues. It shocked him out of his self-indulgent pity.

He arrived at Karen's room on the fourth floor a little after five p.m., refreshed, and eager to see her. She was napping again, but not very soundly. He kissed her gently, she smiled up at him with a dreamy look on her face, and then he sat mostly on the bed and hugged her tightly. "You're the best, Sweetheart. Simply the best. Has Maggie been in? I would love to see her."

"They're bringing her in at five thirty, and I'm supposed to feed her."

"That ought to be good. I'm glad I'll be here to watch."

"We can't sleep together for six whole weeks. I don't know how I'm going to survive it."

"You'll be so busy and tired from what I hear you won't even think about it," he said as he lifted himself off the bed and smiled down at her. "You will come to think of my body as a hockey puck, a considerable annoyance that keeps slapping up against you, leaving you with no option but to deflect, catch, or throw it off into the corner."

"I wouldn't count on that," she said, returning his smile. "Maybe more like something I can check, fall on top of, and hope that the referee puts us both in the penalty box."

"Not bad. I'm impressed with your imagery."

"Wait till you see me skate."

"Then you really will be falling all over me."

"I know, and there will be other people there so it won't be any fun," And then her mood changed abruptly, worry crept across her face, and she said in a voice that was barely above a whisper. "Are we three going to make it? Can I be an effective mother to a handicapped child?" Finally, as if she had turned the volume completely off, "Will I be able to love her?"

"Yes to all three questions, Sweetheart. I had the same questions this afternoon, but I know we can do it. Maggie will be a precious baby, is a precious baby, because you are so precious. Genetics works both ways. Yes she has forty-seven chromosomes, but she will also have your smile. And you love her to pieces already. I can see it every time you look at her."

"I hope so, Pat. I hope so." They were both quiet after that until the nurse brought Maggie in about fifteen minutes later. The fact they were all three together lifted their spirits. They laughed over the fact Karen was totally incompetent when it came to feeding Maggie. Maggie was awake for at least part of the time, but she too seemed to have no clue as to what to do. When she fell asleep, they took turns holding her and wishing they could hold each other. The nurse took her from them a little after seven. Patrick held Karen's hand for another two hours.

Two weeks to the day after Karen was discharged from the hospital, the telephone rang. Patrick was sitting on the living room couch proof reading one of his software training manuals. Karen had just finished nursing Maggie, they had both made enormous progress in that endeavor, and was trying to put her to sleep. Maggie still needed a lot of help with the sleeping part of her otherwise rather simple routine. Because the phone was right next to where Patrick was sitting, he answered it.

"Hello."

"Is Karen there please?" Patrick immediately recognized the voice as belonging to Frannie Vrooman.

"Yes, she is. Just a minute please. Karen the phone is for you." Karen picked Maggie up from the crib, brought her into the living room, and handed her to Patrick. Because she was a little fussy, Patrick moved away from the phone and walked with her around the house.

"Hello," Karen said. And then, "Oh, hi Frannie. How are you doing?"

"I'm fine Karen, although I wish I didn't have to make this call. Maggie's test results arrived today, and they came back positive. As we suspected, she has Downs Syndrome."

"We are well prepared, Frannie. I'm afraid it's only my mother who believes in miracles," Karen responded as tears, uncontrollably, welled up in her eyes.

"I'm so sorry," Frannie said. "We need to get together and talk further about this, and I would like Pat to be there. Frank has a meeting at the college tomorrow night, so I was wondering if I could come over to your home sometime after dinner. We're not more than four or five miles apart."

"That would be so nice, Frannie. Let me just check with Pat." As she placed her hand over the receiver, she looked across the room at Patrick and said: "The tests on Maggie were positive, and Frannie wants to talk to us about it tomorrow night. Is that okay with you?"

"Fine. That's so nice of her to do it that way. What time is she coming over?"

"That's fine with Pat, Frannie. What time is good for you?"

"How about eight?" Frannie responded.

"That's a good time for us. Thank you so much for doing it this way."

"You're more than welcome. I'm looking forward to making my first house call."

After Karen gave her directions to the house, the two women said their goodbyes and hung up.

~

Frannie arrived precisely at eight o'clock. She was dressed casually in blue jeans, a white turtle neck, and a light green sweater. She was a slight woman, 5'4" tall, a hundred pounds maybe, with soft brown eyes and brown hair, cut at a short, pageboy length. Patrick found her cute, very professional looking, perky, though certainly not beautiful in the way Karen was. He was holding Maggie when she arrived, pacing back and forth throughout the house, trying to get her to fall asleep.

"Ah, she's such a beautiful baby," Frannie said as she moved toward Patrick to look at her. "She does look tired though. Maybe you could put her in her crib and let her fuss for a little while. I think of fussing as a way a two week old exercises. Give her ten or fifteen minutes and then if she doesn't fall asleep, you can hold her again."

"You're the doc," Patrick said with a nervous smile as he turned to walk toward the nursery. As he placed Maggie into the crib, he realized from his response he was a little nervous about tonight. In fact, he felt a little like he was being judged, that he was for some reason being placed on trial. He didn't like these feelings. They seemed to contrast so markedly with the way Karen was handling the situation. She seemed to be looking forward to this meeting. So Patrick delayed his return to the living room for a brief moment while he collected himself.

After pouring Frannie a cup of decaffeinated coffee, Karen and Frannie sat down together in the living room. Patrick soon joined them. Maggie did continue to fuss, but the conversation became so engrossing they were able to ignore her. She eventually fell asleep, offering both Karen and Patrick a lesson if they had been paying attention, but it was lost on them.

"Okay," Frannie said after the three had spent five or ten minutes exchanging pleasantries. This time had not been wasted because Patrick had become considerably more relaxed than he had been when Frannie first arrived. "Let's get down to business. First, I want to know how you both are doing?" Karen looked over at Patrick and responded first.

"I guess I'm doing alright. I can't really speak for Pat. I must admit I spend a lot of time crying. Silly thoughts keep floating through my head. I cry when I think about birthday parties. Yesterday I was watching her sleep in the crib, and I started crying when I thought she would probably never drive a car. That's what I mean by silly. I wish I could put those thoughts out of my mind."

"Parents of a handicapped child tend to worry about unknowns, about future events that are out of their control. Just wait till Maggie gets a little older and you are faced with school. Such worries are understandable. It's also very normal for the mother of a handicapped child to cry. I would be concerned more if you weren't having these little attacks. You seem to be coping pretty well."

"Coping is the right word for it. There is so much to do I don't have much time to think."

"That's what makes your adjustment to this situation so much easier. What about you, Pat? How are you doing with all of this?"

"Wow, Dr. Vrooman. I've..."

"Frannie please."

"Sorry Frannie. I keep getting confused as to whether you are my friend or our doctor."

"Both I hope."

"Well, as I was about to say, this thing has put me on a roller coaster. I thought it would be easy at first. Simply a matter of deciding to love her. Instead, I have gone back and forth from being a good husband and father, and a pitiful jerk. Some of the feelings I've had over this thing have been embarrassing."

"You're an honest man, Pat. Do you mean feelings like why did the 24th chromosome come from me and how am I going to love a handicapped daughter?"

"Yes, but it has been even worse. " Patrick was amazed at her ability to name some of his recent feelings. It made this discussion so much easier. She had broken the ice for him.

"I wouldn't be able to point to feelings like guilt and shame unless they were so typical."

"That's all good to know, but I've even wondered why she had to come into this world." Patrick paused, looked away from both women, and as tears began to form in his eyes, he continued in a voice that was rapidly trailing off into incomprehensibility. "I really can't believe I'm telling you all this."

"Again, Pat," she said in a voice filled with caring, "that is typical, normal really. I had a mother when I was in residency who didn't want her nine month old son with Downs to survive a rather tricky heart operation. Then after the operation the woman was consumed with guilt when the son survived, but now she is fine. She went through her own roller coaster of emotions. All of this is perfectly normal."

"You can come over any time Frannie," Karen interjected with a smile. "You're making us both feel so much better. I've had some of those horrible thoughts too."

"I think I'm going to make it, Frannie," Patrick said, now more composed and at ease with the direction of the conversation. "I want to tell you about this dream I had about four nights ago. It really has been helpful. I haven't even shared it with Karen."

"Wives are the last to know about things like that."

"I call it maleness, Karen. Frank is such a nerd about sharing important things with me."

"Are you ladies going to beat up on men or do you want to hear about my dream?"

"The dream, please Pat. We both ask your forgiveness for our outbursts. Don't we Frannie?"

"Yes we certainly do. And I want to say again," and she looked directly at Patrick with a sheepish grin, " I am impressed with your honesty. It isn't easy to talk about feelings you find embarrassing and don't fully understand."

"Thank you ladies," Patrick said as he glanced quickly at both of them. "After all this buildup, my dream will probably be a big disappointment. Here's the setting. I'm in a suburban neighborhood, not anything like where we are living now, and there are these neat, well manicured houses all around. I'm standing on the curb of the road looking at all the nicely kept lawns, and then I look at my own. It's uncut, wild, way overgrown, with weeds throughout, and yet in the middle stands this tall, red flower which is absolutely beautiful.

"So there I am, standing on the curb, confused as to how I feel about the stark contrast between our lawn and the neighbors', sometimes it disgusts me and sometimes I have a strange feeling of pride, when my next door neighbor comes over to me. Actually she looks a lot like you Frannie, but I seem to remember from the dream I had never met her before. That's strange too, because I should have met my next door neighbor. Anyway, to make a long story short, this woman comes up to me and says, 'I like your lawn. It's so original and interesting. We need more lawns like yours in the neighborhood.'"

Karen could hardly wait to let him finish. She had been sitting at the other end of the couch, but she jumped across and threw her arms around him. "That was beautiful, Pat. I'm so proud of you." And then she showered him with kisses. Patrick was embarrassed, of course, with Frannie in the room, and Karen, sensing it, retreated back to her original position on the couch.

"Wow, Pat," Frannie enthused. "You are going to be fine. Absolutely fine."

"I think so too," Patrick said as he looked over at her and smiled. "I can literally feel my heart beginning to open to her."

"I'm proud of both of you. Now let me get to some of the medical issues. About half of all Downs children have heart defects, some of these problems can be very serious. From the tests we did on Maggie in the hospital, her heart looks perfectly normal and healthy."

"Praise the Lord on that," Patrick said as he burst out laughing. "That's a company slogan I've been learning. Please excuse my lack of reverence."

"You're excused, Pat," Frannie said with a grin. "This situation with Maggie's healthy heart illustrates something I feel quite strongly about when it comes to parenting handicapped children. I highly recommend you not rush off and read a lot of books about Downs children. These books will only scare you and shake your self-confidence. Maggie could very well have some physical complications related to Downs further on down the road, but we can deal with each situation when it manifests itself. That's my job to detect things. I see no point in your worrying about conditions that may never occur in your child. Right now all I can tell you is that you have a very healthy Downs child."

"I see what you mean," Karen interjected. "It sounds like good advice."

"The same goes for behavioral issues. There are lots of expert books on the psychology of Downs Syndrome children. Again, I would leave them on the shelf. The problem is you then begin to treat your child as a statistic rather than as an individual which is the worse thing you can do. There is no one way to raise any child, and this is also true when the child has Downs Syndrome. Love her, provide sound discipline, trust your own instincts, and she will turn out just fine. In many important ways, a Downs child is no different from any other child."

"Can you explain for me the mental retardation part?" Karen asked. "What can we expect in that regard?"

"Downs children have lower IQs than normal children, in some cases much lower IQs. We won't know the extent of Maggie's loss until she is tested at a much older age. What Downs kids lack is cognitive ability. They can't reason in depth because the part of the brain that puts together information is damaged. Memory is rarely a problem, just cognitive skills. The good news is there are lots of things you can do to improve Maggie's mental ability. In some ways, Downs is a treatable condition. We recommend you see a developmental psychologist about these issues at about six months."

"Should I be writing this down?" Karen asked as she looked over at Patrick.

"No, I don't think so," Frannie responded. "You'll know when Maggie is ready. We watch her closely too. It's a team effort in that sense. But I would say she'll be ready at eight or nine months.

"You know, one thing they say about Downs kids is that they develop more slowly—slower to walk, slower to talk, that kind of thing. While that's certainly true, you won't have to worry about it because this is your first child. You have no standard for comparison.

"As I said earlier, love, discipline, and a healthy trust in your own instincts are all that is required. One thing I should elaborate on is the discipline part. All children need discipline. What sometimes happens with Downs children or any handicapped child is the parents feel guilty and so they overindulge the child as a means of compensation. That's something you'll have to watch out for."

"Frannie, this is all very helpful and reassuring," Patrick interjected. "But I must tell you that you are making it sound so easy, which violates those instincts you are asking me to trust."

" You certainly are a straight shooter, Pat," Frannie said as she looked over at him with a warm smile. "When I came over here, what I really wanted to do was reassure both you and Karen. Having a Downs child can be devastating, so the first thing I like to do is reassure the parents. You and Karen seem to be coping well with the situation, and so let me make one final point and we can call it a night.

"Your instincts are right on target. There is nothing more difficult than raising a handicapped child. Raising children is never easy, complicating the situation with a handicap makes it far more difficult. So, I do have one final bit of advice, and I think you will love me for it, Pat.

"The best thing the two of you can do for Maggie is keep your marriage healthy. Bringing a handicapped child into a family can destroy a marriage. It happens all the time which is so, so sad. Parents become consumed with guilt and coping. So what is the antidote? The answer is simple. Spend some time alone, or with friends without your child, and maintain an active, healthy sex life. That means joyful, lusty love two or three times a week."

"Is that your prescription, doctor?" Patrick inquired with a sheepish grin.

"Yes it is Pat. I thought you might like it," Frannie said as she looked over at him and winked.

"Could you write it up on your pad, please? I don't want Karen to forget it."

"Yes, I can certainly do that."

"Don't prescriptions have to be renewed periodically?" Karen interjected, eager to get into the conversation and even with her husband.

"Yes they do. The law requires once a year."

"Can we then have this conversation again in twelve months?" Karen asked, barely able to contain her laughter.

"You guys are too much," Frannie said, joining the merriment. "Speaking of sex, I do have a happy confession to make of my own. I'm four months pregnant. Due toward the end of September."

"That's horrible news, Frannie," Karen blurted out as her emotions quickly shifted one hundred and eighty degrees. "We're going to lose you as our doctor."

"Oh, thank you Karen. That was so nice. You won't lose me. I'll continue to work in some capacity after the birth—probably part-time. What I'm really looking forward to is strolling our babies around 'Dirty Woman Park.' Don't you love the name! I called the Chamber of Commerce about it a while back. The receptionist told me the park was named after a woman who was a potato farmer and always dirty. This woman loved children and donated her land to the town when she died. It's less than a ten minute drive for me too."

With that Frannie stopped being a physician, and the two women talked for another hour and a half. Poor Patrick didn't know what to do. He wanted to be polite, but it was obvious he had little to contribute to the conversation. So he took the easy way out and nodded off to sleep right there on the couch.

Interestingly, he didn't sleep long or it didn't seem that way because Karen was suddenly all over him. "Time to take our medicine, Mr. McGovern," she said as she smothered him with kisses. After recovering some and breaking out in a grin that covered his entire face, Patrick said:

"Isn't it a little early for this. I thought Lovejoy's handout said six weeks."

"I hate smart asses," Karen replied as she started unbuttoning his shirt. "We can do everything but," she said matching his grin.

"You're the best, Sweetheart, simply the best!"

It was mid June, Maggie was sound asleep, and Karen and Patrick were enjoying a night alone on their deck. They were sitting on a wooden glider, slowly rocking, with her head nestled up against his shoulder, and the outline of Mount Herman clearly visible in the distance. Patrick had not been looking forward to this evening, not dreading it necessarily but a little anxious nonetheless, because they had to discuss the recent offer on his townhouse. The sale would net them $42,500, which was considerably less than they had expected or at least hoped for.

Karen's advice was to accept it. It was only the second offer they had received, and the money was fine with her. She joked about his cleaning the bathrooms for the next fifty years, wishing they had purchased a house with three bathrooms instead of two. The only dispute they ended up having over the matter was who would advise her on how to invest the money. She wanted Patrick to start taking more responsibility for her investments, but he pleaded total ignorance.

"Your Dad has done a wonderful job for many years. He pays a lot of attention to these things, and forty-two thousand dollars is a lot of money. You need to invest it wisely."

"I know all that. I just don't want to depend on Daddy for anything. Maybe I should start learning more about this stuff myself."

"That's probably a good idea," Patrick said removing his arm from around her shoulder and taking her hand. "I think everyone should take full responsibility for their own money. I do have one idea for you, though," he said with a twinkle in his eye she was unable to detect because of her position beside him. "You know my project with Noah is to introduce software into all the stations. Well, that will require each station purchasing four or five new PCs. Jason and I have done a lot of research on the PC market, and we have chosen Dell. Their machines are top of the line. You might consider putting some money there. Noah Communications will certainly be spending a lot of money with Dell over the next two years."

"I like that. I have always wanted to own a computer company. I will call Lucie at Dean Witter and ask for her recommendations. This is perfect. I'm firing Daddy as my financial advisor. It really feels good." And then Karen abruptly changed the subject and said: "Don't move from here. I'll be right back." With that she walked briskly into the house, took an extra blanket from the linen closet, and hurried back to the glider.

She had become a little chilly with the outside thermometer registering at fifty-five degrees. She reclaimed her position next to Patrick, spread the blanket around them, and snuggled up close. They remained in that position for several minutes absorbed in their own thoughts.

Finally, Patrick broke the ice. "A penny for your thoughts," he said as he shifted his position slightly to become more comfortable.

"I was thinking about my cousin Stephanie. Do you remember her from the wedding?"

"Not really. I remember talking with her and thinking what an attractive woman she was, but not much else. Quite tall, if I'm not mistaken."

"Probably five nine or five ten. Anyway, we should have gone to her law school graduation. It's a pretty big deal to graduate in the top five percent of your class from a place like Penn. I was thinking about her because she starts her first job in two weeks."

"She ought to do very well. What type of law is she going to practice?"

"She likes women's issues, whatever that means."

"Probably cases involving domestic disputes and children," Patrick interjected.

"You know she is like my sister."

"I suspected that a little because of the time you two spend on the phone. Tell me a little about her mother and her relationship with your Dad? Don't the two of them own Noah Communications together?"

"I don't know much about the legal relationship between them, but I assume you're right. Dad and Uncle Peter were equal partners in Philadelphia before he died. I don't really think Daddy and Aunt Harriet are very close. He thinks of her as a spoiled Philadelphia socialite which is really unfair. Yes, she is a mainline type person, not outwardly religious, which I'm sure bothers him no end, but she has done a wonderful job as head of admissions for the Baldwin School."

"The Baldwin School?"

"It's a girl's prep school in Philadelphia. Both of my cousins graduated from there. It must be pretty good because they did extremely well in college. Stephanie has told me many times how grateful Aunt Harriet is for the financial help Daddy has provided. I guess it's probably more Noah Communications than Daddy. Anyway, I'm sure Daddy loves thinking he is the patriarch of the family, the protector of his brother's legacy. But our two families live so differently. I have often wondered how Daddy and Uncle Peter got along? They obviously worked well together, but they were so very different. Their wives certainly are."

"I've occasionally wondered if your Dad resents paying Stephanie's family all that money. He's the one who works six days a week, twelve hours a day. Maybe that's why he sees his sister-in-law as a spoiled socialite."

"Could be. Daddy is full of all kinds of resentments. I have often thought one of the reasons he works so hard is because he doesn't like himself very much. He's always looking for trophies to fill his lack of self-esteem, at least that was the opinion of my therapist. Noah Communications is a trophy. Their house in the Springs is a trophy, the condo in Vail is an extension of that. I was a trophy that suddenly lost its luster. Maggie is not a perfect child. I'm sure she has been very difficult for him to deal with."

"It's been difficult for us too."

"I know Pat, but that dream of yours said it all. I think about it all the time. That beautiful red flower inside all the wildness and weeds. I wish my parents could be more like that neighbor."

"Maybe they will in time. Your Mom certainly is. We have had to change our expectations quite dramatically. Before Maggie was born, I dreamed if it was a girl we would become pair skaters together. I have always wanted to put on figure skates. The crowd I grew up with as a kid thought figure skates were for little girls and sissies."

"You certainly do have interesting dreams my dear. I guess we won't be taking her to the company condo in Vail anytime soon for a skiing vacation. Steph and I used to plan our two weeks together over Christmas for weeks through the mail."

"I just can't help but love her. It's instinctive I guess. When I hear her cry, I want to hold and protect her. When she starts to smile for real, I'll be a captured man."

"You're so different from Daddy, Pat. So secure with who you are, and kind. I'm sure subconsciously that is the reason I picked you."

"It was all hormones, Sweetheart. We're just lucky it's working out so well."

"Most of the time. The biggest stress on our marriage has not been Maggie, but your work schedule."

"I know, and I feel badly about that; but there is so much to do, and I love the challenge."

"Well, at least we take our medicine—most of the time—and speaking of that..."

"I'm a lucky guy," and he hugged her tightly.

"I'll race you to bed," she said as she disengaged herself from him and fled the glider. "If you beat me, I'll clean the bathrooms next month."

"I can't lose with you no matter what happens," and he gathered up the blanket and followed her inside, thinking that Frannie deserved the Nobel prize for medicine. Petty annoyances disappeared when her prescription was faithfully executed.

◠

Their first summer as a family of three went well. Maggie did acquire a captivating smile. It covered her entire face, which unraveled her poor father. Karen and Maggie were also developing comfortable routines together. Karen walked often with her friend Alex and was looking forward to adding Frannie to the list.

The two women, doctor and friend, spoke frequently together on the telephone. As fall approached, they started getting together for lunch as Frannie reduced her work schedule in preparation for the imminent arrival of their first child. One early afternoon in late September after cleaning the dishes and moving Maggie and Frannie to the living room, Karen said: "You wait right there for a minute and keep an eye on Maggie. I'll be right back," and she quickly left the living room, leaving Maggie lying on the carpet in the middle of the floor and Frannie watching her from the sofa. She quickly returned with a new stroller.

"Oh, it's beautiful," Frannie said. "Is it for me, I hope?"

"Yes, it is," Karen said as she brought the stroller to a stop in front of Frannie. "Every time we get together it's like having a free appointment. This is the least we can do."

"Thank you so, so much," Frannie said as she got up from the sofa to hug Karen. "Just two or three weeks, and we'll have both of them at 'Dirty Woman Park.'"

"We'll be twins," Karen said as she rolled the stroller away from the sofa, placing it nearer to the front door. "It's just like mine." As Karen was returning to her seat on the couch, she glanced over at Maggie, smiled, and said to Frannie: "Can you hear the little growl from Maggie? The erh, erh, erh. Isn't it cute? She started doing that about two weeks ago."

"I did notice it while we were eating lunch. It is cute, but it may suggest hearing loss. Downs kids at Maggie's age frequently growl like that, and it often indicates they are not hearing as well as they should. It's about time to have Maggie's hearing checked."

"Oh dear, and we seemed to be doing so well."

"You're doing remarkably well. She is a very healthy, beautiful little girl. The only other problems you have had are colds and ear infections. As I explained to you when we talked at the office, Downs kids often have poorly developed immune systems which leads to these types of problems. On the other hand, colds and ear infections are typical in all babies Maggie's age.

"You know, as I sit here watching her, I think it is also time to make an appointment with a developmental psychologist. She looks ready, which is a good sign. There is a really good one in the Springs named Harold Midway. Call up Andrea tomorrow morning at the office and get his number."

"What kinds of things does he do?"

"He will give you some mental exercises, games really, to do with Maggie. Working on her cognitive skills every day for twenty or thirty minutes can be crucial for her later development. It will require patience on your part, but this kind of work pays huge dividends. Remember what I told you that first day about Downs. In many ways, it is a treatable condition."

"That's great, Frannie. Patrick has been wondering when we can start doing this kind of thing. He cheated a little and read a few books," Karen said with a sheepish grin.

"Good for him," Frannie said as she looked at her watch and decided it was time to think about leaving. She had appointments from three to five in the afternoon, and it was nearing two thirty. "I like parents who are proactive with their children; and, you know, I was probably too strong on my advice about books. I just don't want Maggie to become a statistic."

"She won't, Frannie. Patrick and I both feel strongly about that. Now I noticed you checking your watch, and I know about the afternoon appointments," she said with a smile. "Let me show you how this stroller folds up. It couldn't be easier, and then I can help you put it in your car." The two women accomplished their task with relative ease, hugged each other, and Frannie was on her way. Karen was aglow with warmth as she watched her friend make her way out of the driveway and along Schilling Road. She then rushed into the house to check on Maggie who was busy staring at her hands and wiggling her tiny legs. She was a long way from crawling which had enabled Karen to personally escort Frannie to her car; but when Maggie looked up and saw her mother staring down at her, her face broke out into a wide grin and the tempo of her little legs increased by half. Karen melted into tears, got down on the floor, and tickled Maggie from one end of her body to the other. Maggie's happy squeals made all of her prodigious efforts both that day and in the past more than worthwhile.

~

When Patrick came home for dinner on the eleventh shopping day before

Christmas, his radio stations had been trumpeting this message ad nausium throughout the day and every previous day for the last two weeks, Karen was again on the living room floor with Maggie. She had just returned that afternoon from her first appointment with Dr. Harold Midway, a PhD from Northwestern University, and was eager to try one of his recommendations. She had taken one of Maggie's favorite toys, a mouse that squealed, it was a toy marketed primarily for puppies but you never know what will excite the mind of a child, and had attached nylon thread to the base of the mouse with the other end of the thread tied to the arm of her eight month old daughter. The purpose of the exercise was to get Maggie to pull the mouse toward her.

"Pat, hi honey, you're right on time. Maybe you can sit on the floor with Maggie. We'll attach her other mouse to your hand, and you can show her how to do it."

"Sounds fun," he said as he got down on the floor, kissed his wife and tickled his daughter after kissing her too, "but what are we doing here?"

"This is one of the games Dr. Midway recommended. He's a very nice man. Said some encouraging things about Maggie too. I'll tell you all about the appointment later."

"Okay, hook me up." Patrick demonstrated the exercise for Maggie by pulling the mouse toward him several times, each time picking the mouse up as it reached him, and making it squeal. Maggie laughed and clapped her hands with each squeal, but could not make the same connection to her mouse. Patrick tried it many different ways, going through assorted antics in an attempt to make the show funny. Maggie loved the show, she loved practically everything her father did with her, but she did not pull her own string.

"We'll try this again tomorrow," Patrick said to Karen as he detached the strings from his hand and the hand of his daughter. "Our goal will be to master this game before we leave for Massachusetts on the twentieth. That gives us a week."

"You're so patient," Karen said as she bent down to kiss her husband. She had been watching the show from the couch and was a little discouraged. "Maybe you can be Maggie's coach for these exercises. Both Frannie and Dr. Midway suggested we work with her about half an hour a day."

"I've always wanted to be a coach," he said smiling up at her. "You coach me, and I'll pass it along. I like the idea of having a concrete game to play with Maggie."

"I'll explain some of the other exercises after dinner."

"Do you want some help?"

"No, but thanks for asking," she said as she retreated toward the kitchen. "I'll have things ready in fifteen minutes."

"Good. I'll get a beer and come back here with Maggie. It's another one of my goals to have her crawling by Christmas."

~

Christmas with the McGoverns had been fabulous. They had all been good with Maggie, especially Patrick's mother Kathleen. Though not surprised, Karen was definitely relieved. It was Maggie's first visit with the McGovern clan en masse, Kathleen had come for a two-week visit in July by herself, and Karen felt blessed to be a part of Patrick's raucous family again. The contrast with her own family was painful, so she chose not to think about it.

But today was Valentine's Day which called for a different type of celebration, and Karen had an exciting plan, though definitely a little crazy, in mind. Patrick had called around lunchtime, promising to be home by five o'clock, which put the first part of the plan in place. One side effect of Downs Syndrome for Maggie was that she was a relatively passive child. She would often lie in her crib or playpen and stare contently at her hands for what seemed like hours at a time. Karen figured she needed half an hour, maybe forty-five minutes of cooperation from Maggie, to complete phase two of the operation.

At four thirty in the afternoon she took off all of her clothes, painted purple hearts on her nipples with lipstick she had purchased that morning for the first time in eight or nine years, and put on Patrick's long, gray trench coat. At 4:55 she put Maggie in her crib. She then went into their bedroom to sit on the bed and wait.

One of the advantages of living on a gravel road is that you can hear a car approaching your home long before it arrives. Ten minutes later the sound of the crunching gravel was music to her ears. He's right on time, she thought. This is going to be so great.

When there was a knock at the door, she ran from the bedroom, a little confused, and screamed excitedly, "Come in, come in, you dummy." As the door flew open, she flung the gray coat into the air, threw out her chest, and screamed in a gleeful voice, "Happy Valentine's Day." Her brother Billy stood there in shock.

"Oh my God, oh my God," she screamed, this time in horror, as she leapt backward, scooped up the trench coat from the floor, and flew into the protective haven of her bedroom. "What are you doing here? I thought it was Patrick," she yelled out in disbelief.

"I guess so, Sis," Billy said as he entered the house more than a little disoriented. "I just left Patrick at the office. He told me to come by and present my plans to you personally. He said to expect him by six at the latest."

That son of a bitch, she thought as she struggled to put on her clothes and to keep from crying. Her anger with Patrick threw a dark cloud over her mind, which prevented her from seeing the humor in the situation. He never comes home when he promises. What am I going to do with Billy out there? This confirms his worst suspicions about me. Please start crying, Maggie. I need a diversion, but Maggie was busy with her hand games and was no help at all.

Billy must have been reading her mind as he continued to speak to her from the other room. "Where is Maggie, Sis? I was looking forward to seeing her."

"She's in the nursery, in her crib," Karen responded, struggling now to reduce her heart rate and to answer back as calmly as possible. "Go in and see her if you like." As Billy slipped into see Maggie, Karen slipped out of her bedroom and waited on the living room couch for him to return.

"She's a beautiful baby," Billy said as he returned to the living room a few minutes later. That's an encouraging comment Karen thought as she tried to smile over at him. "She loves to look at those hands. It's so cute to watch."

"I'm sorry for what happened ten minutes go," Karen said as she was finally able to smile sheepishly over at him. She felt she should get up and give him a hug, but she couldn't make herself do it. "I was expecting Patrick, and what you saw was my Valentine's card to him. Your dumb sister popping out of a box. Married people in love do stupid things."

"That's okay," Billy said as he sat down across from her. "Maybe someday, sometime, someone will pop out of a box for me."

"I hope so. You certainly deserve it."

"Let me get right to it, Sis. I need to be leaving before Patrick gets home."

"There's no rush now." The mood had been completely broken. Valentine's Day was now just like any other day. "Why not stay for dinner. There's plenty."

"Thanks for the offer, and I'll take a rain check. I have a church meeting at 7:30 tonight, so I can't stay long. Anyway, here's what I've been thinking about. I talked it over with Mom and Dad the other night, and they think it's a good idea too. Palm Sunday will be here before we know it. How about we baptize Maggie then? I would love to get you and Patrick back to church."

"That's a lovely idea, Billy, but Maggie has a Catholic father. We thought we might baptize her in Chelsea, Patrick's old church, this summer." Karen was lying to her brother. She found it easy to do, and was pleased it had come so effortlessly. She and Patrick had not even discussed the possibility of a baptism. Karen had no idea what the silly ceremony was all about, and she certainly did not want to be placed on stage again at the Abundant Life Assembly of God Church.

"Oh, Karen. You can't ruin her life in that way," Billy blurted out with some passion.

"I think Downs Syndrome did a pretty good job of that," Karen said, her sympathy for her brother rapidly draining from her heart.

"Downs Syndrome was God's punishment for the sin you and Patrick committed on Prince Edward Island," Billy said in an even voice as if he were preaching to her. "This baptism will provide Maggie with a whole new chance to erase that sin." Billy's remarks stung Karen. She sat there in stony silence trying to believe he didn't mean it, and then something snapped. She exploded.

"Is that what you believe, you son of a bitch?" Karen said in a voice of cold fury as she grabbed a glass bowl filled with sea glass she and Stephanie had collected on the beach over more than ten joyous summers together at her aunt's summer home at Stone Harbor on the Jersey shore. Without thinking about its precious meaning to her, she rose to her feet, and, with both hands, threw it at her brother. She missed her target by three or more feet with the glass bowl hitting the arm of the sofa, shattering the bowl, and spreading the sea glass all over that side of the room.

"Have you gone crazy?" Billy said as he jumped up from the couch and ran toward the front door. Karen did not pursue him until he was outside, opening the door to his car. She then screamed out at him one last time.

"Don't you ever come back here you mean, self-righteous bastard unless you do so on your knees in apology. What Patrick and I do in our personal lives is between us, do you hear me, and has nothing to do with your petty, vindictive God." With that, she slammed the door shut and fell into the sofa, burying her head beneath the pillow in an effort to muffle her uncontrollable sobs.

～

Patrick arrived home twenty minutes later to a rather strange scene. The two women in his life were definitely out of sorts. Maggie was screaming from her crib in the nursery while her mother was picking up sea glass that was scattered throughout the left hand corner of the living room.

"Will you deal with her, please? I've got my hands full here or haven't you noticed," Karen said in a voice full of tension and hurt. Patrick picked his way to Maggie, trying to make some sense of the situation. His first thought was Maggie was being punished for picking up and throwing the sea glass bowl, but that was not possible. Maggie was still unable to crawl or to pick herself up. He held Maggie and kissed her, and, as so often was the case, she recovered her composure quickly when held. He then walked into the living room, hoping to work the same magic on Karen.

As he entered the room with Maggie, Karen looked up at him from her position on the carpet and burst into tears. "Oh, Pat, I've done it this time."

"What have you done, Sweetheart? Do you want some help with the sea glass?"

"I threw it at Billy half an hour ago."

"Just because he wanted to baptize Maggie?"

"No, not that. I lied and told him we had plans for Chelsea."

"What did he say about that?"

"Please come here and hold me." Patrick went back to the nursery to pick up a blanket, returned to the living room, and placed Maggie on the floor on the blanket. He then joined Karen on the love seat where she clung to him and sobbed. Finally, after many soothing words from Patrick, she recovered and related to him the story of her intended Valentine's surprise.

"I missed a great Valentine's treat," Patrick said as he continued holding her.

"Oh, Pat. You should have seen the look on his face when I threw off the coat," Karen said as she moved to shift her position on the love seat and was able to focus on the humor of the situation for the first time. "Obviously he was in shock, but I detected a little whoa Sis!"

"I bet," Patrick said as he turned her face toward him for a kiss. "Did he notice you are pregnant?"

"Of course not silly," Karen said, having recovered in the arms of her good, strong husband. "It's hardly been two months yet."

"I know, but did you tell him?"

"No, I haven't told anybody. But let me tell you what happened next. After I was dressed, he asked about the baptism. When I indicated that we had plans for a Catholic baptism, he accused me of ruining her life." Karen was now talking so fast that Patrick had to concentrate hard on listening. "I said Downs was responsible for ruining her life, and then the bastard said Downs was God's punishment for our premarital sin, " Karen concluded as she burst into tears again. "Can you believe that shit?"

"And then you threw the glass bowl at him?"

"Yes," she said in a voice muffled by tears. "Do you see now how my family pushes my buttons?"

"The bastard deserved it. Too bad you didn't hit him." Patrick was becoming angry too.

"Well, that's it for my family. It's just you and me kid," she said as she squeezed him tightly. "They'll never speak to me again after this."

"Billy will be too embarrassed to tell your parents."

"Don't count on it. He loves to make me look like the wicked witch from the west."

"He certainly has a narrow, judgmental outlook."

"Tell me about it."

"Your Mom is too shy to mention it, and your Dad too distant."

"The funny thing is Billy said it was their plan to have Maggie baptized in the church. Maybe that means they are coming around to Maggie? Boy, did I mess that up?"

"Sweetheart, your brother and father were coming around only if you and Maggie conformed to their view of the world. You didn't blow anything with them because you find it impossible to live in that world. Your mother loves you and Maggie anyway. I know you think of her as a weak person, but she really is sweet and kind. And maybe you don't give her enough credit. This whole thing won't make any difference with her. If Billy does tell her exactly what happened, I bet she'll be able to see your point of view." They were quiet for awhile until Karen said in a soft voice.

"For a guy with an engineer's mind, those are pretty deep thoughts. Thank you, so so much for being here when I needed you. I hope you are right about my Mom."

"I thought that's what husbands are for."

"Yes, but most aren't very good at it."

"How do you know that?"

"Soap operas."

"You need a second child to consume more of your time."

"Let's celebrate Valentine's Day, big boy," she said as she stood and lifted up her shirt. Patrick smiled when he saw the lipstick and reflected briefly on the many complex parts that made up his wife. There was a little baggage there, but it really had nothing to do with him or their relationship. She worked hard on separating her family problems from him. He admired that, was thankful for it, and was so much in love with her that minor problems of this sort didn't matter to him in the least.

"With Maggie in the room?" he asked with a smile and little conviction.

"She has her hands to play with. When she hears me squeal in joyous passion, she'll think her mouse has come to play."

"Karen, you are the wicked witch from the west," he said as he pulled off his pants.

"I'm just oozing with sin and love for the most beautiful man I know. Praise the Lord for Valentine's Day," she said as she leaped on top of him.

"Praise the Lord for beautiful sinners," he responded as he threw his arms around her and hugged her tightly. Spontaneous, fun, vulnerable. He was undone.

Karen was excited as she pulled the white Dodge Caravan into the driveway at 9:30 on a crisp morning in early April. She was returning from the grocery store with lots of goodies because it was Maggie's first birthday. They were celebrating at two thirty that afternoon. She had invited Frannie and little Andrew, Alex and her mother, and two mothers with small children she had met at the park walking with Frannie.

There was one additional family member present. No, it wasn't Patrick. He was out of town on business. No, it was not Virginia. She was sick with a mild case of the flu and was worried about passing it on to the babies. Rather it was Tucker. Tucker was a six- week old chocolate lab Patrick had bought for Maggie when he celebrated her birthday two nights ago. Patrick claimed Maggie needed greater incentive to crawl. She was close, poised to excite her parents no end, as she would lie on the floor and scoot ever so slightly forward like an inchworm, but she wasn't quite there. Patrick argued she would instinctively chase after a puppy.

Karen countered that Patrick just wanted a dog, but she certainly had no complaints. Tucker was adorable. He was still tiny, about the size of Maggie's stuffed dog that was a permanent fixture in her crib, and all brown fur with the most enchanting brown/blue eyes that joyously laughed out at you. The dog was not without his problems in that he obviously wasn't house broken, and he still cried from time to time at night, they had only picked him up two days ago, but with respect to Maggie he was a huge success.

They fell in love immediately. That first night when Patrick brought him home Maggie was sitting up on the living room carpet. As Patrick released him, he waddled up to Maggie wagging his tail, and licked her face. Though Maggie lost her balance and fell onto the carpet, she was grinning from ear to ear. As he pranced around the room, her eyes followed him like a hawk, and when he came bounding up to her she giggled with glee.

Although Tucker was a disaster at Maggie's party, he was into everything and all over the place, chewing anything that would fit in his mouth, he was also the party's biggest hit. All the little kids loved him, and he was the dominant topic of discussion. It was a strange party, Karen thought because all of her women friends were busy taking care of the little ones they had brought with them. And she was the worst offender with Maggie, an out of control Tucker, and all those people to feed.

So there wasn't much visiting time for her. But the important thing was Maggie had fun even though she had no idea what it was about. She received several thoughtful presents, and enjoyed immensely watching all the candles Karen placed on her cake.

～

Karen's social life was more successful on a one-on-one basis with her two special friends, Frannie and Alex. She and Alex had a particularly intriguing routine. They would walk in the morning while Karen's mother watched Maggie and Alex's mother babysat her store. Then the four women would get together for lunch at Karen's house with Alex closing the store while they ate. You don't really lose customers in a small town by closing the store occasionally, Alex reasoned. They come back another time.

The only difficulty was juggling schedules. When Alex called one evening in early June indicating she had her mother on board for the following Wednesday, Karen, though seven months pregnant, was eager for some girl time. Her mother was rarely a problem. The plan was to walk from Karen's home along a National Forest trail to the base of Mount Herman and back, a distance of a little more than four miles. The two friends would walk slowly, stopping often to look and to chat. Karen had no qualms about being able to make the hike.

Her mother arrived at their home a little after nine on the appointed Wednesday morning, and Karen and Alex set off about half an hour later. Karen allowed Tucker to go with them. He was just big enough to make the trip with no problems, even though he would travel eight or ten miles to their four. Karen relented because he was good company, and the exercise was exactly what he needed.

Alex was Karen's seeker friend. She had traveled all over the world, read a million books, and like Karen, enjoyed a good philosophical discussion every now and then. The weather was splendid for any kind of discussion or outdoor activity, the temperature in the mid sixties, though threatening to climb much higher with all the sun and deep blue sky. In addition, the scenery was picturesque with patches of brown in places due to the lack of rain.

As they said goodbye to Karen's mother, Alex almost immediately began praising Maggie. It was an easy thing for her to do because her sentiments were genuine. She really did believe Maggie was a remarkable baby.

"That makes my day, Alex," Karen said as they turned off of Schilling Road onto the trail. "She is a good baby. You know I was reading a book about Downs kids that Patrick recommended. This author says handicapped children respond in terms of how they are treated. If they sense fear and judgment, they misbehave. With Downs kids Maggie's age, that often means temper tantrums. We're so lucky about that. She has never had one. On the other hand, when these kids are loved to death, they respond back in loving ways."

"That's really a parable about all humans," Alex responded as she laughed to herself with regard to Tucker. Tucker was running ahead and then sprinting back. His tail was constantly wagging, he had a look of wonder in his eyes, and for the brief moment that he was with them, he would jump up for reassurance. Love and goofiness seem to go with this family, she thought.

"As you know, I was brought up in a traditional Christian family; and, like you, all the bull shit dogma drove me away from the church. Despite my earlier failures as a Christian, I have found there really is an easy answer to the spiritual life I have made so difficult for so many years. All you have to do is look out on the world through the eyes of love rather than fear.

"It's like the author of your book says. If you see another person through the eyes of love, they will return that love. The lives of both people are enriched. If, on the other hand, you choose to look at a person through the eyes of fear, resentment, jealousy or anger, the relationship reflects those qualities and both individuals lose."

"That's it?" Karen asked as she smiled over at her friend. "Is that the gospel of Alex?"

"That's the gospel of Alex," she responded laughing. "Every morning when I get up, I spend fifteen minutes thinking about all the love that's part of my life. Then I go out and the world is beautiful even if the weather is shitty or I have accounting work to do.

"I'm reprogramming my mind. Most people have no clue how the mind works. They think lousy situations or mean, ugly people put them in a foul mood; but the truth is, they choose to see the world that way. On some strange level, they enjoy a world of negativity. Their minds are programmed to see things as bad."

"Where does all this stuff come from? You? Are these ideas original?"

"Nope. I've reconnected to one of the first books I ever read in college, *Man's Search for Meaning*, and damn if the name of the author hasn't slipped my mind. We have several copies at the store, though.

"The book is about a holocaust victim, a Jew in a Nazi prison camp. His situation is of course unbelievable, filled with horror, and at first, at least as I remember it, he is very depressed. Then one morning he wakes up and concludes there must be a better way. And there is. His mind invents it. He decides to see his world from the perspective of love—his fellow prisoners, his Nazi guards, the camp administration, you name it—all the aspects of his prison world. Under the most horrible conditions, he reprograms his mind. He loves, he becomes a spiritual person, he finds meaning for his life, and it makes all the difference. Humans create the psychological world in which they live."

"What an incredible story?"

"I'll give you a copy as a present when number two arrives. You've got all the baby books you need."

"What about children of your own? You'd be such a great mother."

"I think I would make flower children," she said with a laugh. "You know I do worry about making babies from time to time. When I look at you, I sense it's a part of what I'm meant to do here, and I'm not getting younger. I was thinking recently, though not too seriously, laughing about it really, of inviting Bruce back into my life. He was such a great lover. Maybe he could get me pregnant and then move on."

"That doesn't sound like an ideal solution, at least it wouldn't appeal to me."

"That's why I've been laughing about it. Maybe Patrick could introduce me to one of his handsome, jock friends. People always say opposites attract."

"It certainly happened in our case. He's so secure, easy going, happy with who he is."

"Don't put yourself down like that, Karen. I know you guys are different in ways, but you are so loving, it radiates from you like the sun, and you are full of spiritual integrity. You are going to search until you find something real. No phony baloney, no pretending so it looks good, only the real thing."

"And you're telling me today all I have to do is choose it. Choose love rather than hate or fear. That sounds so easy."

"Start with prissy little Billy boy, and you'll see you have some work to do."

"But its so much fun hating him," she said with a laugh. She had come a long way since Valentine's Day.

"That's Frankl's point. The guy's name is Viktor Frankl. He says you chose to hate because there's a part of your mind that likes to hate, wants to hate, but the relationship dynamics that results from hate brings down both parties. There must be a better way. That's my new mantra. When you learn to look at Billy through the eyes of love, you'll be flying, soaring, beating to the wonderful music of a different drum. Billy will probably think you're on dope or something even stronger, but that's Billy's problem. He will probably choose to see your journey through the threatening eyes of resentment and fear. Deep down most fundamentalists, and it doesn't matter if they are Christian, Islamic or Jewish, see the world through the eyes of fear. Anyway, what you don't want to do is to allow Billy's problems to become your problems. So you look at him through the eyes of love, and behold a miracle may happen. He may fall in love with you too."

"That would be a miracle. All I need is love? The Beatles seem to be speaking to me."

"That's it. And when your mind wants to slip back into old habits, when you see situations through eyes darkened by fear, anger or resentment, remember Frankl. He was a Jew in a Nazi prison camp who turned his life around because he chose to love rather than hate. You see, everyone's mind is like a computer. The central question is the background music that beats your drum, which provides the raw material for the program that your mind runs on. If you want to see goodness and beauty, change the music to love. Restructure your mind around love. God made a world with love in it. All we need to do is choose to see it."

"Can we work on this together?" Karen asked with an eye out for Tucker. He was becoming a little too self-confident Karen decided.

"Absolutely. We'll share books and confessionals. We already do it now."

"You're the best friend," Karen said as she turned toward Alex to hug her. "You make my day every day we're together. Now all we have to do is find Tucker and head ourselves toward home."

"That's what seeing the world through love is all about. Returning home, returning to our natural predisposition to love. Look at Tucker," Alex said as he came bounding around the corner at them. "That's how he sees the world. All we have to do is follow Tucker, the reincarnation of the historical Jesus. That's how I see Jesus: laughing, loving, caring for every person that came within his orbit. Jesus, Tucker, Viktor Frankl: the three male heroes of my life. It's time for me to rethink men, Karen. The thought of babies is so appealing. Thanks for planting that awesome seed." The two women returned to their mothers in a state of heightened awareness, the contagion of love between them was bursting out all over their individual and shared worlds.

～

Justin Faircloth McGovern was born on August 8th, 1994 at two in the morning. Frannie came in to see Karen at ten the next day to pronounce him one hundred percent healthy. Karen breathed a sigh of relief, and hugged her friend. Again, it had been a routine delivery with Karen arriving at the hospital around 10:30 p.m. on the seventh. Patrick had been with her this time from labor to delivery, and Maggie had spent her first night with Bill and Virginia Hathaway.

With two infants at home, Karen and Patrick lived in a state of perpetual tiredness. About four weeks into their new routine, they took advantage of some rare alone time. It was a little after 8:30, both kids were asleep in their bedrooms, when Karen took Patrick's hand and led him away from his work to their deck and the warm September night. After several moments of silence between them, Karen broke the ice with some gentle nagging. "You know, Pat. You put in incredibly long hours at work."

"I know I do, and we keep talking about this with no resolution to the issue. Our division is developing the software products that will change the way radio stations operate. In a year or two, we will be generating incredible profits for your father, but it's so damn time consuming."

"I'm sure Daddy loves the idea of all those profits."

"He does, and he's smart enough to leave us pretty much alone. I know you have some problems with him, but he's a good businessman. In fact, he's a really good businessman!"

"What makes him so good? I know he's smart and mean," Karen said as she snuggled up closer to him.

"He works incredibly hard. The company is his family, his obsession, his empire. I often think that is exactly how he views it, as his empire."

"I know he's driven. My therapist's take on things was that Daddy was really insecure and out to prove something."

"I don't know anything about that, but I do know he's decisive and certainly willing to take prudent risks. He sets reasonable goals for the company and then goes out and finds the right people to accomplish those goals. You say he's insecure, but he doesn't micromanage. He's not always looking over my shoulder. I really appreciate the fact that he pretty much leaves me on my own."

"That's because you're so good. I bet he's ruthless with those who don't perform."

"You may be right about that. I haven't been around long enough to see that side."

"You will. Just wait."

"So far things are flying. He was so smart to get into Christian broadcasting. We are gaining stations, market share, and advertising revenues by leaps and bounds."

"Why?"

"Because the message our stations put out is so carefully crafted. We broadcast shows that are entertaining in a tasteful, uplifting, inspirational way. Nothing controversial is ever broadcast. Your Dad is very careful about that. What our listeners get is the fifties, Ozzie and Harriet stuff. We preach a message of unbounded prosperity for those who play by the rules. The point is to feel good about your life and yourself. God will reward you if you work hard. God will bless your marriage if you remain faithful to your spouse. God says that pay day is coming, keep the faith, praise the Lord."

"That stuff is so trite, Pat. It's garbage really. I want to throw up. I can't believe you buy into it. Do you know what Carol says about all that bullshit?"

"Carol?"

"You remember. My friend who's writing the book about the Family."

"Oh, yes. What's her take on things?"

"She refers to Daddy in the book as the Goebbels of the movement."

"You mean the Nazi propagandist?"

"Yes. I gather from Carol that Daddy is responsible for generating the Family's message."

"Are these guys really fascists?"

"No, I don't think they go quite that far. They see that Hitler did evil things, but they also see him as a great man. Great men are the ones that count. They are the ones that re-write history."

"Noah certainly does market a distinctive message."

"It's the hypocrisy that nauseates me."

"You'll love this. We have this station manager in Russell Kansas, married with two kids, and yet he bangs the receptionist three times a week. I don't know where he gets the energy. You meet with him in the office and it's Christ this, and Christ that. Christ led me to do this."

"He probably has some Christian justification for his infidelity. Jesus loves me so why not. The mind can play all kinds of games. I've heard that bull shit all my life. Our Washington office was full of it. So the point is what do these beautiful values produce? The bottom line is not much, at least as far as I can tell. I have often wondered if Christian couples are more faithful than non-Christian couples. Probably not, as is evident from your station manager."

"I'm sure you're right. Our corporate message is way too simplistic, and yet lots and lots of people buy into it."

"I know they do, and I don't want to argue with you about it. It's such a stupid topic really."

"I don't think we're arguing, and I also agree I'm working too hard. How about we take a vacation, just you and me, as soon as you're finished nursing Justin."

"That could be another nine or ten months."

"Okay. I see your point. I'll try to do better on a day-to-day basis. That's more important really."

"I love it Pat. We will be living the family values Daddy preaches."

"With you, Sweetheart, remaining faithful does not require divine intervention. It's a piece of cake," Patrick said as he squeezed his wife more tightly.

"I hope so. Can you wait two more weeks?" she asked in a voice that was saucy and irreverent. "Maybe Lovejoy won't know the difference if we cheat a little."

"I can wait, and we're not going to cheat a little."

"You're so boring, Pat," she said in a teasing voice as she got up from the glider. "Anyway, as you can hear, Justin's not cooperating."

"He didn't sleep very long. Maggie was so easy that way. Bring him out here. It's such a beautiful night."

"I will as soon as I check his diaper. That's probably the problem," she said as she stepped back into the house. "You stay put, and we'll be right there."

"No rush. I'm not going anywhere," he said as he looked out at the starry sky. There was work to do, but nothing that couldn't wait till morning.

Ten days later William Hathaway proved himself to Patrick once again. Half an hour after arriving at work, Patrick received a call from Nora Clooney, Mr. Hathaway's receptionist, informing him the boss wanted to see him as soon as possible. He left immediately.

William Hathaway's office was located on the fourth floor, the top floor in the building, an office not noticeably different from those occupied by other Noah Communications executives. Its one distinguishing feature was the large window behind the wooden desk that looked out on Pike's Peak. The office was formal and austere like its occupant with a few family pictures strategically placed around the room, but not one of Maggie. That rather conspicuous omission burned Patrick, but he kept it from his mind today and most other days he was in the presence of the President of Noah Communications.

William Hathaway looked up from a large stack of reports he was perusing and smiled at Patrick as he was ushered into the office. "Good morning, Sir," Patrick said as he glanced over his father-in-law's shoulder at Pike's Peak in the distance.

"Thanks for coming so promptly, Patrick. I trust all is well at home."

"Everything is fine. Justin is thriving as a result of his mother's good care."

"That's good to hear. I'm sure he'll be a fine boy. Maybe a hockey player like his father."

"I'm looking forward to coaching him in whatever sport he chooses to play," Patrick said as he sat down on a comfortable upholstered chair and looked across at his father-in-law.

"Well, Patrick. I'm very pleased with what you are doing with Paradigm Software, and I have some exciting news. But, before I get to that, I want to hear how things are working out with Jason."

"We have an excellent working relationship. Actually we've become quite good friends in the last year and a half. He works mostly at home as I guess you know, but we get together at least two or three times a week. Usually for lunch. I think we're finally ready to go with our entire package. Jason has corrected all the bugs reported to us from our test stations. So I think we're all set."

"That's fine, Patrick. Right on the schedule we set twelve months ago. What's the next step? What will you and Jason be doing next?"

"He's been talking about developing interactive software so our listeners can talk back to us on the internet."

"Great. Splendid idea. We'll be the first out with that program too. Once people become more comfortable with the internet, the feedback should be enormous."

"I hope so," Patrick said as he laughed to himself thinking if they could only plug into God, they could really make money.

"When does Jason plan to have it ready?"

"He won't be pressured, Sir. That's one reason he likes working for us so much. I don't pressure him. He's really a programming genius. What I find so impressive is how his mind works conceptually. He takes difficult problems and devises simple solutions for them, solutions the average bloke can easily implement. So I don't pressure him. I provide the encouragement and the sounding board he seems to need. He has strange work habits, but he certainly does deliver."

"You have good instincts for managing people. That is why I'm making you President of Paradigm Software. You now report directly to me."

"Thank you, Sir," Patrick said as he enthusiastically rose from his seat to pump his father-in-law's hand in appreciation. William Hathaway responded by partially rising from his seat. He did not meet his son-in-law half way, but he did make an effort by smiling and returning the hand shake with more than his generally tepid response. "You have been a good addition to our company and our family," William Hathaway said while returning to his seat. Patrick was pleased with his father-in-law's rare display of warmth, if that's what it was. It was hard to read William Hathaway, but he had to admit his fondness for the strange man before him. He was a very good person to work for. "I want you to prepare a revised budget for Paradigm Software. You'll need to create a sales force for the new software and an advertising budget. We want to go nationwide with these products as soon as possible."

"I'll do it, Mr. Hathaway. Again, thank you so much for everything."

"Let's get back together in a week. We can talk about your revised compensation then." Patrick rose from his seat. It was obvious to him the meeting was over. William Hathaway did not waste time with small talk. As he moved toward the office door, he looked back at his father-in-law, smiled over at him, and said:

"This is a great place to work, Sir. Making the switch was the best decision I have made with the exception of marrying your daughter."

"I'm glad you feel that way, Patrick," William Hathaway said as he smiled back at his son-in-law one last time before turning his attention to the stack of reports that still remained before him.

Stephanie Hathaway's recent call on a fall Sunday night surprised Karen in a few respects. The call was rather routine in that the two talked with each other on a fairly regular basis. What was surprising was her announcement of an unexpected visit the following Thursday, November 10th, and her request to keep the visit secret, just between them. For some reason she didn't want Karen's parents to know she was coming to town. And that was strange! When Karen asked why she was coming, Stephanie responded simply that she had legal business. Karen was a little perplexed about that too. Why was a very junior member of the firm, she had been working there for less than four months, specializing in family law, coming to Denver?

On the other hand, she was excited to see Stephanie. They had not been together since the wedding, which had certainly not been much of a visit. So she put aside her questions and stuffed the kids into the car for the ride to the airport a little before noon on Thursday. Karen was allowing for plenty of time, the plane was due at 1:30 that afternoon, and the ride to the airport took about an hour. Her plan was to meet Stephanie outside the baggage claim area so the kids could remain in the car and she would not have to leave them. Because she arrived half an hour early, she was forced into playing a cat and mouse game with the parking authorities, parking right outside the sliding doors leading to the baggage claim, then driving around the airport automobile loop, and finally returning to the spot she had recently vacated.

Karen made two trips around the loop before Stephanie came through the sliding doors at 1:50. Stephanie was tall and thin like her mother with long brown hair, the mark of a Hathaway, and a wholesome, expressive face that suggested she would be a fool to play poker. Karen spotted her immediately, she was quite striking really, and jumped out of the car to hug her and welcome her to Denver.

After placing her small travel suitcase in the trunk, Stephanie opened another sliding door to look in at the children. "Oh, Karen. They are both so precious." Justin was sound asleep while Maggie was playing with a red, spinning toy attached to her car seat. She broke into a big smile as Stephanie reached across to stroke her hair. Stephanie was duly impressed. As she closed the sliding door and moved forward to enter the front seat alongside Karen, she said: "I can't imagine you a mother with two kids. Will we ever be able to ski again at Vail?"

"I hope so Steph," Karen responded as she pulled away from the curb. "Maybe when we both have kids. It would be such fun to bring the two families together."

"It may be awhile, though I'm finally dating a really nice guy," Stephanie said as she looked over at Karen and smiled. "I hope I look as well as you do after two kids."

"Thanks Steph. You look great too. How's Aunt Harriet and Audie?"

"They're both fine, and send you their best. How's that handsome jock you married? I'm looking forward to getting to know him better."

"He's fine, though he's working too hard."

"Does he like working for your Dad?"

"Yes, and I often wonder why. The two have about as much in common as a cat and a mouse."

"No. You and your Dad are the cat and the mouse," Stephanie said with a grin. "Remember the time we were skiing in Vail. I must have been thirteen or fourteen. Anyway, we met this really cute guy at lunch, and he skied with us that afternoon."

"Yeah, and he wanted to take me out bowling that night. I hate bowling, but I sure did want to go out with him."

"And your Dad wouldn't let you."

"He doesn't go to our church, Karen, was my Dad's lame excuse. The last thing I wanted to do was go out with a guy from my church."

"You're right, Steph. My Dad can be an asshole. We're still wary of one another. I just kinda lie low in Monument, and I guess that's what you'll be doing this weekend. Lying low." And the questions again floated through her mind which she tried to ignore.

"You're so good to be putting me up. I hope Sunday is not too long a stay?"

"Heavens no. I wish it could be longer. We have a lot of catching up to do."

"You're right about that. I kept my schedule for the next week totally flexible. If my work here takes an unexpected twist, I may have to extend a few days."

"That's fine with me. I kept your visit from my parents as you suggested. Maybe we can all get together on Saturday."

"You can decide that tonight," Stephanie responded. "I really do appreciate your keeping my arrival just between us."

After hearing Stephanie's story, a family dinner on Saturday night was definitely out of the question. In fact, Karen was so mad at her father she didn't care if she ever saw him again. The two young women were finally able to talk seriously after Karen got Justin down for a nap a little after 4:30. It was late for Justin to be napping, but Karen sensed from Stephanie's demeanor since their arrival in Monument she had something important on her mind, and so she wanted to minimize any interference from the children. Maggie, who had napped briefly on the way home from the airport, joined them in the living room and played quietly with her dolls and stuffed animals that Karen arranged for her on the floor within easy grasping distance.

"I don't know quite how to begin this, Karen. I hope when I'm finished I haven't ruined the special friendship that has existed between us since we were little girls."

"Get to it, Steph. Nothing can destroy that," Karen replied as she looked across at her cousin with a feeling of trepidation rising inside her. There had been something spooky about this visit from the first moment Stephanie informed her on the phone she was coming to Denver.

"I certainly hope not," Stephanie said as she briefly looked away from Karen. "As you may have suspected, I am not here on firm business, but rather on a matter that pertains to our families. Your father has cheated my mother out of our inheritance, and I suspect we're talking about millions of dollars." With that, as she promised herself she would not do, Stephanie burst into tears.

"You can't mean it," Karen responded in a state of shock. "What are you talking about?" After quickly regaining her composure, Stephanie continued.

"I mean that over the last fifteen years my mother's ownership of Noah Communications stock has dropped from fifty percent to less than seven percent today. Here's what happened, and please let me be a lawyer for the next thirty minutes so there are no misunderstandings. After I'm finished, we can hug and become cousins again."

"That would be nice," Karen said as she smiled over at her cousin in an attempt to communicate that things were still fine between them, that despite what she had to say they would remain special friends.

"Okay, here's what happened. When Dad died in nineteen seventy-six, my mother inherited fifteen thousand shares of what was then called Hathaway Communications. At that time your father was the only other shareholder with the same number of shares. Because your father became both President and chief executive officer at that time and because my mother trusted him, she did not stand in the way when the corporate headquarters were moved to Colorado Springs and the focus of the company changed.

"Beginning in nineteen seventy-eight, the company began to buy back shares from my mother in one thousand share increments. This practice has continued to the present time, leaving my mother with current holdings in Noah Communications of one thousand shares. The problem is, and here's where fraud enters the picture, my mother had no idea she was selling her shares."

"How could such a thing happen?" Karen asked in a quiet voice of disbelief.

"Simple," Stephanie responded in a voice that was still laced with tension. "My mother has always signed tax returns and other legal documents without reading through them. It was a practice she engaged in even before Daddy died. Every March your father or one of his trusted accountants brings a stack of documents for Mom to sign. These papers, all marked with yellow stickies, have included her tax returns and documents pertaining to her selling Noah Communications stock back to the company."

"I can see that happening," Karen said as she looked sympathetically at Stephanie. "I always sign my tax returns without going over them."

"In one sense your father has been generous to our family. He has paid mother an annual salary which obviously she has not earned. He paid for Audie's and my college tuitions, and then my tuition at law school. He also paid mother what he claimed were dividends from her ownership of the company stock. The point is when you add up all the money mother has received since Daddy died, and I admit it's a lot, that sum is only a fraction of what she was actually due. Or at least that is what we suspect."

"How can you be sure your mother did this unknowingly?"

"Because she was shocked when I brought it to her attention. She had always told us her stock was our inheritance."

"Wow, this is awful, Steph. I know you would not be here unless all that you say is true. Daddy is being a shithead as usual. You know, I'm a little surprised he cheated you out of all that money, but I can see he would want absolute control. As Patrick says, he thinks of the company as his empire. Nobody crosses him. Tell me one more thing? How did you find this out?"

"I want to tell you several more things," Stephanie said in a more relaxed voice, the tension leaving because she was reassured Karen was not angry with her or jumping to the defense of her father. She even managed to smile across at her cousin for the first time since the discussion began. "With respect to your question first," Stephanie continued, "Mom received a letter from the IRS at the end of January indicating they were auditing her 1991 returns. She mailed the letter to your father who took care of things as usual. He explained to Mom they had miscalculated her dividends for the year, and he had the company pay the additional thirteen thousand dollars she owed.

"I spent June and July living with Mom until I could afford my own place. One night we were talking, and she expressed all this gratitude for your father. When I pressed her for details, she told me about the income tax problem. She was grateful the company had paid the thirteen thousand dollars. Though I didn't say a word at the time, I was immediately suspicious about the dividend explanation. I was also worried about mother's admission she never reviewed the documents she signed for your father. But the real problem was the dividend explanation. No accountant, even an incompetent one, would miscalculate dividends to the extent thirteen thousand dollars is owed. So I looked through her returns for '91, and then checked through all her returns since Daddy died. For all those years, she had not been paying taxes on dividends from Noah Communications but for capital gains resulting from the sale of Noah stock."

"Oh, I'm so sorry, Steph. I'm embarrassed too. I can't believe Daddy would do such a thing."

"I couldn't believe it either until I consulted a senior lawyer in our firm who deals in such cases. He told me such things happen all the time in closely held corporations—especially when family is involved. 'How do you think I can afford a second home on Cape Cod,' he concluded our discussion with a grin."

"What is a closely held corporation?"

"It's usually a smaller company where the stock is held by a very few individuals, and the stock is not publicly traded. This last characteristic is the crucial one."

"Will Daddy go to jail for this?"

"No because we are not pressing criminal charges."

"I guess that's good," Karen responded with a face that expressed both embarrassment and real sorrow.

"But we do plan to sue in civil court if your father does not return the fourteen thousand shares."

"It really sounds like theft to me," Karen said fighting back tears.

"White collar malfeasance is rampant and you're right. It is theft. Now let me briefly explain to you the legal issues. There are two main ones. The first is whether my mom knowingly sold the stock. This is our weakest one. It will be her word against his. We will try to point out Mom never initiated any of these sales, but it may not be convincing. Your father had a fiduciary responsibility to explain to my mother exactly what she was signing, and your father will claim he fulfilled the requirements of his fiduciary responsibility."

"What does all that mean? I've never heard of the word fiduciary before."

"A fiduciary is a person who has a legal responsibility arising from a relationship of trust to make fair decisions on behalf of another person. In this situation, your father as fiduciary was required by law to fully inform mother as to what she was doing when she signed those papers, and then to sell the stock, if that was her wish, for the highest possible price.

"And this brings us to the second and far more important legal issue from our point of view. That of valuation. What was the true value of Noah Communications at the time mother sold her stock. Did she receive a fair price?

"This is a controversial question when dealing with closely held corporations because there is no public market to set the price of the stock. We have hired a valuation expert from a prominent consulting firm in Boston. He will make a determination of the value of Mom's stock for each year she sold it. If the value he sets is far more than what she received, we have a problem. We will then file a legal complaint against your father demanding he return the fourteen thousand shares to my mother within thirty days. If he fails to comply, we go to court, and we will notify the press. This could get nasty, Karen."

"It sounds like it could. I can't believe Daddy could be that dishonest. If he gets battered in the press, he will only have himself to blame."

"Oh, Karen. I was so nervous about today, but you took all this just as I told Mom you would. That's it for the lawyerly stuff. Now we can go back to being cousins again," she said as she crossed the room to hug Karen. Karen was in tears, struggling for control. "It's not your fault, Karen," Stephanie tried to reassure her.

"I know, but I'm so embarrassed and sorry about all of this. Is there anything I can do?"

"Yes there is," Stephanie said with a twinkle in her eye as she moved along the couch to the other end. "You can help me pull a Watergate-like caper," she said smiling over at Karen.

"Will I go to jail too?" Karen asked with a smile.

"I hope none of us will," Stephanie said returning the smile. "What we need is some information from Noah Communications, and I don't want your father knowing about it. The valuation expert has given me a list of documents he will need. We will somehow have to get the information without anyone at the company knowing about it."

"That shouldn't be too difficult. Patrick can help us. I've never done detective work before. I hope we can pull it off."

"I hope so too," Stephanie said as she looked down at Maggie who was quietly amusing herself on the floor. "Here's our thinking on this. Mom doesn't want to open a hornet's nest unless we have a real problem. So we'll get this information secretly and have our expert make a preliminary assessment. If there is a problem and we decide to go to trial, we will get the same information legally through the discovery process. This way your father will never know we betrayed him. There's no need to worry about that."

"What's involved with the discovery process?"

"The law allows the plaintiff to ask the defendant for certain information through what are called interrogatories. An interrogatory is a series of questions the other side in a trial is required by law to answer before the trial begins."

"So if your Mom received a fair price for the stock, Daddy will never know about this. If she didn't receive a fair price, there will be a trial and you will get this information legally?"

"Precisely."

"I like that strategy. It doesn't sound like we're doing too much wrong if we can get the same information legally. This way there's a chance we won't open a huge family wound. I certainly don't want to make the problem worse between Daddy and me."

"I think we can do all this without Uncle Bill suspecting your complicity," Stephanie said as she left the coach to sit with Maggie on the floor. It had been years since she had played with dolls, and she dove into the task with a relish that was fueled by the relief she felt that the last forty-five minutes had gone so well.

~

Stephanie was energized again with relief because gathering the information they needed from Noah Communications had been so easy to obtain. Karen had engaged a babysitter for Saturday evening, and the three of them left for the office at 6:30. Patrick quickly scanned the parking lot for cars of employees who might cause problems; and, finding none, opened a door at the back of the building with his keys and disarmed the security system. He sometimes came to the office on Sunday afternoons to prepare for a busy Monday, and so entering the locked building presented no special problems.

The most difficult task was finding where the information they needed was stored. Eventually they located it in the basement in neatly stacked boxes labeled with black magic marker. That accomplished, Patrick and Stephanie began the tedious process of finding the tax records and the other documents required for the valuation for each of the fourteen years in question. When the necessary information for each year was found, it was taken up two floors to Karen who was responsible for making copies. The three left the office at one on Sunday morning giddy with their success.

The mood on the trip home from the Denver Airport later that day was less sanguine. Stephanie had blown into their lives like a cyclone leaving behind a wreckage of conflicting emotions for both of them to deal with. For Karen, this task was easier because her father had been cheating her all of her life. For Patrick, his world had been shattered. Though certainly not a hero, William Hathaway was his mentor and teacher. He had agonized on Friday night about whether he could betray his boss, asking Stephanie several probing questions, which she was able to answer with lawyerly dispatch. Patrick could understand William Hathaway's need for full control of the company. What he had difficulty understanding was the part about cheating his brother's heirs of all that money.

"Pat, Daddy lives in La La land over at Noah. Everyone sucks up to him. They flatter his ego. He has no idea what it means to live in the real world. The rules are not made for him. In his mind, he earned that money. He was taking what was legitimately his."

"Nope. That's not it. Jesus told him to screw Stephanie's family," Karen continued in a voice of bitter sarcasm. "He must have had one of those cute little prayer meetings. 'It's not stealing,' Jesus said to his humble servant who eagerly awaited his marching orders. 'Harriet Hathaway will squander all that money. Only you can be trusted to use it to build my kingdom.'"

"Are you kidding?" Stephanie asked in a tone of disbelief as if Karen was putting her on. "You're making it sound like Uncle Bill is delusional."

"Both delusional and fucked up," Karen replied as she burst into tears. Patrick wasn't willing to buy the delusional argument. The convenient fiction the information could be attained legally at a later date also held no sway with him. He did become convinced, however, during the course of that long evening that William Hathaway had cheated his family out of a lot of money for whatever reason, and this conclusion made him really angry.

"What am I going to do now?" Patrick asked as he guided the car out of the airport parking lot. "I certainly don't want to work for a man who belongs in jail."

"Daddy belongs in jail, alright," Karen said as she shifted her focus from Justin in the back seat to Patrick. "On the other hand, there's no crisis and you don't want to tip Stephanie's hand. Maybe the valuation man will say that Aunt Harriet received a fair price."

"I doubt it. Stephanie has done her homework."

"I agree, but there's still no crisis. I would do your job and start thinking about a different future. Whatever you do, you will do it well. I'm not the least bit concerned about that."

"Thanks, and your advice is good. Right now I have too much on my plate to worry about what might or might not happen. But I will start thinking about a different future. Maybe we should do it together."

"I like that idea, Pat. I've been thinking a lot about this thing already, and this is the calm before the storm. The whole mess could really get nasty if Daddy decides to fight it. Stephanie plans to go to the press and then, of course, there will be a public trial. I'm also concerned about Mom. But most importantly, we need to think about us and that means keeping our marriage healthy no matter what happens in the next six months. Frannie gave us the same advice when Maggie came into our life. We have a great thing going with two beautiful children. Whatever happens, I don't want it to effect our immediate family."

"Maybe this problem will help me spend less time at the office."

"That certainly would be nice—a silver lining. We've only talked about it for the last year."

"And we'll do our planning together at night."

"I hope we'll do more than that."

"You've got a deal. I feel so much better about this already." And they drove the last forty-five minutes to Monument with the feeling they were a team and more in love than at any time in their marriage.

∼

The storm broke six weeks later with another call from Stephanie. "Merry Christmas, Cuz," announced the cheery voice on the other end of the line. "Do you have all your shopping done?" It was the twenty-first of December, and Karen was well prepared with regard to Christmas.

"Yup. I finished it all last week. How are you doing?"

"Fine. I'm not as conscientious as you are, but I will be by tonight. Listen, I won't keep you long, but I just got back from Boston and the news isn't good. The valuation guy has determined mother received less than ten cents on the dollar—actually somewhere in the neighborhood of seven and a half. So we'll be serving your father's corporation with the legal complaint on the 27th."

"That's quite a Christmas present he'll be receiving—at least it will be late."

"Yeah, I'm afraid 1995 will be an interesting year."

"Well, Pat and I have been preparing ourselves for this ever since you left last month. We'll be fine. I'm worried about Mom, though."

"Maybe there won't be a fight."

"I wouldn't count on it. You don't know Daddy like I do."

"We're preparing for the worst. If a fight unfolds, we'll be ready. Now listen, I've got some errands to do and some presents still to buy, so I better run. You guys have a wonderful Christmas, and I'll be in touch."

"You too, Steph. Hug Aunt Harriet and Audie for me."

"I will. Bye. Oh, I almost forgot. Find that handsome jock of yours under the Mistletoe and kiss him for me. He's a gem."

"Thanks, Steph. I will. Bye."

The next call came on January 10th. "It's war, Karen. Your Dad won't even discuss the problem with our lawyers."

"I know Steph. Pat got the same message last week at work. Daddy is irate, fuming in self-righteous anger; and, according to Pat, preparing for battle. The entire corporate establishment is preparing for a fight. Pat is outwardly expressing his loyalty, but his real sympathies are with us. He's mostly doing his job and trying to distance himself from this mess as much as possible."

"Good. I love you guys. I was also calling to tell you that I'm coming next week to hire a local lawyer."

"Great. Stay with us. What day are you coming?"

"Thanks, but not this time. It's too risky, and I don't want to put you in a bad position with your family. I'll call when I get there."

"Maybe we can still get together clandestinely. I can't even believe I'm using that word. I hate this stuff, Steph. I really do."

"Me too, Karen, and we do need to get together. There are some additional parts of the puzzle I want to discuss with you. I'll call when I get to the Springs."

"So I'll see you soon?"

"It looks like it, Cuz. I look forward to hugging those precious babies."

"Maggie is finally crawling and pulling herself up. We're so excited. It's like she's won an Olympic medal."

"I can't wait to play dolls again."

"Bye Steph."

"Bye."

∽

Stephanie's instinct about staying at a hotel during her upcoming trip to Colorado Springs was a good one. On January 4, 1995, William Hathaway summoned Philip Duke, the head of security for the company, for an 11 a.m. meeting.

Philip Duke had been with Noah Communications from the beginning. William Hathaway recruited him from the Denver Police Department where he had been a detective. Like several key employees at Noah, Phil was a member of the Abundant Life Assembly of God church. But his loyalty to William Hathaway had deeper roots. The greatly increased compensation he received from Noah and the benefits gained from William Hathaway's friendship took he and his family to a new social level.

Philip Duke arrived at William Hathaway's office for their private meeting promptly at the appointed hour. There were no introductory pleasantries or questions about family. William Hathaway got right to the point. "We're in a fight for our lives, Phil. My sister-in-law wants control of this company."

"I know, Sir. This is a dangerous situation. What can I do to help?"

"We have to find the Benedict Arnold that is feeding the enemy all these lies. Someone in Noah is betraying us. Here is a list of people I suspect. You may add anyone you suspect to it. Pay particular attention to my son-in-law. He's most likely consorting with the enemy. We need to catch and fire the traitor, whoever he is."

"I will see to this immediately, Mr. Hathaway. We will monitor the corporate email and the phone calls of the people on your list."

"Thank you, Phil. This is a top priority. Please report any suspicious activity to me immediately."

Philip Duke knew his boss well. By William Hathaway's look and the tone of his voice, he recognized the meeting was over. As he stood up to leave, Duke concluded: "You can count on me, Sir. We will win this war for you."

"I hope so, Phil. You just do your job," and the President of Noah Communications reached across his desk for the phone to call his appointments secretary.

∽

The first article pertaining to the law suit appeared on the front page of the *Denver Post*'s business section on January 17th. It was a factual article that discussed the history of Noah Communications and outlined the complaint of Peter Hathaway's heirs. William Hathaway responded four days later. He invited a sympathetic reporter to his office and unloaded. He lashed out at his accusers in no uncertain terms, claiming Harriet Hathaway knew full well what she was signing, that she was bringing this complaint because she had sold her shares when the company was worth five million dollars and now that it was worth more than five hundred million she was consumed with greed. The article painted Harriet Hathaway as a spoiled Philadelphia socialite who had never earned a penny on her own in her life. In contrast, William Hathaway was described as a hard working Christian, generous to both the family of his dead brother and to many worthy Christian causes he supports on a regular basis. He was further seen as a man who had built his company through his own hard work and with his own money. "Harriet Hathaway has never invested a penny of her own money to further our efforts. She has been a taker, pure and simple," the paper quoted him as saying.

Karen finished the article and stuck her finger in her mouth in mock disgust. I need Alex, she thought, and so she dialed up the store.

"Covered Treasures."

"Do I have to forgive Daddy too?"

"Karen, I've been thinking about you all morning. Your father does have a self-righteous streak. Are you okay?"

"He is nauseating."

"Add him to the list, Sweety," Alex said with a laugh. "Can I come over sometime in the afternoon? I've got a high school kid coming to babysit the store after school lets out. I'm dying to talk. Right now isn't a good time. We're still up to our ears in coffee and bagels."

"That's what I hoped you would say. I bet I'm the talk of the store."

"Your name has been mentioned, but I'll see you later. I love you Karen, and that's not because I'm high on coffee."

"Thanks Alex. I love you too. See you soon. Bye."

❧

Unfortunately Karen had to cancel her get-together with Alex because Stephanie was coming. It was another surprise visit. Half an hour after hanging up with Alex, Stephanie called from the offices of Pell, Kleintop, and Zempel on East Vermijo Street, right next to the El Paso County Judicial Building. She had hired a dynamic woman, Sophia Houghton, to represent her family. She was in her mid forties, a senior lawyer in the firm, who has specialized in cases of civil fraud for the last ten years. Karen smiled at the news and her cousin's enthusiasm over Ms. Houghton, thinking Stephanie was a bit of a feminist. Stephanie claimed Sophia had a reputation for being a tough professional and a great performer. Performance is a key aspect of trial success she concluded over the telephone.

Stephanie was flying back to Philadelphia the next day and was anxious to meet with Karen and Patrick before returning home. The plan was for the women to get together that afternoon, Alex was invited to join them but declined, and then they would conduct their business when Patrick came home from work. Karen insisted they stay with this agenda, taking Stephanie to 'Dirty Woman Park' and keeping the conversation light and lively, focusing on the day-to-day aspects of living she so reveled in. Stephanie enjoyed the break from all of her legal concerns.

After a good dinner of Cornish hen and an assortment of vegetables, no potatoes because Patrick was on a diet, there had been little exercise for him over the last year and lots of caloric business lunches, the three co-conspirators assembled together in the living room. Karen nursed Justin in hopes of putting him to sleep, and Maggie snaked around the living room, not crawling really because she was unable to raise her tummy off of the floor, but moving nonetheless to the great pride of her parents. Patrick broke the ice and focused the chatter around the central purpose of Stephanie's visit with the comment: "Well, I'm sure you saw the article in the *Post*, Steph. They're planning for war at the office. The old man is furious and telling everyone he has been unjustly attacked."

"I gather that," Stephanie said as she looked up at Patrick from her position on the floor alongside Maggie. "We'll be ready. Sophia Houghton is a superb lawyer. We're hoping for a trial date in early June."

"I can't wait to get it all behind us," Karen said.

"Me too," Stephanie replied with a grunt as she lifted herself from the floor and took a seat on the sofa across from Patrick and Karen. "Let me fill you in on the valuation report. There are several ways to arrive at the value of a closely held corporation. According to Mr. O'Brien, our opponents will probably use the market model. This approach looks at comparable companies that are publicly held. In this case the valuation expert would look for six or more publicly traded radio station corporations like Noah and value them based on several economic variables. The value for Noah would then be determined by using these same variables and comparing the Noah values with comparable values from each of the six or more companies. It's similar to the way real estate appraisers arrive at a value for a new listing.

"There are a number of problems with this method, the most important of which is finding truly comparable companies over the time period in which mother was selling her stock. The enormous complexity of the method lends itself to manipulating the numbers so that a lower value can be achieved, which is what we will probably find when your father's expert submits his results. Case law pertaining to these questions points out many problems with this approach, so I am confident we can convince the jury this model does not apply well in this situation.

"The model we will counter with is a discounted cash flow model which takes into consideration a whole range of economic factors that apply to the worth of a company. I won't bore you with all the details, but it is this model that determined Mom received less than eight percent of the real value of her securities. We will soon learn how they will approach this issue because we are obligated by law to exchange reports one month before the trial."

"So the whole case will boil down to the testimony of the opposing experts and which approach the jury deems most fair," Patrick said as he looked at Stephanie.

"That about sums it up. Sophia Houghton will send your father's lawyers a lengthy set of interrogatories requesting statistical information on all aspects of Noah's business since the year my Dad died. That means your father will never suspect our little burglary in November."

"I feel very relieved about that," Karen responded with a smile.

"Me too," Stephanie said as she jumped from the couch and moved toward Karen. "Enough of this accounting stuff. Look at my left hand, guys."

"Oh, Steph. You're engaged," Karen said. "Let me see the ring. It's beautiful," and Karen got up to hug her cousin.

"His name is Perry, and he's the chairman of the Math department at the Haverford School. Pat, you'll love him. He was captain of the tennis team at Bucknell."

"I look forward to meeting him," Patrick said as he too got off the couch to hug his wife's cousin. He was gaining enormous respect for this woman. Perry would undoubtedly be a class act too.

"Why have you kept him a secret all this time?" Karen asked.

"Oh, I don't know. The seriousness of the relationship took me by surprise, and we've had all these legal problems to deal with."

"I'm teasing, Steph. This is all so exciting. Some good news amidst all the gloom."

"Mom is so excited about becoming a grandmother. That's all she can think about. I'm happy to have a great guy in my life." As she was completing her sentence, she reached into her purse for her wallet. Removing a picture from its plastic holder, she reached down to hand it to Karen who, like Patrick, had returned to the couch.

"My, he's cute, Steph. Really good looking."

"He's a keeper, Karen."

"When's the wedding?" Patrick asked as Karen handed him the picture.

"We're thinking maybe a year from now during Perry's spring break. That gives us a week for a honeymoon. He wants to go rafting in Costa Rica. But the date is contingent on your being free, Karen. I want you to be a bridesmaid."

"I'm so honored, Steph. I can't wait to see your mother and Audie again."

"You two guys are their heroes. No matter how this thing turns out, you are stars in their eyes. They can't wait to see you too."

"It will be a nice family reunion. You know it's getting a little late, Steph. Are you sure you won't spend the night?"

"Next time, Karen. My plane leaves at 7:23 tomorrow morning. It seemed so much easier to stay right next to the airport. I also didn't want your parents to see me with you guys."

"That's highly unlikely. Actually, once Daddy loses this case, you can charge all these expenses to him."

"You've got a good legal mind."

"I'm looking forward to the day when this is over and we can get back to being family again," Karen said as she smiled at Stephanie.

"Four months. I think we can make it through that," Stephanie said as she raised herself from the sofa. "Because of my early flight in the morning, I think I better hit the road. Thank you guys for everything. You've been more help than you will ever know."

Monday June 3rd, the preliminary date Judge Clarence Bullen set for the trial in late February, came upon the extended Hathaway family more quickly than anyone expected. Perhaps that was because the trial actually started a month prior to that date with several deposition hearings. Karen was relieved she had not been called, she was terrified about anyone discovering her clandestine role in the investigation, and was now confident she would not have to participate in the trial. Patrick was relieved for similar reasons.

When her Aunt Harriet came down for questioning in early May, Karen was excited to see her. Stephanie brought her over to Monument on their way back to the Denver airport. They had a nice visit for almost two hours, and the talk was all wedding.

Karen prepared for the trial by maintaining her routines with Frannie and Alex. Both she and Frannie had organized a morning get-together for moms with small children at "Dirty Woman Park." It was nice to have women friends and regular diversions to relieve her anxiety as the trial date approached. She also engaged a regular babysitter, Kristen McKnight, a junior at Lewis Palmer High School, who lived on Jefferson Street in the Monument historic district and who had a proven track record when it came to dealing with the McGovern children. It was convenient Kristen's last exam was on the Friday prior to the start of the trial on Monday.

Patrick prepared for the trial by becoming a full-time kibitzer. The process fascinated him. He was impressed with Clarence Bullen, the judge who would hear the case. Judge Bullen was the senior judge in the El Paso County system. He was a tall, distinguished looking man, in his early sixties with thin graying hair, and a ruddy complexion that hinted at Irish descent. His reputation for honesty and fairness was legion. The fact he might be Irish added to the confidence Patrick placed in him.

Patrick first saw Judge Bullen in action at the jury selection hearing on Wednesday, May 22nd. The hearing took place in Judge Bullen's courtroom on the fifth floor of the El Paso County Judicial Building. The room looked like a hotel conference room with its soft purple/gray paneling, the light blue industrial carpet, and the hundred or more blue movie theatre-like seats for the audience. The courtroom was rectangular in shape with the judge's bench both elevated and at the back of the room flanked by the American flag on the left and the flag of the State of Colorado on the right. As Patrick looked into the courtroom from the corridor outside, the witness stand faced the judge, the jury box was along the wall on the left, the stenographer's table to the judge's right with the defense table on the right and the plaintiff's table on the left. These tables were relatively small, with space to seat two lawyers comfortably or three thin ones, and Patrick wondered what the William Hathaway team of seven lawyers would do.

The hearing to select the six-member jury and two alternates began at nine a.m. sharp. Eighty potential jurors with summons notices in hand nervously entered the courtroom. The court clerk checked each summons, assigned each person a number, and handed out questionnaires. The questionnaires asked a variety of questions ranging from Christian affiliation, regularity of church attendance, attitudes toward big business, whether a potential juror knew one of the lawyers, and the usual personal information pertaining to age, marital status, and employment.

The lawyers from both sides entered the courtroom a little after 9:30 and were given copies of the completed questionnaires. The lawyers would use this information in making their ten peremptory challenges, which allowed each side to dismiss ten prospective jurors with no questions asked. In an earlier pretrial conference James Lawton, the lead attorney for the defense, had argued vigorously for twenty such challenges and was turned down by Judge Bullen. According to Stephanie, this was merely a tactic on their part to set the grounds for an appeal in the event they lost the case. Stephanie further explained it was a rather silly motion, mostly done to impress William Hathaway that his expensive team was doing their job, because the usual number of challenges was five.

It was interesting, considering the high stakes in the case, that neither side had hired Litigation Sciences, a firm specializing in jury research and selection. Sophia Houghton for one believed such tactics were a waste of money. She knew exactly whom she wanted—single moms like Harriet Hathaway. Obviously James Lawton held a similar view that jury selection consultants were a waste of money, though one member of the Lawton team had begun his career with such a firm in Pittsburgh. Their goal was to seat male businessmen, especially those who were Christian.

Judge Bullen entered the courtroom from the door behind his bench a little after 10:30, and the clerk announced, "All Rise." He welcomed the potential jurors to his courtroom, and immediately stated that everyone older than sixty-five was allowed to leave if they so chose. Four members from the potential pool took advantage of this opportunity, displaying their driver's license to the clerk as they exited the courtroom. The Judge then invited all those with unique physical problems to approach the bench. Two men and a woman in a wheelchair came forward. After briefly consulting with them, he dismissed all three. Finally, the Judge was concerned, as was Sophia Houghton, about the unfair treatment of Harriet Hathaway in the press. He, therefore, asked all those who believed they had formed an opinion about the case from reading press reports to approach the bench. Two middle-aged men came forward and after brief questioning were placed back in the pool.

With these introductory maneuvers completed, the process began in earnest with each potential juror being considered in the order in which they were seated. The lawyers were allowed to ask appropriate questions of each candidate; and if there was no challenge, that person was selected to serve. The end result was a jury that included a grandmother in her mid sixties, later selected to be foreman, a divorced mother of two who was a local branch bank manager, a male computer programmer in his mid thirties, a retired male high school history teacher who had recently turned seventy, a single woman in her mid forties who was the business manager for a large radiology group, and a twenty-seven year old male who worked as a salesman for a local sporting goods store. Patrick gave round one to Sophia Houghton, although he admitted it was clearly a mixed bag, and he worried about the fact that only one no vote from this group would ruin the case for Harriet Hathaway.

Once the jury was selected, Judge Bullen cleared the courtroom, asking only the six jurors and two alternates to remain. He then left his bench and joined the jury members where he began by explaining some procedural matters pertaining to the case. He told them the trial would commence on Monday morning on June 3rd and that they should expect a two-week trial. Although he would not sequester them, he warned them not to discuss the case with anyone and to report immediately any unauthorized contacts intended to influence their vote. He also suggested they bring reading material with them for the inevitable down times they would have to endure. Finally, he thanked them for their patience during the selection process and said he was looking forward to working with them on Monday the third. Eight tired jurors left the courtroom at 4:45.

The next day James Lawton filed a fourteen page motion to the judge asking for a ninety-day extension, pleading the complexity of the legal issues involved in the case. At the last pretrial conference before the start of the trial, the judge denied the motion, stating that the issues were not in fact complex and that it was time to get on with it. Judge Bullen was known as a fair and hard working jurist who was not long on patience. He detested motions for delay and rarely granted them once he had set the trial date. Again, the Lawton team was laying the groundwork for a possible appeal.

∾

Three days before the jury selection process was held in Judge Bullen's courtroom, an important meeting took place at Noah Communications. William Hathaway asked Philip Duke to come by his office after work. He arrived at 5:30.

"Phil, good to see you," William Hathaway said as he looked up from his desk and smiled. "Thanks so much for coming by. If you would, please close my door and have a seat. We shouldn't be long." With that, William Hathaway left his desk, firmly grasped the hand of his friend, and the two men sat down in comfortable leather chairs, arranged along the left hand wall as one entered from the office door. It was not a common practice for the President of Noah Communications to conduct meetings in such an informal manner. Most meetings in his office took place with the boss sitting behind his desk, a symbol of his imperial authority.

William Hathaway looked across at his loyal employee, smiled, and then noticing a change in his face, said: "Are you feeling okay, Phil? Your eyes seem a little puffy."

"Fine boss. Just a rash of some sort. I'm not quite sure what's going on. A minor irritant."

"I've got a major irritant with this trial, Phil. There's no way Harriet Hathaway's getting half of this company. She's been living the good life because of my hard work for the last twenty years."

"You'll win, Mr. Hathaway. You've got a good legal team, and a wonderful reputation in this town."

"I'm not so sure, Phil. Lawyers are lawyers—most of them are blood sucking parasites like my sister-in-law. Have you found the traitor?"

"Nothing conclusive, Sir? It's much the same as I reported to you two weeks ago. Our monitoring of employees has turned up nothing unusual at this point. At your suggestion, we recently planted listening devices in your daughter's house after uncovering the suspicious meeting with your sister-in-law and her daughter in early May. But so far, we have heard nothing that is disturbing."

"Are Karen and Patrick getting along?"

"Seems so. I have received no reports of fighting between them."

"Make sure you keep those devices operational. My daughter is with them for sure. She has been a problem for the last fifteen years. Watch Patrick closely too. I want to know where he stands on all of this."

"We've been doing that, Sir. The only thing I can report is that he is spending some time at the courthouse."

"That in itself is suspicious, but let's move on to another matter, Phil. I've done a lot of reading about juries in the last three months, and Colorado law helps us. Jury decisions in civil cases must be unanimous. One vote against Harriet, and she goes home empty handed."

"We ought to be able to do something about that. Is that what you're getting at?" Philip Duke asked with a sheepish grin. He tried to direct his glance directly at William Hathaway, but couldn't quite do it. He had a hard time doing that with anybody. The sheepish grin did, however, erase some of the deep wrinkles lining his face.

"We can't let Harriet get away with her theft of the company, and I don't trust lawyers as I just pointed out to you—even ones with a good reputation. There are six jurors, and I would like to get to two. We only need one. The second is for insurance."

As was often the case, Philip Duke had read the mind of his boss perfectly. "All we need do is slip them a little money," he said as he shuffled around in his seat.

"Yes, Phil. That's what I had in mind. There certainly will be a large bonus in this for you."

"I never worry about that, Mr. Hathaway. You've taken care of me and my family real well. I almost feel like I need to help you get out of this little jam. I guess the place to begin is with an investigation of the six jurors when they are chosen. We'll have to hire an investigative firm. I would suggest we go outside the Springs just to be on the safe side. Locals may be more prone to talk."

"It sounds like you know how to handle this. Don't worry about expenses. Travel may even be necessary. Have them get as much information on all six as they can by next week so we can make a decision about whom to approach. I think we should have our work done no later than the second day of the trial."

"I'll get right at it tonight, Mr. Hathaway. I may even have a good candidate to do the approaching. This needs to be handled with care, and there is a retired detective friend of mine living in Leadville who might be perfect. As soon as I have the investigative firm nailed down, I'll go see my friend."

"Thanks so much, Phil. This is a top priority for the firm. As I said a minute ago, don't worry about expenses, and come see me if you run into any problems."

"There shouldn't be no problems, Mr. Hathaway," Phil said as he rose from his chair in preparation for leaving. As William Hathaway ushered him out of the office, a flood of relief pulsated through his body. He had dreaded this meeting, fretted all afternoon about how to broach the subject, and Philip Duke had anticipated his desire. What a guy! As he returned to his desk to clean up some paper work in preparation for going home, he couldn't help but compare his son-in-law to Philip Duke. Philip Duke couldn't shoot a hockey puck, but he sure was a loyal employee.

~

As Philip Duke began the work on his high priority project, the inevitable happened. Late Friday afternoon on May 24th around 4:00 Sophia Houghton received a call at her office from Coles Brown, one of the seven lawyers on the William Hathaway team. They wanted to settle. With this in mind, a meeting was set for the following Tuesday, Monday being the Memorial Day holiday, at the Broadmoor Hotel at twelve noon.

Sophia and Stephanie talked long and hard about the possibility of a settlement. The bottom line was they didn't want to settle. They wanted William Hathaway to be exposed for what he was, a fraud and a cheat, and they thought they had a good case. The evaluation report from Montgomery O'Brien estimated the value of Harriet Hathaway's stock, sold over fourteen years in one thousand share increments, should have netted her one hundred and twenty eight million dollars. The money she had received was nine hundred and sixty thousand dollars. The current market value of the 15,000 shares, which she had originally owned before the fraudulent sales took place, was estimated at two hundred and fifty million dollars. The two women decided they would accept two hundred million at the Broadmoor luncheon and nothing less knowing full well such a figure was totally unrealistic.

The firm of Lawton, Reiser, and Farrell had rented a private dining room for the meeting. The room was all decked out with a crystal chandelier, a table set for six, two lawyers from the Hathaway team were still on Memorial Day weekends, with the best silver service and china, and ornately decorated wooden doors to provide for maximum privacy. When Sophia Houghton arrived at the meeting ten minutes late, she found her five adversaries all dressed formally in pinstriped suits, mostly hand tailored in the one to two thousand dollar price range, milling around the table, drinks in hand, in hushed conversation.

"Sorry I'm late, Gentlemen," she said as she stood at the doorway to the room looking in. When there was silence in the room, she continued. "The venue looks great, but I'm on a diet. So let's forget the niceties and get right to it." James Lawton stepped forward, a soft spoken man known for his courtly manners, expressed his gratitude for her coming to the meeting and asked her to:

"Please sit down."

"Thank you, Mr. Lawton, but I have a busy schedule. Mr. Brown spoke to me on Friday about a possible deal. What do you gentlemen have in mind?"

"Well, we were hoping to discuss it with you over lunch. Some of the issues are rather complex as you know." Sophia Houghton agreed with the judge on that point. She saw the issues as being rather straight forward, but she held her tongue for the moment and allowed James Lawton to finish. "So we don't want to rush into anything."

"If you have a figure in mind, Mr. Lawton, let's get it out now because I have a one thirty appointment." She and Stephanie were meeting for lunch.

"Okay, if this is how it must be," he said after hesitating a moment evaluating the situation. "I have consulted with my client Mr. William Hathaway, and he has authorized me to offer the generous sum of ten million dollars in exchange for Mrs. Harriet Hathaway dropping her suit." Sophia Houghton directed her attention to the attractively decorated luncheon table, smiled to herself in recognition, stepped into the room, and latched onto a bowl of peanuts. She then handed the bowl to James Lawton.

"Is that your final offer, Mr. Lawton?" James Lawton was shocked. In thirty-five years of legal practice, he had never been treated this way. This rather unattractive, at least that is how he saw her, brash woman was refusing to play along with the well established, though unwritten, rules of the legal profession, rules James Lawton believed were crucial for the well running of our highly complex society. He felt like throwing the peanuts at her, but instead in a courteous voice that masked his deep frustration:

"I think if you will sit down with us and talk about this situation we may be able to convince Mr. Hathaway that fifteen million is a more appropriate offer."

"Gentlemen, I will see you in court," and with that Sophia Houghton turned and exited as quickly as she could from the Broadmoor Hotel. She was pleased with herself. Her intention had been to get these men mad, to act unprofessionally so they would dismiss her and thus underestimate her legal ability. She was confident she had achieved her goal.

∽

Philip Duke had not been so energized in years. He liked his job with Noah Communications because it paid so well, but it had become routine and not very challenging. After spending the first evening following his meeting with William Hathaway thinking about it, he decided the next morning to conduct the investigation himself. He could always hire extra help late in the game if he got behind, but investigating six jurors seemed to be a rather simple task. He recruited his assistant, Bruce Fetzer, a staunch Hathaway loyalist he could trust, and the two of them set out in earnest the day after the jury was selected. Fetzer was energized in the same way. He had grown tired of monitoring telephone conversations.

They began with a routine background check on all six jurors and were able to eliminate three rather quickly. The retired grandmother, the computer programmer, and the retired history teacher were dismissed as poor prospects because they did not seem to have pressing money problems. That left Kathy Royce, juror number twelve, Ronald Carswell, juror number seventeen, and Gabrielle Coleman, juror number thirty-nine. With these three, they interviewed friends, poured over tax information, ran credit card checks, and interviewed co-workers. Duke even sent Bruce Fetzer on a quick trip to Mapelton Utah where he spoke with Carswell's ex wife.

The two men completed their work in five days. Philip Duke met with Wiiliam Hathaway at the office for a second time at 10:30 on Saturday morning, June 1st, two days before the trial was set to get underway.

"How are things, Phil?" William Hathaway asked as he looked up from a memorandum he was reading and smiled at his security chief. "We tried to settle this thing last Tuesday, but the other side was both rude and greedy. So it's up to you kid," William Hathaway concluded with a smile. He seemed to be both relaxed and in good humor two days before the big trial which amazed Philip Duke. He would have been a nervous wreck.

"Things are in pretty good shape on our end. We have three jurors to discuss, and then we can narrow it to two."

"Good. Who did you get to do the investigating?" William Hathaway already knew the answer to that question, but he wanted an excuse to praise his security chief for his good work and loyalty.

"Bruce and I did the work ourselves. It seemed to make more sense for me to do it seeing as how there were only six jurors involved. We also wanted to take every precaution to keep things quiet."

"Excellent. I know you have saved me some money which I appreciate. What have you got?" he asked as Philip Duke sat down in a comfortable leather chair in front of William Hathaway's desk and opened the first of three files.

"Our first one is juror number twelve. Kathy Royce is forty-eight years old, divorced, with two kids, both boys, in high school. In talking with their teachers we learned they are good kids with good grades. Kathy is attractive, professional looking, with no church affiliation."

"That's too bad," William Hathaway commented as his focus remained riveted on Duke. "A committed Christian may have been of some help."

"She's the branch manager of Colorado National Bank in Woodland Park, and she earns a salary of twenty-six thousand dollars. But here's the key. We think it highly probable she has money problems. Her ex is a deadbeat—provides no support according to the co-worker Bruce interviewed at the bank. Lives somewhere in Idaho. Her modest three bedroom house in Cascade has several problems that need repair. Some, like the roof, are rather expensive. In addition, her mother is seventy-eight, with emphysema. She is not on oxygen yet, but probably should be. She lives in this retirement home which the co-worker described as a dump, and it is really worrying our juror."

"Is that it for Ms. Royce?"

"Yes. Juror number seventeen is a twenty-seven year old male named Ronald Carswell. He was recently discharged from the Army after serving four years, mainly in Germany. He is a Mormon, though he doesn't seem to be currently active in the church."

"A funny religion," William Hathaway interjected.

"You got it right there," Philip Duke said with a laugh. "He grew up in a little town in rural Utah named Mapelton and had some real problems in high school."

"What kind of problems?" William Hathaway asked.

"Academic mostly. We learned nothing about behavioral problems. He graduated by the skin of his teeth. He married a local girl, they have a two and a half year old daughter, and they recently divorced. Bruce talked with the ex wife and gathered one of the main reasons they split is that the wife wanted to return to live in rural Utah while Ronnie, as she calls him, wanted to branch out.

"He currently works as a salesman for STI Recreational Equipment on the corner of Constitution and Paseo for seven dollars and eighty cents an hour. He lives with his girl friend in a one bedroom apartment near Fort Carson. The apartment is run down, and his white Hyndai Accent is falling apart. Most importantly, he has built up a credit card debt of four thousand two hundred fourteen dollars. As Bruce said when we left his apartment complex, "that boy could use an infusion of cash."

"He does sound like a good prospect. What about the third?"

"Gabrielle Coleman is single, never been married, forty-two years old, and not very attractive. She works as the business manager for a radiology group attached to Penrose Hospital. She doesn't seem to have many friends, although she was polite and professional when I went to see her with a problem bill we created. She lives in an attractive condominium complex downtown."

"Doesn't sound very promising. Maybe we better revisit the three jurors you originally rejected. That Royce lady may also be a problem. Seems too wholesome to me."

"Don't be so quick to judge, Sir," Philip Duke replied in a gently teasing way. "I have saved the best for last. I learned the other day that this Coleman woman's one passion in life is gambling. She currently has debts in excess of twenty thousand dollars."

"Excellent work, Phil. How did you find that out?"

"Through a routine credit card check. She gambles in Vegas, New Jersey, and right here at Blackhawk."

"Okay. I think Coleman and Carswell are our best bets."

"I agree. We will approach them as soon as possible. When Bruce was in Utah, I visited my buddy Reese Baldwin in Leadville. He's a retired Denver detective. He kind of took me under his wing when I first joined the force thirty years ago. The good thing about Reese is he likes to spend money and could use some right now. He looks like a kind old grandfather—the type of person one would instantly trust. I think he'll be perfect for the job. I plan to brief him this afternoon."

"You have done this preliminary work well, ahead of my initial deadline to complete the job by the second day of the trial."

"I hope so, Sir. The only thing I need from you now is some guidelines concerning money."

"I was just working some figures in my head. I think we ought to be able to get Carswell cheap. What do you think about five thousand now and an additional five if he delivers for us?"

"That should do it. I'll get back to you if there are any problems."

"With regards to the Coleman lady, we will probably have to offer her considerably more. How about twenty-five thousand now and twenty-five more after the decision when we see how she votes?"

"Fine."

"What do you think we should pay your friend Baldwin?"

"I was thinking twenty-five thousand?"

"That's no problem. Put him on the payroll in a phony position. We'll pay him monthly so he doesn't spend it all at once," William Hathaway said with a laugh.

"I was hoping to give Bruce a five thousand dollar raise for his help in this matter."

"Do it. Tell him I am very pleased with his work and that he can expect a generous end of the year bonus. I've already raised you ten thousand, and there will be a nice bonus for you too."

"Thank you, Mr. Hathaway. I guess that's it. I'll report back when everything's in place."

"Excellent, Phil," William Hathaway said, smiling one last time at his security chief before returning to his desk work. Philip Duke wanted to shake the boss's hand, but decided the best strategy was for him to leave quietly from the office. He was pumped, though. The meeting had gone well, his boss was pleased, and he had received a handsome raise. The rest was up to good old Reese, which meant he could feel fairly comfortable about the execution of the plan.

Karen and Patrick left for the courthouse on June 3rd at eight fifteen in the morning. They wanted to make sure they got a seat, and they just made it. By 9:20 every seat was taken, and people were standing at the back of the room. Opening statements were scheduled for 10:00.

Karen surveyed the scene from her seat on the right-hand side near the back of the room. Melanie James, Sophia Houghton's paralegal, was sitting on the left side, the plaintiff's side, toward the front. Her mother and brother were sitting seven rows in front of them. William Hathaway was conspicuously absent. He was determined to stay away from the court until he was required to testify which was tentatively scheduled for Thursday. As he stated to colleagues, he was too busy at work to consume his time over what he regarded as a bogus lawsuit.

Karen was worried about her mother. She wanted to smile at her in reassurance, but she was unable to catch her eye. Virginia Hathaway kept her focus toward the front of the courtroom, it was frozen in that direction, she rarely looked right or left. Karen wanted to cry for her. Virginia Hathaway was scared.

Karen suspected her mother knew where her allegiance lay. Her mother was well aware she and Stephanie were close, like sisters really, that they talked at least every other week on the phone. Virginia Hathaway also knew neither Karen nor Patrick had offered words of encouragement or made even the smallest gesture in defense of her father. Karen felt like she had betrayed her mother in this regard, and for that she also wanted to cry.

The press was there too—reporters from the *Colorado Springs Gazette*, *The Denver Post*, *The Rocky Mountain News*, several television stations, and, of course, a well seasoned news team from Noah Communications. The press was loving this case, Karen thought as she shifted uncomfortably in her seat impatient for the trial to begin. Noah Communications was big business, with listeners throughout the entire country. The story was ideal—a family feud with lots of money at stake. The only thing that really angered her was the subtle digs at her aunt. They were so unfair she thought, and seemingly unrelated to the facts of the trial. That's what really made her mad. How could the image of Harriet Hathaway as a spoiled, irresponsible, Philadelphia socialite, an image that couldn't be further from the truth, affect the votes of jurors who did not know her. Yet people are people, she concluded. They love to focus on gossip and the negative.

There was a brief hush in the crowd as six of the seven lawyers for Noah Communications entered the courtroom. Three of them squeezed around the defense table on the left hand side, and the other three sat nearby on the front row. They were dressed almost identically in hand tailored suits, perfectly pressed, with clean and crisp white shirts, colorful ties, their only concession to individuality, and shoes that were immaculately shined. Several shook hands with Virginia Hathaway and Billy Junior before littering the defense table with manila folders and yellow legal pads. At 9:55 Sophia Houghton entered the courtroom, alone, dressed in a navy blue suit with a yellow scarf with blue sequined stripes. She carried with her one manila folder, a single legal pad, and her purse. That left the plaintiff's table virtually clear with the exception of a vase of red roses in the center.

Karen loved the "David v. Goliath" strategy Sophia and Stephanie had devised. The stark contrast of the lone woman facing the seven Noah Communications attorneys, the single mother battling the wealthy corporation, was part of the picture Sophia Houghton wanted the jury to see. It was an illusion in many respects. Sophia Houghton had consulted senior law partners from her own firm and from other firms in Colorado that specialized in civil cases like this one. They had hired one of the best and most expensive corporate evaluators in the business. Stephanie and her mother were willing to commit the necessary resources to this case because they were angry at William Hathaway, and because they were confident they would win.

A permanent hush came over the room as Clarence Bullen entered the courtroom from the private door behind his bench, and the clerk announced, "All Rise." Judge Bullen surveyed the room and asked those standing in the back without seats to please leave the courtroom. Once that was accomplished, he announced the case, *Harriet S. Hathaway v. Noah Communications*, in a deep, distinguished, baritone voice, welcomed the spectators and press, while warning them that unruly behavior would lead to immediate dismissal from the courtroom, smiled over at the six jurors and two alternates, and stated that opening statements would begin with Ms. Houghton.

Sophia Houghton waited a minute before rising from her chair and walking around the table toward the jury. She was without notes, and she spoke directly to the six member panel in a soft, professional voice, for a little less than twenty minutes. "Ladies and Gentlemen of the jury," she began. "This is a simple case in which a trusted family member, Mr. William Hathaway, while appearing to be a generous guardian of his deceased brother's family, in fact acted in a manner over a period of several years to cheat his brother's heirs, Mrs. Harriet Hathaway and her two daughters, Stephanie and Audie, out of their lawful inheritance. The value of that inheritance today based on the current value of Noah Communications amounts to more than two hundred and fifty million dollars. I want you to keep this simple premise forefront in your minds throughout this trial, especially in the face of any attempts from the opposing side to confuse the issues with legal complexities."

After presenting a brief summary of the facts of the case involving the fraudulent sale of Noah Communications stock, she went on to explain that William Hathaway was a fiduciary as an executor of his brother's estate and as an officer of Noah Communications. A fiduciary is defined by law as a person who has a duty arising from a relationship of trust to make business decisions for another, she explained to the jury. "The law requires the fiduciary make the fullest possible disclosure of the terms and conditions of any transaction involving the person with whom he or she has this special relationship. It also requires the fiduciary to obtain the highest possible price for that person for the sale of any class of assets. We will show that Mr. Hathaway and his representatives failed in both respects to fulfill their legal obligations as fiduciaries for Mrs. Harriet Hathaway."

In a clear voice, again speaking directly to each jury member, Sophia Houghton concluded her presentation by praising Harriet Hathaway as a single mother who has been able to balance effective parenting with a successful career. As she returned to her seat behind the plaintiff's table, Karen wanted to stand up and cheer. She felt relief it had gone so well. Stephanie had explained to her over the telephone the other day that opening statements in a short trial, and both she and Sophia expected the trial to be short, certainly less than two weeks, were important because they were remembered by the jury. Patrick leaned over and whispered, "Impressive."

James Lawton waited for the inevitable stir of the audience provided by a break in the drama to subside before rising in response. He was also impressive, although more along the lines of a distinguished college professor. He presented the jury with a detailed analysis of the facts of the case and the legal issues involved. His discussion of the facts emphasized that Harriet Hathaway knowingly sold her fourteen thousand shares of Noah Communications stock because professional people, and Harriet Hathaway was a consummate professional, do not sign legal documents unknowingly. He also spent a considerable amount of time inflating William Hathaway, arguing that the success of the company was the result of Mr. Hathaway's hard work and incredible business acumen. He spoke for thirty minutes, and Karen hoped his excessive reliance on details bored the jury and caused their minds to wander.

~

As James Lawton returned to his seat in the middle of the defense table, the judge surveyed the audience, checked his watch, and declared a two hour recess for lunch. Although it was a little after eleven, which meant there was still plenty of time to begin the formal proceedings of questioning witnesses, the judge, Patrick deduced, was either hungry or did not want to break for lunch in the middle of the testimony of a witness. At any rate, judges are sovereign in their little domain and can declare a recess whenever they so choose, Patrick concluded as he rose from his seat to stretch.

The judge's decision suddenly placed Karen in a position of panic. She did not want to eat lunch with her brother and her mother, especially Billy, and yet she didn't want to hurt their feelings. As Patrick took her hand and guided her outside the courtroom through the maze of retreating people, a miracle happened. "Hey guys, let's go Chinese, and I'm paying," Alex said as she moved against the grain of the traffic toward Karen and Patrick.

"Alex, when did you get here?" Karen asked in both relief and genuine surprise.

"Too late to get a seat. I've been out in the hall listening to all the gossip. I know a little Chinese restaurant around the corner. Let's hurry so we can still find a table." The three fled the judicial building, turned right on Vermijo Street, and were soon seated at Hunan Express. "Tell me about the opening statements," Alex asked as she took out her reading glasses to look over the menu.

"Sophia was brief and to the point," Patrick responded. "She spoke directly to the jury in a tone that was both friendly and credible. Lawton was the scholar—erudite and long-winded. He lived up to his intellectual reputation as a graduate of Yale Law School, but we're betting on Sophia."

"I would too," Alex said looking up with a smile, "but I must tell you the rejects in the hall, those like me who weren't lucky enough to find seats, think your aunt is greedy, after your Dad's money now that he's made it so big."

"Who are these rejects?" Patrick asked as he closed the menu and looked over at Alex. He had decided on the buffet. If he ate enough, he reasoned, maybe he could sleep through some of the afternoon testimony.

"They sounded like Baptists to me," Alex said, smiling back at Patrick.

"It's a good thing there are no deeply committed Christians on the jury," Karen said, "or I think our case would be in trouble."

"I'm getting the buffet," Patrick said as he got up from the table to leave.

"Me too," said his two female companions in unison as they too got up from their seats, laughing at the synchronicity of their comments. The lunch was fun, a healthy diversion for Karen, and possibly an important breakthrough for Alex.

"You know, by all rights Pat, as the only male here, you should be paying," Alex said as she handed the waitress her credit card at the conclusion of a meal in which all three felt they had eaten too much.

"I know. I'm feeling very guilty and quite poor at the present moment."

"All you have to do is find me the right guy. I keep bugging Karen about it and nothing ever seems to happen."

"I do have one for you, Alex. He's a high school guidance counselor in Denver. Loves to read, loves to talk about big ideas, and he's a great racquetball player. We played all the time when I was single. Probably five or six years older than you…"

"Beggars can't be choosers," Alex interrupted.

"You're not a beggar, Alex," Karen said, smiling at her friend. Patrick readily concurred with that. He found her quite attractive looking with her long, sandy blond hair, well endowed figure in a five foot six inch frame, and her careless, flower child attire. He quickly came to her defense.

"No, I'm the beggar. That's why you're paying for lunch."

"Let's get together, the three of us with your friend," Karen said as she reached over and took Patrick's hand.

"Fine with me. Maybe we can play mixed doubles racquetball," Patrick said.

"Give me a chance with this guy, Pat. I couldn't hit a ball with a racquet if it was a beach ball and I was strong enough to swing a shovel."

"Maybe we better play golf, then. David likes that too."

"Putting a silly round ball into a tiny little hole is not my concept of fun. I wouldn't be able to count high enough to figure my score." Alex said as she picked up the receipt the waitress left on the table with her credit card.

"You wouldn't have to put the ball in the hole to win with David. All you'd need do is make his putter rise," Patrick said with a chuckle and a twinkle in his eye that he directed at Alex.

" If I get your drift, one look at me would certainly do that," Alex said as she smiled back at Patrick.

"That's what I was thinking."

"Patrick, enough of that. I can't believe you two."

"You're starting to sound like your father, Sweetheart," Patrick said as he looked across the table at Karen, "and he's on trial for fraud."

"Well I don't want to miss the show so I think it's time we get out of here before all the seats in the courtroom are taken," Karen said in a voice of some irritation. The three friends left the restaurant and hurried along Vermiijo Street to the judicial building. As they proceeded into the building and toward the nearby elevator located along the left wall, Alex said to her friend. "I hope the afternoon goes as well as the morning."

"Me too," Karen said as she pushed the button for the fifth floor. "Thanks for lunch, Alex. It provided a wonderful diversion from all of our problems over the last few days."

"Everyone needs a trip to Disney Land once in a while," Alex said as the light above the elevator door flashed three. "I was glad I could help."

"You're a good friend," Patrick said as he moved aside so the two women could enter the elevator. "I think you and David might do well together." Alex smiled over at him as the door closed. The three rode up to the fifth floor in silence. As the metal door opened, they turned right and moved rapidly down the hall to Judge Bullen's courtroom and were grateful to have seats, their ticket of admission to the second act.

～

The second act for Monday afternoon involved Harriet Hathaway. She was the first witness Sophia Houghton called in making her case against Noah Communications. After Harriet had sworn to tell the whole truth and was seated, Sophia led her through a series of questions pertaining to her residence, the demanding nature of her job as Director of Admissions for the Baldwin School, and her relationship with William Hathaway. She testified he was both generous toward them and interested in the lives of his nieces. In this regard, Harriet pointed out William Hathaway had attended the high school and college graduations of both of her daughters.

The key to her testimony, however, related to the question of whether she knew she was selling her stock back to the company. Here Sophia wanted to make four points. First, that Harriet had signed the documents placed before her by William Hathaway each year without reading through them because she trusted him. This situation was no different from when her husband was alive. Second, that she was told she was signing tax returns, which, of course, she recognized, and corporate documents pertaining to dividend distributions as well as her annual salary. At no time was she ever told by Mr. Hathaway or his representatives that she was signing documents related to her ownership of Noah Communications stock. Third, were there any circumstances in which she would have considered selling the stock? Yes, she replied, if there had been a financial emergency, but during the fifteen years in question such an emergency had never arisen. She stated emphatically that in many ways she considered herself a trustee for her children and that ownership of Noah Communications was their inheritance from their father, not her own. Finally, Sophia Houghton made the point that the meetings between Harriet Hathaway and the representatives from Noah Communications always took place around tax time. This was important because it suggested Harriet Hathaway never initiated these meetings, that if she had intended to sell stock the meetings would have taken place at various times during the year, that from her perspective these meetings were routine affairs pertaining to her taxes.

Karen's was proud of her aunt's testimony. She was articulate, soft spoken, and credible; but Karen knew this was the easy part. She became very nervous when James Lawton stood up to cross-examine her, even though she knew Stephanie had been preparing her mother for this for weeks.

Lawton's strategy was a clever one and somewhat surprising. He was not at all interested in getting Harriet to change her testimony or to paint her as a greedy Philadelphia socialite. Instead his questions centered around portraying her as a highly competent professional, an administrator in a prestigious secondary school with a record with which anyone would be proud. He also probed her stewardship of the other investments in her portfolio, despite Sophia Houghton's repeated calls of objection which Judge Bullen consistently overruled, to show that she managed her finances meticulously and was well informed concerning matters of equity investing. Her articulate answers to these questions played into his strategy which was to suggest a person of her general competence would never sign documents about which she knew nothing.

Though puzzled at first, Karen eventually saw into this strategy, recognized its merits, but when her aunt left the stand at 3:45 in the afternoon, tired and obviously relieved to have the ordeal over, Karen was proud of her performance. She also believed that, though Lawton may have sown some seeds of doubt, the jury would end up believing she did not knowingly sell her stock. The women on the jury would certainly have signed documents without paying careful attention to what they were signing.

After her aunt stepped down from the witness stand, Judge Bullen adjourned the court until nine a.m. the next morning. Houghton and Lawton remained to argue motions in the Judge's chambers over the scheduled testimony of Stephanie Hathaway the following morning. The defense team argued that Stephanie was a lawyer working for Sophia Houghton and therefore should not be allowed to testify. Sophia Houghton countered by saying there was no contract between her firm and Stephanie Hathaway, that Stephanie was receiving no compensation from Houghton's firm, and that she had important evidence to present. After hearing oral arguments supplementing the motions, Judge Bullen decided to allow Stephanie to testify.

As she stood up to stretch after her aunt's testimony, Karen had a problem of her own to solve. She took Patrick's hand, walked into the courtroom against the crowd, and hugged her mother. Billy moved the other way and pretended to talk with a Noah Communications employee. Karen was so focused on this peace offering with her family she forgot to say goodbye to Alex whom she called later to apologize and to thank again for lunch.

The meeting was easier than she had anticipated because her mother did all the talking, her brother remained conspicuously absent, maybe thinking she might disrobe again or do something else a little crazy, and the talk was all about the children. Bless her mother, Karen thought. She was a mouse that couldn't roar, but she had a loving heart. Her mother naturally wanted them for dinner, but it was easy to say they had to return to Monument to relieve the babysitter and that a trip back to the Springs would be too much. Her mother, though disappointed, certainly seemed to understand. They left the courtroom together, said their goodbyes on the street, Billy actually shook Patrick's hand and smiled over at his sister, and went their separate ways. Perfect Karen thought. The distance they had created for themselves in Monument had never been more welcome.

Reese Baldwin was anxious to get to work. He needed the money to placate his wife who was constantly nagging him about a trip to Alaska. His repeated reply was that their combined retirement incomes left little at the end of the month for trips to Alaska. Philip Duke's little job would solve that problem nicely.

He left Leadville at nine on Saturday morning June 1st in his 1990 blue Ford truck for the two and a half hour drive to Colorado Springs. He met with Philip Duke at 3 p.m. in his office at Noah Communications where he was briefed extensively on the two jurors he was to approach. He left Duke's office at 3:45 for the short drive to Carswell's apartment. His plan was to make the two contacts before the start of the trial on Monday. Both men agreed the sooner this job was completed the better because things could go wrong and time would be of the essence if other jurors had to be approached.

The meeting with Carswell went extremely well. Baldwin found him at his apartment watching a baseball game. The two met in a deserted picnic area that was part of the inside courtyard of the apartment complex. His appeal was direct and to the point. The offer was for five thousand now, and five thousand after the trial—all in cash. He further explained to Carswell there was no way he could lose. His client could not implicate him without implicating himself. After briefly considering the offer, Carswell accepted it with a smile on his face. They arranged to make the first payment on the following Saturday at 10:00 a.m. at Monument Valley Park.

Gabrielle Coleman was a little more difficult to approach because she seemed to spend a considerable amount of time away from her condominium. Reese Baldwin finally made contact with her at 4:00 on Sunday afternoon. He told her through the intercom system he had an important package to deliver. When he entered her condominium empty handed, a look of terror flashed across her face. "Please, Ms. Coleman, you can relax. I lied about the package in order to get to see you. I have a proposition to present to you which will take no longer than ten minutes. Then I'll be gone."

Gabrielle's first instinct was to run past him, out her door, and to seek assistance from a neighbor. Her panic was eased somewhat by his gentle manner, his soft, grandfatherly good looks, and the fact there was no gun in evidence. "Okay, Mr."

"Curtis Baufman," Reese Baldwin interjected, and he thrust out his right hand to shake hers, which caused Gabrielle to step backward to maintain some distance.

"Okay, Mr. Baufman, you have ten minutes, and it better be good." She led her uninvited guest into the living room where he sat on the sofa which was adjacent to a large picture window with a view of the downtown area. Gabrielle remained standing in a direct path to the front door which she had left open.

Again, Reese Baldwin went directly to the point. "My proposition, Ms. Coleman, relates to the Hathaway trial. My client is willing to pay fifty thousand dollars to influence your vote." Gabrielle gasped, and quickly ran outside through the front door. She ran past her neighbor's place, headed for the garage and her car, when she paused, out of breath, and turned slightly to see if she was being followed. Seeing no one behind her, she relaxed for a second time and began to reconsider the situation. Maybe this will be another way to nail them, she thought. As her mind cleared and her fear dissipated, delicious new strategies bubbled up from inside her. Slowly she walked back to her condo and met Reese Baldwin as he was leaving.

"I'm sorry I panicked, Mr. Baufman, but your proposition startled me. Please come in and let's talk. I can at least hear you out."

"Don't worry about panicking. This kind of thing doesn't happen every day. I promise to be brief." After the two were seated in the living room, Reese Baldwin continued. "As I said a few minutes ago, my client is willing to pay you fifty thousand dollars to influence your vote on the jury—twenty-five thousand now and twenty-five after the trial."

"Which client do you represent, Mr. Baufman?"

"Mr. William Hathaway." Gabrielle Coleman smiled inside. She couldn't believe her good luck. She paused briefly to consider the situation one last time and could not see how she could lose. The worst that could happen is she could change her mind in the next twenty-four hours, report the illegal bribe to the judge, and be released from the jury.

"Okay, Mr. Baufman. I'm willing to vote against Mr. Hathaway's sister-in-law for fifty thousand dollars. I was uncommitted until you came barging in here," she felt comfortable lying to him, a return in kind for the lies he was obviously spinning, "and fifty thousand dollars seems like a fair price."

"Thank you, Ms. Coleman."

"Here's how we'll do it. You call me tomorrow night, and I will give you the name of a bank in the Cayman Islands." She smiled inwardly again. She had read too many John Grisham novels. "I will give you all the necessary account information. Once I receive confirmation the twenty-five thousand has been properly deposited, you will have my vote."

"Thank you, again, Ms. Coleman," Reese Baldwin said as he raised himself from the couch in preparation for leaving. "Your vote for the defense will ensure justice is served in this case." As soon as she had closed and bolted the door, Gabrielle Coleman sat back down on the living room couch, her heart racing. Unfortunately for the defense, Philip Duke had failed to pick up one crucial bit of information pertaining to Gabrielle Coleman. She had a female lover in St. Louis Missouri, and she hated Christian Fundamentalists because of their self-righteous views concerning homosexuality. She was thrilled to have been chosen for the jury, and had fully intended to punish

William Hathaway with her vote. The money would have no affect on her vote. She had not been successfully influenced, but rather her revenge would now come with an added twenty-five thousand dollar gift. She had no expectation of receiving the rest.

That gift would allow her to pay off her gambling debts and to move to St. Louis. The balance after the debts were paid would give her two months to find a new job. A door was finally opening for her she thought as she left the couch to phone Jennifer with the good news.

$\sim$

It was almost too easy. By seven o'clock on Monday evening, Gabrielle Coleman's assets had increased by twenty-five thousand dollars. Reese Baldwin had called almost immediately after she returned home from her first day at the trial. The bank in the Cayman Islands confirmed the transaction via email half an hour later.

Gabrielle decided to celebrate her good fortune with a strong bourbon and water before dinner. After pouring the drink, she called Jennifer in St. Louis to ease her mind that everything was now in place. The two women decided Gabrielle should remain in Colorado Springs until after Labor Day to avoid any unnecessary suspicion.

"Boy, you sure do get paranoid in situations like this," Gabrielle mumbled to herself as she nibbled on some leftover chicken and worked on her third bourbon and water. And then a dark cloud descended over her. What if the son of a bitch has bribed other jurors? she thought. It only takes one vote for the bastard to win. The judge had explained that to them at their first meeting following their selection to the jury.

Gabrielle immediately called back Jennifer. "What if Hathaway has bribed other jurors, Jen? It only takes one vote for him to win."

"He probably has," Jennifer responded into the phone. "He's a fat cat with unlimited resources."

"I know, and I can't stand the thought of his winning."

"Maybe we can have it both ways," Jennifer said after a brief pause while she thought the problem through. "Why not transfer the money to my bank here. That way no one can ever suspect you. I'll pay off your gambling debts. Then you can drop a hint Hathaway is tampering with the jury. If they catch someone else, Hathaway goes to jail. That's even better than his losing all that money."

"Perfect, Jen. I'll call Sophia Houghton right now."

"Be careful, Baby. I don't want you to land in jail too."

"They'll never be able to trace the money. You're so smart, Jen. I'll call you right back."

"I love you, Baby."

"I love you, too, Jen. Bye."

It took Gabrielle two hours to make the right call. The problem was Sophia Houghton had an unlisted number, which led her to initially give up. As she was brushing her teeth in preparation for bed, an important thought flashed through her mind. Houghton was receiving legal help from a member of the Hathaway family. She remembered reading it in the paper a few weeks back.

She instantly went online to reread the newspaper and found the information she needed in less than thirty minutes. Stephanie Hathaway was both helping Houghton and staying at a local hotel for the trial. After three misses, she finally connected with Stephanie at the Antler's Hotel at 10:45. Satisfied her revenge was now complete, she collapsed into bed and slept for eight fitful hours. As she drove to the courthouse the next morning for day two, she was in a state of panic she had gone too far, that her desire for punishing William Hathaway would put her in jail.

～

Karen also had misgivings about attending the trial on Tuesday. She missed the children, and hated the sight of her mother in the courtroom, feeling both guilty because she was supporting the other side and sad her mother was going through all this. But Stephanie was first up to testify this morning, which meant she had to be there to support her. She hoped her cousin would perform as well as her mother did yesterday, but she wasn't really worried. Her cousin had some real steel in her character, which Karen wished she possessed in greater amounts.

Because the session was starting an hour earlier, they left at 7:30 in the morning so they could be sure of getting a seat. On the way into town, Patrick raised a subject Karen had carefully put out of her mind. "I admire the way you have conducted yourself through all this. It hasn't been easy."

"Thanks, Pat. It hasn't been easy for any of us," she responded as she reached across for his free right hand.

"You know, you must have thought of this. You have a lot at stake in this trial. If your Dad wins, you will one day inherit several million dollars. That's a lot of money."

"Maybe, but the way Daddy feels about me, you never know. Anyway, I try to focus on the fairness of the case, and the fact that Stephanie is like my sister. Money can't replace her."

"I know what you mean. She is a super girl. I'm looking forward to meeting Perry."

"Me too. I think someday we ought to travel together as couples. Maybe we could introduce them to Prince Edward Island. We could continue as couples what Steph and I did as kids."

"Nice thought. I'd love to go back to Prince Edward Island. We still haven't finished the bike trip."

"Maybe we should go soon and make one more baby there. I think three is going to be our magic number."

"I like the thought of three kids too. We should think about taking some time after I resign from Noah and before Jason and I get going full blast on the new company. The first few years setting it up could be quite hectic."

"When are you planning to leave Noah?"

"Not for at least six months if I can hold out that long. Jason needs time to get the bugs out of our new software. I really do feel a little guilty about cheating your father. Jason hasn't worked on Noah stuff in two months."

"I wouldn't worry about cheating Daddy. You have already done so many things to help his business."

"But I still feel some loyalty to him. He has taught me everything I know. In a funny way, he's been a good guy for me to work for."

"What does Jason think about Daddy?"

"He considers him a crook. He has no problems working on programs for the new company."

"I couldn't agree more. What are you and Jason working on? Is it exciting stuff?"

" Jason is designing software that allows different makes of computers to talk to each other. The market for this type of thing is enormous."

"That does sound exciting. Maybe we should consider moving out of Colorado. You could locate this company anywhere it seems to me. I would miss Monument, but creating more distance from my parents would not be a bad idea."

"It may come to that," Patrick said as he turned off of interstate twenty-five and headed for the judicial building. They were mostly quiet after that, but they walked hand-in-hand from the parking lot to the courtroom feeling a closeness that was such a special part of their marriage. Adversity had forged them into a close-knit team.

The morning session was dominated by two witnesses—Stephanie Hathaway and Conrad W. Lane, Jr., Harriet Hathaway's stockbroker. Stephanie was asked a range of questions, but the two most important pertained to her discovery of the problem and her mother's intentions. She explained in detail how her mother's recent tax problem had triggered her interest. She did not understand how thirteen thousand dollars could be owed on miscalculated dividends. She also stated her mother's intention with regard to her Noah Communications holdings was to save the stock for a financial emergency with the idea that whatever remained at her death would be the inheritance of her two daughters.

"She told me on at least two occasions this is what my father would have wanted."

"Was there ever a financial emergency that you were aware of?"

"No. My mother has been a good mother and a good provider. Our family has been financially blessed."

"I have no further questions, Your Honor." James Lawton tried to suggest Stephanie was a member of Sophia Houghton's legal team, but Houghton objected to the question and Judge Bullen ruled in her favor. Lawton's final series of questions related to the financial help William Hathaway had given to Stephanie's family over the years. Stephanie readily admitted her uncle had been generous.

Conrad Lane had been Harriet Hathaway's stockbroker for twenty-five years. He was a graduate of Princeton University and the Wharton School of Business. He was impressive looking and articulate Karen concluded as she struggled with sleep. The most important point he made for the plaintiff was that he never got the idea when Harriet Hathaway purchased stock she was reinvesting money gained from the sale of Noah Communications stock. James Lawton chose not to contest that point in his cross-examination. What he wanted the jury to hear was that Harriet Hathaway was a savvy investor, a point Conrad Lane fully supported. A draw, Patrick concluded, and he was ready for lunch.

The first witness to testify in the afternoon session was boring, at least as far as Karen was concerned. Richard Settering was currently employed as an accountant at Noah Communications who had had the job six years ago of delivering Harriet Hathaway's papers to her for her signature. Despite Sophia Houghton's probing, Settering insisted he had fulfilled his fiduciary responsibility in explaining to Harriet Hathaway exactly what she was signing. Patrick wondered how much his father-in-law was paying for this testimony. James Lawton did not bother to cross-examine him. There was no need.

The story on Fred Cummings, the second witness, turned out differently. Fred had been an accountant for Noah Communications until he retired four years ago.

He had made the trip to Philadelphia in 1985. When asked if he had performed his fiduciary responsibility, he responded it had not been necessary. Harriet Hathaway knew exactly what she was signing.

"Let me get this straight, Mr. Cummings. Do you mean to say when you met with Mrs. Hathaway on April second, nineteen eighty-five you did not provide her with a detailed explanation of exactly what she was signing?" Sophia Houghton inquired in a puzzled tone.

"I asked her if she had any questions, and she said she did not."

"She then proceeded to sign all the documents that were marked for her signature. Is that what happened, Mr. Cummings?"

"Yes it is."

"Did she study the documents carefully before signing them?"

"No, not that I remember. Our time together was brief. Fifteen or twenty minutes, certainly no more."

"I have no further questions, Your Honor." James Lawton tried as best as he could to repair the damage, but he was not very successful. It was obvious Fred Cummings's testimony would have benefited from more coaching by the defense team.

∼

Wednesday was an important day for Sophia Houghton. Montgomery O'Brien, the valuation expert, was scheduled for the entire day. Karen begged off—too much accounting, and she was still struggling with all the guilt from the cross pressures of family loyalties. She kept the babysitter engaged, why waste a good thing, and she and Frannie took a long walk. Patrick headed for the courthouse at 7:45 a.m. He was hooked on this family soap opera.

Sophia Houghton and Montgomery O'Brien had worked together for hours deciding on what cases to present to the jury that supported their approach to valuation and how best to destroy the market model of the Hathaway team. Sophia Houghton was pleased with Stephanie's choice of O'Brien. His credibility as an expert was beyond reproach, and he had many hours of experience testifying in court cases like this one. His rumpled gray hair and ruddy complexion reminded Sophia of her father. She estimated they were of a similar age.

Sophia began her presentation with a series of questions to demonstrate Mr. O'Brien's credibility—Stanford BA with honors, Harvard MBA, and thirty years of experience in the business of valuing companies. She then had him explain to the jury some of the issues of valuation that pertain to a closely held corporation—why it is so difficult to derive a value for such companies, what are some of the standard methods for valuing a company like Noah Communications, and why his discounted cash flow model was the most appropriate. In answering the last question, he cited several academic studies to support his conclusion.

"Okay, Mr. O'Brien, let me summarize the findings of your report and we can get to the bottom line. According to the figures you present, Mrs. Harriet Hathaway has received nine hundred and sixty thousand dollars for the sale of fourteen thousand shares of Noah Communications stock from nineteen seventy-nine through nineteen ninety-three. Is that correct?"

"Yes it is."

"What do you estimate the true value of those fourteen thousand shares to be?"

"Our discounted cash flow model estimates the value of that stock to be a hundred twenty-eight million. What we did was establish a value for the company for each year beginning in nineteen seventy-nine and ending in nineteen ninety-three using the discounted cash flow model and the figures that were given me. Then for each year we determined the value of one share of Noah Communications stock and multiplied that figure by one thousand. Finally, we took these results for each of the fourteen years in question, added the totals, and determined the sale of these shares was valued at one hundred and twenty-eight million dollars."

"I have no further questions, Your Honor," which ended the proceedings for the morning session. The afternoon was consumed in its entirety by James Lawton, who tried to poke holes in Montgomery O'Brien's testimony. He questioned his figures, his assumptions, and tried to show his findings were exaggerated. Mr. Lawton had obviously done his homework, but O'Brien's carefully worded, well thought-out defense of his findings, was impressive. He was aided by the fact that the questions were technical, arcane, the testimony boring, and in places difficult to follow. Mr. Lawton also tried to suggest that a discounted cash flow model was not an appropriate way to value a corporation like Noah Communications, but Montgomery O'Brien was able to swamp him with judicial and professional opinion to the contrary.

Sophia Houghton, though pleased with O'Brien's defense of his report in the face of Lawton's detailed assault, fumed over her opponent's tactics and the phrasing of several of the questions in a leading and argumentative fashion. Such tactics violated the norms of courtroom procedure, but Sophia held her tongue. She did not formally object because she did not want to give the jury the impression she was trying to suppress information based on some legal technicality. It was a good strategy because O'Brien's testimony held up well. Patrick left the courtroom at 4:45 reassured that the Harriet Hathaway family had survived Lawton's cross-examination.

Thursday morning was a typical late spring morning for Colorado Springs with a cloudless blue sky and temperatures in the mid fifties as Karen and Patrick headed again for the judicial building a little after seven. This was the big day. It was the first day for the defense, and William Hathaway was the lead witness. The court session was set to begin at nine o'clock sharp, as they had all week; and Karen and Patrick wanted to get there while there were still seats. They made it with plenty of time to spare, although when Sophia Houghton entered the courtroom at 8:55, this time dressed in a solid gray suit with a blue scarf, Patrick smiled when he saw the scarf thinking it must be a good luck charm, it certainly was her signature, there was not a seat to be had in the room.

William Hathaway, dressed in a conservative blue business suit, his uniform for life Karen thought with some disappointment, was duly sworn in and seated at the witness stand. James Lawton began with the usual questions of name, residence, and occupation. With these preliminaries completed, he went right to the legal requirements of a fiduciary. He began by asking him to define for the court his understanding of a fiduciary relationship. To no one's surprise, he had a full and complete understanding of the concept. Lawton then went on to ask:

"Are you confident, Mr. Hathaway, you fulfilled your fiduciary responsibility with respect to your sister-in-law on the twelve times you met with her? Did you explain to her on each occasion that she was selling one thousand shares of Noah Communications stock back to the company?"

"Yes I am. Harriet was given full knowledge of all the details and consequences of each transaction."

"Are you confident your two subordinates on the occasions they met with Mrs. Hathaway for similar reasons also carried out faithfully their fiduciary responsibility toward her?"

"Yes I'm sure they did."

"Thank you, Mr. Hathaway. I have one further question, Your Honor. Over the last several years, Mr. Hathaway, your company has enjoyed considerable success, growing an average of twenty-two percent a year. Why has this happened? Can you explain to the court what has led to this impressive growth?"

"Certainly, Mr. Lawton. The simple answer is we have plowed all of our profits back into the company. In order to keep our profits high, I have kept my salary low. We have also made some good decisions. Recently, for example, we purchased a small software company with products that create substantial efficiencies in the operation of radio stations. The result is our stations are the most efficient in the industry, and we are now beginning to sell this software to other corporations. I could go further, but I think that answers your question."

"Thank you, Mr. Hathaway. Your witness, Ms. Houghton. Sophia Houghton rose slowly from her chair and smiled across at William Hathaway.

"I too applaud you for the impressive success of Noah Communications. You are certainly a very effective business executive."

"Thank you, Ms. Houghton."

"I do have one question concerning your phenomenal growth record, however. You just testified one reason for that success is that all profits were plowed back into the company. Does this mean no dividends were paid out during the period under question?"

"Yes it does, Ms. Houghton."

"Then why was Harriet Hathaway told that she was signing papers related to dividend payments over the last fourteen years?"

"Harriet Hathaway was not given that information. She was told she was selling one thousand shares of Noah Communications stock back to the company."

"I see Mr. Hathaway. Let me explore another issue with you. Tuesday afternoon Mr. Fred Cummings, a former accountant with your company, testified that his meeting with Mrs. Hathaway on April second, nineteen eighty-five in which he asked her to sign papers related to her tax returns and the sale of Noah Communications stock was exceedingly brief. According to Mr. Cummings's testimony, he merely asked Mrs. Hathaway if she had any questions pertaining to the documents requiring her signature. When she stated she had none, he asked her to sign them. Do Mr. Cummings's actions meet the legal requirements of a fiduciary, Mr. Hathaway?"

"I cannot speak for his actions, Ms. Houghton, because I was not at the meeting he held with my sister-in-law. However, I can assure you he was instructed by me to give Harriet a full and detailed explanation of all the relevant issues pertaining to the documents for her signature."

"Thank you, Mr. Hathaway. Finally, let me direct your attention to a related matter of interest. The typical investor tends to sell stock throughout the year, at different times depending perhaps on the price of the stock on a particular day or because of specific economic issues the individual faces. In the case of Mrs. Hathaway, the fourteen transactions in question occurred during what is commonly referred to as tax season, between the last week in March and the first week in April. That's a very narrow window, Mr. Hathaway. Is there any significance to this?"

"Yes there is, Ms. Houghton. I'm glad you asked me that question. About a year after my brother, Peter, died, I met with Harriet to discuss the future of our company. At that time I told her of my plans to move to Colorado Springs and to focus the company in a new direction. She had no objections to that strategy. She also expressed her wish at that meeting to diversify her assets. Because she had no interest in becoming actively involved with Noah Communications, she thought her long term economic welfare would best be served by selling her ownership in Noah Communications on a systematic basis and then reinvesting the proceeds from the sale of her stock into a diversified portfolio of companies. It was at that time I suggested the idea of selling one thousand shares a year. Such a strategy was important to us because it enabled us to afford both continued internal growth and the redemption of Harriet's shares. We jointly agreed to conduct these transactions around tax time as a matter of convenience."

Karen couldn't believe her father would make up such a story. She had never heard him lie before, and he was obviously good at it. It all sounded logical, it seemed to come easily, it just rolled off his tongue. She was so mad at him she wanted to jump up and scream liar. Her anger was somewhat assuaged when Sophia Houghton pointed out the inconsistency between her father's story and Harriet Hathaway's testimony.

"I see, Mr. Hathaway," Sophia Houghton responded. "Although you were not in the courtroom to hear Mrs. Hathaway's testimony, I would like to point out to you and to remind the members of the jury that she has a very different view of this issue. According to her testimony, she viewed her ownership of Noah Communications stock as the rightful inheritance of her daughters, and she stated very clearly to this court she would never have sold her shares in the company without first discussing it with them."

"I guess she and I see the results of that meeting differently. If I had known differences of this nature would emerge fifteen years later, I would have had notes taken of the meeting. You would think such formalities when dealing with family would not be needed, but I guess I was wrong." This last statement was made in a sanctimonious tone Karen found nauseating. Her anger was definitely rising, and it was not helped by Sophia's polite response. Why doesn't she expose the bastard for who he is, she fumed. If Patrick had been able to read her thoughts, he would have counseled patience.

"I agree with you, Mr. Hathaway. Detailed notes of that meeting would have been helpful. I have no further questions, Your Honor."

Karen grabbed Patrick by the hand and led him quickly out of the courtroom. On the elevator down to the first floor, she said: "That's it, Pat. I'm through with the trial. I'm going home to the children."

"I know it's been difficult for you, Sweetheart, and I certainly understand. Would you mind picking me up when the afternoon session is over?"

"Sure. Give me a call. I'll be at home waiting," and she hugged him tightly for the brief moment it took the elevator to reach the first floor.

The afternoon session was dominated by Dr. Kevin Thompson, accountant, and senior partner at Thompson, Leventhal, and Daniels, a respected consulting firm in Denver. It was Dr. Thompson's role to convince the jury a market approach was the fairest way to determine the value of Noah Communications stock. His testimony took the entire afternoon, and there were times when Patrick wished he had gone home with Karen. Valuation is a boring subject.

The basic point of Dr. Thompson's testimony was that the fairest way to establish the value of a share of Noah Communications stock was to compare it to similar companies that were publicly traded using various economic variables in making the comparison. He made it sound so simple. "It's the same thing a realtor does in establishing a price for a house that is going on the market," he said in response to one of James Lawton's questions.

Patrick was amazed it took over an hour of testimony for Dr. Thompson to establish this point. He was nervous the pure simplicity of it would appeal to the jury. The real estate analogy was one every juror could identify with. He felt better about things when Sophia Houghton hammered away during her cross- examination. Her attack was brutal.

"Dr. Thompson," Sophia Houghton began. "You compared six publicly traded companies in making your estimates. Is that correct?"

"Yes it is."

"Four of these companies had not been in business for fifteen years. The most successful of the six achieved an annual growth rate of twelve percent, far less than the twenty-two percent achieved by Noah Communications. Is this a fair comparison?"

"Everything is relative Ms. Houghton. This was the best we could do. Finding comparable companies that are publicly traded which specialize in Christian broadcasting was not easy."

"I see, Dr. Thompson. To use your real estate analogy, with Noah Communications being by far the most beautiful house on the block, doesn't that tend to reduce its value?"

"It could, but not significantly." A rather lame response, Patrick concluded. He hoped the jury also saw it that way. Sophia seemed to be making a good point.

"I guess that's in the eye of the beholder, Dr. Thompson. Moving to another issue, I noticed from the material you provided us during discovery that your figures discount the value of Noah Communications stock for its lack of marketability. Is the percentage figure used in making such a discount a subjective number?"

"Yes, and it's also a standard practice in arriving at valuations for closely held corporations."

"I understand that Dr. Thompson. The thing that bothers me is the percentages you used are well above IRS norms and accepted case law on this matter. The net effect is to greatly reduce the value of my client's holdings."

"The problem, Ms. Houghton, is marketability." He jumped on his inquisitor before she had time to finish her question. "Our assumptions were based on the fact that the market for stock in a Christian broadcasting company is not large."

"I don't know of many companies that are growing at an annual rate of twenty-two percent, Dr. Thompson. It sounds like a good investment to me, but yours was a subjective call. Is there any significance to the fact that the percentages for each of the fourteen years chosen happened to produce a price quite close to what Harriet Hathaway received?"

"In which transaction, Ms. Houghton?"

"All of them, Dr. Thompson."

"The percentages were based on what we determined the market would bear at the time Harriet Hathaway sold her stock. That's all I can tell you."

"I have one final question Dr. Thompson. As you may have read, the *Denver Post* reported last month that the value of Noah Communications was estimated to be worth five hundred million dollars. My client received less than a million for the sale of her stock. Does this amount seem fair to you based on your detailed knowledge of the company's finances? From what Mrs. Hathaway received, it seems obvious that

Noah Communications wasn't worth much ten years ago. What happened? Did the company take a quantum leap forward in the last year or two?"

"I can't answer that question, Ms. Houghton, because I did not read the *Post* article in question. I have no idea what their assumptions were based on."

"Thank you, Dr. Thompson. I have no further questions, Your Honor." As Kevin Thompson left the witness stand, he feared for William Hathaway. Patrick bolted from his seat at the back of the courtroom to call Karen. Thompson's testimony ended the session for the day, and Patrick was convinced his answers to Sophia's questions would provide the final nail in the coffin regarding William Hathaway's defense.

∾

One thing Patrick loved to do was mountain bike. It was a crisp Saturday morning, about fifty degrees with a deep blue sky, and he had Maggie on his back. Karen trailed behind with Justin. They had left the Keystone Lodge about 9:30 that morning and were headed for the tiny mountain village of Montezuma about ten miles away. By prearrangement, Karen and the kids had picked him up at the courthouse at 2:30 p.m. on Friday. Then the four of them had fled Colorado Springs for Summit County and the lovely mountain resort at Keystone.

On the ride there that Friday afternoon Patrick filled Karen in on the latest developments regarding the trial. "As I told you at dinner, we won Thursday afternoon. That accountant was a disaster, but things didn't go quite so well today. There were four testimonials."

"I bet that cost Daddy a lot of money."

"It may have. The morning witnesses were two guys from work—Stephen McRae the executive V.P. and Jeffery Halligan the CFO."

"What is a CFO? It sounds like an alien from another world."

"Jeff is the chief financial officer. He's a sharp guy."

"I guess I have heard of that. Did Sophia get him to admit under oath that Daddy is a thief?"

"They painted this picture of a Christian entrepreneur. The same old story line—hard working, ethical, fair to subordinates, brilliant in the execution of strategy, and frugal with his personal finances. Much of that stuff I agree with."

"Don't you dare become a traitor, Patrick McGovern," Karen said with a laugh.

"That's not new, Karen. I've always felt that way about your Dad. I might have added cold and ruthless, but that would not have fit the picture. Their point was Noah has thrived because of your Dad's skill and willingness to keep his own salary low so profits could be plowed into future growth. The implication was Aunt Harriet has already received more than she deserves."

"I'm going to be sick," Karen said as she looked over at Patrick and scowled.

"The afternoon session was even worse. The President of Colorado College and the Commandant of the Air Force Academy took the stand. I left before the Air Force Academy dude finished, but just his being there was impressive. Their mission was to paint your father as a Christian philanthropist."

"Does that end it for the defense?" Karen asked as she turned to check the kids in the back seat, smiling at Justin who was sound asleep and so cute in his distorted position in the car seat.

"Yes, the closing arguments are set for Monday morning. Then it's up to the jury."

"That's good. At least we'll get some closure on all of this."

"Actually I'm not really that worried. I still think your aunt is going to win. Testimonials are nice, but the law is the law, and your Dad has real problems there."

"I hope so," Karen said as she smiled over at Patrick and thought a little about taking a nap herself. They arrived at the Keystone Lodge a little after 5:00 p.m. with bikes, backpacks, and a profound need for a change of pace.

The bike ride the next day from Keystone to Montezuma provided the change of pace they were looking for. It is not an easy ride because you climb one thousand feet. That is the bad news. The good news is that the road is wide, there was minimal traffic on that second Saturday in June, and the McGoverns were in no hurry. Their goal was to arrive at the little General Store in Montezuma by lunchtime. The kids cooperated for the most part, at least they had no problems adjusting to the change in altitude which was a relief to Karen.

They arrived at the little store at 11:15 where they purchased sandwiches and drinks for lunch and received directions to a pretty mountain meadow about a half hour hike from the store. After diaper changes for both kids and allowing Maggie a few minutes to wander around the store in her drunken sailor fashion (she had started walking about two months ago around her second birthday), they set off on the hike. The meadow was half way to St. Johns, an abandoned mining town, and, because it was mostly uphill from the village of Montezuma, Karen decided maybe getting to the meadow would be enough. They could make the full trip to St. Johns another time.

She worried too about whether they would ever find the meadow, but forty minutes later as the trail leveled out there it was, on the right hand side, lush and green, about five acres in area with early spring wildflowers scattered in clumps here and there. They quickly found a place that was shaded by a large pine tree which Karen leaned up against and began nursing Justin. "I'm going to take Maggie and explore a little," Patrick said as he lifted Maggie from his pack and placed her on the ground.

"We'll be here," Karen replied. "Please stay within hollering distance."

"We will," Patrick responded as he leaned down and kissed Karen. After patting Justin gently on the head, he picked up Maggie in his left arm and the two proceeded across the meadow. When they reached the other side, Patrick spotted a fairly large stream that paralleled the edge of the woods. "This is just what I was looking for, Magster," he said as he looked over at her and smiled. She returned his smile and wiggled her legs in eager anticipation. "I think it's time you learned how to throw rocks."

Patrick sat Maggie down on the bank of the stream and gathered five or six small stones. He then sat beside her and made two tosses into the stream. Maggie clapped her hands with glee. "Now it's your turn, Sweetheart," and he placed a stone in Maggie's little hand. She looked at the stone, squeezed her fingers around it, but kept it in her hand. Patrick tossed another rock into the stream, Maggie smiled over at him, but the stone remained in her hand.

"Here, Sweetheart, let me show you how to do this." He picked her up and turned her so she was facing the stream. Then he took her arm and thrust it forward, but Maggie continued to cling to the stone. "Let me do it a few more times, and I think you will get it," he said as he placed her away from the water and returned to the water's edge to collect more rocks. With several additional rocks in his arsenal, he continued this process of throwing rocks himself and then helping her do it for ten minutes before she succeeded in doing it herself.

"Wow. You're the best, Sweetheart," he said as he clapped his hands with gusto. Maggie giggled and threw another rock into the stream. After three more successful launches, he picked her up and hugged her tightly. "Let's go back and show Mommy what you can do."

"Okay," she shouted in a high-pitched voice filled with excitement and enthusiasm. When they arrived at the tree, Justin was sound asleep on a blanket next to the tree and Karen was sipping a diet coke.

"Ready for lunch, guys," Karen said as they came within hearing distance.

"I'm starved," Patrick responded, "but Maggie wants to show you something first." He placed her on the ground, took a rock from his pocket which he placed in her right hand, and said, "Okay, throw it, Sweetheart. Show Mommy what we've been doing at the stream." Maggie looked over at Karen, smiled, and continued to hold the rock. "Watch this, Maggie," Patrick said as he crouched beside her, took another rock from his pocket, and threw it into the tall grass. He repeated this process two more times before Maggie finally was able to do it on her own.

"Oh, Maggie, I love you, baby," Karen said as she swooped her into her arms and tickled her. Karen then sat her down on the blanket in front of the tree, and the three of them enthusiastically had their lunch.

After lunch Karen told Maggie her favorite story about a monkey named "Curious George," which worked its magic and she was soon asleep. Karen then checked on Justin who was still sleeping soundly beside the tree. Patrick had wandered back over to the trail, and she went after him next. She came up behind him and engulfed him in a hug. "Remember, you said we could have one more, Pat?" she whispered in his ear.

"Absolutely. I wouldn't mind four, although educating them all would be expensive."

"Can we begin making him now? We seem to do our best work in the strangest places," she said as she hugged him tighter.

"Are the kids asleep?" he asked as he broke away from her and turned around.

"They're both sound asleep. Justin should last at least another hour, and Maggie just got started."

"You're amazing, Sweetheart," he said as he took his finger and circled her forehead, placing a strand of brown hair back behind her ear.

"Come with me," she said with a smile. "I know just the spot," and she took his hand and led him to a circle of pine trees not more than twenty-five yards from where the kids were sleeping. He slowly undressed her, kissing her from the neck on down while admiring her body, which had returned to the amazing curves and shapes that had so attracted him three years before. After reaching her toes, he stood up and she stepped toward him, duplicating the process he had recently completed, taking her time, and kissing gently every part of him she found so exciting. Half an hour later they walked arm-in-arm back to the tree to check on the children who were both still sleeping soundly. After gazing at them in wonder for a few moments, they returned to the circle of trees and began all over again.

"Twice in one day, Patrick McGovern. I think the seed has been successfully planted," she said lovingly as she peered down at him.

"I hope so, Sweetheart," he said as he looked up at her full breasts that were still aching to be caressed by him. "You sure do make beautiful babies."

"I think one more will be just right," she said as she rolled from him and went in search of her clothes. He lay on his back for five more minutes soaking up the sun and thinking how wonderful this break from the trial had turned out to be. He then got dressed himself and wandered back toward the children, smiling deeply when he noticed Justin had replaced him as the center of her attention and affection.

～

While Patrick got lucky in Montezuma, Stephanie hit pay dirt of another kind on that same Saturday morning. It was a victory that only came after a tense inner struggle. When the drunken juror had called late Sunday night with the charge of jury tampering, Stephanie was stunned. Her initial reaction was to call Sophia Houghton, but it was too late. She settled for Perry instead. "Hi, Pere. I hope I'm not calling too late."

"No, Steph. It's never too late. But you did get me up. I guess you forgot I'm two hours ahead."

"Oh, my God, I'm so sorry."

"That's okay. What's up?"

"You won't believe it. I just received a call from a drunken juror claiming she was offered fifty thousand dollars to vote against us."

"You're kidding. I guess your uncle will do anything."

"I guess so. I started to call Sophia, but it was too late."

"What can Sophia do about it?"

"She can lose her license to practice law if she doesn't report something like this to the judge."

"Do you want your uncle to go to jail?" Perry inquired after pausing a moment for reflection.

"Well, I don't feel as strongly about it as Karen. Really, all Mom and I want are the shares back."

"I may have an idea for you. Why not hire an investigator to find out which jurors were approached. If you nab one, you can pose the devil's question to your uncle: either return the stock or go to jail. If you don't uncover the tampering but still win the case, it doesn't matter. If you lose the case, you can leak to the press the idea of jury tampering and see that a larger investigation takes place. Just be careful the investigation can't be traced to you."

"That's a good point because I could lose my license over this too."

"Well, you're not the practicing attorney in the case, so maybe not."

"You may have something there. You go back to bed, and I'll think about it some more."

"Keep me posted, and be careful."

"I love you, Pere. You'd make a great lawyer."

"I have my hands full with my students. I miss you. Talk to you soon. Bye."

Stephanie agonized over this new development for the next two hours. She paced her room and tried to think of every contingency. The bottom line was she wanted to win the case badly, and the possibility of jury tampering provided them with a new avenue of approach. She hired an investigation firm after her testimony in court on Wednesday morning. She waited until then because she wanted to be absolutely sure about her decision. She told no one.

When the phone rang in her hotel room at 10:45 on the following Saturday morning, she was reading a novel in her room, trying to gain some distance from the trial.

"We got him," Darrell said. Darrell Reynolds was one of the investigators Stephanie had hired last week. Darrell was about the age her father would have been, not too bright, but a thoroughly pleasant man. She had spent considerable time working with these guys over the last week and had become a little discouraged they had not found anything. "I nailed Ronald Carswell being handed a sack of money at Monument Valley Park about thirty minutes ago. I got two pictures of the transaction."

"Wonderful. I think I finally have a good reason to get going this morning. Do you know where the Antlers Hotel is?"

"Sure. Right downtown."

"There's a Revco around the corner with a one hour photo service. I think if we offer them a little extra money we can get the pictures developed right away. Can you meet me there?"

"I can be there in less than ten minutes."

"Good. I'll see you there." The pictures were good quality, though not absolute proof a crime had been committed, and so Stephanie made a bold decision to confront Carswell. "Do you have a microphone and recorder I can hide in my clothing?" Stephanie asked as she placed ten copies of the incriminating prints in her pocketbook. She and Darrell were standing outside the store on the sidewalk.

"At the office," Darrell responded.

"Let's get them, and you can show me how to use them."

"What do you have in mind?"

"These prints are great, but we need a confession. I'm going to interview Carswell."

"I'll be happy to remain outside the apartment in the event of problems."

"That would be great," and for the first time Stephanie wondered if she had gone a little crazy. She smiled when she thought about Karen and anger, and hoped her personal reasons for pursuing this case were not clouding her ability to think clearly.

They arrived at Carswell's apartment at 1:15 p.m. and were relieved to find his white Hyundai Accent parked alongside the curb. Darrell parked his blue Ford Taurus directly across the street with a clear view of Carswell's second story apartment. He came armed with a wireless receiver that could pick up Stephanie's conversation for up to half a mile and a shoulder holstered revolver.

Stephanie left the car with heart pounding. After climbing the twenty steps to the second floor apartment, she paused a moment to collect her breath before knocking on the door. When Carswell answered her knock, her heart jumped, and the next thing she knew she was standing in the hallway of a dingy building. "Mr. Carswell, my name is Stephanie Hathaway, and we need to talk."

"Oh, my God, I'm bein' hit by both sides," he said in a barely audible voice. Darrell picked up the comment, and smiled, relieved that his equipment was working flawlessly and that they already had the confession they needed.

"May I come in?" Stephanie asked, gaining some confidence. "What I have to say won't take long."

"Sure. Come in and sit. My lady is off with a friend." Carswell led her into a three room apartment that was badly needing a new coat of paint and presentable furniture. After staring at her for a moment, Carswell broke the ice. "What you got in mind?" He was beginning to think his ship had come in for a second time.

"Mr. Carswell, I have direct evidence the defense in the Hathaway case has tried to influence your vote. We have pictures of you receiving money at Monument Valley Park three hours ago. I'm sure you are aware that such actions are against the law."

"Shit, man. It wasn't nothin' but a little money to get me out of this dump. I didn't mean no harm. The man who made the deal promised nothin' bad would happen." Stephanie had her confession. Tension eased from her body. She got up to leave.

"The man who made the deal is probably right. I don't think the jury will get to vote in this case. If I'm right about this, you can keep the money and no one will ever learn about what you did. If there is a jury vote and you vote for the defense, I will present my evidence to the judge." With that, Stephanie exited the apartment in haste. Carswell continued to sit in his badly stained sofa, stunned, and staring blankly into space.

Stephanie and Darrell hurried back to his office to make four additional copies of the tape after first erasing her last comment. The edited tape ended with Carswell. Once that was done, she typed a letter to her uncle giving him an ultimatum: he would either make a statement in open court before the closing arguments in which he admitted he had failed in his responsibilities as a fiduciary and was returning all fourteen thousand shares of Noah Communications stock to her mother or she would submit the evidence of jury tampering to the proper authorities.

In taking these actions, she knew she had embarked on a high stakes game. If her uncle was smart, he could counter with a threat to disbar her for withholding the evidence from the judge. Stephanie was gambling her uncle would fear the prospect of jail more than his desire to harm her professionally. In the final analysis, she decided she could find a life outside of the law if the worst happened. After signing the letter, she went in search of Darrell. He was in the reception area of the office reading a magazine. He looked up as she entered the room.

"Okay Darrell, there is one more job for you to do and then a great big bonus will come your way. In this manila envelope is a letter for my uncle as well as copies of the tape and pictures. Please deliver it to him personally. Tell him the envelope contains important new information about the trial that demands his immediate attention."

"That should be no problem, Ma'am. You do good work. If you ever need another job bein' done, let me give you one of my cards." Reynolds returned the magazine to the coffee table and reached into his pocket for his keys.

"Actually I have two jobs for you," Stephanie replied smiling back at him. "Can you take me back to the Antlers?" She arrived back at her room at 5:15 p.m. with an important call to make.

"You did it, Pere. Your plan worked flawlessly. We caught my uncle red-handed." She then changed the conversation to more personal matters. She missed him terribly, and couldn't wait till the trial was over. The tension was finally getting to her. As she lay there on the bed talking with Perry, she couldn't help but conclude she had acted rather recklessly these last few days.

There is a longstanding tradition in courtroom procedure that closing arguments are made in reverse order from the opening statements. This meant Sophia Houghton was scheduled to have the last word. What happened at 10:00 a.m. on Monday June 10th had no precedent in this longstanding tradition. James Lawton rose from his seat at the defense table and approached the bench. He spoke with Judge Bullen in a hushed tone. Sophia Houghton watched the conference with some concern. She was soon invited to join them.

"Mr. Lawton has requested his client be permitted to briefly address the court before we begin the closing arguments. He claims Mr. Hathaway has something important to say that pertains to the case," Judge Bullen said while looking directly at Sophia Houghton.

"Do we know what Mr. Hathaway plans to say?" Houghton asked.

"No we don't," Mr. Lawton replied.

"Will I have the right to cross-examine?" Houghton asked.

"Yes, I can allow that, but only if it relates to this new information."

"Then I have no objection," Sophia Houghton said.

"You may proceed, Mr. Lawton." As the two lawyers returned to their seats, Judge Bullen invited William Hathaway to again take the stand. He walked slowly from his seat in the front of the courtroom, looking tired and uneasy. The courtroom was packed, and there was an eager air of expectation among the spectators, sensing something unprecedented was about to take place.

William Hathaway took his seat on the witness stand, was duly sworn in, and paused briefly to gather strength. He glanced quickly at his wife, Virginia, and then turned to face Judge Bullen directly. In a quiet, controlled voice, he began.

"After considerable reflection over the weekend, Judge Bullen, I would like to change a portion of my testimony. After consultation with my two accountants, Mr. Richard Settering and Mr. Fred Cummings, we now feel we were negligent in our duties as fiduciaries with respect to Mrs. Harriet Hathaway." There was collective shock in the courtroom, a stunned silence among the spectators as they hung on every word. Karen grabbed Patrick's hand, and stared in disbelief at her father. "Further, we agree that Mrs. Hathaway may have legitimate reasons for claiming she was confused about the documents we asked her to sign during the years in question."

Stephanie looked across at Ronald Carswell and wondered what was going through his mind. She also wondered about the female juror that had tipped them off.

It was a remarkable ending to this ordeal, and she was both relieved it was over and ready to go home.

"Therefore, Your Honor," William Hathaway continued, "I believe it is only fair the company return fourteen thousand shares of Noah Communications stock to Mrs. Harriet Hathaway. We will begin this process tomorrow morning."

"This is a remarkable turn of events, Mr. Hathaway," Judge Bullen said as he looked directly at the President of Noah Communications. "Were you coerced or influenced in any way in making this statement?"

"No, Your Honor, with the exception of the gentle tug of my conscience which grew louder as the weekend progressed." Karen liked that answer and wished it was a statement of truth because that would mean her father was indeed a human being. She doubted it though, and was dying to ask Stephanie for an explanation of this bizarre turn of events.

"Thank you for your statement Mr. Hathaway. This case is now closed with the exception of the matter of expenses. Ms. Houghton, how much money did Mrs. Hathaway receive for the sale of the stock she did not know she was selling?"

"Nine hundred and sixty thousand dollars, Your Honor."

"Please submit a copy of all your expenses to me, Ms. Houghton. I rule the defense is responsible for paying all trial expenses in excess of nine hundred and sixty thousand dollars." He then turned to address the jury, thanked them for their service, and told them they were now released from their duty and could return to their normal lives. He rapt his gavel one last time and left the courtroom through his private door behind the bench.

Karen caught the eye of her cousin and looked at her in disbelief. Stephanie smiled back at Karen, though she was upset with the Judge's final ruling about fees. She then proceeded to the plaintiff's table to congratulate Sophia Houghton.

William Hathaway arrived at work at 7:30 on the Tuesday morning after the trial. He called a brief senior staff meeting for nine in the conference room across the hall from his office. He entered the room at 9:05.

"Gentlemen, we had a bad week," he said after taking a seat at the head of the small table and smiling at each of the six men in attendance. He wanted them to know beyond a shadow of doubt where his mood was. The image he projected was upbeat, and he was clearly back to making money. "So we have some catching up to do. Jeff," and he directed his glance at Jeffery Halligan, the chief financial officer of the company, "I want you to oversee the transfer of fourteen thousand shares of company stock to my sister-in-law. This will end this sordid matter, and there will be no further discussion of it. I also want you to begin the process with the SEC of taking Noah public. It is time we have stock with real market value."

"I'll get right to it, Sir."

"Thank you, Jeff. Stuart," Stuart Womple was the Vice President for Development, "do you have any new acquisitions for me to consider?"

"We are looking at stations in Omaha and in Colby Kansas. I'm not sure the numbers are right with the Kansas station, but the one in Omaha looks promising. I'll have a recommendation on your desk by the end of the week."

"Good. Finally, Patrick, how is your sales force looking?"

"We're about seventy-five percent there."

"Finish up please. We need to get those software sales off the ground. Recently you've been on a paid vacation. It's nice to see you back at work." There were a few snickers in the room in response to that last comment. Patrick didn't like the sarcasm in his father-in-law's voice or the snickers from his colleagues, but he dutifully responded.

"Yes, Sir.

"That completes it, Gentlemen. We all need to get back to work. Phil, would you remain for a few minutes, please?" As the other five corporate officers went their separate ways, Philip Duke moved his chair closer to his boss. He was pretty convinced what they had to discuss needed privacy, and more than a little nervous his boss would blame him for the recent turn of events. When the room had emptied,

William Hathaway spoke in subdued tones to his security chief. "Do you have any idea what went wrong, Phil?"

"Nothing concrete, Mr. Hathaway. Reese Baldwin reported everything went well with his part of the operation."

"The Coleman lady must have betrayed us somehow," William Hathaway said. "The only other possibility is Houghton became paranoid and hired people to watch all the jurors. If that is the case, she went fishing and got lucky."

"I agree with you about Coleman. We must have missed something big about her in the investigation. It would have helped if we had had more time."

"Don't blame yourself, Phil. You may be right about the time element. There's no way we should pay the rest of that money, is there?"

"Absolutely not, Sir. Carswell and Coleman can't implicate us without getting in trouble themselves."

"That's my thinking too. This damn case has already cost me plenty."

"I know what you mean, Sir?"

"That leaves one more thing for you to do. Can you remove those listening devices from my daughter's house? I'm already in enough trouble with my family. The last thing I need is for one of them to stumble on those things."

"We'll watch the house, and remove them as soon as it is empty."

"Good Phil, and thank you again for all of your efforts. It's a comfort knowing I have at least one loyal friend."

"You have many loyal friends, Mr. Hathaway. Don't you dare let this thing get you down. You'll come roaring back. I'm convinced of that."

"I hope so," and William Hathaway stood to shake hands with his security chief and then returned across the hall to his office.

After lunch, a week to the day following the bizarre end to the trial, about half an hour from the time she had put both kids down, Karen heard a car on the gravel road approaching the house. She looked out the window expecting to see Patrick and was surprised to see her mother's car coming up the driveway. As her mother opened her car door, Karen ran outside to greet her. The two women fell into each other's arms. "I love you, Mom," Karen said as she slowly broke away from her. Virginia Hathaway burst into tears as she hugged her daughter for a second time.

"I love you too," she finally said.

"How's Daddy?" Karen asked as the two women ascended the front steps.

"All business. It's as if nothing happened last week. The only thing he said to me about the trial is that he won't talk about it. There is nothing left between us."

"I'm so sorry, Mom," and Karen embraced her Mom and held her. After soaking up her daughter's compassion, Virginia said.

"We need to talk, Sweetheart. Are the kids napping?"

"Yes, both are sound asleep."

"Good. My timing is perfect."

"How about the deck? It's such a nice day."

"That sounds good. I need your gentle wisdom." After the two women were comfortably seated on Karen's deck, Virginia continued. "What happened last Monday, Karen? This strange man came to the house late Saturday afternoon, and your father went immediately to the office. He didn't get back home until after eleven, and he looked tired and beaten. I tried to get him to talk about what was troubling him, but he only said I would learn about it on Monday. I didn't learn a thing except that his confession was totally out of character. Does Stephanie know anything about this?"

"They caught Daddy trying to influence the jury. Stephanie wouldn't provide details, but the long and the short of it is that Daddy tried to buy a verdict."

"I can't believe that, Sweetheart. Your father has become a monster," Virginia said as she burst into tears again. Karen reached across and took her hand.

"This is all so sad, Mom."

"I'm leaving him, Karen. This jury thing is the last straw. I've always liked Harriet and never thought of her as a liar. I can't believe your father would try to take away her inheritance. Thirty-five years ago I married a nice Christian man and now he has become a monster. I'm terrified of leaving him, Karen. You'll have to help me. That's why I'm here."

"What about living with us? Have you thought about counseling?"

"He's the one who's leaving. I'm going to tell him tonight as soon as he gets home. I'm so scared this will become permanent. I have never loved another man."

"I think you both need counseling, Mom."

"Can you see your father going to a marriage counselor? I need counseling. I'm the first one to admit that. One of the things I want you to do is ask your friend Frannie to recommend a psychologist for me."

"I'd be happy to. Maybe Daddy will come with you when he really hits bottom?"

"That would be nice, but right now it's as if nothing has happened. I can't believe he could be that cold and ruthless."

"Would you ever go back with him?"

"Absolutely. I can't picture myself living with anybody else, but he must become a human being again. When he learns to hug Maggie, then I will welcome him home."

"Me too Mom."

"He's been so hard on you, Sweetheart."

"I know, but it has been my fault too. I feel so guilty about this trial, like I betrayed both of you."

"You certainly didn't betray me. Stephanie is like your sister, and Harriet was wrongfully cheated. I really suspected that from the beginning. There is a part of me that is pleased with the result of the trial. Maybe it can serve as a catalyst to turn your father around."

"I hope so Mom. You are a very special lady," and Karen got up from her chair to embrace her mother. "Let's go check on the kids."

～

Three hours before he received his eviction notice from Virginia Hathaway, William Hathaway received a disturbing call from Ronald Carswell. The receptionist hesitated to put the call through, but there was something in the tone of Carswell's voice that led her to change her mind. "Am I speaking with Mr. William Hathaway?" Carswell asked, trying to fight off his nervousness.

"Yes you are," replied the voice on the other end.

"Where's the rest of my money, man? We had a deal."

"Bribery is against the law, Mr. Carswell." William Hathaway instantly recognized who he was talking to and became deeply disturbed.

"So is messin' with juries." Carswell was gaining confidence. He loved the fact he was screwing a big shot, and he wanted more money. "Maybe we both belong in jail. You certainly do, and I wouldn't mind puttin' you there. Here's the thing, man. I get off of work at 5:00 on Friday. From there, I'm drivin' directly to Monument Valley Park. Same place your goon gave me the first five. I'll wait till five thirty. If I don't leave with another five grand, you're going to jail." And then he abruptly hung up the phone. William Hathaway buried his face in his hands. Fifteen minutes later he instructed Philip Duke to meet the demands. The thought of jail was terrifying.

～

On Thursday after the July 4th weekend, Virginia Hathaway drove to the Cheyenne Mountain Presbyterian Church for a nine o'clock appointment. She was meeting Rev. James W. Yount, a retired minister, whose former church allowed him to keep an office there. Yount supplemented his retirement income with a part-time psychology practice.

Yount was a slight man, sixty-eight years old, with a wealth of wisdom and compassion. He greeted Virginia with a firm handshake and a warm smile. After seating her in a comfortable office chair, Virginia began her story by relating all the sordid details of the recent trial with the exception of the jury tampering information. "I remember reading about it in the paper, Virginia. It must have been a trying time for both families."

"It certainly was that Reverend Yount."

"Jim please. I no longer preach advice, but rather I try to listen as best as I can."

"I need advice Jim, and lots of it," Virginia said as she smiled shyly over at him. "My husband and I have been separated now for almost three weeks, and he hasn't even called me. I want him back, Jim, but I want the kind man I originally married," and Virginia burst into tears.

"The first step is to get him here, Virginia, and for the two of you to start talking again. Just because he hasn't called, don't think he isn't also hurting. His entire life has collapsed. There is often a process involved in coping with stress of this kind. The first thing that happens is denial. Your husband probably went right back to work as if nothing had happened."

"That's exactly what he did." Virginia was beginning to feel better about being there. This man certainly seemed to know his business. Bless you Frannie for getting us together, she thought.

"If the process unfolds in the usual pattern, there will come a time when he begins to lose his ability to cope, and then there's a crisis. Once the crisis occurs, we may have a chance to save him and your marriage."

"That would be wonderful, Jim. There's something about my husband I want to share with you I have never discussed with anyone before. I do it only because the one thing I know about psychology is that childhood trauma often produces lasting consequences."

"Unless it is properly dealt with, that is often the case."

"My husband had an awful experience when he was eight years old. My mother-in-law told me about it right after we were married. There were three of them—Bill was the oldest, Peter two years younger, and Katherine, the sister, was four years younger than Bill.

"In preparation for Halloween, Bill's mother had taken them all shopping for costumes. As they were walking back to their parked car on a fairly crowded street, Bill's mother told him to take Kate's hand. He did, but as they came up to a traffic light, she leapt away for some reason, ran in front of a car, and was instantly killed. Bill has carried that guilt with him for the last fifty years, and the situation was made worse because his father never really forgave him."

"Wow, that certainly was a lot for an eight year old kid to deal with. It may explain some things. Do you and your husband attend a church, Virginia? I hate to get personal, but it is part of my job."

"Yes, we are members of the Abundant Life Assembly of God Church."

"Have you always been members of that church?"

"No, we actually started as Episcopalians."

"Who made the decision to switch? You or your husband?"

"It was mostly his decision. I was perfectly happy where we were. All this happened when he moved the company from Philadelphia to here."

"Are you happy with your current affiliation?"

"That's hard to say. Our son is the associate pastor. He is furious at me for leaving Bill so I've stopped going to church for the time being. Our daughter Karen won't set foot in there. She claims it opposes everything good about modern life."

"She may have a point there, Virginia. I want to be very careful here because I don't want to malign your faith, but it all adds up. Your husband may have sought a more fundamental approach to scripture because of all that guilt he has carried with him since he was a child. The flip side of guilt is salvation, and churches like the Assembly of God put more emphasis on that part of the Christian message than more mainline churches do. Let me ask a related question. Does your husband have issues of control?"

"I'm not exactly sure what you mean, but he certainly can be controlling. I was speaking with my daughter a few weeks ago, and she thinks her father's motivation for cheating Harriet had much more to do with control of the company than money."

"She might be right about that too. This undoubtedly goes far deeper than his company. Gaining control of all aspects of his life is a strategy for keeping guilt at bay. He is probably also very competitive. His need to win could very well be driven by a need to show his father."

"I think you have my husband pretty well described, and now I'm beginning to feel a little guilty myself. It doesn't seem fair to be saying all these unkind things behind his back, and some of our problems as a couple may have a lot to do with me."

"Thank you for that, Virginia. Let's hope your husband will come too so we can deal fairly with him. I also admire your honesty. Marriage relationships involve two as you suggest, and both partners usually share responsibility for failure."

"How do we get to my part of the problem?"

"That's a very good question. From what I have seen of you thus far, you seem to be quite psychologically healthy. Are there any psychological skeletons hanging in your closet?" he asked as he looked across at her and smiled.

"None that I'm aware of," Virginia replied, shifting her glance away from him a little nervously.

"Good. Here's how I like to work. I believe most psychological health is gained from self-learning and reflection. So I'm going to give you two books to read about marriage. Then I want you to come back, and we'll discuss them in terms of how they apply to your marriage. How does that sound?"

"It sounds fine. I want my marriage back, and I'm certainly willing to make changes."

"Then there are lots of reasons for optimism."

"Thank you, Jim. I can't wait to get started on this."

～

Two weeks later Karen engaged Kristin McKnight. Kristin was a little bleary eyed at eight o'clock in the morning, but Karen wasn't too worried. She wasn't going very far, and Sheila, her neighbor, was right next door. She instructed Kristin to pick her up with the kids at the Covered Treasures just before lunch.

She arrived at the store a little before 9:00 after an invigorating three mile walk, and immediately joined two other female customers for a cup of gourmet coffee. They talked about their children and husbands, and events taking place in the little elementary school. Karen asked lots of questions about the school because, although Maggie was only two and a half, she was already starting to worry about her at school.

Alex came and went, and it wasn't until 10:30 that she was finally able to join Karen for real conversation. The other two women left a little before ten. "Can you tell me about the trial, Karen? The ending was a tad bizarre."

"Not really. Stephanie said little about it except that they discovered some new information they confronted Daddy with." It bothered her she couldn't be totally honest with her best friend, but Stephanie had warned her that nobody could know about the jury tampering. She felt a little guilty about telling her mother. "That information somehow made him change his mind."

"It must have been some pretty damaging stuff because your Dad is no patsy."

"You're right about that. They must have somehow given Daddy the 'devil's choice,' you know damned if you do and damned if you don't, and I use that analogy because that's how I think of Daddy."

"You mean as a devil?"

"Yes, if asshole is its modern equivalent," and she burst into tears. Alex moved closer to her on the sofa so she could hug her friend.

"This thing still has you all torn up."

"You bet it does. He's blood you know," she continued through her tears. "I can't seem to shake him loose, to get him out of my head and my life."

"Blood certainly does complicate things. You know we've talked a lot about forgiveness in the past, and it seems the burden has been placed solely on you. A relationship involves two. It sure would be easier if your father would move a little toward you."

"If he would only hug Maggie and mean it, my heart would melt. My mom used that example the other day, and she hit the nail on the head. That would mean he is a human being with emotions, feelings, and a heart that works."

"I know it would make a huge difference for you. You are one of the most loving people I have ever met."

"I knew I would feel better coming to the store to see you this morning," Karen said as she smiled warmly at her special friend who had resumed her original place on the sofa.

"Listen, I've got to get back to work, but I have a favor to ask. I called David, remember Patrick's racquetball friend we joked about that first day of the trial. He would love to meet you and see Patrick again. So I invited him to dinner. I thought the four of us could get together next week."

"Sounds wonderful. What can I do?"

"Invite him to spend the night after dinner. I don't want him staying with me yet, and I also don't want him to have to drive back to Denver late at night."

"No problem. If things work out, you can join us for breakfast the next morning."

"Thanks, Karen, I knew you'd come through," Alex said as she stood up from the sofa. "I'll call him tonight and let him know that's an option." Karen smiled at her friend as she returned to the checkout counter. She reached across to pick up the latest issue of *Woman's Day* which would occupy her time for the next hour until Kristin arrived with the kids.

∾

Patrick left work early on the first Wednesday in August. Karen was working outside weeding the flower gardens around the house when Patrick's car came up the driveway at 3:45 p.m. He found Justin busily engaged in his playpen, and Maggie following behind her mother with a small plastic trowel. He leaned over to kiss his two favorite women, walked over to the deck to gather up Justin, and returned to join the gardeners.

"It's still war at work, Sweetheart."

"What do you mean?"

"I'm the bad guy, the crook, the traitor. Nobody smiles at me or comes by the office to chat. I've become persona non grata at Noah Communications. They question my loyalty, and blame me for your father's downfall."

"You better leave there as soon as you can," she said as she came over to Justin and tickled his nose.

"I agree. Jason and I talked about it for two hours over lunch. He feels like the new software is almost ready for me to go to venture capitalists and bankers. I also want to get rid of all this guilt I have about cheating your father. I really should give him a percentage of the new company."

"If you do that, you can say goodbye to me," she said as she looked up at him and laughed. "I want to be your first investor, anyway."

"I hope I can find other people to take that risk."

"I hope you can't. Even if you get backers, I want to be a part of it."

"Do you understand what you'd be investing in, Sweetheart? I've learned a lot about fiduciary responsibilities in the last few months."

"Yes, as a matter of fact, I do," she said as she looked over at him and smiled. "I would be investing in you and Jason, and I can't think of a safer bet."

"I don't know if I could take the pressure of you being my boss."

"No, Pat. A silent partner."

"I love you, Karen. That's such a nice offer even if I never take it. Let's take the kids over to the lake. You can walk with Justin on your back, and I'll throw rocks again with Maggie. I want to keep working on that."

"Sounds like fun, as long as we're back before 5:30. I still have a few things to get ready for dinner.

Patrick gave notice the next day. He thought the one thing his father-in-law deserved was a personal meeting. He knocked on William Hathaway's office door at 5:10.

The closed door was the first thing he found to be unusual. When William Hathaway invited him in, he found the office in disarray. Papers cluttered his desk, and the coffee table was littered with file folders and more papers. "Yes, Patrick. What can I do for you? As you can see from the mess of papers around here, I'm way behind. I guess I've lost some motivation for all this hard work."

"You've had a tough two months, Sir."

"You could say that. Whose side were you on anyway? I've been trying to figure that out from day one."

"Perhaps it's most honest to say I was neutral," Patrick said as he stepped further into the office. "Torn between my loyalty to you and to my wife."

"Your wife and her cousin got their revenge, didn't they?"

"I'm not sure I would call it revenge."

"Call it what it was, Patrick. That's always the best policy. So, what's up? To what do I owe this rare pleasure?" These last words were uttered with such bitter sarcasm Patrick wanted to flee. He had never heard William Hathaway speak in that way. Though sometimes distant, he had always been polite, his instinct was to act as a gentleman. The only solution was to get right to the point.

"I will be brief, Sir. I have my letter of resignation with me, and I thought the least I could do was give you a personal explanation. The software project is completed, the sales force in place, and I'm not sure I'm a good fit for Noah."

"I can agree with you on that. There's no need for you to give the letter to me. It will only get lost among all these other papers. Put it on Nora's desk as you leave, and she can deal with it in the morning. Is Jason going with you?"

"Yes Sir. We're forming our own company."

"So you're stealing him too." Patrick couldn't wait to get out of there. He was both embarrassed by the tone of the conversation and extremely uncomfortable because of the partial truth of that last statement. All that guilt was resurfacing. Deciding not to respond to that last barb, he simply stated.

"Before I go, I just want to thank you, Mr. Hathaway. I have learned a lot in the last two years, and you have paid me well. I wish you the best of luck, Sir," and with that, he turned quickly and bolted from the office. William Hathaway left the office to go home to his stark, one bedroom apartment fifteen minutes later.

～

Two weeks following his meeting with Patrick, William Hathaway sat behind that same desk trying to decide what to do. It was only a little after four p.m., far earlier than his usual time for going home, but he was merely going through the motions at work, putting up a good show, and he knew it. Maybe he could quietly leave unnoticed. Maybe a new setting would lighten his mood.

He arrived at his new home on East Untah Street fifteen minutes later. His sparsely furnished apartment was both an oasis and a source of dread. The President of Noah Communications watched Fox news while he waited for his prepackaged meat loaf dinner to warm in the microwave.

The news was hard to focus on. He had little interest in learning about the Clintons's vacation on Martha's Vineyard, although he did wonder briefly about what he would do in similar circumstances. He wasn't a golfer, and sitting on a beach had little appeal. He worried about his lack of hobbies other than work, and decided he needed to acquire some.

Living alone was not easy especially when dinner was over at 5:45, and he was having difficulty with sleep. After leafing through a few magazines, he headed back to his car a little after seven.

The drive to Gabrielle Coleman's condominium on East Kiowa Street took less than ten minutes. At a conscious level he had no idea why he was driving there. He certainly didn't want to run into her face-to-face. At a subconscious level, he was afraid to speculate as to what he was doing. There were so many new things about his life that were mysterious and quite frankly a little scary, but at least this little jaunt would fill some time.

The condominium complex consisted of three, eight story buildings, arranged in triangular form with a large swimming pool in the middle. The upper floors provided great views of the city and mountains, and the landscaping was meticulously maintained. He drove two blocks beyond the complex to a Walgreen's pharmacy where he parked his car. He decided against the visitors's lot, which was located just inside the security gate.

He walked back toward the complex trying to regain a picture of Ms. Coleman in his head. He remembered Philip Duke's detailed description of her as being in her mid forties, somewhat overweight, with short, curly brown hair, and large, professional looking glasses. He had spent a brief moment during the last day of the trial looking over the jurors, trying to pick out who had betrayed him. Carswell was easy, and he thought he had recognized Gabrielle Coleman too.

How had she betrayed him? Why had she betrayed her own interests and given up the rest of the money? Maybe in fact she had not betrayed him. Maybe the Stephanie Hathaway cabal had been lucky with Carswell, but he suspected Coleman had tipped them off. He wondered how he would have responded if she had tried to blackmail him like the Carswell kid had done. It's only money, and Harriet has most of it now, he thought with real bitterness as he passed by the complex with his eyes firmly focused on the sidewalk.

Stephanie and her mother had struck it rich, that's for sure, he mused as he turned the corner, which took him away from East Kiowa. There are always two sides to a story. He had earned that money with his hard work and sound strategic decision making. And yet maybe they had a point, he thought as his dark mood softened somewhat. What would his brother Peter think about the mess he had created? He was glad Peter was one person he didn't have to provide with answers. A wan smile flashed across his face. He was relieved for the moment that he remembered how to smile.

As he came up to a Ben and Jerry's store on the next block, he purchased a double scoop of butter pecan ice cream. He sat down on one of the small metal tables outside trying to people watch and extend his lightening mood. He smiled at the first few passersby, and then abruptly left. Sadly, he wasn't really interested, not even in the ice cream. With little else to do, he returned to his car and drove home. He dreaded the thought of sleep, of lying on his bed and staring up at the ceiling for what seemed like endless hours of anxious insomnia, but even fitful sleep was better than watching people.

~

September of 1995 was a beautiful month in the Springs. With moderate temperatures and clear blue skies, the Colorado outdoors was crying out to be enjoyed. The first problem for William Hathaway was that he had no idea what to do with his weekends. In addition, he somehow missed seeing the clear blue skies. His world was clouded in gray.

At least today was Sunday, and there was church. He had promised Billy at a recent dinner outing he would make a greater effort to get back to church. Billy had assured him the warm community of the Abundant Life Assembly of God Church would do wonders for his declining spirits. He wasn't sure about that, but he felt it was important to do this for Billy. Billy had been his one lifeline as he struggled to get his life back together.

He was proud of his son. He could not remember ever having an experience of felt dependency on another person until his recent change in fortune, but he was becoming comfortable with this new situation. It felt good when Billy helped him make a decision or just came over to spend some time.

So he left his apartment at 9:15 a.m. for the short walk to the church feeling energized and believing he had a real need to get right with God. One important reason he and Billy had chosen this apartment was because it was within easy walking distance of the church.

Located on Palmer Park Road, the Abundant Life Assembly of God Church was a large, attractive, sprawling, two-story structure of white brick with gold trim. The sanctuary was built to seat a thousand people in comfortable movie theatre-like seats. The pulpit was situated at the center of a large stage with the choir and six piece band located toward the back of the stage in front of a white neon cross. A gym/ recreation center flanked one side of the sanctuary with an auditorium flanking the other side.

William Hathaway smiled in recognition at the greeter inside the main door of the church who handed him a bulletin. He took a seat on the right hand side toward the back. Two-thirds of the seats in the sanctuary were taken, and congregation members were quieting down in anticipation of beginning the service. Billy was seated on the left side of the stage, and his father smiled over at him in an attempt to gain his attention. Unfortunately, the two Hathaway men were unable to connect. Though disappointed, William Hathaway was not surprised. Billy would not be looking for him in the back of the church because the family always sat front and center.

When Pastor Ty asked the members of the congregation to join him in prayer, William Hathaway's mind began to wander. His energy drained, and his upbeat mood dissipated as he bowed his head and tried to think about a God who cared for him. He stood with the congregation as Pastor Ty announced the opening hymn and the words of "Jesus Is The Sweetest Name I Know" flashed up on the movie screen. There were no hymnals. And then, as an overwhelming sense of panic engulfed him, William Hathaway abruptly left the church, and returned to his apartment in a haze of fog-like dread.

≈

"Mom!" Karen said in response to her mother's answering her telephone.

"Hi, Sweetheart. I've been missing you lately. What have you guys been up to?"

"Oh, the same old stuff. Pat's been working long hours setting up his new company. The kids's are fine. Justin's having a ball with those new toys you got him for his birthday. He seems to be getting into more things daily. Maggie's so easy! Bless her heart."

"I'm glad Justin likes the toys. He's a precious little boy."

"I can't believe we're already into October, and we haven't taken the kids or ourselves to the mountains to see the Aspens. I bet all the leaves are down by now."

"Probably getting pretty cold up there too."

"I'm sure you're right about that. Listen, Mom. Let me change the subject for a minute. I just got off the phone with Billy, and he's real worried about Dad."

"Funny, he never called me."

"We're both persona non grata. He probably debated long and hard over which one of us to call."

"What did Billy have to say?"

"Mostly that Dad's not doing well. Says he's lost weight and looks rather fatigued from lack of sleep."

"That's interesting. Your father's never had a problem with sleep."

"According to Billy, he's pretty down on himself and discouraged. They went out for dinner last night. Billy said he was shocked at the change."

"His past seems to be finally catching up with him," Virginia Hathaway said without really intending to be mean-spirited, but it came out anyway.

"Should we do anything about this, Mom?"

"Do you want to do something about it, Sweetheart?"

"Absolutely not. I have no idea what I would say to Daddy."

"I don't either. Jim Yount told me your father has to hit bottom before anything can be done to help him."

"How do you know when that happens?"

"I'm not sure, but I'll talk to Jim about it on Wednesday. I have another appointment at nine."

"How are things going with him, Mom?"

"Great. He's teaching me what it means to be a partner in a good marriage. He's also helping me learn to stand up for my own interests. I hope your father and I get a second chance."

"Me too. It's not much fun thinking of the two of you divorced."

"I know what you mean. Have you heard from Stephanie recently?"

"Nothing really since the trial. Maybe it's time for me to call her."

"Give them all my best when you do."

"Don't forget we're doing our thing with Alex and her Mom next Monday."

"I have it on my calendar, Sweetheart. I'll let you know what Jim says about your Dad. I worry about him all the time. I just can't believe we got ourselves into this big mess."

"You're the best, Mom. I better hang up and change Justin before he loses that sopping diaper. Talk to you soon. I love you."

"I love you too, honey. Thanks for filling me in on Dad. Hug those two wonderful kids. Bye."

"Bye." Virginia Hathaway had put up a good front with Karen on the phone. In truth, she was really shaken by this recent news about her husband. She immediately called Jim to report the latest developments. He reassured her this was part of the process of dealing with a stressful loss, that he may in fact be entering a final conflict phase, and that the worse thing she could do would be to run over and comfort him. She wasn't fully reassured, but she resisted for the time being the urge to run to him.

Billy took a different approach. He worked with Nora Clooney, his father's trusted receptionist and keeper of his schedule, to literally kidnap William Hathaway. The office was becoming scared too. Nora cleared her boss's appointments for the Friday before the Thanksgiving holiday, and scheduled the corporate jet to take Billy and his father to Washington DC. The plan was to spend Friday night and most of Saturday at Ivanwald, one of the twenty-four homes owned by the Family. The weekend prayer retreat to heal William Hathaway was to be led by Scott Hildebrand, the charismatic leader of the organization.

Scott Hildebrand grew up in a small town in Southern Ohio. He attended Ohio State University where he led a schizophrenic life. On the one hand, he was handsome, friendly, a leader in his fraternity, and a ladies man with a legendary reputation. On the other hand, he was a committed member of Campus Crusade for Christ.

Scott graduated from OSU in 1958, married his high school sweetheart, Betsy Tilson, and remained in Columbus where he became a fundraiser for the OSU chapter of Campus Crusade. Success at the local level led to promotion to Campus Crusade headquarters in Orlando Florida in 1963. While in Orlando, Scott was introduced to the Family. He became an active member in 1965, and its leader in 1981.

Scott Hildebrand has spent more time counseling Presidents than Billy Graham. His organization has established prayer groups in every Congressional district in the country, and throughout the world. His members form an underground of Christ's men in government whose goal is to establish a Christian world order led from Washington. As the Noah Communications jet touched down at Dulles Airport at 5:30 p.m. on Friday November 19th, he was there along with Senator Tom Brownstone from Kansas to welcome William and Billy Hathaway to Washington.

Friday evening was kept low key by design. The Hathaways had dinner with Scott, Senator Brownstone, Justice Paul Dugan of the Supreme Court, and Congressman Jackson from the Springs. The dinner was held at the Cedars, the Family's main retreat center in the DC area. Conversation during the affair alternated between prayerful appeals to Christ for humility, forgiveness, and guidance, and locker room banter that focused on professional sports. The entire group retired early to Ivanwald, a handsome, two-story colonial in Arlington Virginia.

The main event of the weekend began at 10:00 sharp on Saturday morning. In a small conference room off from the living room at Ivanwald, twelve men met around a solid, dark oak table. In addition to the six dinner companions from Friday night, the group included the senior Senator from Mississippi, two members of Congress from Iowa and Georgia, an army Lieutenant General, the former Secretary of Commerce under Ronald Reagan, and Frank Segwick, the CEO of General Motors.

Scott Hildebrand opened the Bible study session with prayer. "Heavenly Jesus, those gathered here this morning are among your chosen servants who carry out the work of establishing your Kingdom. Keep us humble in disposition and ever obedient to your word. Of special interest this morning, we express our gratitude to brother Hathaway for his dedicated work in spreading your message to the world. He has presented that message truthfully, and with the sole intention of furthering your glory. Help us this morning to heal his heart, and to re-energize his spirit so he can continue his important work on your behalf. We make this petition in your name, God's glorious and only Son, our Master and Savior, Jesus Christ. Amen."

As Scott opened his eyes to the brothers at his table, he continued: "Senator Nicolls, would you please begin reading our scripture lesson for today from First Samuel, chapter sixteen, verses one through thirteen." Senator Nicolls, after a brief pause to allow those present to open the Bibles before them to the appropriate passage, began in a deep baritone voice:

> Yahweh said to Samuel, "How long will you go on mourning over Saul when I have rejected him as King of Israel? Fill your horn with oil and go. I am sending you to Jesse of Bethlehem, for I have chosen myself a King among his sons."

Brother Nicolls faithfully recounted the story of Samuel's trip to Bethlehem where he interviewed several sons of Jesse whom Yahweh rejected. "God does not see as man sees; man looks at appearances, but Yahweh looks at the heart" (16:8), brother Nicolls intoned. The Senator concluded the first reading with the anointing of David (16: 11-13):

> Samuel then asked Jesse, "Are these all the sons you have?" He answered, "There is still one left, the youngest; he is out looking after sheep." Then Samuel said to Jesse, "Send for him; we will not sit down to eat until he comes." Jesse had him sent for, a boy of fresh complexion, with fine eyes and pleasant bearing.

Yahweh said, "Come, anoint him, for this is the one." At this, Samuel took the horn of oil and anointed him where he stood with his brothers; and the spirit of Yahweh seized on David and stayed with him from that day on.

"Thank you brother Nicolls. Brother Jackson, would you read us the story of King David's sin. Please turn to Second Samuel, chapter eleven." Congressman Jackson read the story of David and Bathsheba, how he saw her bathing on a roof, how he slept with her which caused her pregnancy, and how he sent her husband Uriah the Hittite to his death in battle so he could marry her.

"Thank you brother Jackson. Brother Hathaway," and he looked directly at William Hathaway, "would you conclude our study today by reading First Chronicles, chapter twenty-nine, verses twenty-six to thirty." In a hesitant voice that gained strength slowly as his concentration on the passage at hand increased, William Hathaway read:

David son of Jesse had reigned over the whole of Israel. His reign over Israel had lasted forty years; he had reigned in Hebron for seven years, and in Jerusalem for thirty-three. He died in happy old age, with his fill of days, of riches, of honor. Then his son Solomon succeeded him.

"Thank you brother Hathaway. Gentlemen: how do these passages from our holy scriptures speak to us today?" Justice Dugan was the first to speak.

"From the first reading, it is clear God chose David for a special mission, to be King of Israel. That is how God works in the world. He chooses great men to carry out his purposes."

"And that great man David sinned," interjected Senator Gaylord from Mississippi. "That's no big deal. We all sin. I'm sure if we had more time this morning brother Scott would have had us read about all the great things David did in his service to our Lord. It is those deeds that are truly important, not the fact that he was human and thus a sinner."

"Well spoken, brother Gaylord," General Lewis said with enthusiasm. "Let me add that God sees his servants quite differently than we do."

After pausing briefly to see if other members wanted to comment, Scott Hildebrand looked directly again at William Hathaway. "Let me conclude our session this morning by saying that God only granted old age, riches, and honor to his servants in Israel with whom he was well pleased." William Hathaway bowed his head, and struggled to fight back tears.

"We bless you, brother Hathaway," Scott continued, "for your one million dollar contribution last year to my former employer, Campus Crusade for Christ."

"The Navigators would be unable to continue their important work of spreading the gospel of Jesus Christ without your generous support," Justice Dugan said as he stood up from his seat beside William Hathaway to embrace his friend.

"Diddo for Focus on the Family," said brother Segwick from across the table with a big smile. "Your financial support and Board dedication are without equal."

"As every Board member of the Family knows," Scott Hildebrand said, again looking directly at William Hathaway, "our operational budget would not survive without your generous support. Your obedience to Christ is unparalleled. Your work at Noah Communications inspires us all." And after a final pause, Scott concluded: "Gentlemen, please join me in prayer. Lord Jesus, we thank you for your special servant William Hathaway. May he continue to serve your Kingdom by proclaiming your message and through the generous donations of the fruits of his labor. It is clear to all of us at this table that you bless him, that you honor him, and that you continue to guide him in his efforts to serve you. We praise your name Lord Jesus, and we thank you for the trust you place in us for the building of your Kingdom. May we always be humble and willing to obey your commands. Amen." Eleven men rose from their seats at the table to embrace the President of Noah Communications.

≈

After a light lunch and warm goodbyes from his ten brothers, William Hathaway and Billy left the Ivanwald grounds for a walk in the park across the street. As they climbed the gentle hill along the gravel walking path, William Hathaway paused, turned toward his son, and said: "The sky is blue Billy. You have given me my life back." And then he threw his arms around his son and hugged him for the first time in more than twenty-five years.

"Dad, it's so great to have you back," Billy said as he separated himself from his father. "I really started to get scared when you bolted from church last month."

"You are a loyal and a good son," he said as he turned into the path and began walking again.

"You know, Dad, how Jesus speaks to Family members?"

"In our special prayer groups," William Hathaway responded.

"Well, he's talking to me now too. When I asked him in prayer three weeks ago about you, he said: "Take him to Washington.""

"Thank you for obeying son. You and Jesus have made me a new man."

"Mainly Jesus, Dad," Billy said smiling. "Wow, was that an impressive bunch. Is General Lewis really the Family's main man with General Suharto of Indonesia?"

"He and Scott."

"What do they do over there?"

"Pray together. Jesus and our Family members have helped the General to understand the real nature of the Communist threat in his country."

"I know they have killed lots of them."

"Thousands," replied his father.

"That's good. It's important that atheistic Communists die. You know that wonderful Mr. Segwick gave me a sermon last night."

"What did you and our friend from General Motors discuss?"

"Free market capitalism. Recessions and economic downturns generally are caused by human meddling and the work of Satan. Getting the government out of the way, allows God and the guiding wisdom of the market to provide prosperity for all."

"He's a smart one," William Hathaway said as he checked his watch and quickened their pace somewhat. "My favorite though is Justice Dugan."

"What does he do for the Family?"

"He conducts special prayer groups for judges throughout the system—both at the state and the federal level."

"You're right. He is important. We can't bring in God's Kingdom without getting the courts under control."

"That's exactly the point. Getting our men in there. The courts decide the most important policy questions in our society." They were silent for awhile, steeped in their private thoughts, when William Hathaway broached a more personal topic. "Billy I have one more favor to ask of you. I want your mother back. Can you serve as a go between until we start communicating a little better?"

"Sure Dad. There's nothing I want more than for you and Mom to get back together. The two of you are the guiding lights of my life. Well, of course, we have to add the Lord. You three make quite a team."

"Thank you son. Your Mom and I have had one conversation on the phone, and she wants us to seek psychological counseling. It almost sounds like a precondition of our getting back together."

"Was it a threat, Dad?"

"I wouldn't quite say that, but she seemed pretty adamant about it. She's seeing some guy named Jim Yount, a retired Presbyterian minister from the Cheyenne church."

"I don't know anything about him, but I think you would do better with us or New Life."

"Maybe New Life would be a good compromise. She'd think I was stacking the deck if we went to Abundant Life."

"I know a great guy named Matthew Rigley at New Life. He runs their marriage and family ministry."

"Try to get us an appointment with him. If the appointment is made, I think your Mom will come. It would be a good start."

"I'll do it as soon as we get back. Listen Dad. I saw you looking at your watch a while back, and it's almost two. Hank wanted to leave Dulles by four this afternoon. Maybe we'd better head back, and pack up."

"I guess you're right. Thanks again for everything son," and William Hathaway turned toward Billy and hugged him one more time. "As I said half an hour ago, you have given me my life back."

"I love you, Dad," and there were tears in his eyes. The two returned to Ivanwald, mostly in silence, but convinced Jesus had performed a miracle over the last two days. They walked easily together, past flower gardens maintained by Family members as an expression of humility, feeling that everything was now right with their world.

≈

It was a quiet Christmas for William Hathaway. Virginia invited him over for the day, mainly to put on a good show for Whitney Hastings who was staying with her. Whitney and Billy had recently announced their engagement, with a June wedding planned in Kansas City. Bill senior respected Billy for returning alone each evening to his townhouse during Whitney's stay at the Hathaway home. In fact, he couldn't help making the comparison with the contrasting behavior of his daughter prior to her marriage.

He was also pleased to be at the helm again at Noah Communications. For six long months the corporation had been rocked by strong headwinds, but the tide was turning, and the corporation was finally back under full sail.

They had replaced Patrick with an older man whose resume suggested he would make a good fit. Francis Slocum was a decorated Vietnam War veteran, with degrees in software engineering and a MBA, both from Colorado State University. Most importantly, he was a committed Christian, and a new member of the Abundant Life Assembly of God Church. It felt good to have his energy and focus back.

He felt especially optimistic as he left home at 7:00 a.m. on the first business day of the new year. The first item on his schedule was a staff meeting of his senior people at 9:00. The meeting was traditional, held annually at this time, but William Hathaway believed this year's meeting was of particular importance. He wanted to convince his team he was back, to energize them in their work, and to reemphasize the Christian values and focus that had made the company so successful. It was part of God's plan. His brothers at the recent Family retreat had reassured him about that.

After his brief pep talk, James Ryan, the Vice President for Advertising, spoke first. "I have a proposal to increase our sales staff by fifteen percent. I will have it on your desk by the end of the week. Not only is the number of our stations growing, but the interest in a Christian endorsement for consumer products is rising. The left preaches all things green. I prefer selling products that have the Lord's blessing." Nods of agreement spread across the table. "We need to ride this up and coming wave of the future."

"I agree with you, Jim, and look forward to seeing that recommendation."

"In a similar vein, Sir, I plan to come by your office soon to discuss a new focus for our expansion efforts," piped in Stuart Womple, VP for Development. Of course, we are still looking for new stations to buy, but we're thinking that a partnering focus makes great sense. There are many independent stations that would benefit from our products and services. Francis and I have been talking about such an approach in some detail."

"How are things going in your shop Francis? Did my son-in-law provide any transition help?" William Hathaway asked in a tone of sarcasm.

"Things seem to be proceeding on target at this point," Francis Slocum replied. "Patrick was in fact helpful, and I continue to call him occasionally when a question comes up. Our problem has been in finding a new Jason. That problem should become clearer when we establish a new direction for our software efforts."

"I'm not sure Jason fulfilled his contractual obligations with us, but the matter, as you all know, is complicated by family considerations."

"Speaking of family, Sir," Jeffery Halligan the chief financial officer interjected. "Your sister-in-law has given all her shares to her two daughters. Your niece, Stephanie, has petitioned the SEC to sell her holdings."

"Good. She will be paying a lot of taxes. She might then see that we run a pretty good ship around here. In any event, it would be beneficial if the corporation purchased her shares rather than their being sold on the open market. Can you handle that negotiation, Jeff. I'm not quite up to making the call."

"We've already been in contact with her. I don't expect any problems."

"That's a nice change. She certainly was aggressive in her pursuit of my demise." After finishing, William Hathaway looked around the table and with no further comments forthcoming, he concluded the meeting. "Gentlemen, I know you have busy schedules so let's get back to work. I appreciate very much your dedicated effort and loyalty. Let's make 1996 our best year ever." As the boss turned from the table and headed across the hall to his office, Philip Duke rose with the rest of his colleagues. He was pleased there was no private meeting to follow, and that his general was back. He was ready to follow.

～

"Karen, where are you?" Patrick called out as he came bursting through the front door. He was late as usual. It was after seven p.m., but he was pumped up from a very productive day at his new offices.

"I'm in with Maggie. We're getting ready for bed."

"Magster," Patrick cried out with enthusiasm as he entered her bedroom.

"Daddy, Daddy, Daddy," she replied clapping her hands from on top of her dressing table. Karen smiled as she wondered what would happen next between these two clowns. She felt a little remorse in always being the heavy with her kids, but the feeling was fleeting. She couldn't harbor such thoughts for long because Patrick moved quickly across the room to kiss her tenderly. He'd be on top of her if the setting had been a little different, she thought as she smiled deeply in appreciation for Patrick's lustful and expressive love.

"Is Justin down?" Patrick asked as he left Karen to swoop his daughter into his arms. "You girls come with me. I've got some exciting news to report."

"Please do it quietly, Pat," Karen said as she picked up Maggie's little T-shirt and placed it in her dresser. "Justin may not be fully asleep."

"Hush, Maggie, hush," Patrick teased as he hurried with her into the living room. They wrestled together on the floor with Maggie on top of Patrick, pounding her little fists into his tummy with glee. Karen soon found her way to the sofa, sitting down to enjoy a brief respite and to watch the antics of her two oldest children.

"I think you've extended Maggie's awake time by at least an hour," she said grinning over at the two of them.

"I've missed her, Sweetheart. Whoa, Tuck," he said as Tucker pranced across the room to shower the two of them with kisses. Maggie giggled as she tried turning away toward her mother.

"Maybe I should put the final touches on our dinner."

"No, sit tight. I'll get some toys for Maggie and join you on the sofa. I've got news, kid! After I'm done, you can finish dinner, and I'll read Maggie a story." Karen leaned her head back on the sofa, closed her eyes, and dozed briefly. She was awakened by the feel of Patrick's hand on her thigh."Tired, Sweetheart?"

"A little I guess."

"Are you feeling okay?"

"Pretty good. Actually I'm fine. No nausea today," she said with a smile as she reached down and took his hand.

"That's good. We can start telling people—don't you think?"

"I told Stephanie this morning when she called."

"Did she say anything about the business?"

"No, she just wanted the number of your new office."

"She's going to finance the whole thing. Unbelievable. Her Mom has given away her shares of Noah to both Steph and Audie. Well, Steph wants no part of the company so she's selling all her shares on March 1st back to the company. 'I could give a rats ass about the taxes', she said. She wants an outlet for some of that gold, and she's prepared to invest ten million in our company. I couldn't talk her out of it."

"You certainly gained her confidence last summer."

"I was thinking maybe she just wants to thank us for our help with the trial, but there's more to it than that. Perry's involved too. He somehow got Jason's phone number, and the two have discussed the project extensively."

"Why all the secrecy?"

"I guess they didn't want to hurt our feelings if they decided against investing. Can you believe it? No banks, screw you venture capital firms. This is a godsend."

"Does Steph want to become involved in running the company?"

"Just like you. A silent partner. She's planning to invest another chunk of the money in starting a nonprofit in education. The idea would be to provide services to schools which they need but can't afford. Her dream is to open branches in cities all over the country. It's nice for her she's leaving the practice of law a winner. She was involved in one legal case and won."

"Steph has always had a big heart."

"Huge. I think she looked at the law in real life and said not for me. She did hint that someone in the family needed to make money. I suspect Perry might get involved in the company at some point which is fine with me. He's got a good mind for computer software. I'm falling more in love with your family every day."

"We're a pretty good group with the exception of you know who."

"He'll come around," Patrick said as he hugged the beautiful and fertile woman in his life. "He's been through a rough six months."

"Maybe. You go get *Curious George*, and I'll finish our dinner."

"Hi, Mom. It's time I told you some good news. We're expecting again. It's a little more than three months. This one will definitely be the caboose."

"That's wonderful, Sweetheart. Three is a perfect number."

"I hope so. I know for certain I'll be busy."

"There's no greater contribution you can make to our society than to be a loving mother to those children. I wish your Dad could focus more on the precious little things in life. He's so obsessed with changing the world."

"Any progress between you two?"

"Not really—well maybe a little, I guess. We're going to see a psychologist on Monday."

"Reverent Yount?"

"No, some guy Billy picked out from New Life."

"Oh, my God, Mom. Pastor Ted's place. You've got to be kidding me."

"At least it's a start."

"It's all about Daddy, Mom—his life, his worldview, his need to control. What about you?"

"We'll see, Sweetheart. As I said, at least it's a start. Jim's been helping me understand what I want in a marriage. I won't be impressed by your father's charm or by phony solutions."

"Good Mom. I'm proud of you. I really do hope it works out. There's a small part of me that wants Daddy back too."

"I'll keep you posted. Thanks again for that special news. Right now I'm on my way to Century 21. Remember Wendy Clement? Didn't you go to school with her?"

"She was a class ahead."

"Well, she's Billy and Whitney's realtor. Billy wants me to look at a house."

"Nice. I guess things are progressing well with those two."

"Seems to be. Anyway, I better run."

"Love you, Mom."

"Love you too, Sweetheart. Bye."

Colorado Springs is the city of fundamentalist religion, and the home of New Life Church. New Life was founded by Pastor Ted Haggard in the 1980s. It is a nondenominational, Protestant, Evangelical church that has flourished under Pastor Ted's leadership.

Located in the northern section of town near the Air Force Academy, it represented a twenty minute drive from the Hathaway home. William Hathaway picked up his wife at 9:30 a.m. on the last day of January. Their conversation on the way to the church was conducted on safe grounds, mainly dealing with Karen's pregnancy and the new home Billy was thinking of making an offer on.

William Hathaway, dressed for work in a blue flannel suit, turned off of New Life Drive and followed the signs to the Chapel, slowing down the speed of his car dramatically as he navigated his way through the New Life complex. Matthew Rigley's office was located directly across from the Chapel in a building that housed the World Prayer Center.

Pastor Rigley was one of fifteen staff ministers with primary responsibility for marriage and family counseling. He received his bachelor's degree in psychology from Liberty Bible College in Pensacola Florida in 1975 and his Master's degree in Theology and Counseling from Oral Roberts University two years later. He greeted Virginia and William Hathaway in his office at 10:00 o'clock sharp.

"Welcome to New Life," Pastor Matt said as he stood up from his large oak desk to shake the hands of his new clients. After directing them to a large couch across from his desk, he relocated to a leather backed chair alongside them. "Can we begin with prayer, please. Heavenly Father, I am honored to be with this upstanding Christian couple this morning, our brother and sister in Christ, William and Virginia. Expand their hearts, and help them come back together through the love of your Son, our Lord and Savior, Jesus Christ. Amen."

Upon completion, he looked over at them and said: "I have learned a little about you both from your wonderful son, Pastor Bill. I understand you've been married for thirty-five years, that you have a daughter Karen in addition to Bill, and two grandchildren."

"There's one more on the way," Virginia interjected with a smile.

"God continues to bless you," Pastor Matt responded, returning her smile. "Isn't that wonderful. Now, as I understand it, you've been living separately for the last six months. What precipitated the separation?"

"I was asked to leave, Reverend Rigley," William Hathaway stated in a rather manner-of-fact manner.

"What kind of problems led you to make that request, Virginia?"

"We certainly weren't communicating very well," Virginia said.

"I was going through a difficult time at work."

"You do such wonderful things for Christ and his Kingdom, William. We are all very proud of you at New Life."

"Thank you, Reverent Rigley. I appreciate those kind words of encouragement," William Hathaway said with a smile. After some hesitation as she struggled for a sense of control that eluded her, Virginia blurted out:

"But you have a family too."

"Yes, I know that Dear. I think I have provided for you very well."

"That's so unimportant, Bill. I really don't think you get it. You're proper with me; but when it comes to Karen and Maggie, you're a cold, self-centered bastard. Oh dear, I shouldn't have said that," and she burst into tears. "I'm so sorry Reverend Rigley."

"Dealing with raw emotions is part of the healing process, Virginia."

"I do admit to having some problems with Maggie," William Hathaway said in a soft voice that may have contained some contrition.

"Who is Maggie?"

"She is Karen's precious three year old daughter with Downs Syndrome," Virginia interjected with some passion.

"Karen and her husband Patrick had sexual relations before they were married, Reverend Rigley. Maggie resulted from that sin."

"I can't stand this anymore, Bill Hathaway," Virginia shouted out as she stood up from the couch and moved toward the door. "Is there a receptionist in this building, Reverend Rigley?"

"Yes, just down the hall on the right."

"Good. Maybe she can get me a taxi. Don't call me again, William Hathaway, until God gives you a new heart." And she stormed out of the office fighting back tears. William Hathaway buried his face in his hands briefly, rose from his seat to shake the hand of Reverend Rigley, and returned to work.

Alex and Patrick's friend David were doing remarkably well together as a couple. They had started dating soon after the trial. Karen loved it because when David was in Monument the four of them often did things together. She and Patrick were dating again. Well, almost she thought with a smile. It's hard to think of an outing as a date when you have two children and are five months pregnant with number three. Anyway, tonight the four of them were going to an early movie and then out to dinner. Karen was looking forward to it.

Patrick loved Alex's success with David because he had his racquet ball buddy back. He arrived home from work a little before noon on the second Saturday in March, had a light lunch, and then put Maggie down for her nap. With mission accomplished, he quickly changed into his tennis shorts and peeked his head into Justin's room where Karen was reading him a story. She looked up from the book, and smiled over at him.

"Be back by three-thirty, Pat. We need to leave by four."

"I will, Sweetheart. I'm not in the shape I used to be. An hour and a half with David will probably do me in. Tonight should be great."

"I hope the movie is good."

"If not, I'll put my head on your shoulder and nap," he said with a smile.

"You won't sleep long because I'll need more popcorn. My tummy hormones are out of control."

"That's nice to hear, but I better go. Love you."

"Bye Pat. Have a good game," she said as she returned her attention to Justin.

"You're beginning to look a lot like your father, little buddy. I wonder if you too will be a racquet ball player," she said as she gently squeezed Justin before continuing the story. "Show me the moo cows, Justy. Good for you," she said as Justin placed his tiny finger on the book. "Now look. There are three of them. One, two, three," she said as she pointed out the cows with her finger. The two of them read together for another twenty minutes until both were asleep.

Karen's nap abruptly ended when she heard a car crunching the gravel on her road. Maybe it's Mom, she thought as she placed Justin in his crib and looked out the window to see who was coming. "Oh good, it's Alex," she mumbled to herself as she hurried toward the front door.

"Nothing was going on at the store," Alex said as she climbed the front steps. "Megan's there, and she's going to close up anyway." She gave Karen a big hug.

"Oh, I'm glad you're here early. Both kids are napping. We've got a little girl time. Can I get you some coffee or a small glass of wine?"

"Small glass? What's that all about?" she asked with a laugh as the two women entered the house.

"Well, I don't want you sleeping at the movie."

"I'm fine. I can hold off on the drinking till later. Tonight will be fun. On the way over, I called David on my cell, and told him to come here with Pat. I brought him a change of clothes."

"Good. So let's talk," Karen said as she plunked herself down on the living room sofa.

"Yes, let's, and I've got some news," Alex said as she sat in the easy chair across from Karen.

"The big news?" Karen asked with a broad grin as she looked over at Alex's left hand.

"No, not that, but good news nevertheless. David and I had a long talk last night about marriage. It's nice we're on the same page. We've dated now for a little more than seven months, and if we make it a year it's either shit or get off the pot."

"You're both not getting younger."

"That's the point. He really wants children too. At least we have a few things in common."

"Most important from my perspective," Karen interjected, "is that he's a great guy."

"I agree. I am in love for the first time since Bruce. He could care less about my playing sports, especially with Pat around. We enjoy walking together, discussing books, and partying with friends. That seems to be enough."

"Would you move to Denver?"

"No, I don't think so because he loves Monument. He's going to look into jobs around here."

"So it's pretty definite."

"I wouldn't say that quite yet, but we're moving in that direction."

"I guess it's kinda sad in a way. My parents are moving in the opposite direction."

"That is sad. I guess your Mom is finally standing up to him."

"She is. Actually I'm quite proud of her, and a little surprised."

"Your Dad needs to learn how to love. For some reason, he has a damaged heart."

"His religion has certainly been a disaster. Mom says it reinforces all the things about him she can't stand."

"Religion for most people is about belief. Christianity, Islam, Judaism: it doesn't matter. They're all the same in that regard. Beliefs are invented by humans to explain the world, to answer big questions, and to provide some hope of a life after death. People love religion because it takes them on a trip to Disney Land. The problem is religion as belief does not teach you how to love. Religions tell you to love and many practitioners pretend, but religions fail in the how-to department for many people.

"For me, organized religion misses the point. It's a waste of time. Love is a matter of the spirit. It shines on us like the sun. Everyone has equal access. All we need to do is to learn how to go outside and bask in it."

"Okay," Karen said. "You and I have danced around this issue for more than a year now. We've got at least half an hour with the kids napping. Give me a how-to lesson. How do I become a spiritual person? How do I learn to bask in the sun? Can you explain that to me in half an hour?"

"No problem. This stuff is not rocket science. It's difficult to put into practice sometimes, but the how-to part is quite simple to understand. We've discussed certain aspects of it before. Let me see if I can tie all the strings together.

"The first thing spirituality posits is that love is real. It is part of the structure of the created universe. Remember that Frankl book I keep coming back to. I'm going to give you a copy tomorrow. I've promised to do it for more than a year now. Anyway, Frankl related to his wife with deep love in a Nazi prison camp. He had no idea if his wife was still alive. It didn't matter. Love never dies. He focused on loving his wife by relating to her in his mind under the most terrible conditions, and it transformed him. It made all the difference.

"Love sees goodness and beauty. It brings joy, abundance, peace. It doesn't judge, compare, or compete. It washes away fear. There is no need to defend oneself. It heals hate.

"One place where I differ from some thinkers on this subject regards the place where love resides. I don't find it deep within myself. We are biological creatures through and through. Love is not part of what makes us human. It is built instead into the structure of the universe as I said before. It's like a form of energy. But what is really neat is we can choose to bring it into our awareness. It lies outside us, but we can decide to make it part of our conscious awareness.

"As the domination of ego over awareness recedes, love floods in. When we decide to see others as good, love floods in. When we allow others to define themselves without judging, love floods in. When we serve the needs of our neighbor, love floods in."

"Love floods in where?" Karen asked as she shifted her position on the sofa.

"Good question," Alex responded with a smile. "Love floods into our awareness, our mind. It comes from outside, and changes the way we perceive. It creates different background music for guiding the mind's operation and perception. As the ego recedes from our awareness, love floods in to replace it."

"Let's talk about the ego for a minute. That's obviously very much related to all of this. I kinda know what the ego is; but it's also, at least for me, a slippery concept."

"Your ego is the biologically driven perspective that comes from the organism's strong will to survive. You need it. Your ego organizes your body around survival. It also helps you attain important goals. It certainly isn't all bad.

"But it can be your worst enemy. It wants to defend you so it invents conflict in an attempt to do just that. It defines the world in self-centered, self-interested ways that distort reality, that prevent you from perceiving your real interests.

"The ego manufactures resentments. It craves stuff. In this sense, it creates desires that can never be fulfilled. You become attached to the ego's needs, which makes it more difficult to move beyond them."

"How do you move beyond the ego? That seems to be the key to the spiritual process."

"It is. There are two crucial steps. You must first want to change. It needs to be a primary focus for your life. You don't dabble in the spiritual life if you want to succeed. Once you make the firm decision to seek a spiritual life, there is no way you can fail if you persist at it.

"Step two is about learning how the ego functions in your life. Once you learn how it operates, you can start pushing it aside. So, you need to watch it. Pay attention to how you react to things. Go to a quiet place and examine your resentments, your grievances. Examine in a gentle way the cause of your negative emotions, your jealousies, and fears.

"Journaling can help. Put into writing important experiences and your reactions to them. When you read about several experiences later, as a collection, when the emotion is drained from them, patterns leap out at you. You will see your ego at work.

"Affirmations can also help with certain ego related problems. They are short, pithy statements you repeat over and over. The best way to get a handle on affirmations is to look at how the brain operates.

"The brain works mostly on automatic pilot. We breathe without thinking. We can learn a sport, or at least some of us can, and it becomes natural. The many complex motor skills involved in playing the sport are performed with the brain working at the subconscious level. A problem can arise if we acquire certain beliefs, mostly as children, which are limiting. These beliefs can dramatically affect our ability to choose love. They work at the subconscious level too.

"This is part of your problem. You learned from your father you are only a good person if you are behaving in a certain way."

"Doing what he wants me to do," Karen interjected.

"Yes, exactly," Alex responded with a reassuring smile. "Parents can give children the message that the world is a dangerous place, which paralyzes them with fear. Fear activates ego. It is impossible to love if fear dominates your awareness.

"These limiting beliefs operate like a computer program that governs the way you see the world. The first step in moving away from limiting beliefs is to understand them. You are there. You have done a good job with that. It's a big achievement," she said while giving Karen another reassuring smile.

"I hope you're right. I sure have spent a lot of time in therapy."

"It was time well spent. Now what you can do is recite an affirmation to change the limiting belief. Something like I am beautiful and good. Or you can focus on a goal you want to aspire to. I choose to love.

"It's a form of meditation. Go to a quiet place, relax, close your eyes, and begin reciting the affirmation. Repeat it over and over for ten or fifteen minutes. Make sure to recite it with conviction."

"Even if I don't really believe it?"

"Yes. Again, what you are doing is reprogramming your subconscious mind. It doesn't work if you don't repeat it with conviction. Say it also with loving, compassionate emotion for yourself. Continue with the affirmation daily, ten or fifteen minute sessions are all you need, until you notice a real change in the way you see yourself. When that change occurs, you can more freely choose to love."

"How am I going to remember all this stuff? It's fascinating, but I know I'm going to forget a lot of it."

"Well, you always have me."

"My best friend," Karen said as she moved across the room to hug her.

"That's what best friends are for," Alex said as she held onto Karen with conviction. "I'm going to beef up the spiritual section in the store," Alex said as Karen moved back toward her seat on the sofa. "I'll give you books to read, and then we can discuss them."

"That's so nice," and Karen was close to tears. "How am I ever going to repay you?"

"Love is not about paying back as you know all too well when you think about your children. It's about giving. When you give to another, love is returned to you.

"But there is one more part to this, and then the lecture is over. Humans are decision makers. We can choose what story we want to listen to. We can decide whether to allow love in or to see the world from the perspective of ego.

"It's a little like dieting. The thought is so tempting to have a hot fudge sundae, and yet you know afterwards it will set you back. It feels good in a similar way to judge another person, to choose to see them in a bad light; but it creates a perspective, a way of seeing the world, that is unfulfilling in the long run. So humans must decide."

"Let's not talk about dieting. Dieting is hard. I spent my life as a teenager starving myself so I could look good in a skimpy bathing suit."

"The spiritual life is not a free lunch. It's like deciding to go on a healthy diet for the rest of your life, a diet of choosing to see others with love."

"I think I can do that."

"I know you can. Let me make one more point about Frankl. When he was in those Nazi prison camps, he lost everything. They took everything away from him. But what he learned there is they couldn't take away his power to decide how he was going to respond to his circumstances. He chose love, and it made all the difference. He chose to love his wife, to focus on her goodness and beauty, and it changed him.

"When he decided to help others as a doctor, love and inner peace ruled his life. He noted the few prisoners who were givers, ones who shared their meager rations with a starving friend, were the happiest ones in the camp. The type of person one became in the camp was not dependent on the circumstances of camp life, but on decisions individual prisoners made on how to respond to these circumstances.

"Humans have two propensities: to act from love or to act from self-centered egoism. You decide. You decide what background music you want playing inside your head. It's an important decision because whatever music you choose organizes the way you see the world."

"So love is out there, and one must decide to allow it in."

"Precisely, and there is one additional spiritual practice which can help in this regard. Meditation is a way of disciplining the mind, of getting it under your control. With a disciplined mind, you are more able to decide to love. When ego thoughts enter your awareness, and they always will, a trained mind gently pushes them aside.

"That's it. If you want the sun to shine down love, learn how to let the sunshine in. There's nothing to believe in. Not even God if you don't want to. The test is not what you believe, but the size of your heart. If you are better able to love, then your spiritual practice is working. The true test of the spiritual life is your ability to live love."

"Fantastic," Karen said as she left the sofa one last time to hug her special friend. "Let me check on the kids, and then take a quick shower while they're still asleep."

"Take your time. I'm all set. Do you have an apple or a banana? All this talking has stimulated my appetite."

"Both. Take your pick, and anything else you see in the kitchen. I'll be back soon."

"No hurry like I said. I'll take my fruit onto the deck, and soak up all that good Colorado sunshine."

Seven hours later Karen reached over to kiss Patrick goodnight, arranged her head on the pillow, closed her eyes, and began thinking about her father. There must be a better way she concluded. I can choose to love Daddy. And she thought about what her mother had told her over the phone last week, the tragic story of the childhood death of her Aunt Kate. That's where that guilt and fear comes from that fuels Daddy's ego. No wonder he has a damaged heart, and empathy for her father flooded her awareness for the first time in as long as she could remember. "Thank you Alex, my best friend and teacher," she said to herself as she hugged her sleeping husband and then turned away to go to sleep.

On the following Sunday, the last Sunday in March, Karen and Maggie set off on a special trip. They arrived at the apartment on East Untah Street a little before four o'clock. Karen had taken a chance. She had bet on her father's innate shyness, that without her mother he was without a social life, and she won. He was there.

She knocked on the door of his first floor apartment and waited with heart pounding. He answered her second knock, dressed casually in slacks and an open sports shirt. That's nice, she thought to herself with a smile. It had been awhile since she had seen this look.

"Karen, this is indeed a surprise. Were you out exploring the neighborhood? Please come in."

"Thanks, Daddy," and she took Maggie's hand, leading her through the door of the stark, one bedroom apartment, and wishing she had the courage to reach out and hug him. She was a little disappointed he stepped backward, retreating into the apartment, also unable to initiate a less formal greeting.

"We won't stay long, Daddy, but Maggie has something she wants to ask you." Karen had been training Maggie for two days on this little speech, and Maggie was hiding behind her right leg, chewing nervously on the hem of her dress. "Maggie. This is Granddad. What do you want to tell him?"

William Hathaway couldn't help smiling. They had decided on a personal name for him. It sounded nice. It was the first time he had been addressed in that way. He took a step forward, got down on one knee, and smiled at his granddaughter.

With the hem of Karen's dress still in her mouth, Maggie peered from behind her mother; and in a halting voice, garbled: "Granddad."

"Sweetheart, what's with the dress? You can do better than that," and Karen gently removed it from her mouth. Slowly, Maggie found some words.

"Granddad, my party."

"What about your party?" William Hathaway replied in a soft voice.

"My party, my party," his granddaughter responded.

"What do you want Granddad to do, Magster?"

"My party, my party," she repeated with greater authority, looking up at her mother. After an awkward pause, Karen intervened to supply the missing information.

"Maggie wants to invite you to her birthday party, Dad." William Hathaway again smiled over at his granddaughter.

"Do you know when it is, little Maggie?" he asked. Again, Karen had to fill in the gaps for her tongue-tied daughter.

"Next Sunday. We'll probably get started around five."

"Will your mother be there?" William Hathaway asked, rising to his feet and looking toward his daughter.

"She certainly is planning on it."

"Great. That sounds like a fun afternoon. I look forward to coming."

"That would be wonderful, Dad. I plan to ask Billy too. Maybe you guys could ride together."

"That would work out well for me because he knows where you live. Can I bring anything?"

"How about a nice big salad. Just kidding, but it is for dinner. Pat has a barbeque planned."

"Sounds good," and he directed his attention back to Maggie. "And how old will Miss Maggie be?"

"Can you show Granddad three fingers, Magster? No, not your whole hand. Just three," and Karen bent down to help Maggie display three fingers.

"You've become a real old lady, little Maggie. See you on Sunday."

"Okay, Mags. Say good bye to Granddad. Tell him you love him." And Karen picked up her daughter and started moving slowly toward the door.

"Love woo!" Maggie said.

"Wave goodbye." Karen smiled as she watched her daughter vigorously wave her little right hand, and then she said: "Thanks, Dad. I look forward to Sunday."

"Me too, Karen. Thanks so much for coming." William Hathaway closed the door, and returned to reading the Sunday paper.

∾

As soon as Karen arrived back at her house, she called her mother. "Mom, Dad said he would come."

"That's nice, Sweetheart."

"He implied he was coming because you would be there."

"That's interesting, but I won't hold my breath."

"He smiled, and was gentle with Maggie; but there were no hugs or kisses."

"I'm not surprised. He has a long way to go Karen."

"I guess so. He plans to come with Billy, so I better call him."

"Let me do that. I need to send an olive branch to Billy. I haven't been to church since this whole thing started nine months ago, and I'm not intending to anytime soon. I'm terrified that I'm losing him too," and she sounded like she was ready to cry.

"Fine with me. It should be an interesting party. Tell him five o'clock. Well, I better run. Pat and I are going over to Frannie and Frank's for dinner."

"Have fun, Sweetheart. I'll talk to you soon."

"Bye Mom."

Patrick was relieved the weather was cooperating for Maggie's party. They had invited all their friends, both neighbors and new colleagues from work, so it was helpful everyone could be outside. He was also relieved Jason had taken a rain check. Jason was not quite ready to face William Hathaway.

As he set up tables and chairs on both the patio and adjacent back lawn for the twenty-five or more expected guests, he knew he was ready. He was in fact looking forward to making peace with his father-in-law. He was also hoping things had improved between Karen and her father. Family tension was both alien to his experience and his nature.

At 4:15 Alex and David arrived, a little early so they could help if needed. Alex immediately went to the kitchen to lend Karen and her mother a hand. David stayed outside with Patrick and Maggie, who was dressed in a blue smock dress that tied from the back with a yellow ribbon in her curly brown hair.

"Want a beer, Bud? We're all set out here," Patrick said as he smiled over at his friend.

"Sure. That sounds great."

"Your usual Coors light?" Patrick asked as he reached into a large cooler that held an assortment of both beer and soft drinks.

"Sounds good. Maggie, I like your dress. Where can I put your birthday present?" Maggie smiled at David, and then looked up at her father.

"How about we put them all on this table. Can you thank David, Mags?" Maggie managed to smile up at David as he handed her the present, and then she ran off across the lawn. "No Maggie. Come back with the present. We'll leave it on this table. It won't be long till there are lots of them here. Then you can open them." And Patrick chased after her, scooping her up with lots of tickles, which aided in dislodging the present he was then able to place on the table.

"If things keep progressing on their current course, it won't be long till we will be going to a birthday party at your home," Patrick said to his friend after first pausing to catch his breath.

"I know. It's a little scary."

"I tell you what. Why don't you start practicing now. Can you watch Maggie for a few minutes while I take care of the arriving guests?"

"No problem. It would be an honor to escort the birthday girl," David replied as he moved toward Patrick for the handoff of Maggie. As he set her down on the ground, David took her hand and said:"Let's go play on your swing set over there. I bet some of your friends will come join us in a few minutes."

As the guests arrived in a flood of cars, Patrick welcomed them, offered them a drink, and placed their presents on the table. He was joined outside by Karen, who visited with the mothers, before directing them to take their kids and join Maggie on the swings.

William Hathaway and Billy arrived at 5:30. Patrick greeted them warmly, offering each a diet coke, and then engaging Billy in a conversation about the house he and Whitney would be closing on in early June. William Hathaway briefly left the conversation to place his present on the table.

"Sounds like a good buy, Bill," Patrick said following Billy's detailed description of the house. "You must be getting excited about the wedding."

"We are, Pat. It won't be long now."

"How are things at your new office?" William Hathaway asked as he rejoined the conversation.

"We are right on schedule, Sir. We hope to launch our first software package by July fourth. I should come by Noah, and give you a detailed presentation of our business plan."

"Oh, that won't be necessary. I'm just glad to learn things are proceeding on schedule."

"Hi Daddy. Hi Billy," Karen interjected as she joined the three members of her extended family. "It's so good to have you both here."

"Glad to do it, Sis. Maggie looks pretty in that little blue dress."

"I'll save it for you, Billy. I hope it won't be long before you and Whitney need it."

"We plan to start having babies right from the get go. I'm not getting any younger."

"They'll be handsome babies, Billy," Karen said smiling across at her brother. "Listen, Pat. I could use your help at the table. Maggie is excited about opening her presents."

"Fine, Sweetheart. I'll catch you guys later," and he patted his father-in-law on the shoulder before moving toward the table with all of the presents on it.

"Can you announce it, Pat?" Karen asked as she followed after him.

"Absolutely. Hey you all," Patrick shouted out. "Let's gather around this table and watch Maggie do what she loves to do best. Open presents." As the guests gathered around the table, William Hathaway and Billy retreated to the far end of the lawn. They quietly exited the scene fifteen minutes later.

~

The postmortem began at 9:15 when Alex and David left after helping with the dishes. Patrick excused himself to prepare for Monday. Virginia was spending the night; and as she followed her daughter into the living room, there were tears in her eyes.

"It was a great party, Karen, but your father ruined it for me," Virginia said as she sunk into the sofa. She was both tired and distraught.

"I know, Mom, and I just don't get it. Why did he leave so early?"

"Because he sensed this was your life and not his. You guys are so easy and flowing. He doesn't feel comfortable without rigid boundaries. As I said on the phone the other day, he has a long, long way to go, and I'm tired of waiting. Nine freakin' months. I don't believe it. Again, I've come to a decision point. I'm putting the house up for sale tomorrow, and the hell with Abundant Life Assembly of God Church. That place has about as much real life as a funeral parlor." Karen was taken aback by her mother's tone. She had never heard her talk this way. Eventually she managed to ask.

"What if Daddy doesn't want to sell the house?"

"Then he can buy me out. I own half."

"Wow, Mom. You sound like you've given up."

"I haven't totally given up, but I'm not going to spend my time in a big, lonely house, waiting for a middle aged man to learn how to love me. I've also had it with all the self-righteous bull shit."

"Mom!"

"It feels good to say self-righteous bull shit because it's true," Virginia responded with a sheepish grin.

"I'm lovin' the new you, Mom, but I want to keep trying with Daddy."

"You try, Sweetheart. As far as I'm concerned, he can come to me. He can make the effort for a change. It takes two to tango."

"Will you still keep seeing Reverend Yount?"

"Every other week. He's my lifeline. I may even join his former church. Now before I go to bed, I want to share with you something a little more positive. I start work part-time at Daybreak in three weeks."

"You mean the nonprofit that runs that center for handicapped adults?"

"That's it. I'm going to be the new cook."

"Oh, Mom, you're such a hot shit if you'll pardon my French." And Karen jumped across the room to hug her. After returning to her chair, she continued: "Why the cook? This is so amazing."

"Because I know how to cook, and enjoy doing it. And, most importantly, the current cook is leaving soon. There's a therapeutic aspect to the work in that clients are assigned to help me. The job is only twenty hours a week. I do breakfast and lunch. My afternoons and weekends are free."

"I just can't believe it. Who gave you the idea?"

"Jim Yount. If he was single, I might be tempted; but that is a really stupid thought."

"What if Daddy comes back, if he changes?"

"Then he can have the new me."

"He'll be lucky to get you. I'm so proud of you, Mom."

"Thanks, Karen. I can finally imagine a life without your father. It's not my choice, but it will be okay. I will be okay."

"I think so too, Mom," and she left the couch to hug her one last time before the two women headed off to bed.

Describe the causes of the conflict between Karen and her father. Was progress made during the course of the novel in healing her psychological hurt?

After the trip to Prince Edward Island, would you be willing to exchange a Carnival cruise for one on a tall ship?

Discuss the major issues resulting from the parenting of a Downs Syndrome child. Grade Karen and Patrick on their efforts.

List the central issues in the trial involving Harriet Hathaway and Noah Communications. Was the outcome of the trial credible?

William Hathaway is a stereotypical character. Is he human enough to be real?

What is it about Karen's life that enables her to grow as a woman? Virginia grows as a woman too. Are their situations similar?

Patrick must make some difficult choices as the corporate scandal unfolds. Evaluate those choices.

Describe the activities of The Family. Do these activities pose a credible threat to democratic government?

Karen chooses love. Is her choice credible?

Contrast religion and spirituality as approaches to creating meaning.

www.ingramcontent.com/pod-product-compliance
Lightning Source LLC
Chambersburg PA
CBHW060244030726
47493CB00025B/2094